The Post Office Girls

The Post Office Girls

*Book One in the
Post Office Girls Series*

POPPY COOPER

HODDER

First published in Great Britain in 2021 by Hodder & Stoughton
An Hachette UK company

1

Copyright © Kirsten Hesketh 2021

A CIP catalogue record for this title is available from the British Library

Paperback ISBN 978 1 529 31026 9
eBook ISBN 978 1 529 31027 6

Typeset in Plantin Light by Palimpsest Book Production Limited,
Falkirk, Stirlingshire

Printed and bound in Great Britain by Clays Ltd, Elcograf S.p.A.

Hodder & Stoughton policy is to use papers that are natural, renewable and
recyclable products and made from wood grown in sustainable forests.
The logging and manufacturing processes are expected to conform to the
environmental regulations of the country of origin.

Hodder & Stoughton Ltd
Carmelite House
50 Victoria Embankment
London EC4Y 0DZ

www.hodder.co.uk

To John, Tom, Charlotte, O and O. With love.
And in loving memory of Grandpa George.

Dear Reader,

I hope you enjoy this first book in the Post Office Girls series. I've loved researching and writing it – and I'm so excited to share the adventures of Beth, Milly and Nora with you.

My grandfather, Joseph 'George' Biggs, served in the First World War. He never talked about his experiences but, at the end his life, he was right back in those trenches, hiding from the shells. That haunted me and taught me, more than anything, what the men in the Great War endured and how it must never, ever be forgotten.

What Grandpa George *did* talk about was the post office. Before the war, he was a teenage assistant postman near Liverpool, but after the war he came down to London and worked his way up the ranks at Mount Pleasant Sorting Office. The loveliest of grandfathers, apparently he ruled his section of the sorting office with a rod of iron – even, at one point, turning down an opportunity to head up the postal service in the Bahamas. My sister still has the clock he was given when he finally retired in 1956; it has pride of place on her mantelpiece. My own childhood took place before the internet age, so writing and receiving letters was a big part of my growing up and so my grandfather's job helping to run London's main sorting office seemed terribly romantic to me. All those letters . . .

When I heard that the Army Post Office had constructed the biggest wooden building in the world at that time – the Home Depot – in The Regent's Park during the First World War, I knew it would make a wonderful setting for a story. During the war, soldiers and their families sent over two billion letters and 140 million parcels to each other. Much of this went through the Home Depot, where it was sorted by thousands of postal workers – many of them, by necessity, women as their menfolk (like my grandfather) were away at the front. It was an opportunity for many of these women to leave their traditional roles for the first time and heralded the beginning of a huge social revolution that persists to this day.

Beth, Milly and Nora are fictional characters, but the descriptions of the Home Depot and wider events in WWI are very much based on truth and I hope capture the spirit – if not all the detail – of the age. The Home Depot seems to have been dismantled shortly after the Great War and details of when exactly it was built and what exactly went on within its wooden walls remain sketchy so, in some instances, I have gone with a 'best guess' given the information I had available. There is no recorded evidence of a fire at the Home Depot but such fires were unsurprisingly far from unknown.

I thoroughly enjoyed developing the characters in this book, especially Beth, Nora and Milly, and their journeys against the backdrop of such a turbulent part of our history. I hope you grow to love them as much as I do and that you will come back to discover what happens to them as the war progresses.

Poppy x

The Post Office Girls

The War Maiden at Home

When the soldier's tramp is o'er the land
And 'Civvies' do not count,
When Luxury's severely banned
And prices upward mount,
When each man over forty-one is put upon the shelf
The thoughtful maiden sits up straight and says unto
  herself:
'Now where's the place where I come in?
How can I lend a hand?
I'll knit and sew, but can't I take
A still more useful stand?'
While all around the soldiers gay in every house were
  billeted:
The people hardly knew their homes, but said the
  place was filleted.
There! These conditions do provide
The maiden's useful part – To do the undistinguished
  jobs
With all her willing heart. She won't get the Victoria
  Cross – no, not by any means!
But the fighting man can't fight without the help
  behind the scenes.

Anonymous WW1
Published in *St Martin's Le Grand*,
the General Post Office staff magazine

Prologue

October 1915

Beth stood very still and the world stopped with her, grinding to a halt while she decided what to do next.

She had a choice.

A stark choice.

And what she did next mattered. Really mattered. Mattered more than anything that had ever happened to her. Indeed, it mattered more than anything that would happen in many people's lives – even if they lived to be one hundred years old.

If she ran for help, an innocent person would die. And they *were* innocent; in spite of everything, deep down she was absolutely sure of that. They might have made mistakes, huge mistakes, they might have teetered on the edge of disaster but, at the end of the day, they were innocent and as much a victim of the war as if they had been fighting at the front.

But if she stayed and tried to save them there would be devastation and loss beyond measure – it might even affect the outcome of the war.

So, what to do?

One special person versus the greater good.

The greater good versus one person.

A crash, a moan, and the world started to speed up at the very instant Beth leapt into action.

At the end of the day, she knew – had always known – exactly what she needed to do.

I

April 1915
Woodhampstead, Hertfordshire

I'm eighteen years old today.

The words beat like the clatter of hooves on cobbles through Beth's head, tightening across her skull, making her temples throb.

I'm doing nothing to help.

These words were higher, shriller, like a knife dropped onto a plate. They made Beth's breath catch and her hands shake – almost as though they belonged to someone else . . .

'That's under, Elizabeth.' Mrs McBride's voice was sharp. 'Don't you dare be tricky with the butter – not today, not ever. There's a war on, don't you know!'

'No, Mrs McBride. I mean, yes, Mrs McBride.'

Sweat prickled the roots of Beth's plait under her neat, white cap. Nerves. Indignation. She was never tricky with the butter. She was never tricky with *anything*. It wasn't in her nature and, anyway, Ma would have something to say if she tried. Ma loved a quote, especially from Queen Victoria, and 'honesty guides good people' was one of her favourites. The family shop – J.A. Healey, General Provisions of Woodhampstead – was *built* on honesty. Everyone knew that. It was what kept customers coming back. Well, that and the fact that there weren't any other grocers in Woodhampstead.

Mrs McBride was right, though. The piece of butter Beth
had taken off the main block was well under half a pound.
There was an art to cutting it and Beth was usually pretty
accurate – better than Sally, better even than Ma – but today
her eye was out. Biting her lip, she added more with the
wooden pats. It took several attempts, but finally the scales
were balanced and she smacked the misshapen lump into a
smooth, neat rectangle. And, all the time, Mrs McBride kept
talking. About how the war was dragging on and the casualties were mounting. The new front opening up in the
Dardanelles – wherever that was. The dreadful use of poison
gas by the enemy. And how it was probably a good thing
that Beth didn't have a sweetheart away at the front because,
well, no one knew what the future held, did they, dear? On
and on she droned, until Beth felt like screaming – *do you
think I don't know?* – but she kept her head carefully down
while she wrapped the butter in a square of waxed paper
and tucked the edges under, just so.

She wondered if she should interrupt and tell Mrs McBride
that today was her eighteenth birthday. But no, there was no
point. The old lady wouldn't care – after all, Beth was neither
coming of age nor coming out – and it might just prompt a
whole load of extra questions about what her twin brother
Ned was going to do next.

It was only when she had quite finished wrapping the
butter that she allowed herself to look up. 'Will there be
anything else?' she asked with a polite smile, putting the
butter into Mrs McBride's basket and entering the purchase
into the ledger in her small neat hand.

'I don't think so.' Mrs McBride didn't move. 'Although
the butter's not too salt, is it, dear? I'm making lemon curd
to send out to my great-nephews at the front.'

Really?

After the butter had been weighed and wrapped?

The war is raging and I'm discussing lemon curd with Mrs McBride.

'I tried it this morning and I think you'll find it isn't salt at all,' said Beth calmly. 'But if you'd like a taste for yourself . . .'

I'm doing nothing to help.

Without waiting for an answer, Beth pared off a small sliver and put the little curl on a scrap of paper. Mrs McBride sampled it leisurely. Eventually, she smacked her lips and pronounced it just the right side of acceptable. Then she picked up her basket, nodded to the other shopper and swept out into the rain. As the doorbell clanged, Beth allowed herself the luxury of a tiny sigh of relief.

'Coo, she doesn't half go on, does she?' giggled the next customer as Mrs McBride's ample back view disappeared up the street. It was Florence Emmett, a pretty red-headed acquaintance of Beth's from school. Florence worked in the kitchens at Maitland Hall, the mansion on the outskirts of the village where Beth's brother, Ned, was a gardener. Florence rarely came into the shop – in fact, Beth had barely seen her for months – but now here she was, putting a couple of baskets onto the counter and tucking a stray Titian-coloured curl behind her ears.

'She's lonely,' said Beth diplomatically. She could think of various other – and possibly more apt – words to describe Mrs McBride, but Ma took a dim view of gossiping in the shop, and especially about the customers.

Florence shrugged. 'There's a lot of people lonely nowadays,' she said dismissively, 'and most can keep a civil tongue in their head. Anyway, never mind her. Cook's sent me in because she needs a few sundry items. Although she was gabbling that fast, I'll be blowed if I can remember the half of it. There'll be hell to pay if I forget something. We definitely need tea. And sugar . . .' She trailed off, rosebud mouth pinched and worried.

Beth smiled reassuringly. 'Didn't Cook write down what she wanted?' she said. 'Ivy usually brings in a list.'

'I've got a list,' said Florence, 'but Cook's writing looks like a couple of spiders have been at the sherry.'

Beth laughed. 'Shall I have a go?' she suggested, holding out her hand. She was used to deciphering even the densest of scrawls. Four years of working in the shop and seeing to all manner of shopping lists had seen to that.

Florence handed over a torn-off piece of paper and Beth scanned the list. Cook's writing was difficult at the best of times, but today it was even worse than usual. It didn't help that the list had got wet in the rain, which had made some of the letters run.

'What happened here?' Beth asked in amusement.

'Cook couldn't find her specs,' said Florence.

Squinting at the letters, it didn't take Beth long to confirm that Cook needed tea and sugar – rather a lot of each and maybe more than their depleted stocks could supply – as well as flour, coffee and a variety of packets and tins. Soon Beth was scurrying around the shop, climbing up the ladders to get things from the top shelf, weighing and measuring, gradually assembling the order.

'Why's Cook sent you today?' asked Beth, stacking the last tins of crab onto the counter. 'Where's Ivy?'

'Gone.'

'Gone?' echoed Beth, bemused. Surely, steady, sensible Ivy hadn't got herself into trouble? 'Gone where?'

'Gone to "do her bit",' said Florence, mimicking Ivy's distinctively high voice. 'She just upped and offed without so much as a by your leave. Cook was not happy. None of them were.'

Beth stared. Girls didn't just *leave*. They stayed where they were – where they'd been put, to be more precise – until they got married. And then they left to look after their husband and to have babies. It was just the way things were. It was the way things had always been, like it or not. You didn't just march off and try something different. You certainly didn't just decide to 'do your bit' all of your own accord. It wasn't right. It wasn't . . . seemly.

'It's left us all in a dreadful pickle,' Florence was saying. 'Cook's trying to hire someone new but there's no one around.'

Now Beth knew the world really had gone topsy-turvy. A matter of weeks ago, any job in service would have been in high demand. As Ma always said, it was a roof over your head, all your meals *and* a wage. Beth herself might have ended up working in one of the big houses had her sister Sally not got married and stopped working in the shop.

And now even Maitland Hall couldn't fill Ivy's position? The world had gone mad.

And I'm just here.

Selling tins of crab to servants from the big houses.

Beth shook her head to clear her thoughts and started entering the purchases into her ledger. 'Any news from Ralph?' she asked.

Florence had been stepping out with one of the footmen at Maitland Hall for a couple of years. Enlisting as soon as war was declared, he'd put a ring on Florence's finger just before he marched away.

'Got a letter this morning,' said Florence, starting to pack away the groceries. 'Thank goodness! I worry like anything when I don't hear from him. I'll pick up a few things for him now I'm here and send them on to him.'

'Where is he now?' asked Beth. 'Close enough to send perishables? Because everyone says this ham is wonderful.'

Florence paused, then gave a nervous little laugh. 'I'm not sure,' she said.

'Didn't he say?' asked Beth, nonplussed. Surely Ralph

would have mentioned where he was and where he was
going? Unless he wasn't allowed.

Florence's eyes darted around the shop and came to rest
on Beth's face. 'To be honest, I can't read most of what he
writes,' she said. Her green eyes brimmed with tears and she
dashed them away. 'I'm so stupid . . .'

Suddenly Beth remembered Florence crying in the school
playground, nursing whipped hands for getting her reading
or her spellings wrong. 'Oh, Florence,' she sighed.

'Ivy was helping me,' said Florence. 'But then she upped
and offed and I didn't know who else to ask. I mean, I'm
sure Cook would help, but . . .'

Beth understood. Who would want a dry old stick reading
out their love letters? The romantic bits would be bad enough
but God forbid there was anything saucy.

'When's your afternoon off?' Beth asked.

'Tomorrow,' said Florence. 'Why?'

'Tomorrow's my afternoon off too,' said Beth. 'If you
haven't got anything else on, would you like to come here
and I'll read Ralph's letters to you? That is, if you wouldn't
mind me seeing them.'

Florence paused in her packing and looked up, beaming.
'I'd like that very much,' she said. 'Thank you.'

The door to the shop jangled and both girls looked around.
It was Sam, the junior postman, dominating the space with
his height, his breadth . . . his *manliness*. Most of the girls in
Woodhampstead were sweet on Sam Harrison – had been
ever since they'd all been at school together – and Beth felt
herself blushing. It wouldn't be a delicate flush either; she
knew she'd have gone scarlet from her neck to the roots of
her hair. There was just something about Sam with his curly
dark hair, his deep blue eyes . . . his uniform. The ridiculous
thing was that she often saw him several times a day and she
knew she blushed every single time.

'Afternoon, ladies,' said Sam with his charming lop-sided grin.

'Afternoon,' said Beth.

At least she hadn't stammered.

'I need a couple of signatures from you,' said Sam, 'but I can wait until you've finished serving Florence.'

'Thank you.' Beth quickly finished parcelling up the last few items. 'I could write a letter to Ralph from you too, if you'd like?' she added quietly to Florence. 'To go with the package you're planning to send him.'

'Oh, Beth, *would* you?' said Florence, eyes shining. 'He's been having a right moan to his Ma that I don't write to him enough and I haven't liked to tell her why.'

'Of course,' said Beth. 'Come at half past one tomorrow.'

Florence nodded and left, weighed down with her purchases, and Beth watched the lad who had been sent from the hall jump down from the pony and trap to help her stow her parcels. The jingle of bridles, the swish of wheels through puddles and all was quiet again.

Beth turned to Sam. 'Hello,' she said, shyly.

'Raining cats and dogs out there,' Sam replied cheerfully.

Suddenly Beth couldn't think of a thing to say.

'Yes, it's very inclement, isn't it?' she said finally.

Inclement?

Inclement!

Who said inclement nowadays?

Sam chuckled. 'It is,' he said. 'Very . . . inclement. Now, I've got a right little haul for you this afternoon. Something tells me that today might be a special day?'

'Yes,' said Beth, feeling her blush intensify. 'It's our birthday. Mine and Ned's. Eighteen today.'

'Well, happy birthday to you both,' said Sam. 'And what's Ned going to be doing now that he's eighteen?'

'I don't know,' said Beth hurriedly. She didn't want to

discuss what Ned might have decided now he was old enough to sign up. She didn't even want to think about it. She and Ned had talked about it, of course, but still. She didn't want to talk about it today. And she certainly didn't want to talk about it to Sam, who was nineteen but who had a perfectly valid reason for not signing up because he was an only son and his father had died the year before.

'Of course,' said Sam, giving her an understanding smile. 'Well, as I say, I've got a right little haul for you both here.'

Beth beamed. She loved the daily post – birthday or no birthday – and she would have loved it even if Sam hadn't been the one delivering it. The post brought in the exciting, the luxurious, the useful – the things that couldn't be bought in Woodhampstead. The post brought invitations, gossip and, most importantly, it brought news.

The morning delivery hadn't contained much of interest but this one more than made up for it. That rectangle would be the nature book she'd ordered for Ned. The smaller one would be the skirt pattern she'd bought for herself. There were several other interesting-looking parcels and a handful of cards for both her and Ned. And – oh, look! – here was a card addressed to her from her cousin Charlotte! Beth would recognise those big forward-slanted letters anywhere – almost falling off the page in their hurry to be somewhere else. She snatched it up and held it to her nose, fancying she could catch a whiff of the heady perfume that Charlotte loved to wear.

Then her eyes met Sam's and she realised what a clot she must look, standing there clutching a letter to her face and inhaling deeply.

How immature.

How unsophisticated.

How *humiliating*.

No wonder Sam was laughing.

'I'm afraid I haven't got a birthday present for you,' he said, brandishing another envelope at her, 'but here's a little something that stumped the chaps in the sorting office this morning.'

Confused, Beth took the letter from his outstretched hand and resisted the temptation to fan her glowing cheeks with it. Then she realised it was one of *those*. An envelope with writing so impenetrable, it was almost impossible to decipher. Sam brought them in from time to time – had done ever since he'd come across Beth trying to interpret a shopping list he deemed officially impossible to read. Beth had never failed to deliver the goods.

Yet.

Beth duly studied the envelope, aware of Sam's deep blue eyes on her. At first nothing made sense. The writing was dense, the up and down strokes exaggerated, and the ink blots and smudges didn't help. She paused for a minute, waiting to get her eye in, for some clue to the puzzle to emerge . . .

Nothing.

Absolutely nothing.

Just a series of squiggles – apparently too many for a regular address.

Beth was tempted to take out the magnifying glass that Pa used to check that strangers' coins and notes were genuine, but Sam might think that was cheating. Maybe she should at least open the hinged counter and go over to the shop window for some proper light? That wouldn't be cheating, but it would leave her without the safety of a barrier between her and Sam. She was only wearing her second-best skirt that day and the hem was a little ragged on one side . . .

Oh, for goodness' sake, Beth.

Concentrate.

Still nothing. Was she going to have to admit defeat?

Ahh . . . but she'd already given herself the clue.

Too many lines for a normal address.

The writer was one of those who split words randomly onto two lines. Yes, there it was: Woodha on one line, mpstead on the next. And then Hertfo on one line and rdshire on the following. Not even a logical break in the words – but at least it gave her something to go on. And – aha! – it was obviously an elderly writer because she or he was using the old long 's', which looked more like a 'f'' in the double-s words. Mrs McBride used it sometimes and it made molasses look like molafses. And – yes, again! – they were using the old letter 'c', which looked more like a capital 'e' with its elongated tail.

Beth looked up and smiled at Sam. 'Jessica Carter, Baronsmead, Nomansland, Woodhampstead, Hertfordshire,' she rattled off triumphantly.

Sam slapped his hand against his thigh. 'You've done it!' he said. 'You're a marvel, you really are. And it's close enough that I can just drop it off now. You really should join the post office – you're wasted in here!'

Beth laughed. She loved it when Sam teased her and his eyes went all crinkly at the corners. 'Lugging those great big bags around in all weathers?' she said. 'I have enough trouble with the tea and the flour here, thank you. And I burn some-thing rotten in the sun.'

The door jangled behind Sam and a couple of women came in, chatting intently.

'Well, goodbye then,' said Sam.

And he was gone.

The rest of the afternoon was busy.

Really busy.

It seemed that the whole of Woodhampstead had left it until four o'clock on Wednesday afternoon to go shopping which, to be honest, they probably had because the rain was finally letting up and a pale April sun was trying to peek through the clouds.

In they came, gently steaming from the rain, chatting about the weather and over-buying just about everything that happened to be in stock. Mrs McBride came back to complain the butter *had* been too salt but she would take another half a pound anyway. Mrs Lovell needed condensed milk – as much as possible – to make coconut pyramids for the village fete that weekend. Mrs Collins wanted to tell her, in great detail, about her cousin's friend's neighbour who had just lost a leg in France. Beth didn't mind the crowds, didn't mind the gossip; it made the day go faster, and took her mind off what Ned might or might not have decided to do. But where the dickens was Ma? Ma *always* worked in the shop in the afternoon with Beth but she had taken off somewhere and Beth had no idea where she'd gone. And on her birthday to boot!

By five o'clock, the crowds of shoppers had dwindled away and Beth was exhausted. She lifted up the hinged counter and walked across to the door, flipping the shop sign from 'open' to 'closed'.

Drained, she leant her head against the glass and stared out across the street. The view hadn't changed since, well, *ever*. The rain had started up again and was bouncing off the dirt road and dripping from the eaves of the cottages opposite. Even from here, and with the door closed, Beth fancied she could smell the heady scent of the sweet peas in their front gardens. School had finished for the day and children had filled the streets as they did every day, rain or shine, winter or summer – their homes too small to stay cooped up indoors. The boys were playing football and the girls had formed a long line across the road and were playing a complicated game of catch, which Beth remembered from her own childhood. Everything looked as it had always looked. Pretty soon, Pa would arrive home and Mayfair, the lovely old mare who pulled the delivery cart, would take a deep draught from the trough outside. Pa would wave to her and then lead Mayfair through the arch beside the shop and into the stable behind and then old Mr Hiscock would arrive with his ladder and the paraffin oil to light the street lamp and another evening would begin . . .

And yet, despite the gentle rhythms and routines that had punctuated her eighteen years, below the surface, *everything* had changed.

Most of the young men had gone.

Her older sister Sally's husband Bertie. *His* brother Reginald. Florence's fiancé Ralph. Farm labourers, gravel-diggers, gardeners, coal merchants, brick-layers, railway porters, errand boys . . . the small town had lost them all. Almost two hundred of them. Less than a week after war was declared, they'd been swallowed up by the Beds, the Royal Engineers, the Army Service Corps, the Labour Corps, the Egyptian Expeditionary Force and goodness knew what else and marched off to an uncertain future. Some had died. And throughout the year, more and more boys had turned eighteen and signed up.

And here was Ned, squelching up the street, shoulders hunched, hands in pockets, sandy hair forming little peaks in the rain. To an outside observer, there would have been nothing unusual in the way he pushed the door open, said hello to Beth and disappeared through the counter into the storeroom and the house beyond. But, to Beth, everything was different. It was what Ned *hadn't* done. He hadn't made a silly face. He hadn't attempted to ruffle her hair or to pull her plait. He hadn't even tried to filch a piece of ham or a sliver of cheese.

Beth sighed deeply and looked around at the rows of

colourful tins and shining jars on the wooden shelves. The shop, as usual, was immaculate. But, beneath the surface, things were shifting beyond recognition.

I'm eighteen years old today and everything is changing.

2

Supper was fit for King George himself in honour of Beth and Ned's birthday.

Ma had reappeared and she and Agnes-the-daily had been busy, rustling up a fine shoulder of lamb with anchovy and caper sauce, roast potatoes and three different types of vegetables – all served on the only-for-best china. It was certainly fit for a celebration and everyone was acting as if it was a celebration too; faces bright and rosy, the conversation punctuated by loud bursts of laughter.

Rather than relaxing her, the fancy food and crockery just put Beth more on edge. She looked around the dining room almost as if seeing it for the first time. Like the rest of the family's rooms, it was neither as smart nor as tidy as the shop at the front of the house. The heavy oak furniture and brown wallpaper had been there her whole life, as had the soot stains shadowing the gas lamps, the cream embroidered tablecloth and the picture of Queen Victoria casting a malevolent eye over them all.

Then she looked around the table at her family. Ma and Pa, her and Ned and her older sister Sally. Sally and Bertie had moved into a cottage on the edge of the village when they married, but now that Bertie was in France with his brother Reggie, Sally found it lonely living there by herself and often came round to the family home in the evening after she had finished her shift at her in-laws' pub. How similar Pa and Sally were with their dark wavy hair, brown eyes and broad, square faces and how different to Beth, Ned and Ma, who were all fair with a smattering of freckles. It was hard to believe they were all members of the same family.

Once Pa had said grace, Ned smoothed a crumpled piece of paper onto the table. 'The recruitment officer came into the estate office and gave this to me,' he said with a little grimace.

Beth leant forwards, squinting at the paper. It was a flyer, printed in green ink with '6th Battalion Bedfordshire Regiment' emblazoned in huge letters across the top. The Beds – the same regiment many of the local boys had joined. The army, it explained, was in urgent need of more recruits to complete the battalion and an earnest appeal was being made to all men of military age. There followed details about who could enlist and how to do so, terms of service (four years or the duration of the war) and rates of pay. At the bottom were several signatures that meant nothing to Beth and an exhortation: 'God Save the King'.

'God save the boys' would be more appropriate, thought Beth with a lump in her throat. After all, she hadn't noticed His Majesty or any of his signatories volunteering to fight alongside the British Expeditionary Forces. And why was Ned being so calm – so *casual* – about all of this? Why wasn't he looking her in the eye?

'They might at least have addressed you by name,' she said. 'Surely they should have written you a proper letter. In an envelope.'

Ned laughed. 'You and your letters, Beth,' he teased. 'Maybe the recruitment officer should have sealed it with a kiss!'

Everyone laughed and Beth felt herself go pink.

'You know what I mean,' she said crossly. 'These things are so . . . impersonal.'

'It's a war, sis,' said Sally. 'No time for niceties.'

'Yes,' said Ned. 'Everyone's going. And now it's my turn.'

Icy water ran down Beth's spine. 'You've signed up?' she said.

You didn't tell me first?

'I have,' said Ned. 'Ma came to the recruitment office with me this afternoon.'

So that's where Ma had been.

A good enough reason for leaving Beth alone in the shop that afternoon, she supposed.

Ned finally met her gaze and in that moment Beth understood. He didn't want to go to France. He *really* didn't want to go, but he felt he had to and he was putting on a brave face. That was what was giving his words and actions the brittle edge she didn't recognise. No one had been surprised when some of the local boys had signed up as soon as the war started. They had sensed excitement, adventure, camaraderie – a way out of Woodhampstead.

But Ned was different.

Gentler.

Poor Ned.

Ned had already turned his attention back to his lamb. But, Beth decided, if he could put on a brave face on things, then so could she. Enough of her pathetic comments about letters. Time to show some backbone.

'I know everyone said it would be over by last Christmas,' she said, smiling round the table. 'And I know they were wrong. But I'm sure it will be over by this Christmas and we'll all be able to celebrate together.'

Ma smiled back at her. 'Of course it will,' she said staunchly. 'It will be over and it will be a victory. As good Queen Victoria said, "we are not interested in the possibilities of defeat".'

'Too right we're not,' said Pa. 'The Hun won't know what's hit them with my boy giving them hell.'

Ned looked up. 'If the war's finished by Christmas, it had

better be the biggest and best Christmas we've ever had,' he said. 'I shall expect the tallest tree, the biggest plum pudding, and mince pies to be coming out of my ears.'

Beth laughed. 'Ma and I will make a whole dozen,' she said. 'Just for you.'

'With cream?' said Ned.

'Of course.'

'And cherries?'

'No self-respecting mince pie contains cherries,' said Beth, parroting the cookery books. 'But, if you insist on being a heathen, I shall stuff each one of yours full of them! Oh goodness, I can't believe you're going. Really going. Off to serve King and Country. Maybe I should be doing something too. Doing my bit.'

Beth hadn't meant to say that. The words seem to have arrived fully formed, missing out her brain. And what a silly thing to have said. After all, what could she, sensible, logical, play-by-the-rules Beth, possibly do to help? She bit her lip and glanced around the table. Would her parents scold her? Worse still, would they laugh?

But Ma just gave her a smile. 'You *are* doing your bit dear,' she said. 'After all, what could be more useful than helping in the family shop? And you've got a very important role to play in curbing all this over-buying. I looked at the ledger today and Mrs McBride is buying a ludicrous amount of butter for someone who lives on her own, and as for Maitland Hall suddenly buying all those tins . . . It's very unpatriotic and we're going to end up with real shortages if we don't put a stop to it.'

Beth signed inwardly. Stopping people buying too much tea and tinned crab wasn't really making a difference, was it? Not really the sort of difference she had in mind, anyway.

But at least Ma hadn't laughed.

★　★　★

Beth knew exactly where she'd find Ned once supper was over.

And, yes, there he was – in the fragrant, dusty storeroom between the hallway and the shop. He was sitting on a wooden crate in the corner, legs bent and chin resting on his knees, just like he'd always done after a fight or a beating or when he needed some time to himself.

Without saying anything, Beth reached for the jar of sherbet lemons. They hadn't pinched any for years, but tonight it seemed the right thing to do. She shook out two and she and Ned tucked in in companionable silence. Then, as the tartness hit, they sucked their cheeks in as hard as they could until their faces were distorted. Ned – as he had always done – crossed his eyes for good effect and Beth – as *she* had always done – tried and failed to do the same. By the time the sweets were finished, both of them were smiling.

'You don't want to go, do you?' said Beth.

She never had to mind what she said to Ned; she could say what she felt.

What she *knew*.

Ned paused and then shook his head. 'No,' he said. 'I don't want to go. I know that makes me a coward, yellow—'

'It doesn't make you either of those things,' said Beth fiercely, sitting up straighter and tucking wisps from her plait behind her ears. 'And, anyway,' she added, because it was worth a try, 'I know you've already signed up, but you don't *have* to go.'

'I do,' said Ned flatly. 'You know I do.'

'It's voluntary,' said Beth. 'Couldn't you claim essential work or something?'

Ned gave her a sideways look. 'For what?' he said, with a snort of laughter. 'Tying up the roses? Pruning the privet?'

'Rosehip syrup is very good for warding off colds,' said Beth. 'So that's essential medicine production.'

Ned smiled. 'And I guess the privet is to poison the enemy?'

'Exactly,' said Beth. 'No one can argue with that!'

Ned laughed and stood up to dig out another two sweets. 'Write, Beth,' he said, suddenly serious. 'Promise me you'll write?'

'Of course I will,' said Beth.

'But write to me *properly*. Tell me things that really matter. The bad stuff as well as the good.'

'I promise,' said Beth. 'And you must do the same. Promise me you'll save the King and Country stuff for Ma and Pa and let me know what's really going on. Even if it's awful. *Especially* if it's awful.'

'I promise,' said Ned. 'Even though I'm not really one for letters, I promise to do my best. I don't think I'll be able to get through whatever's coming without someone I can share everything with.'

'You can be honest with me,' said Beth. 'And I promise to be honest with you, too.'

And Beth vowed she would keep that promise.

Whatever was happening in her own small, useless life, she would keep her promise.

3

Two days later, Ned was gone, swallowed up by the Beds and off to training in Northamptonshire. His departure left Beth feeling bereft. Oh, she was close enough to Sally, of course – she loved her sister – but there was no one she could talk to quite like Ned.

For the next few weeks, Beth fought abject terror. There was no other word for it. She could be doing something quite ordinary – slicing the bacon, plaiting her hair, helping Ma around the kitchen – when a physical pain, like a knife through butter, would strike under her breastbone, making her catch her breath. It was the helplessness that was the worst. Here she was, languishing behind the counter, packaging goods, dispensing credit, totting up the ledger, while her brother had gone off to an uncertain future and there was nothing she could do about it. He was only training at the moment, but what happened next?

It was awful.

In the meantime, life went on as normal. The shop was as full of customers as it was increasingly low on stock. Pa reported that more and more wholesalers didn't have the goods to supply them and people were buying more than usual. It was so silly, Beth thought. Everyone had more than enough to worry about without adding unnecessary food shortages – couldn't they just buy what they needed and leave the rest for someone else? She'd heard Ma and Pa discuss how the government should introduce rationing but, for now, it was every household for itself.

It certainly wasn't the responsibility of the shop to start rationing but Ma was very good at making the odd casual comment to try and make people think again about what they were planning to buy. 'My, that's a lot of sugar for someone who lives on their own,' she said when Mrs Collins tried to buy several pounds of granulated. Or 'Do you have the whole Hertfordshire Regiment coming for elevenses?' when Mrs Johnson tried to buy enough tea leaves to sink the Armada. Or when Mrs Richardson requested a ridiculously large amount of flour, she'd say gently, 'There's more coming on Tuesday – no need to struggle home with it all today.' And Beth noticed that on most occasions the shopper reconsidered and bought less.

'Give it a try, Beth,' Ma said gently.

But that sort of thing didn't come easily to Beth. She was too young, too meek – it wasn't in her nature. Besides, the idea of saying something felt strange when Ma was by her side. Surely such a reprimand to a customer, however mild, should come from her?

'I've got to pop to the post office and the greengrocers,' said Ma, 'so what about giving it a whirl then?'

'All right,' said Beth. Luckily the shop was reasonably quiet that day. 'I promise I'll have words with the very next customer who tries to buy too much.'

With a bit of luck, she thought, there wouldn't be anyone else in the store to witness her attempts.

Ma duly disappeared. The next few customers only bought a few things – nothing she could possibly find fault with – and then Mrs McBride walked in. Beth willed her just to buy some ink and writing paper or maybe a packet of custard.

'Three pounds of flour, Elizabeth, please,' said Mrs McBride, fixing Beth with her dark, beady eyes.

Oh no! There was no way that Mrs McBride needed that much flour. She would have to say something. She would plaster on a bright smile and try *two* of the lines Ma had used. Hopefully that would do the trick.

'My, that's a lot of flour for someone who lives on her own,' she said. 'Perhaps you would like to leave some of it for next Tuesday when we have another order coming in.'

There was a silence that stretched and lengthened until you could have heard a mouse squeak from the storeroom.

Then Mrs McBride banged her stick on the ground.

Once, twice, three times.

'Such impertinence, Elizabeth,' she hissed. 'I did not expect that from you.'

Beth, stung by embarrassment, hung her head in silence. Thank goodness there was no one else in the shop to witness her humiliation.

But Mrs McBride hadn't finished. 'I assume you are implying that I'm hoarding, young lady?' she said. 'If you must know, I'm baking apple pies for the harvest fete at St Helen's in aid of the soldiers. Is that a good enough reason for you?'

'Yes, Mrs McBride,' Beth whispered, reaching for the flour. 'I'm so sorry.'

'Just be grateful I'm not going to tell your parents on this occasion,' said Mrs McBride.

With flaming cheeks, Beth entered the purchase into the ledger and Mrs McBride staggered out, tutting loudly.

Beth rested her head in her hands on the counter, tears prickling at her eyelids.

That had been terrible.

She had been terrible.

She wanted to do her bit but she couldn't even manage

to ask an old lady to buy less flour so there was enough to go around.

She was hopeless.

Maybe Ma and Pa would actually be better off without her in the shop – but what would she do then?

Then again, maybe *she* should be the one to be getting angry. The war had been started by old people who expected the young to put their lives on hold at best, and at worst to make the ultimate sacrifice – and yet they were still expected to be seen and not heard.

Why shouldn't they have a view?

A voice?

It just wasn't fair.

'Afternoon, Beth.'

Beth looked up. She had been so caught up in misery and confusion, she had barely heard the shop door jangle. It was Sam, bringing in a burst of fresh May fragrance and holding out a little stack of letters.

'Hello, Sam,' replied Beth, straightening up and hoping it wasn't too obvious that she had been close to tears.

'Lots of letters for you all today,' said Sam, apparently oblivious to any drama. 'Looks like a couple from Ned as well.'

Beth fairly snatched the letters from him. She had written to Ned most days and sent him a few parcels but she didn't hear back from him very often and she was tempted to rip the envelope open in front of Sam.

'Thank you,' she said, almost absentmindedly. 'See you later.'

There was a pause.

'You won't actually,' said Sam.

'Oh. Is it your day off? I thought—'

'No,' said Sam. 'I've signed up.'

Beth stared at him, her mind going nineteen to the dozen. What had he just said?

'For the army?' she said at last. She couldn't think of anything else to say.

'Yes, the army. I've joined the Post Office Rifles.'

'But you can't,' Beth blurted out, not caring what he thought of her.

'I can,' said Sam simply. 'And I must. I'm nineteen. I should have gone before now—'

'But who will deliver the post?' said Beth, clutching at straws. 'Doesn't it count as essential work?'

'They can manage without me,' said Sam. 'In fact, I've got to give my uniform back tonight. That's why I'm not doing the evening round.'

'Oh, no!' Beth's hand shot involuntarily to her mouth. Wasn't taking his uniform back terribly cruel? Didn't it imply that the uniform would never need to be worn again?

'I know,' said Sam, correctly interpreting her thoughts. 'Ma almost collapsed when I told her. But the Post Office donates the material to make war uniforms. Nothing more to it than that. Anyway, they've already recruited my replacement.' He paused and then grinned. 'Don't you want to know who it is?'

Not really, thought Beth. It would be someone old, someone past recruitment age. It wouldn't be Sam with his curly hair and dancing eyes . . .

'It's Ivy Hastings from Maitland Hall,' said Sam, without waiting for a reply. 'Her father works in the Welwyn Post Office and . . .'

Beth shut her eyes, trying to take it all in.

Ivy Hastings.

Ivy – with her marvellous curls and dark smoky eyes – was going to be the new Woodhampstead postman. Or should one say post*wo*man? Oh, sub post offices round about had been run by women since time immemorial; indeed, the Woodhampstead Post Office further up the high street had been run by Mrs Nash from her greengrocery ever since

Beth could remember. But *delivering* the post? That was quite another matter.

Ivy's leaving to do her bit and I'm just standing here.
I'm doing nothing to help.
But never mind all that. Sam was leaving.
Leaving!
'You should think about joining her,' said Sam. He held up his hand as Beth opened her mouth to protest. 'Not doing the rounds. They're looking for girls like you to help sort the letters going to chaps in the army.'

Sam didn't look like he was joking. He was looking at her quite seriously with his head on one side.

'I'm needed here,' Beth said simply.

'Of course.' Sam was pulling his sack back onto his shoulder. 'With your brother away . . .'

Beth nodded. It wasn't because her brother was away, of course; Ned hadn't even worked in the shop – he was useless at adding up. It was just that working in the shop had always been her job, ever since she'd left school at fourteen. Oh, there had been a chance of a scholarship to the school in St Albans but Ma and Pa had waved that away. She was needed here.

It was just the way things were.

And now Sam was leaving – on a sunny May Day when nothing bad should happen – and she hardly had time to say goodbye because Mrs Mason and Mrs Jones had come into the shop and were waiting to be served and, besides, she couldn't possibly find the right words to say goodbye to a young man who was barely even a friend and yet she minded what might happen to him.

Then Sam leaned over the counter and Beth found she was holding her breath. What on earth was he going to say?

'I couldn't help overhearing you offering to read Florence's letters from Ralph the other week,' said Sam.

'Er . . . yes.' Whatever Beth had imagined Sam had been going to say, it hadn't been *that*.

'Only, I wondered if you'd mind very much helping my mother get started. Just to begin with. Her writing's pretty good but she might need help with addressing the envelope the new way until she gets used to it.'

'I'd be happy to,' said Beth.

Sam smiled. 'Thank you,' he said, turning to leave. Then he turned back around, one big hand on the counter. 'Please feel free to write to me as well,' he said with his wonderful smile.

The two locked eyes for a second longer than Beth fancied was strictly necessary. She gave him the smallest of nods before Sam swung around, nodded to the other shoppers and was gone, the doorbell jangling with finality behind him.

That evening, at supper, Pa read out Ned's letter to the family. As usual, it was full of bland news about his training and stoic platitudes about the war. There was no trace of the disillusionment and fear he confessed in the separate letter he'd written to Beth. He had enclosed some hedgerow flowers for her too, carefully pressed between the pages. Lovely Ned, who so loved nature and the turning seasons. Beth stared down at her chops, mash and carrots and her heart broke for her twin.

'He's safe, praise the Lord,' Ma said, hand to heart.

'Of course, he's *safe*, Ma,' said Sally with a laugh. 'He's training in *Northamptonshire*. He's probably as safe there as he is at home.'

There was an edge to her laugh, though. Reports were reaching home of a new French battle at a place called Festubert.

Beth put her hand on her sister's. 'No news, today?' she asked, and Sally shook her head.

'You'll hear soon,' said Pa. 'He'll write as soon as he can, I'm sure, and chances are he's miles from Festubert.'

'Either way, it will be over soon and it will be a victory,' added Ma.

No one responded. Beth knew that none of them really believed that the war would be finished any time soon. Not anymore.

Beth took a deep breath. 'Sam Harrison has signed up to the Post Office Rifles.' She said it as much to change the subject as anything else, but she couldn't wait to share the news. It had barely left her mind all afternoon.

Of course, everybody else already knew. News in Woodhampstead travelled faster than the time it took for Mrs McBride to find fault with the world.

'So, Sam's finally going, is he?' said Pa. 'Some would say it's not before time.'

'It's been hard on his mother with him still being around,' said Ma. 'Julia Harrison has hardly been able to look me in the eye with Ned signing up as soon as he was able. But it will be hard on her, without a husband and now without Sam. I'll drop round hers with a little something tomorrow.'

'I told Sam I'd help his mother write back to him,' added Beth, as casually as she could.

She found she rather liked saying Sam's name out loud.

Ma smiled and murmured, 'That's kind, dear' and Pa just grunted as he shook out his newspaper. But Sally, of course, gave her a sharp, enquiring look. Sally might not have excelled at school – might have been desperate to get married as soon as she could – but not much got past her where relationships and matters of the heart were concerned. Beth wondered what Sally would say if she knew Sam had also asked Beth to write to him, and decided that she wouldn't tell her. Not yet, anyway. For all she knew, Sam had asked half of Woodhampstead to write to him. For all she knew, he'd also asked Sally. Except that Sally was married and had her own little cottage around the corner and that wouldn't have been at all appropriate . . .

Oh, stop *overthinking* everything, Beth! she thought to herself. Why on earth would Sam ask *Sally* to write to him?

'Ivy Hastings is going to deliver the post,' she said, to shift the subject from Sam and to stop Sally grinning at her.

Of course, her family were bound to know this too. Had probably known it for days!

Only . . . they didn't!

'Ivy?' said Sally with a little giggle. 'Fancy! Whoever heard of such a thing?'

'I know,' said Beth. 'Imagine *Ivy* lugging all those sacks about!'

'Will she carry them?' pondered Sally. 'Or ride a bike?'

'Heaven knows,' said Ma. 'Either way, she'll probably take an age and we'll be down to one post a day before we know it! And I can't imagine the women liking their drawers and whatnots being delivered by a *girl*. She might take a peek and it would be all around the village like a shot.'

Beth smiled but she felt a little stab of protectiveness towards her gender. We aren't all gossips and airheads, she thought. Some of us know how to keep a secret. Not that she had many secrets to keep, but she had never told when Ned had sneaked out of his bedroom window and climbed down the ivy to look for badgers one night or had 'borrowed' Mayfair to ride to the river in search of otters.

She hadn't told a soul.

Pa put his paper back down on the table. 'Is Ivy that little slip of a thing from Maitland Hall?' he asked. 'I suppose she's one of *them*. Those suffragists or suffragettes or whatever they're calling themselves nowadays. Dreadful women. Throwing themselves in front of horses and blowing up postboxes and generally stirring up mischief.'

Beth and Sally exchanged a glance.

'I don't think Ivy Hastings is a suffragette,' said Beth mildly.

'Queen Victoria said that when women claim equality with

men, they "unsex" themselves and become the most hateful, heathen, and disgusting of beings,' said Ma, apropos of nothing.

Beth found herself suddenly battling a strong desire to laugh out loud, which would not only be disrespectful to her mother but most unseemly at the supper table.

But . . . really.

Beth wasn't particularly interested in the suffrage movement – rich ladies with nothing better to do with their time as far as she was concerned – but Ma didn't half have some strange ideas sometimes. And as for funny old Queen Victoria . . .

'I am sure Ivy Hastings considers herself suitably "unsexed",' said Sally, with an infinitesimal wink at Beth.

Oh dear.

That was too much.

Too, too much!

Beth didn't dare look at Sally. She cast her eye around the room and tried to concentrate on something – *anything* – to stop herself laughing out loud. She settled on Queen Victoria's malevolent eye and finally she had herself under control again. She wiped her mouth demurely with the corner of her napkin and risked a tiny glance at Sally. Sally gave her another almost imperceptible wink in return.

'Queen Victoria also said that women would surely perish without male protection,' said Ma, seemingly oblivious to the mirth.

Beth banished a vison of Sam shielding her from unseen dangers and started speaking before her brain was fully engaged. 'But that's just the point,' she said hotly. Well, hotly for her anyway. 'There aren't any men around *to* protect us. I'm absolutely certain Ivy Hastings isn't a suffragette. She's just stepping forward to help keep things going. Maybe she's doing the right thing. In fact, maybe I should be—'

'That's enough, Beth,' said Ma sharply. 'Your father is still here to keep things going for us and *your* place is in the shop.'

'Cutting up the butter and being shouted at by Mrs McBride . . .' muttered Beth, surprising even herself. What on earth had got into her?

'Quiet, Beth!' cut in Pa. 'Keeping things running smoothly is more important than cutting loose and leaving everyone in the lurch as Ivy seems to have done. When our boys come back, do you think they want to see everything changed?'

'No, Pa,' said Beth dutifully, staring at her plate.

'There you are,' said Pa. 'You have important work to do here. Let's not be hearing any of this nonsense again.'

'No, Pa,' repeated Beth.

She didn't dare say anything else, but her mind was working feverishly. Everything around her was changing – but not for her. Oh, she didn't mind working in the shop; it was all she had ever known. But she had worked there for four years, ever since she'd left school, and maybe, just maybe, she no longer wanted to be stuck behind the glass, on the inside looking out, watching the world go by. With her long blond plait, she fancied she was rather like Rapunzel or the Lady of Shalott – only there was less and less chance of a handsome prince riding by to rescue her. Especially now Sam Harrison was off to the war.

Who was she?

Where did she fit it?

Everything was changing and surely that meant desperate measures.

The thought came from nowhere, beating a tattoo into Beth's skull.

Britain was at war with Germany and Sensible Beth, Play-by-the-rules Beth, was going to make sure that she played a proper part in it.

4

When Beth went to bed that night she had wondered if she would wake the next morning feeling differently about things.

It wouldn't be the first time; after all, how many times had she had a furious row with Sally or Ned and gone to sleep vowing that she would never speak to them again only to wake the next morning realising that the argument had been so trivial that was not worth thinking about?

Well, this time it was different.

Beth woke the next morning feeling just as, if not more, determined to do her bit. The trouble was, it was all very well deciding to do something, but how on earth was one supposed to set about it doing it? And, in particular, how was one supposed to do it without the whole village finding out and reporting back to her mother and father before she'd got her thoughts together, let alone got something off the ground.

She had to do something.

She had to make a difference and, if she wasn't able to do it in Woodhampstead, she would damn well do it elsewhere.

'Were you planning to see Julia Harrison on your half day?' Ma asked when the two of them were alone in the shop later that morning.

'No.' Beth was surprised. 'I was planning to leave it for at least a week after Sam goes.'

'Ah,' said Ma. 'Only I've put aside a couple of things for her and I wondered if you'd mind dropping them off for me.'

Beth's heart leapt. Might there be a chance to see Sam before he left? She had already decided that Sam had just been being friendly when he'd asked her to write to him; it didn't mean that he was sweet on her – and it certainly didn't mean that they were stepping out together. But it would be lovely to say goodbye. It was a nice day and maybe he'd ask her take a stroll along the river. She would tuck her arm into his and then, where the river narrowed and the willows kept their secrets, he would turn to her, blue eyes dancing and—

Oh, stop it Beth.

'I'm happy to go anyway, Ma.'

She'd go as soon as she finished work. She'd wash her face and hands in the scullery and re-plait her hair. The important thing was to do it quickly because time was of the essence. Who knew when Sam would actually leave?

And then, with a sinking heart, she remembered. She'd arranged for Florence to come around with her latest letter from Ralph. It was far too late to send Florence a message and she couldn't possibly not be at home when Florence arrived. Beth sighed and cursed herself for being so proper. She knew that many would just rush round to Sam's and hang the consequences. But not her. Not Sensible Beth, Play-by-the-rules Beth. She would just have to wait and to go around to the Harrisons once Florence had gone.

She would just have to hope that it wasn't too late.

In the event, Florence was late.

Beth had already finished her soup and bread and cheese and was pacing impatiently when Florence finally knocked at the back door.

'I'm right sorry I'm so late,' she panted. 'Our dinner seemed to go on for hours and hours today.'

It wasn't Florence's fault. No need to take it out on her.

The latest letter from Ralph – like the others before them – wasn't particularly exciting or saucy. It was quite short and written in a childish hand, riddled with misspellings and grammatical errors. Like the others, it gave some sparse details of what he'd done over the past few days. He was out in the Dardanelles and, even though he hadn't seen any action, the flies, the food and the water were making his life hell. He expressed his fervent desire to give the enemy a good bashing, asked after her welfare, professed his love and the fact he was missing her and begged Florence to write back to him and to send him socks and tobacco. Probably the most interesting thing about the letter was the way the stamp had been applied in the bottom left-hand corner of the envelope. Beth didn't comment but she was secretly appalled. Everyone knew that stamps went at the top right corner.

Florence, of course, lapped it all up.

'Shall we get some tea and then I'll help you to write a letter back?' said Beth.

She mustn't, she told herself sternly, think about Sam. Helping Florence was more important and Beth didn't want her to feel rushed.

But – oh! – time was ticking by. By the time the letter was written and addressed and Beth had practically slammed Florence's hat onto her head for her and bundled her out of the door, it was mid-afternoon. Beth sprang into action. She gathered up the provisions her mother had set aside and packed them carefully into a basket, covering it with a cloth. As an afterthought she ran into the storeroom and shook some sweets for Sam's younger sisters into a paper bag. Dora, she recalled, was very partial to Vinegar-Flats while Elsie and

Lucy liked Yanky-Pankies. She added lemon bonbons for good measure because she vaguely recalled that Sam liked them.

And then she was off, walking briskly up the high street, past Blacks the tailor, Nash the greengrocer and Parfitt the china shop, nodding and greeting people by name. Up past the blacksmith, and the butcher and over the bridge past the mill and the road to the station. By the time she got to the side street that the Harrisons lived on, she was as close to running as would be seemly.

School was already finished for the day and Sam's sisters were outside the cottage. Thirteen-year-old Dora was sitting on the low cottage wall between the hollyhocks and half-heartedly knitting a sock and the younger girls were playing marbles with friends in the rutted cart tracks in the road. Beth hurried up to them, planning to offer some bland good wishes about their brother's imminent departure or maybe to say something about the weather, or the sweets she had brought for them . . . but in the event her mouth over-rode her brain. She came to a halt in front of them all and blurted out, '*Sam?*'

Dora looked up.

'Gone,' she said shortly and Beth could see that she had been crying.

'Gone?' echoed Beth. Her legs went weak, the stuffing knocked out of them and she sat down heavily on the wall next to Dora. 'Oh, Lordy! Gone when?'

'This morning,' said Dora, flatly.

Gone.

After all that worry, all that stress, all that chivvying of Florence – and Beth had never had the chance of saying goodbye. Beth battled a strong desire to join Dora in her tears. She mustn't though – she knew she mustn't. Sam was Dora's *brother*, for goodness' sake, and she was just a foolish shop girl who had had her head turned because Sam had asked her to write to him. In the relative scheme of things, she had no right to cry.

So, with a great effort, Beth tilted her chin and turned to Dora with a smile. 'I'm sorry he's gone,' she said. 'I'm sure he'll be safe.'

Dora looked at Beth through her brother's blue eyes and Beth could see that she didn't think Beth's comment worthy of reply. She had a point. How could Beth possibly know Sam would be safe?

'What's in the basket?' said one of the younger girls.

Beth stood up. 'Provisions for your mother,' she said. 'And there might be some sweets for you and your sisters too.'

That got more of a favourable response. Dora smiled and the marble-players clustered around, whether or not they happened to be related to Sam. She left them exclaiming over their little haul of sweets and walked up the short path to the front door. It was ajar, but she rapped tentatively all the same, not wanting to barge in on a day like today. After a moment, Mrs Harrison appeared and Beth was relieved to see that, while pale, she looked composed and was, as ever, very neat and proper. Her hair was up in a little bun and she had troubled to put gold rings in her ears, and to have a neat, tight waist and a whale-bone collar.

'Hello, Beth,' she said with a little smile.

'Good afternoon, Mrs Harrison,' said Beth politely. 'My mother has sent me round with some provisions because . . . because . . .' She trailed off. What could she possibly add? Because your son has gone to war and you may struggle to put food on the table? Because your son has gone to war and may not come back?

Fortunately, Mrs Harrison seemed to realise her dilemma. 'That's very kind of your mother,' she said. 'Would you be kind enough to take the basket through to the kitchen?'

Beth followed Mrs Harrison down the passage. Despite the bright summer day, the kitchen was gloomy with its brown wallpaper and the oilskins on the table and it took Beth's eyes a while to adjust.

'I'm so sorry Sam's gone,' Beth said honestly as she began to unpack the cheese and ham and assortment of tins.

Mrs Harrison smiled. 'I've been telling him to go and do his duty for a while but he's always said a family needs a man at its head. And with his father dead . . . I told him that we'd all pull together without him but he wouldn't listen.' She paused, then gave a little laugh. 'In the end do you know what got him to go? It certainly wasn't me. It was a girl in St Albans!'

'Oh!' Beth's hand fluttered to her chest.

A girl.

Of *course* Sam had a sweetheart!

'Yes,' said Mrs Harrison. 'He was walking down the street, minding his own business, and she tapped him on the shoulder and handed him a white feather!'

'*Oh*,' said Beth again but for quite a different reason. The enormity of her relief that the girl hadn't been a sweetheart took her totally by surprise. 'How perfectly horrible of her – especially not knowing his circumstances.'

'He was terribly upset,' said Mrs Harrison, 'and he looked into enlisting that very same day. And now he's gone and the girls are all devastated, but I know his papa would think he was doing the right thing.'

Beth didn't know what to say. In the end she said, 'Sam asked me to come in from time to time and to read his letters to you.'

Mrs Harrison started putting the tins into the pantry. 'I know he did,' she said over her shoulder, 'and I'm very grateful for your kindness but I shall be perfectly fine. My reading and writing are better than he thinks, and I have the girls to help me.'

'Of course,' said Beth feeling a little deflated. She picked up the empty basket and turned to go. 'Well, goodbye, Mrs Harrison.'

'Goodbye, Beth. And thank you.'

Beth had reached the door when Mrs Harrison called after her. 'Oh, I almost forgot. Sam did give me a message to pass on to you when I next saw you.'

Beth paused with her hand on the door handle and swung around round, her heart pumping painfully in her chest. What could Sam possibly have wanted to tell her? If it was through his mother, it wouldn't be anything too personal or intimate . . . but, then again, needs must.

Oh, stop it, Beth!

'I need to make sure I get it right,' said Mrs Harrison, wrinkling her brow. 'It's all very mysterious and I'm not sure if it will make any sense to you. But he said that if you change your mind – and he hopes you do – you need to talk to Mr Webb at St Albans Post Office.'

5

She'd go to St Albans.

Of course, she would.

The whole thing felt almost like it was meant to be. After all, she'd been wondering how she could do more to help and Sam had presented her details of how to go about it on a plate.

Why *wouldn't* she go?

On the other hand, it was a ridiculous idea. Ma and Pa had already made it abundantly clear that her future – her *duty* – lay in the shop, helping the family business. She loved and respected her parents and had no wish to anger or disappoint them, especially with Ned away and emotions running high. She should just get on with working in the shop and fold bandages and knit socks for the soldiers in her spare time like everyone else was doing.

Of *course*, she wouldn't go.

Oh, but then again, the shop was so dull and the world was so big and . . .

Round and round she went, going over and over the same ground. At last she came to a decision. She would talk to this Mr Webb, whoever he was, and at least find out more about what the job entailed. That much she felt she owed to Sam. But she wouldn't make any hasty or impulsive decisions without thinking it all through carefully and talking it over with her family. And, of course, the position may not be suitable or she may not be offered it or it might already have been filled. There were a thousand and one ways it might not work out.

It was one thing deciding to go and talk to Mr Webb. It was quite another thing actually *getting* to St Albans in order to do so. St Albans was over five miles away – too far to walk, even on her half day – and it was a tricky train journey, involving changing at least once and often twice. It would probably be months until she could devise a plan to get there and then the job would be gone and that would be that. Maybe it was for the best.

But then Pa unwittingly came to the rescue. Less than a week later, he idly mentioned that he was going to St Albans the very next day to try and find some additional flour suppliers to boost the shop's dwindling stocks.

'Oh, I'd love to go to St Albans,' said Beth, feeling horribly deceitful. 'To have coffee in a cafe and to go to the haberdashery and the bookshop. Ned asked about sending him some books in his last letter.'

The last bit, at least, was true. Beth wouldn't lie about Ned.

'Believe me, I won't be doing any of *that*,' said Pa. 'I shall be haggling with mulish millers and I promise you there won't be a cup of coffee, a ribbon or a book in sight.'

Everyone laughed and then Ma unexpectedly came to Beth's rescue by saying, 'Why don't you go with him, Beth? You've been working so hard recently; you deserve a little treat.'

'I shall be most of the day, Rose,' warned her father. 'Are you sure you can spare Beth for that long?'

'Just this once,' said Ma with a smile. 'After all, it's been tough for her with Ned gone and she has been working very hard.' Ma leant over and patted Beth on the knee.

Oh, the guilt!

Couldn't her parents see it written all over her face?

She almost wished her mother had protested that she *was* needed in the shop, and of course she couldn't just swan off to St Albans. Then she could paint her mother as an ogre and rebel against her with impunity.

Life was so *difficult*, sometimes.

Beth dressed with extra care the next morning.

No one commented. Ma just pressed some money into her hand as she waited for Pa to finish harnessing Mayfair.

'It's not much,' she said, kissing Beth on the cheek, 'but buy yourself something pretty with it.'

Beth nodded – she didn't trust herself to say anything – and climbed up onto the front seat of the cart next to Pa. By nine o'clock, they were off, looking at the world between Mayfair's ears and nodding and smiling at friends and acquaintances. Beth usually loved these trips with Pa, and was proud to be seen beside him on the delivery cart with its smart dark-green paint and J.A. Healey, General Provisions of Woodhampstead painted along both sides in gold script. Today, though, she couldn't relax. She stayed quiet, deep in thought, as Mayfair picked her way along the rutted village road and then sped up into a steady clop-clop-clop as they reached the newly made-up road to St Albans.

She should, she realised, have written to Mr Webb in advance and made an appointment to see him. That, of course, would have been the sensible, the *business-like*, thing to do. After all, the position, whatever it was, might already have been filled or Mr Webb might be off sick or in meetings or . . . or . . . *anything*! Beth cursed her impulsiveness, her lack of planning. It was very unlike her. Sensible Beth, Play-by-the-rules Beth, would usually think everything through . . .

'Ah, the wonderful whiff of manure!' said Pa, cutting through her thoughts.

He was sniffing the air with a smile on his face and pretending to savour the aroma. There was no wind and the smell of horse dung brought in from London to fertilise the watercress beds was more pungent than usual today.

'A most magnificent smell,' agreed Beth, with a little giggle.

Pa turned to her with a wink. 'Never tell your sister,' he said, 'but that smell always makes me think of Bertie.'

Beth burst out laughing.

She couldn't help herself.

Sally's husband worked on the watercress beds and, no matter how often or how well he washed, the faint acrid tang of manure always seemed to cling to him.

Beth settled back into her seat feeling much more cheerful. It was a lovely late May day, the sun bright but not too fierce, and everything was fresh and verdant. The cow parsley was growing high beside the road, bees and butterflies were buzzing around and the air was fragrant and blowsy. And now they were passing the golf course where rich folk came out from London to play at weekends and where Bertie's brother Reggie used to caddy. And here were the fields, high with summer crops and being tended by girls because the agricultural labourers had signed up as soon as war was declared, the promise of a regularly full belly more than sufficient incentive. Every twist and turn of the road reminded her of people who were not here to enjoy the perfect English late spring day and she realised that her problems were tiny compared to theirs.

So she wouldn't fret and fuss that she hadn't made an appointment at the post office. She would relax and just see how the day unfolded.

Half an hour later, they were trotting through the outskirts of St Albans and ten minutes after that, Pa dropped her off at the crossroads in the centre of the city and agreed to meet her in same place a few hours later.

Beth stood on the corner for a moment, trying to get her bearings. Oh, she knew St Albans – had been coming here on and off ever since she was a little girl – but every time she visited, something was different. Today it was the number of men in uniform. St Albans was a garrison town and every time she visited, there seemed to be more and more of them. Today there were soldiers everywhere – marching down the street, on the back of lorries, chatting in small groups. Instinctively, Beth started scanning the faces. Ned, she knew, was a long way from here but there was a very small chance she might see Sam . . .

And the number of motorised vehicles! They were every-where you looked and almost outnumbered the horses. Beth saw automobiles around Woodhampstead, of course – all the big houses had them – but there weren't many in the centre of the village and one parking outside the shop would still invite attention. But here they were, the noisy, smelly things, and it looked like everyone was taking their life into their hands every time they tried to cross the road. She would have to keep her wits about her.

Finally, Beth's eyes went to the women. It had been a few months since she was last here and she noticed that, despite the war, fashions had shifted. Not hugely, and not as much as the ads in Pa's newspapers would suggest, but there had been a definite change. Skirts were definitely shorter – well above the ankle – and the new fuller shape seemed to be growing in popularity and colours were more muted. She would have to make some alterations when she got home . . .

Enough of gawping.

Time to make a plan.

Beth longed to go to a tearoom and steady her nerves, but she knew the most sensible thing would be to go straight to the post office. That way, if Mr Webb wasn't available straight-away, she could at least make an appointment to come back later in the day. She knew exactly where the main city post office was – it was the Georgian building on St Peters Street, less than two minutes' walk away. She'd strolled past it lots of times but never had a reason to go in.

Beth walked up the steps and strode in with a confidence she didn't feel. Inside, a long wooden counter ran the length of the interior and behind it were half a dozen clerks, hard at work. At that time of the morning, it wasn't particularly busy and she didn't have to wait long until it was her turn to be served.

'Can I help you, Miss?' the ginger, pimply young man behind the counter asked. The sign on his desk said his name was Herbert Mason.

'Good morning,' she said. 'I'd like to talk to Mr Webb.'

Mr Mason put his head on one side. 'Mr Webb?' he said with a little frown. 'I'm not sure I know who you mean.'

Oh Lordy.

Don't say she'd got the wrong post office.

Maybe Mrs Harrison had said Luton or Harpenden or Hatfield. She should have written it down. Or maybe Mrs Harrison herself had got it wrong herself. In which case . . .

'Mr Webb,' she repeated, for want of anything else to say. She said it very slowly and clearly and with more than a hint of desperation. As if any of that would make a jot of difference.

Mr Mason pursed his lips and shook his head slowly and Beth's heart sank. What a blooming waste of time. But then he suddenly said, 'You don't mean Mr Web*ster* from the sorting office, do you?'

Did she?

Beth really had no idea.

But Sam had mentioned they were looking for women to help deal with the war letters, so the sorting office definitely made sense. It had to be worth a try, anyway.

'Yes,' she said, trying to sound business-like. 'Mr Web*ster*.'

'And, do you have an appointment, Miss . . . ?'

'Miss Healey. Elizabeth Healey. Well, no. Not as such. At least, not a meeting with an actual time.'

Mr Mason suppressed a grin and leaned forwards mock-conspiratorially. 'I hate to be the one to break the news to you,' he said, 'but that's usually what an appointment is. A meeting with an *actual* time.'

Despite the situation, Beth couldn't help laughing. 'Yes, I know,' she said, lowering her voice to match his. 'And, no, I don't have an appointment with an actual time, but a friend mentioned that I should talk to Mr Webster, so he might have been expecting me to come in at some point for a meeting *without* an actual time.'

Mr Mason laughed and got to his feet. 'If you'd like to take seat over there, Miss Healey,' he said, gesturing to a group of chairs, 'I'll go and see if Mr Web*ster* is free to see you for a meeting without an actual time.'

Beth smiled at him gratefully. 'Thank you so much,' she said.

She wasn't holding out much hope as she sat down. The best she could wish for was that she would be told to come back later, but even that was unlikely. But, if all else failed, at least she could write and tell Sam that she had tried. Apart from anything else, it would give her an excuse to write to him for the first time . . .

'Miss Healey?' A girl not much older than Beth and wearing the dark-blue post office uniform had arrived from seemingly nowhere and was standing in front of her. Beth scrambled to her feet. 'Mr Webster will see you now.'

Beth smiled her thanks to Mr Mason, who was retaking his seat behind the counter, and followed the girl out of the front door and onto the street. The post office was on a corner of two streets and the girl led Beth down the side street and then turned left through some wide gateposts. This gave way to a courtyard and a hive of almost frenzied activity. People were rushing about, carrying sacks and wheeling trolleys and there were more motorised vans and lorries than Beth had ever seen in one place before. Through the windows that surrounded the courtyard, she could see into the large rooms – halls, almost – where people were sorting letters into cubbyholes. All those letters! All that news! All those human stories setting out on, or finishing, their journeys. Beth felt a surge of excitement and her energy levels ratcheted up a gear.

Instead of taking her into one of the halls, however, the girl led Beth through a door and then up a narrow flight of stairs. She motioned for Beth to stop and rapped on the door.

'Miss Healey to see you, sir,' she said in response to a gruff voice from within, and then she was holding the door open and ushering Beth inside.

Gosh!

Beth's first thought was that Mr Webster had one of the most luxuriant moustaches she had ever seen. In fact, he bore *such* a striking resemblance to Lord Kitchener in that war recruitment advertisement that Beth almost expected him to shoot out an arm and boom 'Your post office needs you'. And so she was stifling a giggle when Mr Webster gestured to the chair in front of his desk and invited her to sit.

Nerves, she supposed.

'What can I do for you, young lady?' Mr Webster asked in a voice that was as deep and resonant as she had imagined it would be.

'Thank you for seeing me at such short notice,' Beth replied, trying to sound confident – but not *too* confident. 'I'm here about the job.'

'Job?' Mr Webster looked utterly nonplussed and Beth's heart sank. 'What job?'

'The job sorting the letters,' she said, trying to keeping the tremor from her voice and feeling more than a little stupid.

'There must be some mistake,' said Mr Webster, impatiently. 'I haven't got any vacancies for sorters. Not at the moment. We've just had a big recruitment drive and we're fully staffed.'

Well, that was that, then. All that way, all that subterfuge, for nothing.

Now, to get out of there with what was left of her dignity intact.

'I'm sorry for troubling you, Mr Webster—' she started, rising to her feet.

'Who told you there was a job here?' interrupted Mr Webster testily. 'Or did you just march in here on the off-chance?'

'*No*. Of course not. Sam Harrison – the Woodhampstead junior postman – specifically said I should talk to you about a job sorting post to the soldiers. But he must have made a mistake.'

'Ah,' said Mr Webster, flapping his hands to indicate that Beth should sit down again. 'Sam Harrison was talking about opportunities at the new Home Depot.'

'I see,' said Beth, sitting down as instructed but not seeing at all. 'The new Home Depot?'

'Yes,' said Mr Webster. 'I spoke to all the staff about the new sorting office going up in the Regent's Park. That must have been what Sam meant.'

'The Regent's Park, Mr Webster?' echoed Beth.

There wasn't a park of that name in St Albans, as far as she knew, although she wasn't familiar with the outskirts to the west.

'London, girl,' said Mr Webster, blowing out a cloud of smoke.

London.

London!

London was only twenty miles away but it might as well have been another planet.

Beth had been there precisely twice in her whole life.

How could she possibly work in London?

She needed to get out of there, go home and try to forget about the whole humiliating affair. Thank goodness she hadn't told a soul she was coming here. She could just chalk the whole thing down to experience and never make such a ridiculous and impulsive decision again.

Mr Webster leant back in his chair. 'Sam Harrison used to work in the sorting office here. You knew that, of course?'

Beth nodded although she hadn't. Not really. One branch of the post office was much like another to her.

'A very fine sorter he was too,' Mr Webster continued. 'But after what happened to his father – such a dreadful accident and while working for the post office, too – the boy wanted to be closer to his mother and sisters and asked to be transferred to the Woodhampstead deliveries. It was a loss to us and it meant less money for him but I think that just shows the measure of the man.'

'Oh.'

Beth hadn't known any of that. She knew Sam's father had been killed, of course – thrown from a rearing horse into the path of an automobile – but not that he'd been working for the post office at the time. Not that it mattered.

'Tell me, why does Samuel Harrison think you would pass muster at the Home Depot?' Mr Webster asked suddenly.

Beth paused. What could she possibly say that didn't sound embarrassingly childish? That didn't sound ridiculously provincial? *We had a game where I tried to decipher the envelopes . . .*

Mr Webster held up his hand. 'Actually, don't tell me,' he said. 'I have no sway over the matter one way or another. But you are interested in being put forward for the job?'

Say no, Beth.

Just say no.

Her mouth opened by itself. 'Yes, I am, Mr Webster,' she found herself saying. 'I want to do my bit and to serve my country.'

Where had *that* come from?

'Well, then' said Mr Webster. 'I will write and put a good word in for you. It's the least I can do for young Sam and his father.'

Though initially appalled at her own daring, Beth felt quite calm by the time she left. There was no chance of her getting an interview. If the job was in London, they would have the choice of anyone and everyone. Why would they take a shop girl from all the way out in Hertfordshire? But at least she had done her best. She had done as Sam had suggested and now she could move on with a clean conscience. Maybe something else would turn up.

But she couldn't help wondering.

Had Sam known the job was in London?

Had he?

6

A mere matter of days later, a letter arrived from London inviting Beth to an interview.

It was fortunate that Beth had been alone in the shop when it arrived or Ma might have had something to say about the crisp white envelope and the Royal Engineers Postal Service postmark. Ivy had handed it over without comment and Beth fervently hoped that she believed in discretion being the better part of valour or it would be all over Woodhampstead and she would have some explaining to do.

She read the letter in the storeroom in a rare quiet moment in the shop. She was invited to an interview with Sergeant Major Cunningham the following Tuesday, 1st June (only four days' time!) and would she please present herself at King Edward Building in the City of London at noon sharp. Not in the Regent's Park, after all. Not that it mattered. There followed instructions on how to get from King's Cross to the King Edward Building by Underground and a request to RSVP straightaway.

Well!

Almost despite herself, Beth felt a surge of excitement.

They wanted to meet her.

Sergeant Major Cunningham, from the Royal Engineers Postal Service, no less, wanted to meet her!

She wanted to go and meet him, just for the experience, but how could she? She couldn't take the job so there was no point in getting in trouble over nothing.

But then again . . .

Oh, what should she do?

That evening she went around to her sister Sally's cottage for supper. Sally was in fine spirits because she had heard from Bertie and he was nowhere near the front. She'd bought a whole herring to share and, while they tucked in in her spotless little kitchen, Beth found herself unburdening herself to her sister and telling her the whole story.

'Ooh, you are a one,' said Sally when she'd finished. 'How very unlike Goody-Two-Shoes Beth to pull the wool over Ma and Pa's eyes like that.'

'I know,' said Beth with a little giggle. 'I quite surprised myself too. I kept expecting to bump into Pa in the post office.'

'So, what you going to do?' Sally asked. She took the fish head and tail and laid them on the bars over the fire. The fish started to hiss and spit.

'I don't know,' groaned Beth. 'Ma would *not* approve of that,' she added with a grin at the fish. '*Most* inelegant!'

'It's the one good thing about living on your own with no parents, no husband and no servants to care about what you do,' said Sally. 'Besides, if these food shortages continue, everyone will be doing it – and never mind manners!'

She started breaking off little bits of crispy fish, bones and all, and sandwiching them between pieces of bread.

'Pudding,' she said, with a wry grin as she passed Beth a portion. 'Now, do you *want* to go to the interview or not?'

'I think I do,' said Beth. 'But I don't see how I can. It was hard enough getting to St Albans without arousing suspicion so how on earth can I get all the way down to London? It's impossible.'

'The same as you did before,' said Sally, shrugging. 'Don't tell them.'

Beth gawped at her. 'You mean, tell Ma I'm ill and staying

in bed and then shin down the ivy like Ned used to do?' She gave a little giggle. 'I'm not sure that's going to work.'

'No, silly,' said Sally. 'You have to tell them you're going to London. Why not just say the St Albans trip has whetted your appetite for adventure and that you fancy a trip to the big city?'

Beth wrinkled her brow. 'But I would never say that,' she said, 'so Ma would smell a rat immediately. Anyway, she would probably say she needed to chaperone me – if she said yes at all. You know how she feels about London.'

The whole thing was hopeless.

'*I'll* come with you,' said Sally, sitting up straighter and clapping her hands. 'I'm a respectable married woman so I'll be able to make sure no harm befalls my little sister. Ma couldn't possibly say no.'

'Would you, really?' asked Beth earnestly. 'It really would be an adventure. I'll never get the job, but at least I can tell Sam I tried.'

She didn't dare to ask herself what she would do if she actually got the job.

'*Another* trip?' said Ma.

'Beth's only been to London twice,' said Sally. 'I'll be chaperoning her and, honestly, I could really do with a little daytrip myself.'

Beth held her breath, waiting for Ma to say that she couldn't be spared or for Pa to say, chaperone or not, it was out of the question.

'But *London*!' said Ma, with a shudder. 'All those ne'er-do-wells. Why not go to St Albans and have a nice lunch together in the Station Hotel?'

'Your mother is right,' said Pa, lowering his newspaper. 'London isn't safe now the Kaiser has made London fair game for those dreadful Zeppelin attacks.'

'Only east of the Tower,' said Beth, who had been scanning Pa's newspapers.

'Enough, Beth!'

When Pa said something like that, he meant it and so it looked like that was that.

But Sally was smiling, as cool as a cucumber. 'Of course,' she said. 'I'm happy to take Beth to Hatfield instead and to have lunch at the Coach and Horses.'

Beth shot her a quizzical look. Lunch in Hatfield was all well and good – and usually she'd have jumped at the chance – but it wasn't really the point.

'That's a much more sensible idea,' said Ma. 'But, after that, no more gallivanting for a while, Beth. I need you to help me give the whole shop a going-over so that the shelves don't look so bare.'

'Yes, Ma,' said Beth dutifully.

'In the meantime, I will treat you to your tickets to Hatfield. I'll buy them tomorrow when I go to the post office.'

After supper, Beth grabbed Sally and pulled her into the storeroom.

'Well, that didn't exactly go to plan, did it?' she said. 'Ma's buying us tickets to *Hatfield* and we're having lunch at the Coach and Horses? Where *is* the Coach and Horses?'

'I have no idea,' said Sally, sitting on a crate and pulling Beth down beside her. 'I just made it up on the spur of the moment.'

Beth wrinkled her brow. 'I don't understand,' she said. 'Why would you just make up the name of an inn?'

'Because we won't be eating there,' said Sally, looking a little self-satisfied. 'But I wanted Ma and Pa to think I had somewhere precise in mind to take you for lunch. Look, slowcoach,' she added, when Beth continued to stare at her blankly, 'we'll use Ma's tickets to Hatfield and then we'll change trains and continue on to London. We need to change trains there anyway. No one will be any the wiser.'

'Wait,' said Beth, holding up a hand. 'You're suggesting *lying* to Ma and Pa?'

Play-by-the-rules Beth could hardly believe what she was hearing. Oh, some might say she had lied by omission when she had hitched a lift to St Albans, but this was on a whole different level. She was so confused that she stood up and shook a pink sugar ball from one of the jars. Popping it into her mouth, she made a deal with herself. If it was one of the rare ones that had a real farthing hidden inside, she would go. If not, she would forget this ridiculous notion and carry on with her life.

She wanted to do her bit, but this was getting out of hand.

'Maybe London really is very dangerous,' she said, sucking vigorously.

'I thought I was the boring stay-at-home one,' said Sally. 'Look, do you want to go for this interview or do you want to spend the whole war slicing butter for Mrs McBride?'

Beth was still thinking about it when a metallic taste flooded her mouth.

'I want to do it.'

7

Tuesday 1st June came around quickly and dawned bright and sunny.

Beth couldn't help wishing she had something new to wear, but she settled for her fanciest white blouse with its dozens of dainty mother-of-pearl buttons and her smartest navy skirt, which she had secretly altered so it was shorter and had at least a nod towards the new, softer shape. She couldn't claim to look fashionable but hopefully she didn't look hopelessly out of touch. Anyhow, she reminded herself, she was going for a job – a war job, no less. It was her brain and her wits they needed. As long as she was clean and tidy, surely it didn't matter how she looked . . .

'Ooh, look at you,' said Sally when she answered her cottage door. 'How did you get past Ma with all that ankle showing?'

Beth gave her a grin. 'She was already in the shop and barely gave me a look. Come on,' she added, grabbing her sister's hand. 'Let's catch that train before I change my mind about all this scheming.'

The two girls ran hand in hand down the high street, over the bridge and down Station Road. It was nine o'clock and, as usual, Woodhampstead Station was a hive of activity. The bustle of people and freight being moved around never failed to cheer Beth up. One of the sidings served the coal yard while another was used for loading and unloading cattle from the neighbouring pens. Here too was the unloading point for wagons of dung from London Zoo and where the salad vegetables were sent to London and the straw plaits to the hatters in Luton. Beth loved it all. Rather like the post, it was where Woodhampstead met the outside world and it made her feel more alive.

Many of the workers were women. Two girls were leading the horses from the stables to shunt the carriages. Girls were unloading tomatoes and lettuce from a horse cart. One was even driving the cows from one pen to another. The world really was topsy-turvy but today that only added to Beth's sudden 'anything was possible' feeling.

Anything was possible.

Anything was *happening*.

The station was busy with human passengers, too. Tuesday was market day in Welwyn, a couple of stops along the line, and the little platform was crowded.

'It's going to take us an hour and a half to London,' said Beth, looking at the timetable.

'It's a good thing we've got plenty of time,' said Sally. 'But if you do end up getting the job, it's a very long journey twice each day.'

Beth smiled. 'I won't get the job,' she said. 'But, if you go at half-past seven, there's a through train and you can get to London in fifty-three minutes.'

'Off to Welwyn?' asked Grace from the bakery as the train puffed into view.

'We're going to Hatfield,' said Beth. She crossed her fingers behind her back as she said it, but it wasn't technically a lie.

'Oh, well, as long as it's not London,' said Grace.

Beth stared at her departing back and was about to ask her why she'd said that, how she knew they were going there, when Sally grabbed her arm and pulled her onto the train. The guard shut the door behind them, blew his whistle and they were off, the train belching steam as it hauled itself out of the station.

They were on their way.

Beth didn't start getting nervous until fields and woods began to give way to serried ranks of housing. Up until then, she'd felt that she really was just on a day out. She'd even managed a bun in the cafe at Hatfield Station while they waited for their connecting train – although that perhaps hadn't been her most sensible idea as she now had a tiny speck of blackcurrant jam on her shirt, which she concealed beneath Sally's cameo brooch.

But now that the train was slowing down with a protesting squeal of metal and blast of whistles, the first butterflies in her stomach started beating their wings in earnest. She squeezed her new lucky farthing, which she had been clutching the whole way there.

'What on earth am I doing?' she said, turning to Sally. 'I don't know the first thing about sorting the post. Especially the war post.'

'Just be honest,' said Sally soothingly. 'And be yourself. They know you haven't got any experience so there's nothing to be nervous about.'

'I hope so,' Beth muttered, getting to her feet as the train heaved into King's Cross with a protesting hiss.

The two girls disembarked and Beth looked around in wonder. Compared to the single platform and modest brick buildings at Woodhampstead, King's Cross was *huge*. With its two great arches and a soaring, white-pillared ceiling, it was more like a cathedral than the terminus of the Great Northern Railway.

And the *people*.

Everyone else seemed to know exactly where they going and Beth and Sally found themselves being buffeted from all sides by purposeful passengers and harried porters.

Beth took out her letter, trying to stay calm and focused. 'We need to find the Underground and take the Northern Line to Bank Station,' she said. 'Then we have to change onto the Central Line and take it one stop to Post Office Station. Fancy!' she said looking up. 'A whole station named after the post office . . .'

'How far is it?' asked Sally.

'Not far,' said Beth. The letter had included a map too. 'Above ground, not more than a couple of miles.'

'Can we walk, then?' said Sally. 'We've got plenty of time and I don't fancy the Underground.' She gave a little shudder. 'All those *tunnels*. All those rats!'

'Of course,' said Beth. She'd been nervous about braving the Underground herself. It would be like being trapped in a coffin . . .

So they followed the crowds across the concourse and out onto the street. Beth looked around in wonderment. If she had found the traffic in St Albans overwhelming, this was something else entirely. On the road in front of them, motorised omnibuses, packed to the gills, did an improvised dance with automobiles, horse-drawn carriages and hand-pulled carts. How any of them were emerging unscathed was a complete mystery.

And the *noise*.

The countryside was noisy too, in its way – Beth was often roused from her sleep by a fox screaming and cursed the poultry, who slept in the trees outside the stable and woke her up before dawn. But this . . . this *cacophony*! The roar of engines punctuated by bangs and whistles and shouts and neighs. It was all she could do not to put her hands over her ears and sing loudly as she had done when frightened by a thunderstorm as a child.

Which was less dangerous? she wondered. The Underground or the streets?

Arm in arm, the girls set off towards the City of London. The street was lined with imposing Victorian buildings and all different types of manufacturing and warehousing. Beth looked with interest at the various signs and window displays: printing and engraving, jewellery, scientific and technical manufacturing, watchmaking.

It all felt a very long way from home.

Was it safe?

Progress was slow because of negotiating the traffic and the dung – the very dung that might one day make it out onto a Woodhampstead field – on the side streets. Beth was glad of her shorter skirt – it wouldn't do to arrive at her interview with filthy hems – but they would have to get a move on if she was to arrive with time to tidy her hair and to wash her hands . . .

But, wait!

What was that ahead?

Traffic backing up. A little crowd of people.

Something . . . she couldn't see what . . . blocking the street.

Beth and Sally exchanged a glance.

'What is it?' said Sally.

Beth gave a nervous shrug in return.

She stood have trusted her instincts. She should have gone a different way.

They shouldn't have come at all.

The two girls walked closer . . . and gasped.

The top three storeys of a six-storey building had been completely destroyed. The roof had caved in, the windows and some of the walls had been blown out and the blackened interior was on full display to the street. There was a strong smell of burning and the building was still gently steaming. A huge pile of bricks and roof tiles on the road had already been moved to one side and a lone policeman was directing the traffic around it.

Beth clutched Sally's arm as she surveyed the scene. Around her, snatches of conversation ebbed and flowed.

'A Zeppelin raid—'

'No one was killed here, but two men died further east—'

'They say it killed dozens of people. Lord knows how many poor souls were injured—'

Beth watched and listened in mounting horror. How stupid they had been to come here without a care. And worse still, to have deceived their parents in order to do so. Ma and Pa had been right: this was no place for two silly girls. And no one knew they were there. Suppose there was another raid, right here, right now? Beth looked up at the blue, cloudless sky almost expecting to see another airship slide silently into view with deadly intent . . .

Sally touched her sleeve. 'Isn't it awful?' she said. 'But it does remind us why we're here.'

'Does it?' said Beth. She'd just been about to suggest they turned tail and went home.

'Of course it does. We're here so you can apply to do a man's job so the men make sure this sort of thing never happens again.'

Beth hadn't thought of it quite like that, but Sally was right. Suddenly a-tingle with purpose, she joined the queue of people waiting in turn to edge past the pile of rubble.

'Can't we go another way?' she asked. 'Perhaps get onto a parallel street?'

The woman in front of her turned around. 'All the roads are blocked,' she said. 'This is the quickest way.'

The two girls looked at each other and edged forward. After what felt like an age, the policeman waved them through. Beth could taste the ash and debris and, by the time they were clear on the other side, her white shirt had a thin film of grey dust all over it. So much for being spotless for her interview . . .

They hurried on.

Soon, the dome of St Paul's Cathedral loomed into view above the buildings ahead. Beth's spirits lifted and she realised she had been holding her breath. Apart from being heart-soaringly beautiful, surely nothing awful could happen in sight of the ultimate house of God? And, now, they were nearly there. There was more bomb damage to a church so Beth's theory didn't hold up; churches clearly didn't offer any divine protection at all. A second pile of rubble to negotiate and finally – *finally* – they were on King Edward Street.

What a journey!

If King's Cross had been a cathedral, the post office at King Edward Place was a palace. Beth and Sally stood gawping up at it. Five storeys of grey stone, it had more balustrades and arches and royal arms than you could shake a stick at.

'It's the principal post office in London,' said Beth, 'which makes it the principal post office in England and therefore the principal post office of the whole of the British Empire. That's why it's so grand.'

'I still didn't expect it to look like Buckingham Palace,' said Sally, checking her watch. 'Go on, you'd better go; you're just in time.' She pointed at a small public garden on the opposite side of the road, rather thrillingly called Postman's Park. 'I'll wait for you there. And good luck! Although you don't need it. They'd be lucky to have you.'

Feeling very small, Beth gave her sister a shaky smile, walked up the front steps and went into the building. It was safe to say that didn't disappoint. Columns clad in veined marble supported a richly ornamented ceiling and the floor was a white marble mosaic with bands of Irish green. The counter-front – the longest Beth had ever seen – was made of green marble and even the ordinary writing tables had bronze moulded edges.

Beth stood in the doorway and took a deep breath while she drank it all in. She couldn't help comparing it, with a little snort, to the tiny sub post office in Woodhampstead, which always smelt of cauliflower.

Five minutes later, Beth was being escorted 'backstage' for her interview.

It turned out that, as in St Albans, she had come in the wrong entrance. The sorting office was behind the main post office and the entrance was around the corner on a different street.

No matter, the friendly clerk said. There was a high-level bridge between the two buildings and he was happy to show her the way. Beth followed him up two flights of concrete steps, over the bridge, more stairs and down a long corridor, her shoes click-clicking on the dusty wooden blocks.

The clerk checked Beth's letter, stopped at one of the doors and knocked and, before she had time to catch her breath, there was an answering call and she was being ushered into a small, bare office – even plainer than Mr Webster's in St Albans. Behind the plain wooden desk there were two people: a middle-aged man in an army uniform and a younger bespectacled woman dressed in navy.

Neither smiled as Beth put her hat and coat on the stand. Then the man indicated that she should sit down opposite them.

'I'm Sergeant Major Cunningham,' he said. 'And this is Miss Parker, who supervises the women in the Army Parcel Office.'

Goodness.

A woman in a supervisory role.

Quite a young woman at that, and an unmarried one. Miss Parker had a locket around her neck, worn – rather unusually – like a choker and Beth wondered who it might be for.

'Good afternoon, Miss Healey,' said Miss Parker. 'It looks

rather like you must have got caught up in the aftermath of the Zeppelin raid this morning.'

Beth's hands flew to her hair. She suddenly realised what she must look like. Her hair and her clothes were covered in dust, her gloves filthy.

'I was,' she said, folding her hands into her lap. 'We walked from King's Cross and—'

'We tell all our staff to build extra time into their journeys,' interrupted Sergeant Major Cunningham dismissively. 'That way, we can accommodate unexpected delays.'

'Yes, Sergeant Major Cunningham,' said Beth.

It seemed she had failed at the first hurdle. She had arrived on time, but unkempt, even dirty.

It was not a good start.

Sergeant Major Cunningham picked up a letter and flicked it with a finger. It made a noise like a whip cracking and Beth couldn't help flinching.

'Army or post office?' barked Sergeant Major Cunningham, staring at her from under beetling brows.

Beth paused, flustered. She had absolutely no idea what he meant. Did he mean would she rather work for the post office or the army? Or which did she think was better at delivering the army's post? Or something else entirely?

Maybe it was a trick question? One with no right or wrong answer and designed to see what she could come up with under pressure.

Which, clearly, wasn't very much.

'I . . . er . . .' she started. 'I'm not sure.'

'It's a simple enough question,' bellowed Sergeant Major Cunningham, flicking the piece of paper again. 'Have you been sent here from the Army or the post office. Mr . . . er . . .' – he checked the letter – 'Mr *Webster*'s letter doesn't make it clear.'

Ahh.

Well that at least she could answer.

Although, she had a feeling that her answer might not go down well.

'Neither, Sergeant Major Cunningham.'

Was that how one addressed a Sergeant Major? Or should it be sir? Goodness, this really had got off to an appalling start. Beth could feel sweat trickling down between her breasts and knew that her cheeks would be glowing bright red.

'Neither?' blustered Sergeant Major Cunningham. 'Then what on earth are you doing here, girl?'

'Well, Sam – I mean Mr Harrison – and Mr Webster both said I should—' Beth begun.

'I don't care what Mr Harrison or Mr Webster said,' Sergeant Major Cunningham shouted, banging his hand down onto the table and making Beth jump. 'This is the Royal Engineers Postal Service. We are formed of army and post office personnel *only* and we are responsible for delivering millions – *millions* – of letters and packages to the front line. At the moment, we are rushed off our feet recruiting for the new Home Depot at the Regent's Park. What the devil do you think you're doing marching in here and wasting everybody's time like this?'

Beth could feel tears pricking at her eyelids.

This was a disaster.

'What line of work *are* you in, Miss Healey?' asked Miss Parker suddenly. Her tone was, if not exactly friendly, at least more conciliatory.

Beth took a deep breath. 'I work in a general store. My family owns J.A. Healey General Provisions of Woodhampstead . . .' She trailed off, knowing her interviewers wouldn't be impressed by this or by the fact that the store had a smart delivery cart in exactly the same Irish green as in the post office downstairs.

She was right.

'A store? A *shop girl?*' Sergeant Major Cunningham leaned back in his chair and looked round the room with an incredulous look on his face – rather as if addressing an imaginary audience. 'Tell me, Miss Healey, can you even read?'

Beth's humiliation began to transform into anger.

How dare Sergeant Major Cunningham pass judgement on her like that? How dare he patronise and humiliate her and – even worse – her family? Ma and Pa had built the store up from nothing and they worked all hours of the day and night and . . . they didn't know that she was currently in London.

They deserved better than this.

'Yes, I can read, Sergeant Major Cunningham,' Beth said coldly, preparing to get to her feet. 'And now, if you'll excuse me . . .'

She'd get out of there.

She'd go and find Sally and maybe they'd go and have something to eat and drink in a Lyons' Corner House. Although, really, she'd much rather just go home and give her parents a hug.

Miss Parker held up a hand. 'Sit down, please, Miss Healey,' she said. She had picked up Mr Webster's letter and was scrutinising it. 'You've come a long way to see us today and you do come highly recommended. Tell me why Mr Webster and Mr Harrison think you might be suited to a role with REPS?'

Beth paused. What on earth could she possibly say that wouldn't invite more scorn and ridicule.

There wasn't anything. She should just leave.

On the other hand, didn't she owe it to Sam, and perhaps even to Mr Webster, to at least make her case? If she walked out, it might get back to Sam. It might even reflect badly on him somewhere down the line. She needed to say something.

Not that it would make any difference. And not that she wanted the job anyway. Not with that rude, patronising . . . nincompoop.

'Mr Harrison and I used to play a game where he challenged me to decipher the oddest and most difficult handwriting,' she said simply.

And then she stopped. It sounded pathetic and there was no point in trying to dress it up or add details. Sergeant Major Cunningham was already drumming his meaty fingers on the desk top.

Miss Parker, however, pursed her lips and then slid open one of the desk drawers. She pulled out a little pile of letters and put them on the desk in front of Beth.

'So, Miss Healey,' she said, 'why don't we play that little game now. Perhaps you could read out the addresses on these envelopes?'

Beth looked at her, trying to work out if she was being serious or was mocking her. Miss Parker looked back steadily through pale blue eyes magnified many times by her spectacles, and Beth gave her the benefit of the doubt.

She picked up the first letter. It had been sent from a solider in France to an address in Newcastle. The writing, although large and looping, was clear enough and Beth read it out without difficulty.

Miss Parker nodded and gestured to the pile. Beth picked up the next letter. This one was addressed in tiny handwriting – the up and downstrokes almost non-existent – but it was no harder to read than the shopping list from Cook at Maitland Hall. She rattled off the address in Weston-Super-Mare with no problem.

Miss Parker nodded again and Beth carried working her way through the pile of letters. One or two had her initially stumped but she took a deep breath, kept her nerve and tried to pretend she was back in the shop with Sam and not in the primary post office in the British Empire. This way, she managed to read all the envelopes.

Miss Parker rewarded her with a little smile but Sergeant Major Cunningham just made a little harrumphing noise and flared his nostrils.

'And now, Miss Healey,' said Miss Parker, 'perhaps you would like to read the *contents* of this letter out loud.'

'Very well.' Beth slipped two sheets of thin, writing paper out of the envelope that Miss Parker was holding out to her. Unfolding it, she started to read it out loud. The letter was written in a fairly legible script but the page was marred by ink blots and unidentifiable stains. Grass? Blood? Beth wasn't sure. It was from a solider to his mother and it was utterly heart-rending – full of brutal details about life in the trenches and the mounting casualties. Almost worse was the young soldier's fears for his own survival and of not seeing his family again. By the time she got to the end of the letter, Beth's eyes were filmy with tears.

That boy could have been Ned or Sam . . . or any other others.

'Thank you, Miss Healey,' said Miss Parker, her face as expressionless as if Beth had just read out a shopping list. 'And now tell me. Why would that letter be intercepted and not permitted to reach its destination?'

Beth's first thought was: why wouldn't you let that letter reach its destination? What right did anyone have *not* to allow the letter to reach its intended recipient – to stop a frightened son pour his heart out to his mother?

Beth was about to say all that out loud, when she thought a little deeper. The boy had written that there were many, *many* dead. Far more than anyone in Blighty knew about. He had written that conditions were terrible – terrifying – unbearable. What if many such boys wrote home along those lines? What if *everyone* knew how dreadful things were along the various fronts?' Word would get around and what would that do for morale on the home front? What would that do for recruitment, for enlistment which was still – officially, at least – entirely voluntary?'

She explained all that haltingly to Miss Parker, who nodded briskly without giving any other reaction.

'May I just ask something?' asked Beth timidly. 'Was that a real letter, or a fictitious one put together for the interview?'

Were the casualties, the conditions, really that bad?

'Don't be so impertinent, girl,' spluttered Sergeant Major Cunningham. 'Staff here follow orders and don't ask questions.'

Miss Parker glanced at him. For the first time, Beth thought she saw irritation. Dislike, even. She turned back to Beth.

'For the purpose of this interview, you may assume that nothing we are showing you is current and that some things may have been put together purely for the purposes of interview. Do you have anyone fighting?'

'A brother,' said Beth. 'Friends. Acquaintances.'

She said it matter-of-factly because so did everybody else.

She was nothing special.

Miss Parker nodded. 'Now, if you work in a shop then presumably you are useful in packing and repackaging packets and parcels?' she said.

'Yes, Miss Parker,' said Beth. She knew she was good at that. Her parcels never unravelled under pressure, no matter how much they were thrown around.

'Perhaps you could show me?'

Miss Parker reached under the desk and brought out a parcel that was spilling out at the seams, together with some heavy brown paper and string. A typical parcel destined for a soldier, it contained condensed milk, cheese, tobacco, soap and toothpaste. Beth had packed up many such parcels recently, but never as badly as this. She noticed Miss Parker had given her neither sealing wax nor a candle, but that didn't matter. Useful as they could be for sealing knots and crossover points, she was used to working without them at home.

Beth set to work, deftly repacking the parcel and reminding herself that the little handle she usually made out of the string to help the shopper carry her purchases home wasn't needed here. She finished her work, then folded her hands neatly in her lap. Miss Parker stood up, picked up the parcel and dropped it from a height of at least three feet onto the table. It remained intact.

Beth exhaled and allowed herself the ghost of a smile. She didn't dare look at Sergeant Major Cunningham.

Miss Parker sat down again. 'Finally, Miss Healey,' she said, 'can you tell us in your own words why you want to work here?'

Beth hesitated.

Fifteen minutes ago, she hadn't been sure that she did want to work here. In fact, she had been sure that she never wanted anything to do with Sergeant Major Cunningham ever again! But now she felt differently. She wanted this. She really did. And the film of dust that she could still taste in her mouth and see on her skirt reminded her of how important it was and what was at stake.

'Miss Parker,' she said. 'I want to work here because I want to free up a man to go and fight. I want us to be victorious and I want to help stop the terrible bombs that only last night killed and injured innocent people in London. I want to work here because I know from my own brother and my neighbours and customers in Woodhampstead just how important letters and parcels getting through to our brave men at the front is to morale.' She stopped but then ploughed on regardless. She might as well be honest. 'And I think, but

I'm not sure, that I might be of more use in London, working here, than I am in Hertfordshire.'

She stopped and looked from Miss Parker to Sergeant Major Cunningham. Both stared impassively back at her.

Then Sergeant Major Cunningham got to his feet.

'Thank you for coming in, Miss Healey,' he said. To Beth's surprise, he reached over the desk and shook her hand. 'We will let you know the outcome of the interview in the next day or so.'

And that seemed to be that.

The three of them walked to the door of the office.

'I will escort you out of the building, Miss Healey,' said Miss Parker. 'Please come with me.'

Beth started to follow Miss Parker down the corridor. A man pushing a trolley of parcels was coming towards them and Beth moved to one side to let him past. Suddenly, there was a sharp pain in her ankle that made her cry out involuntarily. She clearly hadn't moved over far or quickly enough because the trolley had caught her just above her shoe.

And it hurt.

It really hurt!

She stopped and bent over to inspect for any damage. Then she glanced over her shoulder at the departing trolley. But it too had stopped and the man pushing it was looking at her with concern. He was handsome, she noticed, clean-shaven with short brown hair and a long, thin, clever face.

'I'm so sorry,' he said.

'No, no, it was my fault,' Beth replied, straightening up.

'Mr Blackford!' It was Sergeant Major Cunningham striding down the corridor towards them. He ignored Beth, marched straight up to the young man and jabbed him in the chest. 'How many times do I have to remind you that there is an absolute ban on fraternising with the opposite sex in here?'

Oh! That was so unfair.

Mr Blackford hadn't been 'fraternising'. It hadn't been like that, at all!

'Excuse me,' she said. 'Mr Blackford wasn't fraternising. I just didn't get out of the way quickly enough . . .'

Sergeant Major Cunningham acted as if she hadn't spoken. 'Come with me, Mr Blackford,' he said, and more or less pulled the young man back into the office where she had just had her interview.

Beth stood gaping after them.

Sergeant Major Cunningham was a rude, boorish, over-bearing oaf!

Miss Parker cleared her throat. 'Miss Healey?' she said as if none of that had ever happened.

Beth turned to her, wondering what to say. In the end she decided to say nothing.

What was the point of saying anything?

She would never see any of them again.

Ten minutes later, Beth was back in Postman's Park and reunited with her sister.

'How did it go?' asked Sally, all pink-cheeked excitement.

Beth blew out her cheeks and exhaled noisily. How on earth could she explain all . . . *that*?

'It was a complete waste of time,' she said, slumping down onto the bench beside her sister. 'They're only recruiting people who either work for the army or for the post office already.'

'I don't understand,' said Sally, frowning. 'What was Sam doing putting you forward for it then?'

Beth shrugged. That had occurred to her too.

'I can only assume he didn't know,' she said. 'I just want to forget all about it. Shall we find a restaurant or a cafe and get some lunch?'

'Of course,' said Sally. 'Although would you mind waiting a little? I've nearly finished writing to Bertie and I'd like to post it here so it gets a fancy postmark. Wouldn't that be grand?'

'Very,' agreed Beth fondly. 'And, yes. Take as long as you need.'

Even though Beth wanted to scarper and never come back, Sally had given up her day to escort her here and the least she could do was to wait for her with good grace. In fact, maybe she should write a letter herself. She could write to Ned and tell him about today. Only she was still too het up to sit down and concentrate. She had the beginnings of a headache and feared that writing would only make it worse.

'I'm going to take a little stroll,' she said to Sally.

Over in one corner of the park, a loggia had been built against the wall of the adjacent building. Inside, fifty or so ceramic tablets had been mounted on the wall. Beth stepped inside to take a look. It turned out to be a memorial to ordinary people who had died while saving the lives of others and who might otherwise be forgotten. How wonderful, she thought, taking a closer look at one or two. All those brave and heroic things that people had done with their lives . . . while she seemed destined to spend hers in Woodhampstead.

She took a step back and stiffened. Someone else had entered the loggia. Even though he had his back to her, she was pretty sure it was Mr Blackford. He, too, was busy scrutinising the memorial plaques and, as he turned his head slightly, she saw from his profile that it was indeed him.

What to do?

Should she just creep away? Wait for him to see her?

Speak to him herself?

After all, Sally was less than a hundred feet away so, strictly speaking, she was being chaperoned. Anyway, she had sort of been introduced to him earlier in the corridor *and* he had got in trouble because of her.

Yes. It would be very rude of her not to say anything.

She gave a little cough. 'Hello,' she said brightly.

Mr Blackford turned around and started with genuine surprise when he saw Beth. So he obviously hadn't followed her into the loggia on purpose. Beth wasn't sure whether to be relieved or disappointed by the discovery.

'Good afternoon, Miss . . . ?' Mr Blackford trailed off with a question mark in his voice, and Beth realised that he had never actually heard her name. So, they hadn't been introduced. Not really.

'Oh, Miss Healey,' said Beth, hastily. 'And I'm sorry to be so forward. I just wanted to apologise for what happened in there, just now. I really didn't mean to get you in trouble.'

Mr Blackford smiled. He had a lovely smile that surprisingly revealed two dimples and quite changed his whole countenance. He was very dashing when he wasn't looking so serious.

'I should be the one apologising, Miss Healey,' he said. 'Bashing into you at full tilt with the trolley like that. I do hope that you aren't badly hurt?'

'Oh no, not at all,' said Beth. 'It was just the shock that made me cry out, that's all. I've quite forgotten my ankle now.'

'I'm glad. And it was my fault entirely. That trolley was totally out of control.'

Beth smiled. 'Maybe a little,' she allowed.

'I have an excuse, though,' said Mr Blackford. 'That blasted Zeppelin raid last night hit a house near my lodgings and I was up all night trying to help. Didn't get a wink of sleep.'

'Oh, how awful,' said Beth. 'Did Sergeant Major Cunningham know? He was so beastly to you!'

How odd this was! She shouldn't really be talking to a

strange man like this. Whatever would Ma say? Sally, still engrossed in writing her letter, seemed blissfully unaware.

Mr Blackford was laughing. 'Oh, he knew, all right,' he said. 'But I'll let you into a little secret. Reginald Cunningham isn't really a Sergeant Major at all. He was a postal worker before and he's just been given the army rank for the duration of the war. And the trouble is that he – like a lot of these chaps – takes his new military authority extremely seriously. Too seriously, some might say. They become more army than the genuine army personnel. Most army chaps wouldn't have hauled me over the coals like that just for apologising to you.'

Beth started laughing, too. 'I was terribly afraid of him,' she said. 'Well, I was until he became rude and asked me if I could read.' She paused and added more seriously, 'I do hope you didn't get into terrible trouble on my account.'

'I didn't actually,' said Mr Blackford. 'Not on this occasion. Cunningham actually ran out of steam pretty quickly, which was just as well because the last poor sap who became too familiar with the ladies was shunted off to operate the heavy goods lift. And that really would be a fate worse than death!'

Beth found she was warming to Mr Blackford. 'Well, I don't think Sergeant Major – or should I say plain *Mr*? – Cunningham thought too much of me.'

'Bad luck,' said Mr Blackford. 'What are you, anyway? Army or post office?'

'Don't you ask me that too,' said Beth with a grimace. 'I'm neither. And that was where the trouble started. I didn't even know how to address him!'

'Ah,' said Mr Blackford, sympathetically. 'They're trying to recruit hundreds of people to staff this huge new depot they're building in the Regent's Park but, as far as I know, they're sticking to army and post office personnel. You did well even to get an interview.'

Out of the corner of her eye, Beth could see that Sally had noticed that she was deep in conversation with a strange man and was packing her writing materials back into her basket in some hurry. And now here she was, bustling over to them as quickly as she could. Beth wasn't standing inappropriately close to Mr Blackford but she took a couple of steps back anyway.

'Hello, Beth,' said Sally, 'and Mr . . . ?'

She said it calmly and politely enough but Beth could hear the slight rebuke in her voice.

'May I present Mr Blackford,' said Beth. 'Mr Blackford, this is my sister, Sally. Mr Blackford was . . . involved in my interview.'

Which was true.

In a way.

'Delighted to meet you, Mr Blackford,' said Sally a little stiffly. 'And now, you must excuse us. We are due elsewhere.'

It took all Beth's willpower not to look over her shoulder as Sally led her away.

She would never see him again.

8

Beth woke the following morning with a thumping head-ache.

Her muscles ached, her mouth was dry and she felt queasy. The thought of standing behind the till in the shop was unbearable. The thought of doing *anything* except snuggling back down underneath the eiderdown was unbearable.

Beth wasn't often ill and she put it down to 'too much' of everything. Too much excitement, too much noise, too much *guilt*.

She must have looked terrible, because Ma was sympathy itself. 'Such a shame,' she said, 'Now, you stay in bed. I'll get Agnes to bring you some broth at lunchtime and you'll be right as rain in no time. Sally's going to help me in the shop when she's done her shift at the pub, so you mustn't worry about a thing.'

Beth nodded weakly and shut her eyes.

Ma being so kind, so understanding, somehow made the whole thing worse.

Beth must have dozed off because the next time she opened her eyes, the sun had moved and was streaming through the gap in the curtains. The pounding in her head had been replaced by a dull ache. She really should get up. She should be helping Ma in the shop and there was a small chance that the reply – the rejection – from REPS would arrive by the afternoon post and she needed to be there to intercept it.

She had just wriggled to a sitting position when Ma burst into the room, throwing the door back so abruptly it rattled against the frame.

Oof.

That wasn't going to help her head one little bit.

Then she saw that Ma was clutching a telegram. An icy chill ran down Beth's back and her breath started coming in raggedy little gasps.

A telegram.

Please no.

Not *Ned*.

'Is that . . . ?' she started, her voice barely a squeak. And then she trailed off.

She couldn't say the words.

Couldn't *think* the words.

Ma came over to the bed and, for the first time, Beth looked at her properly. Her face looked different. Scary. It was red and blotchy and all scrunched up with . . .

Rage?

'It is a telegram,' said Ma. Her voice was cold, almost unrecognisable. 'And yes, like you, I thought it must be about your brother and I had a minute or two that I never want to live through again. But then I opened it . . . and discovered it was a message inviting my daughter to start work at the Royal Engineers Postal Service in London on Monday.'

Oh.

Oh!

A dozen conflicting emotions stunned Beth into silence.

Relief – sheer, exquisite relief – that Ned was safe from illness or accident.

Toe-curling embarrassment and shame that she had been caught out. They would never forgive her. She would never forgive herself.

And, somewhere behind those two, a little warm kernel of excitement. She had got the job. *She had got the job*!

Meanwhile, Ma had come right up to the bed and was brandishing the offending telegram in Beth's face.

'How dare you?' she hissed, the veins in her neck bulging. 'You *lied* to us.'

'I'm sorry,' said Beth cowering away.

'And Sally too,' said Ma, slapping the telegram down on the bed. 'I can't believe Sally went along with this deception. Wasn't she able to talk some sense into you?'

'It wasn't Sally's fault,' said Beth quickly. 'It was my idea and I said I'd go whether or not she came with me. Please don't blame her. And I didn't mean to deceive you. I didn't think I'd get the job and—'

'I don't want to hear your excuses,' said Ma. 'I feel like I don't know you anymore. Queen Victoria said that "the greatest maxim of all is that children should be brought up as simply and in as domestic a way as possible." You, my girl, have let us down in the greatest way possible.'

'I just want to do my bit,' whispered Beth. 'I just want to *help*.'

'You *are* helping,' said Ma. 'And if the shop isn't enough for you, there are enough good causes around here for you to help a different one every night of the year. Leave London to the Londoners. Charity begins at home and I forbid you to take that job. Forbid it. How can you even think of leaving us when Ned has just gone?'

And she stormed from the room.

Beth was left reeling.

She lay there, bed clothes pulled up to her chin, for she didn't know how long. Eventually, not knowing what else to do, she got up, dressed and stumbled from the room.

Ma didn't mean it, she told herself as she emptied her chamber pot in the privy.

Ma had just lashed out in the heat of the moment, she told herself, as she washed her face and hands in the scullery.

She'd make it right. She'd go and apologise and all would be well.

Beth went through the storeroom and into the shop.

'Ma, I'm sorry,' she said to her mother's back.

'You will leave, Beth, right away,' muttered Ma. 'Unless you can tell me right here and right now that you have no intention of taking that job, you will get out of my sight.'

'Please can we talk about it?'

'Go,' said Ma quietly over her shoulder. 'Don't make me raise my voice in front of the customers.'

Beth looked past Ma and for the first time registered that the shop was full of people. Most were chatting among themselves but Mrs Harrison, who was being served, glanced at her curiously.

Beth fled.

For what felt like forever, she walked the streets of the village, mind a-whirr, and then she set off along the footpath by the river. Lost in her own misery, she responded with only the curtest of nods to people she knew working on the watercress beds and in the nurseries. It was only when she got as far as Maitland Hall that she realised how far she had walked. She turned around and set off back to Woodhampstead, her head starting to thump again.

Back in the village, she found herself outside Sally's cottage. Weary, defeated, she knocked on the door. There was no reply. Of course, there wasn't. Sally, like every other sensible, reliable, trustworthy person, was where she should be. Where she *said* she'd be. Helping Ma in the store or doing her shift at the pub or with Lady Kemble and the bandage committee. Doing her bit from *within* the village.

Beth sat down on the low wall outside Sally's cottage, breathing in the scent of the early roses and avoiding the worst of the pigeon droppings. Absentmindedly, she stroked a skinny white cat, which deigned to accept her ministrations. If only her life was as uncomplicated. If only—

'Beth. What are you doing here? I thought you were poorly in bed. And what on earth is the *matter*?'

It was Sally, hands to her mouth and looking frightened. Beth realised that she was crying – great heaving sobs that started somewhere in her chest and bubbled free with a wrench. She tried to answer but couldn't; her words drowned out by her misery.

'Come inside,' said Sally putting her hand under Beth's elbow and helping her up. 'Come inside and tell me.'

She unlocked the cottage and shepherded Beth inside and down the narrow passage to the kitchen. Beth collapsed into the sofa and gave in to her tears completely.

'What's happened?' said Sally. 'Not Ned?'

Beth shook her head, feeling even worse. How awful she was to even let Sally *think* that something had happened to their brother. She was so selfish. Completely wrapped up in herself.

What a *terrible* person she was.

'Then I'm guessing Ma found out about yesterday?' said Sally.

Beth nodded and Sally dropped onto the sofa beside her.

'Oh Lordy,' she said. 'You'd better tell me everything.'

Through copious tears, Beth told her sister the whole story.

'What do you want to do?' asked Sally when she had finished.

Beth thought about it. Then she thought about it some more. And she realised, with steel in her heart, that she wanted the job. She *really* wanted the job. She wasn't quite sure how she'd got it and she still wasn't convinced the whole thing wasn't an elaborate joke – but she did want the job. And she realised she was crying not only because she had hurt and angered Ma by defying her wishes and going up to London for the interview but because she was going to hurt and anger her all over again by accepting the job.

Because, whatever it took, that was what she was going to do.

Sally was laughing. 'There's no need to answer my question,' she said.' I can see from your face that you want it.'

Beth gave a small, defiant nod. 'I do,' she said.

'In which case, why don't you *take* it?' asked Sally.

Beth gave her a weak smile. 'Don't *you* want to do something different?' she asked, knowing she wasn't quite answering the question, but curious all the same. She glanced at her sister out of the corner of her eye: her smooth dark hair, her full face and rosy cheeks, the little dimple in her chin. Sally always looked happy, content. Nothing ever seemed to ruffle her world, she moved through it calmly and steadily, always seeing the best in everyone, happy with her lot.

'No,' said Sally, so simply and so straightforwardly that Beth believed her. 'Oh, I was up for the adventure yesterday – it was my idea, for goodness' sake – but all I've ever wanted is to get married and to have children. And Bertie might be away fighting but I have to believe that he will be coming home and my job is to keep the home fires burning.'

'I wish I was more like you,' said Beth wistfully.

'No, you don't,' said Sally, briskly. 'And I've always known that Woodhampstead wasn't going to be big enough for you for ever.'

'Really? I hadn't.'

Sally grinned. 'You got a scholarship to the grammar school, didn't you? I know you didn't go but you're exceptionally clever. You're practical. And you read and write like an angel. You've got a splendid new job in London. In fact, is there anything you *can't* do?'

'I'll always have legs that are too short and stumpy for my body,' said Beth with a little giggle.

'Mine too,' said Sally. 'We can blame Ma for that.'

Ma.

Beth's laughter dried in her throat.

'Ma's furious.' Beth's voice dropped to a whisper. 'She told me to get out. She told I was on my *own*.'

'She's hurt,' said Sally. 'She's probably more upset that we lied to her yesterday than anything else. She'll be livid with me too.'

'I told her it was all my idea.' Beth puffed out her cheeks. 'I said I dragged you along with me.'

'There was no need to do that,' said Sally. 'I'm happy to own my part in it.'

'There was a need,' said Beth. 'We can't have Ma angry with the pair of us. Not with Ned gone.'

Sally blew out her cheeks. 'Yes, you're right. I'm sorry, though. It *was* my idea.'

'I could have said no. I dread to think what Pa is going to say. Maybe Ma will tell him to beat me.' Beth shut her eyes. It must be ten years since her father had last taken his belt to her – Beth was no trouble-maker or rebel – but she could still remember the pain. The stripes had throbbed for days and almost worse had been the terrible humiliation . . .

'I'm sure it won't come to that,' said Sally. 'You're far too old now.'

'I lied to them,' Beth whispered. 'I can't believe I *lied* to them.'

'And you're going to take the job,' said Sally.

A statement, not a question.

Beth paused. 'I am. I can't think of anything more impor-tant than keeping the post running to the boys at the front.'

'It's a long way away,' said Sally. 'That journey. Every day.'

'Even so. I'm accepting it.' Beth gave a little tremulous

sigh and clutched a cushion to her chest. 'Fool that I am, I'm accepting it.'

Sally nodded. 'Good for you.' She got to her feet. 'And *I'd* better go and build some bridges with our mother.'

'I'll come with you,' said Beth. 'I need to tell her I'm accepting the job. I know I'm leaving them in the lurch. They'll find it really difficult to replace me and we're already short-staffed as it is.'

'That's why I'm going over.' Sally smoothed down her skirt. 'I'm going to explain that I'll take your place and work in the shop.'

'*No*,' cried Beth. 'You can't do that. You *won't* do that. I'm not letting you change your life or put your life on hold so that I can do what I want to do. In fact, if it comes to that, I'll—'

Sally laughed. 'Stop being a martyr, Beth! So, you'd happily leave Ma and Pa high and dry, but if I offer to step in and help, you're having none of it?'

'You're right.' Beth gave a rueful smile. 'But I'll be earning money – proper money – and I'll be able to give some of that to Ma and Pa, so it's not all bad news.' The telegram had mentioned a sum. A huge sum. Even after the train fare, it would be far, far more than a shop girl could ever earn.

'That should certainly soften the blow,' said Sally. 'And I'd like to work in the shop. No, really,' she added, waving away Beth's protesting hand. 'If you must know, it's lonely over here on my own and they don't really need me over at the pub – not now that there are so few people left to drink there. And there's only so much cleaning and tidying I can do when there's just me living here and I'm taking most of my meals over with Ma and Pa. So, you see, you'll be doing me a favour. Oh, I'll still do my volunteer work, of course. I'll go and help Lady Kemble with her splints and calico bandages and I'll help Alice Oswald with the Scouts and I'll be on the fete committee, but I still need something to fill my time to stop me worrying about Bertie constantly. And if I'm helping my little sister to do a big important job – well then, I'll also be doing my bit in my own way, won't I?'

Beth took a deep breath. 'Thank you.' If Sally really would step into her shoes, surely Ma and Pa couldn't be too angry. Could they?

'Right, then,' said Sally, bossily. 'You'd better reply to the post office, and I'd better get over to the shop.'

'You're my favourite sister,' Beth said, giving her a hug.

'I'm your only sister,' replied Sally.

Beth had never sent a telegram in her whole life.

She knew how it worked, of course – even a sub post office as small as Woodhampstead had its own telegram machine – but she had never needed to send one before today. But, even now, she hesitated. There was the cost, of course – at a penny a word, it was prohibitively expensive, even for a very short message. And then there was the confidentiality issue. The staff weren't supposed to divulge what was being sent but Beth had never really trusted Nellie Green, not since the time she had told Sam Harrison Beth was sweet on him at school. The whole village probably already knew that Beth had been offered the REPS job and she didn't want them also knowing that she had accepted it before she had had a chance to tell Ma in person.

So, in the end, she wrote a letter, accepting the position and confirming that she would 'report for duty' the following Monday. She'd catch the second post and, with a fair wind, her reply would arrive in London the next morning. Hopefully that would not be too late.

She sealed the letter into the envelope, addressed it in her neat script and was about to head out of the door when she hesitated. Now that she had all Sally's writing things on the kitchen table, why not write to Ned as well? With all the excitement, she hadn't written to him for a couple of days. In fact, why not write to Sam too? Surely she should let him know that she had got the job? It was only polite.

No sooner had the idea popped into her mind than she grabbed a piece of paper and loaded the pen with ink.

Dear Sam,

I hope this letter finds you well.

I am writing to let you know that I went to St Albans and met Mr Webster, as you suggested, and he let me know that the job is actually in London. I went to the interview yesterday and, even though they said that they are only recruiting people from either the army or the post office, I somehow got the job! I start on Monday, which is exciting and scary at the same time. Thank you very much for suggesting it to me. I knew being able to decipher all those envelopes would come in useful sometime!

Anyhow, I'd love to hear where you are and how you are getting on. Please let me know if there is anything you need.

Best wishes,

Yours,

Beth.

She paused before she sealed the envelope, unsure of whether she had got the tone right, unsure of whether she should be writing at all. Was it all too forward? Too bold? Too boring? Just simply inappropriate? She was too tired and too over-wrought to know, so, in the end, she just sealed the envelope, addressed it with his name, number and regiment number and sent it off.

What was the worst that could happen?

Beth had just got back to Sally's and put the kettle on to boil, when she heard knocking and scuffling at the front door.

She went to investigate and found Sally trying to wrestle a large, battered trunk inside.

'What on earth are you doing?' she asked, taking hold of one of the handles and helping Sally manoeuvre it down the passage and into the kitchen. And then realisation dawned. 'It's my clothes, isn't it? Ma wants me to leave.'

'I'm sure it's just for a short time,' said Sally. 'Just until things settle down.'

Beth sat down abruptly. Whatever she had thought might happen, it wasn't . . . this. An argument, certainly. Some sort of punishment, probably. But she hadn't expected her mother to throw her out of her own home.

She would almost rather be beaten.

'But what about Pa?' she said trying to work it all out. 'Does Pa know about this?'

Maybe it was just her mother being irrational. Pa would make her see sense.

Sally shook her head. 'He's back from the deliveries and Ma's told him everything. It's not just the lying and the deception. They can't believe you would willingly put yourself in danger when they've already had to face Ned going off to war. They say that if you take the job, you're not welcome there. And they've asked you not to tell Ned. But I'm sure it's not for long. And, of course, you're welcome here for as long as you like.'

Beth looked at her sister. 'Is it worth it?' she whispered. 'Is what I'm about to do really worth it?'

9

Beth did try to talk to Pa.

She intercepted him the next morning as he was saddling Mayfair. But he waved her away with a dismissive flick of his wrist and turned his back.

Then she wrote to both her parents, apologising for her deception. The message came back through Sally that unless she turned the job down, there was nothing more to say.

Far from putting her off, Ma and Pa's intransigence only served to strengthen her resolve.

A letter from REPS arrived two days after the telegram. Luckily, Sally managed to intercept it before her parents could have salt rubbed into their wounds. It contained all the details she required and what she needed to prepare. Not that there was much to do. She went to the station, copied down the timetable and familiarised herself with the journey as best she could. On the first day, she didn't need to arrive until ten o'clock. Thereafter her hours would be 9am to 5pm.

And so, here she was, on the 8.25am through train from Woodhampstead to King's Cross and feeling a heady mix of terror, defiance and huge, anything-is-possible euphoria. At least she would be able to ease herself in gently without an early start and the journey should be a breeze.

Unfortunately, the Great Northern Railway had other plans for her. Instead of speeding through Hatfield Station en route to the capital, it groaned to a halt. 'All change,' cried the guard, and Beth thought she could detect sympathy in his voice.

The defiance and euphoria disappeared and left Beth only with the abject terror. The next train wasn't due for fifteen minutes and, checking the timetable, she could see that it was scheduled to stop at every darned station between here and King's Cross. Unless she was very lucky, she was going to be late – and there wasn't a thing she could do about it.

As soon as the stopping train finally puffed into King's Cross, Beth was by the door, pushing the window down to open the door from the outside. She was the first to alight and, jamming her straw boater onto her head with one hand, she ran towards the Tube as fast as she could. There was no time to worry about rats or coffins and the four stops west to Portland Road Station passed in an agony of impatience. She bounded up the stairs – gosh, the clock stood at ten minutes to ten – and out onto the busy Euston Road. This, of course, took an age to cross but finally she set off at practically a run up the side of the Regent's Park. On her right were large Georgian houses with wrought-iron verandas and balconies, their brickwork painted so white they looked like they had been constructed entirely out of icing. On her left, through an avenue of plane trees, was the park with its lawns and flowerbeds. Here, people were strolling, two little boys were trying to fly a kite in the gusty wind and nannies were pushing perambulators for all the world as if there was no war on at all . . .

Quicker.

Quicker!

Her heart was racing, her cheeks were on fire and damp strands from her plait were sticking to her face. Still, there was no time to stop. No time, even, to slow down. It was all much, much further than she had anticipated and she was going to be late.

She was going to be late on her very first day!

What did that say about her?

She would never live it down!

At last, Beth came to a road on her left that led straight into the park. She consulted her map – yes, it was Chester Road, the one she needed. She dashed around the corner, then slowed down in the way you do when all is lost. On the right, through more plane trees, she could see a huge wooden structure, not unlike a massive barn or a warehouse, with half a dozen lorries backed up in front of it under a large wooden awning. It certainly wouldn't win any awards for architecture – it couldn't have been any more different to the King Edward Building where she'd had her interview. Beth couldn't help feeling a stab of disappointment. It looked so ordinary, so drab, so run of the mill . . .

Had it really been worth falling out with Ma and Pa to work *here*?

What the building lacked in appearance, however, it more than made up for in size. As Beth reached the corner of the road, she could see just how big it was. It seemed to go on forever – by far the biggest wooden building Beth had ever seen – and the sounds of sawing and hammering and general construction suggested that it wasn't yet finished.

Beth walked briskly up the Broad Walk until she came to a gateway in the metal fence, manned by two soldiers. She showed her letter of employment to one of them and was waved through. The other soldier gave her a little salute and, despite her stress and nerves, Beth felt a little thrill of pride. No one ever saluted her in the shop! She was doing more than just lending a hand. She was a woman of import now.

She was still smiling as she followed a gravel track up to an unprepossessing wooden entrance. Another soldier inspected her letter, waved her in and . . .

Wow!

If the building had been unimpressive from the outside, it took her breath away inside.

Beth's first thought was of a forest. It was the smell, for a start – the sharp resin tang of pine was almost overpowering – but also the wooden columns looked just like tree trunks. Which, of course, they were, in a way. For one heady moment, Beth was back playing hide-and-seek in the woods behind Maitland Hall with Sally and Ned, brushing away the scratchy branches as she crawled into her hiding place . . .

The building was almost empty – just a few men in uniform moving around the vast, cavernous, echoing space – and if Beth looked up at all the wooden columns dividing into wooden supports, it somehow reminded her of St Albans cathedral.

Only it was hot. Really hot. And stuffy.

'Healey? Elizabeth Healey?'

'Yes, ma'am.'

Beth stopped craning her neck at the ceiling and snapped to attention. It was Miss Parker, the woman who had interviewed her, the woman Beth somehow knew was responsible for giving her the job. And she'd already let her down . . .

Miss Parker was glancing at her through her narrow-rimmed spectacles and ticking her name off on a clipboard. 'You're late,' she said, matter-of-factly.

There was a big clock attached to the wooden wall, next to a huge union flag. It showed the time was precisely seven minutes past ten. So yes, she was late. She couldn't argue with that.

'I'm sorry, Miss Parker,' she started. 'The through train stopped at Hatfield Station and—'

'Where you live and how you get to work are of absolutely no interest to me,' interrupted Miss Parker. 'I won't mark it down on your form today, but just make sure you're not late tomorrow. And now, come with me. You're the last to arrive and Sergeant Major Cunningham is waiting to speak to the new recruits.'

'Yes, Miss Parker. Sorry, Miss Parker.'

Beth's anxiety ratcheted up a gear. She'd already blotted her copybook, and now she'd have to deal with that oaf as well.

Beth hurried along behind Miss Parker through the vast open building and over to some doors at the far end. Miss Parker opened the very last door and ushered her into what looked like a small classroom with chairs in a semi-circle facing a large desk. There was even a blackboard on an easel. Beth blinked and looked around stupidly, and a dozen pairs of eyes stared back at her. They all belonged to women, most much older than Beth – closer, indeed, to Ma's age – but there were two girls more Beth's age sitting on the back row together. Beth, almost squeaking with fright, slid into an empty chair directly in front of them. She wondered if they were friends who had signed up together. Oh, how she wished Sally was her with here today.

The door opened again and in came Sergeant Major Cunningham. Or should that be plain Mr Cunningham? Beth found that he was somehow not as scary when she remembered he was only playing at being a sergeant major. Even so, she couldn't help feeling a little intimidated as he marched up to the desk and turned to face them.

At least he hadn't seen her arriving late . . .

He stood facing them until everyone had noticed him and the hubbub of chatter had died away. Then he held up a white envelope. He let the silence lengthen, clearly enjoying the theatrics, and then said, 'What's this?'

For a moment no one answered. A couple of women in front of Beth shot each other a nervous glance.

It was too simple a question.

It must be a trick.

'Come on, ladies,' said Sergeant Major Cunningham, with a tinge of impatience. 'You're meant to be the crème de la crème. Cat got your tongues?'

One of the girls behind Beth cleared her throat. 'It's an envelope . . . sir,' she said in a cut-glass accent.

Silence.

'Yes,' said Sergeant Major Cunningham. 'I think we can all agree it's an envelope.'

He said it with exaggerated politeness, clearly playing it for laughs and there was a sycophantic ripple of laughter around the room. Beth decided she really didn't like him at all. He wasn't kind, and in her world, kindness counted for a great deal.

'And what else might we deduce about this *envelope*?' Sergeant Major Cunningham was saying.

Say something, Beth.

Say it's a letter.

'It's a le'er?' said another voice behind Beth. This voice was quite different: higher, perter and clearly more working class. Without turning around, Beth concluded she was wrong to have assumed that the two girls behind her were friends. They were much more likely to be mistress and servant.

For some reason, the thought unnerved Beth slightly.

'I think you're right,' said Sergeant Major Cunningham. 'I think it is very much a "le'er",' he continued, mimicking the girl's accent. 'And let me tell you a little more about this particular "le'er". It's from a lady – a Mrs Flowers in Shropshire, to be precise – who is writing to her son in France. Mrs Flowers is telling her son how proud she is of him for serving King and Country. And that she will shortly be sending him a fruitcake, some socks and more tobacco. So, what else does that make this letter?'

There was another silence.

This time, no one broke it.

Sergeant Major Cunningham put both palms flat on the desk and looked around the room.

'Very well, then,' he said. 'I'll tell you what that makes it. It makes it one of the most important parts of the war effort. Never estimate the power of the post. This humble letter – the type you write to your father, your brother, your sweetheart, your son – is one of the most powerful weapons we have in keeping morale high. Let me tell you, ladies, getting letters to the front is just as important as getting food and munitions out there, and do not let anyone tell you any differently. What you will be doing is absolutely essential – which is why the government has paid fifty thousand pounds, at a time we can ill afford it, to put up the biggest wooden structure in the *world*. It's the reason you've all been taken on and we are all here today. This humble letter – and millions like it – will do nothing less than win us the war.'

Despite her dislike of the man, Beth found herself moved by Sergeant Major Cunningham's words. What she was doing was important. It *mattered*. Even though it had driven a wedge between herself and her parents, she would be making a difference. In her own way, she would be fighting for Blighty and, for that reason, she was going to give it everything she'd got.

For King and Country.

For Ned.

For Sam.

For all of them.

Sergeant Major Cunningham was still talking. 'Now, what do you notice about this envelope,' he was saying. 'What's unusual about it?'

Fired up, Beth leaned forward to take a closer look. It was the stamp. Definitely the stamp. Just look at it! It was completely crooked – almost at a forty-five-degree angle, for goodness' sake. Mrs Flowers had clearly been distracted or in a tearing hurry or maybe she needed new spectacles and couldn't get any as so many opticians had gone to the front.

It was time for Beth to speak up. Time to join in the discussion and show that she was fully committed.

Beth put her hand up. 'The angle of the—' she started, then stopped with a little squeal. Something – some*one* – had dug her firmly in the back. She swung round, indignant – *furious*—

How dare whoever it was ruin her big moment?

The girls behind were both smiling at her, but the smiles were friendly and indulgent rather than unkind or mocking.

'Shh,' said one, putting a finger to her lips. Beth noticed that she was dark-haired and very pretty with a heart-shaped face, dancing violet eyes and a perfect rosebud mouth. Beth was surprised – shocked, even – to detect the merest hint of lipstick. Not that any of that mattered. Why should she be quiet? Why shouldn't she answer the question? She had as much right to as anyone else.

Beth was about to turn back around and finish answering the question when the other girl put a hand on her arm. She was more striking than pretty with blond hair, large heavy-lidded grey eyes and a wide curving mouth. 'The stamp's *meant* to be like that,' she hissed. 'It's a code.'

Oh!

'A *code*?' Beth whispered back in confusion. 'What sort of a code? Like *spies*?'

Out before she could stop it. But was that what the girl had meant? A message to the enemy? From the enemy?

Florence's Ralph had stuck a stamp on like that. Was he a spy? Was *she*?

The dark-haired girl gave a deep-throated chuckle. 'When you put the stamp on like that, it means "missing you",' she said. 'Nothing more sinister than that, you chump.'

'Oh!' said Beth with a rueful smile.

'Would you ladies in the back row care to stop chattering and join in our conversation?' said Sergeant Major Cunningham loudly. 'Mrs Smythe says the envelope is different because the stamp is crooked, but, charming as that suggestion is, it's not the answer I was looking for. Perhaps you girls have a better idea?'

The ripple of laughter that followed made Beth very glad that she was not Mrs Smythe and she felt a swell of gratitude towards the girls behind her.

As to the 'right' answer, though . . .

'Is it that the envelope ain't got a proper address on it, sir?' said a voice from behind her – the cockney voice that Beth now knew belonged to the pretty dark-haired girl. 'It's just got the soldier's name and number and his regiment.'

'Very good, Miss . . . ?' said Sergeant Major Cunningham.

'Miss Woods, sir,' came the voice from behind Beth. '*Milly* Woods.'

'Quite right, Miss Woods,' said Sergeant Major Cunningham, tapping his stick onto the ground. 'And why do we think the letter might be addressed thus?'

Beth raised her hand, resisting the temptation to say 'oo oo oo' as Nellie Green, the cleverest girl in the class, had been wont to do. Sergeant Major Cunningham nodded at her.

'Because the regiments move around, so they haven't got a permanent address, sir,' she said. 'And because, even if they did have a permanent address, we would not wish that information to get into enemy hands.'

Beth knew this from writing to Ned and to Sam. To be fair, everyone else would know this too, both from writing to their loved ones and because many of them were post office already. Still, she had got in first.

'Excellent, Miss . . . ?' said Sergeant Major Cunningham.

'Miss Healey, sir,' said Beth. '*Liza* Healey.'

Liza?

Liza?

Where on earth had *that* come from?

She hadn't planned to say that and she wasn't even sure that Liza was actually a name. But Beth was just so homely. So dull. So *provincial*.

Liza sounded worldly, sophisticated . . . a million miles from Woodhampstead.

It was too late now.

She'd been and gone and said it.

'Very good, Miss Healey,' said Sergeant Major Cunningham with a little nod. 'That is exactly the case. Each morning we will be informed by Whitehall of the latest battalion movements and positions so that each and every item of mail can be dispatched to the right place at the right time and with the minimum of fuss. The post office was a huge operation before the war, but we have lost nearly a quarter of our workforce and are also dealing with an *extra* twelve million letters a week being sent overseas to the British Expeditionary Force. It is a huge undertaking. *Huge*. But, as the Postmaster General himself said, it is more important to let our men leave in order to beat the Germans than it is to keep the post office operating to the same very high standards of efficiency for which it is famed.'

Just when Beth was beginning to warm to the sergeant major, too! He clearly thought the girls and women weren't going to be nearly as good at getting the post sorted as the men. The way the room shifted and stirred suggested that Beth was not the only one to notice this. No one challenged the sergeant major on his words, though. Even the confident little miss behind Beth stayed silent.

We'll show him, thought Beth fiercely. We'll show him.

Sergeant Major Cunningham was still in full flow, oblivious
to the change in mood. 'This structure has been built because
the current facilities at the King Edward Building and at
Mount Pleasant can no longer cope with the sheer volume
of mail. As you will have gathered, this building is only just
becoming operational and indeed some parts of it are still
under construction. You are the advance guard. The building
is largely empty at the moment, but over the next few days
and weeks, your numbers will increase dramatically. This
building will house a large parcel office and a section to
censor letters coming from the various fronts to complement
other offices elsewhere in London. We will also handle some
– but, you will be very pleased to hear, not all! – of the mail
going abroad to our soldiers. You will report for duty on
time, work hard, and keep what you see and hear entirely
confidential. Understood?'

Everyone nodded, mutely.

'Under*stood*?' repeated Sergeant Major Cunningham.

'Yes, sir,' parroted the women as one.

'Very good. Well, battle stations,' said Sergeant Major
Cunningham, for all the world as if they were fighting for
King and Country.

Which, in a way, Beth supposed, they were.

When Sergeant Major Cunningham had finished speaking,
Miss Parker announced a twenty-minute break. She said that
the new recruits were welcome to go outside, but they were
not permitted anywhere near the unloading bays or the
construction site on the other side of the building. In the
next week or so, a canteen would be opened across the grass
on the edge of the site, which they could visit during their
breaks. For now, rations would be provided only at lunchtime.
There was to be strictly no smoking in the building, no
unnecessary fraternisation with the opposite sex, no larking

around on the wheeled baskets, no eating or drinking while on duty, no going on leave without giving at least a month's notice, no forgetting to get injuries recorded in the Injury Book . . .

And so on.

Rations?

Duty?

Going on leave?

It really was like being in the army, thought Beth.

They were dismissed.

Feeling slightly dazed, Beth followed the others out of the office and then through the cavernous space at the heart of the Home Depot. While they had been in the meeting, the men Beth had noticed earlier had started to arrange baskets and wooden frames into rows and sacks and sacks of mail had been left in – presumably – strategically placed piles. There seemed to be an awful lot of them and Beth started wondering exactly what she had let herself in for. She hoped they weren't expected to process all those letters and parcels today – and there were more sacks being hauled into position by the dozen even as she watched.

The two girls who had sat in the row behind Beth were walking together slightly ahead of Beth, deep in conversation. Beth was trying – and failing – not to feel left out when the taller girl tapped a bucket attached to a nail on a wooden post.

'What's this?' Beth heard her say.

'It's sand,' said the shorter girl. Milly, was it?

'I know, you chump,' said the first. 'It's got *that* written on it in big black letters. But what's it for?'

'It's to put out fires,' said Milly. 'Let's hope we never have to use it.'

They were an odd couple, thought Beth, but she couldn't

help feeling a little jealous of the two of them being together when she was all on her own. Beth wasn't used to feeling left out and she didn't like the feeling at all. Outside – much cooler than inside, despite the sun – she gave herself a good talking to. Even if she was being left out, it was up to her to do something about it.

So she walked up to the two girls with a smile plastered on her face.

'Thank you for helping me out in there,' she said. 'You saved me from making a complete chump of myself in front of the whole room.'

Both girls laughed and the laughs were friendly and warm.

'The woman in the front row won't be thanking us,' said the tall la-di-la one. 'She made exactly the same mistake you were about to.'

'She did,' said Beth. 'Is it very wrong of me to be thanking my lucky stars that she made it and I didn't?'

'Very wrong,' said the pert, dark-haired one with a grin. 'After all, the war is meant to be about self-sacrifice and putting others before yourself. Anyhow, how come you don't know about the stamp code?'

Beth shrugged. 'I've just never heard of it.'

'You're not post office, then?' said Milly.

'No,' said Beth. 'Are you?'

'Sort of. Me uncle runs one of the post offices in Bow so I've just picked things up over the years helping him out over there.'

Beth sighed.

Of course, the girl was post office.

She was just going to have to get used to the fact that everyone was going to know more about, well, everything than she did. Hopefully she would catch up quickly and not make too much of an idiot of herself.

Milly covertly lit a cigarette and nonchalantly blew out a perfect smoke circle. It looked terribly daring and alluring to Beth, who wasn't at all used to women smoking – but somehow in keeping with this new topsy-turvy world where anything seemed to go.

'What did you say your name was?' Milly asked Beth, taking another deep drag.

Beth paused. Now was the time to admit she was a boring old Beth.

'I'm Liza,' said Beth.

Goodness, what was *wrong* with her?

The girls both looked at her, frown lines deepening.

'Do you mean Lisa?' asked Milly.

'Or Eliza?' added the high-class one.

'Neither,' said Beth. 'I'm Liza.'

And now she was.

Liza Healey.

Beth suddenly felt so racy and so daring that she almost asked Milly if she could have one of her cigarettes. She had never smoked before, but somehow she was sure that Liza could blow out a perfect smoke ring without any trouble at all.

'What about you?' Milly asked the other girl. 'What's your name?'

Oh!

'I thought you knew each other,' interrupted Beth. 'I thought you . . .'

She trailed off. Would it be impolite to say 'I thought you were mistress and servant'? Being neither mistress nor servant, Beth found that she had no idea.

'Oh, Gawd, no,' said Milly. 'We just sat down next to each other. We were the only young ones – well, until you came along – so I think we just sort of sought each other out.'

'I see,' said Beth. 'And here was I feeling all left out for no reason.'

The three girls laughed easily together.

Then the tall, high-class girl said 'I'm Nora Benham.'

Beth decided that she actually was quite pretty if you caught her face at the right angle. Otherwise, the main impression was a bit like a very tall baby bird. Big mouth, big eyes, awkward arms and legs. Her skirt was beautiful, though – dark blue like the rest of them but beautifully and elaborately embroidered and divided in the latest style.

'Hello, Nora,' said Milly.

Beth couldn't help thinking that Milly was frightfully forthright in the way she spoke and asked questions. It was a bit unnerving. But for the war, she would be addressing Nora as 'miss'. But if Nora was finding the conversation strange, nothing in her voice or demeanour gave it away.

'And . . . Benham?' said Milly. There was a questioning tilt to her chin that Beth didn't understand.

'Yes.' Nora started to fiddle with the locket around her neck.

'That's your surname?' clarified Milly.

'It is. But—'

'It's also the surname of the man who's in charge of this place.'

Was it? Beth had had no idea of who was in charge. In fact, she'd had half a mind it was Sergeant Major Cunningham. *He* certainly seemed to think he was in charge. But Nora had dropped both the locket and her gaze.

'Is he your father?' persisted Milly.

'No, no.' Nora looked up. 'Nothing like that. He's my uncle . . .'

There was a little silence while Milly took another drag of her cigarette.

'I see we'll have to mind our Ps and Qs around you,' she said finally. 'In more ways than one.'

This was strange. Very strange.

Beth had no idea what to say.

Nora's hand fluttered to her heart and her words started tumbling over each other. 'I promise I'm not here to spy on you or to tell tales or anything like that.'

Milly didn't say anything. She just blew out another perfect smoke ring and Beth was sure that the fact it came perilously close to Nora's face was far from an accident.

'Look,' added Nora. 'I really wanted to do something to help and Mummy wasn't keen on me doing anything dangerous. I'm not sure Uncle Alf – Major Benham – wanted me here at all but Daddy can be awfully persuasive when he puts his mind to it. I had to go through all the same tests and interviews as everyone else, you know. And it does mean I know stuff. Like about the secret language of stamps,' she finished defensively, with a little glance at Beth.

Beth stood there feeling more and more inadequate. Milly's family working for the post office was bad enough, but now Nora being the niece of Major Benham . . . what could she possibly have to offer compared to them?

At least nobody else seemed to be thinking that. Milly was smiling at Nora. 'Well, I suppose we'll have to give you the benefit of the doubt, an' all,' she said. 'At least you didn't try and change your surname to something else.'

'I probably should have done,' said Nora. She had gone all red around her neck and locket. 'Or I probably should have become a canary like I wanted to all along.'

Milly laughed. 'I expect "Mummy" would have had something to say about that,' she said, not unkindly. 'Round where I live, that's what a lot of girls are doing. You can see why they get their name. Yellow as bananas.'

'I'd have gone yellow for the boys at the front,' said Nora, staunchly.

'Oh, me too,' said Milly. 'But I reckoned I'd be more use doing the skilled work here. The pay's much better too. Only, cos I ain't married, it looks like I'm gonna be stuck wrapping bleeding parcels instead of stopping spies.'

'Me too,' said Nora ruefully. 'I'm tempted to invent a husband.'

Beth looked from one to the other. They could have been talking a foreign language as far as she was concerned. Timid Beth might have nodded along, desperate to pretend she was following all the twists and turns of the conversation and equally desperate not to get found out; Confident Liza didn't care. She needed to learn what she could, when she could.

'Canaries? Spies? *Invented husbands*?' she said. 'What on *earth* are you talking about?'

Now both Milly and Nora were laughing.

At her.

'Oh, you really are a darling,' said Milly, linking her arm with Beth's. 'Where on earth did they find you?'

Beth might have been offended.

Liza chose to be amused.

'A general provisions store in Woodhampstead,' she said, matter-of-factly. 'In fact,' she added, out of loyalty to Ma and Pa, '*the* general provisions store in Woodhampstead. There's only one.'

'Oh, I say,' said Milly. 'And, where, might I ask, is Woodhampstead?'

'It's in Hertfordshire.'

Only twenty miles away.

Another planet.

Nora took hold of her other arm. 'Well, Miss Woodhampstead,' she said. 'Canaries is the name given to the girls who work in the munitions factories over in the East End. The chemicals they use make their skin go bright yellow.'

'Oh,' said Beth. '*Fancy!*'

Maybe she should have told Ma and Pa she was planning to work there instead and then 'settled' on the Home Depot. It would have made the post office look positively tame by comparison . . .

'And the bit about the spies is because the Depot behind us is going to house a big censoring department to make sure that there's nothing untoward in the letters that go backwards and forwards to the front. We thought that that was why we was all hired, but before you got here, Miss Parker was telling us that most of the censoring work is going to be done elsewhere and what's here is going to be reserved for women that's married. That's why Nora here wants to invent a husband.'

Beth blinked, trying to take it all in. It was all so confusing. 'But why can only married women censor the letters?' she asked. It didn't make sense. Half the time, it wasn't 'done' for married women to carry on working. That was why Sally had stopped working in the shop.

Nora and Milly exchanged a look over her head. 'Can't have us spotless maidens being shocked by anything saucy, can we?' said Milly archly.

Ah!

Her brother was being asked to risk his life, but they couldn't risk her being shocked by something saucy . . . How ridiculous.

The girls wandered over to the shade of a nearby plane tree, Beth between the two other girls. *Look at me*, Beth thought to herself. Beth-in-the-middle. And she *was* in the middle in lots of ways, she realised. Taller than Milly but not as tall as Nora. She was proud of her fair hair but even though it was much lighter than Milly's, Nora's was even blonder. And, of course, her family was obviously better off than Milly's but Nora's was clearly in a different league altogether.

'Talking about pretending to be married, maybe you should forget that and just go for the real thing,' Milly was saying with a laugh.

Beth looked at her and followed her line of sight, right over to . . . Mr Blackford from the interview at the King Edward Building. Yes, it was definitely him. Head down, cigarette in hand, he was pacing around the glass, deep in thought and apparently oblivious to the three girls watching him from under the trees. Tall, thin and clever-looking, there was no doubt he was a handsome man and Beth felt her heart beat just a little faster to see him again.

'Hmmm, he's very debonair,' agreed Nora with a giggle. 'Do you think it would be breaking the "no fraternising" rule to go over and introduce myself?'

'Perhaps,' said Milly. 'But it's a hot June day and if you were to go over into the sun, maybe you might feel faint and then—'

'I know him,' interrupted Beth. Or was it Liza?

The others rounded on her.

'You know him?'

'Why didn't you say?'

'Well, I don't know him *exactly*,' said Beth. 'But he accidentally crashed a trolley into me at my interview at the King Edward Building – I've still got a tiny scar from the collision – and afterwards we talked for a brief time. A Zeppelin had just landed very close to his lodgings and I think he was quite shaken up.'

'Well, aren't you quite the dark horse,' said Nora.

'Maybe you could introduce us,' said Milly.

Beth was beginning to regret saying anything at all, but she was saved by Sergeant Major Cunningham pompously tooting a whistle. 'Time to report back for duty,' he shouted, before striding back into the building.

The three girls looked at each other with stifled giggles.

'Duty?' said Milly. 'What are we? Soldiers or something?'

'Sergeant Major Cunningham is a bit scary though, isn't he?' said Nora.

'He's not a real sergeant major,' said Beth.

For the second time, the others turned and stared at her.

'Not a real sergeant major?' echoed Nora doubtfully. 'What is he then? Is he lying?'

'No, silly,' said Beth. 'He worked in the post office before the war and he's been given that title.'

'How do you know?' asked Milly as the three went up the ramp into the building.

'Mr Blackford – the man outside – told me after my interview.'

Milly swung round on her heel. 'Liza Healey – for someone who's only had the briefest chat with that man, you seem to have discovered rather a lot!' She was laughing up at Beth as she dropped her cigarette butt on the ground, idly grinding it underfoot.

Only she missed.

There was a thick coating of light brown dust on the wooden floor and an area about the size of a penny burst into flame. Alarmed, Beth pushed Milly out of the way and silently stamped on it herself.

Sergeant Major Cunningham mustn't see. Smoking inside was *strictly* prohibited and Milly would be in terrible trouble on her first day if he did.

But, despite Beth's stamping, the little fire was spreading. Milly and Nora looked at each other, mouths wide with horror. No one said anything, but all three of them started dancing over the little fire desperately trying to extinguish it. The trouble was, every time they got one bit under control, another bit burst into life.

This was terrible. *Terrible!* They would be all be sacked.

That was if the whole building didn't burn down and take them with it.

Beth ran to the nearest wooden column and, reaching as high as she could, wrestled down the metal sand bucket. It was much heavier than she'd been expecting and its centre of gravity shifted, sending her spiralling out of control. Off balance, she tipped the sand over the little fire as best she could before the bucket clattered to the ground with a loud clang. In strained silence the three girls kicked and stamped the sand over the little fires and finally, *finally*, the flames went out.

'What was that?' barked Sergeant Major Cunningham striding back towards them.

Silence.

Milly shifted a little so she was standing on top of a defiant curl of smoke, her skirts hiding it from Sergeant Major Cunningham. Beth moved to cover another wisp and battled a sudden desperate desire to laugh out loud.

'What on earth is going on here?' Sergeant Major Cunningham repeated, prodding the offending bucket with his foot. 'Answer me, girls.'

The silence persisted.

What could they possibly say? Smoking was absolutely forbidden anywhere near the wooden building, and Milly had already broken a cardinal rule.

Then Milly stepped forward. 'Sir, it was—'

Beth found her voice. 'It was *me*, sir,' she said, firmly, pushing in front of Milly and hoping against hope that the smoke didn't give them all away. 'I went over on my ankle and lost my balance and then I banged into the bucket and it . . . it fell off the nail. I'm so sorry, sir.'

Where had that come from?

More importantly, would it wash? Or would Nora tell Sergeant Major Cunningham she was lying?

Imagine getting fired on her first day. Imagine telling them all at home.

She would never live it down.

Nora was talking now. 'No, it's *my* fault, Sergeant Major Cunningham,' she said with quiet authority. 'I tripped coming over the threshold. The reason Liza lost her balance was because I banged into her. It's very kind of her to try and take the blame but if anyone's going to get into trouble, it should be me.'

Despite her cut-glass vowels and quiet confidence, Nora was all coltish, uncoordinated limbs and this made her explanation entirely plausible. The fact that Sergeant Major Cunningham would also know full well that she was Major Benham's niece probably wouldn't hurt, either. Beth breathed a sigh of relief. They were going to get away with it.

Sure enough, the fight seemed to have gone out of the sergeant major. He rocked back on his heels and cleared his throat. 'Right, we'll get someone to clear up the mess,' he said. 'And watch where you're going in future. We can't be having you girls making an example of yourselves by being clumsy. There are enough people who don't want women working here as it is.'

Yes, and chief among them is you, thought Beth. But she just said, 'Yes, sir. Sorry sir,' and resisted the temptation to bob a little curtsey.

'We'll tidy up,' added Nora hastily. 'It's the very least we can do.'

'Yes,' said Milly. 'We're very happy to clear up after ourselves.'

Beth shot Milly a severe look. Milly was supposed to be blameless in all of this and they didn't want to fall at the final hurdle. But Sergeant Major Cunningham just nodded at them all, swung on his heel and marched away.

A little curl of smoke rose from the sand to herald his

departure and all three girls started laughing. Before long the laughter turned slightly hysterical.

'Thank you,' said Milly. 'Thank you, thank you, *thank* you! I thought I was for it then!'

'I thought we were all for it!' said Nora.

'I'm sorry I misjudged you, even for a moment,' said Milly. 'I'm sorry that I thought you might be spying for your uncle. When the canteen opens, I owe you both treats until they're coming out of your ears.'

'I'll hold you to that,' said Beth. 'But in the meantime, I'm going to go and find a broom so that we can get this lot cleared up before anyone else comes along and starts asking more questions.'

As Milly and Nora had anticipated, the three girls were allocated to the Broken Parcel Department along with three older women. Others would be joining them over the next days and weeks – very many others – but for now they were the first.

The advance guard.

A trial run.

The Home Depot was going to be operational twenty-four hours a day, but Beth, Milly and Nora could only work regular hours because they were not yet twenty-one. Beth didn't mind that – she had no real wish to work the night shift – but how silly these rules and regulations were. Ned was hardly being tucked into bed by his sergeant major at ten o'clock every night and he was exactly the same age as she was.

'These are your admission cards,' said Miss Parker, distributing small, dark-blue cards bearing their name to each of them. 'Sign them straightaway, please. They are extremely important and you must look after them carefully. You must show them each time you enter the site and you will not be allowed in without them. If you lose or mislay your card or you think it may have been stolen, you must inform me or Sergeant Major Cunningham straightaway to be issued with a replacement. If you lose it twice, you will be fined. Don't even contemplate losing it a third time!'

Nods and weak smiles all round.

'Will we be getting a uniform?' asked Milly.

Beth had wondered about that too. A uniform would be nice – no need to ruin her own clothes or plan what to wear each morning or buy or make anything new. Ivy had a smart new uniform for her rounds in Woodhampstead – a blue serge skirt, a coat and a blue straw hat – and Beth would feel ever so fancy and important wearing that on the train each day.

But Miss Parker was shaking her head.

'No uniform,' she said. 'You girls aren't from either the post office or the army – and anyway, the post office is donating its material to help make army uniforms. You will wear practical but respectable day clothes – rather as you are all wearing now. Now, follow me,' she continued. 'Think of the department as a hospital for parcels. "A veritable clinic for derelict comforts", as Major Benham himself put it.'

She led her little team over to where several large wooden tables had been screened off from the centre of the Depot. A variety of dented, crumpled and completely disintegrated parcels were already lying on the table. Beth blinked, a little uncomfortable. Like the aftermath of the Zeppelin raid, they revealed interiors that she really had no right to see. Luckily there was more string, paper, linen, canvas and sturdy boxes than Beth could ever have imagined to make their job easier. Glue too. Lots of glue instead of wax and candles, which, given their surroundings, Beth acknowledged made sense.

'Your job is to get the broken parcels fixed up and on their way as quickly as possible,' explained Miss Parker. 'Many, as you will know, contain perishables, so time is of the essence. Sometimes a simple repair is all that will be needed, but often you will need to completely repack the parcel as you will find the original packaging materials are completely unsuitable for the job. It is not our job to pass judgement on this – we all know that packaging materials are expensive and can be in short supply. Be very careful when you relabel these packages to make sure you have transcribed the name, numbers and regiment numbers accurately and clearly.'

Beth was fired up and itching to get going, but it seemed Miss Parker had more to say.

'We are, of course, aware that some of you are unmarried and not yet of age, so I and some of the senior staff will always be on hand should you see anything . . . untoward,' she said, flushing slightly.

For a moment, Beth was confused. Whatever could Miss Parker mean? Could she possibly be referring to undergarments – or should she be all French and à la mode and refer to them as *lingerie*? Either way, who could afford to send their unmentionables abroad at a time like this when everything was in such short supply? It would be most unpatriotic. Beth stifled a giggle and studiously avoided the others' eyes.

'You also need to keep an eye out for any contraband,' Miss Parker was saying. 'It is not your job to check the parcels for prohibited items, but clearly if you see anything of the sort, it must be reported. You will know from sending things to your own loved ones at the front that one can send most things through the post, and there are lists of what is and what isn't allowed pinned to the walls and to the screens. Cigarettes and tobacco are allowed, of course, as are matches – but be careful handling them with all the sacking and dust around. We don't want any accidents.' Beth allowed herself a flicker of a glance at Milly and Nora. 'Any munitions and arms are obviously not allowed. Cocaine and heroin are allowed, other medicines are not. We're really pretty free and easy in this country—'

'You can send people,' interrupted Milly, apropos of nothing.

'*People*?' said Nora, wrinkling her nose. 'How can you send people?'

Beth had a brief vision of herself swathed in brown paper like one of those Egyptian mummies and being delivered to Sam. He'd unwrap her slowly and—

Beth!

For shame. What a time for thoughts like that!

Everyone had turned to look at Milly. 'You really can,' she was saying, laughing gaily. 'Don't you remember? It was about five years ago – it was all over the newspapers and I can remember me ma talking about it. The suffragettes sent two women by post to 10 Downing Street to talk to the prime minister!'

'I remember,' interjected one of the older ladies. 'A Miss Solomon and a Miss McLellan as I recall. They went to the post office and were passed to a telegram delivery boy and escorted to Downing Street!'

'Yes,' said Milly, excitedly. 'But then the butler refused to pass them on to Mr Asquith even though the women had already paid to be sent. So, they were returned to the post office and the telegram boy had to explain why he hadn't managed to deliver them.'

She looked round at the little group, laughing. Beth glanced at Miss Parker's stony face and didn't laugh back.

'Thank you for reminding us of that silly stunt, Miss Woods,' said Miss Parker, coolly. 'I am sure those women had their reasons, but there's a war on and we have absolutely no time nor patience for such time-wasting activities nowadays.'

Milly opened her mouth as though to reply but then coloured and looked down at her feet. 'Yes, Miss Parker,' she muttered. 'Of course, Miss Parker.'

Milly was a bit of a one, Beth reflected. She was friendly and animated – and, of course, had helped Beth out with the crooked stamps that morning – but she had also been careless with her cigarette and spoken across Miss Parker even if it had been funny. Despite herself, Beth couldn't help a stab of admiration. She would never dare behave like that, especially not on her first day when everyone was trying to make a good impression.

She turned to Miss Parker. 'Are the parcels being censored elsewhere?' she asked, both because she was interested in the answer and to get the conversation back on track.

'Not at the moment,' replied Miss Parker. 'The government has just finished a trial censor of a month's parcels and deemed it not essential at this end for the time being. And now, everyone,' she clapped her hands together, 'to work.'

Somewhat nervously, they took their places at the trestle tables.

Beth had never had any preconceptions about where she would be working within the Home Depot and was quite happy with her allocated task. And, once she got over the initial discomfort, it was really interesting seeing what other people were sending their loved ones at the front – a privilege, even. It was almost like having a little window into their family. Into their *world*.

Take the first parcel she started working on, for example. It had been badly battered in transit and the brown paper had ripped open in one corner, exposing the contents. It contained food – a tin of crab and one of condensed milk, some bullseye sweets and four sausage rolls – but also a lock of honey-blond hair, a photograph of two little girls, and a copy of a local newspaper – the *Henley Standard*. Something for mind, body and soul, Beth reflected as she started repairing the packaging so that it would survive the journey to France. She imagined the recipient, Private Tom Richardson, opening it around the campfire one evening, relishing all the connections to home and perhaps sharing the sweets and pastries with his friends and compatriots. She should send Ned some more sweets.

Maybe she should send Sam a lock of her hair . . .

Oh, Beth!

She shook her head and laughed to herself. A lock of her hair! And to a boy who wasn't even her sweetheart. Whatever was she thinking?

Beth carried on, enjoying the work. She was also pleased and relieved to discover that she was rather good at it. She was quick, neat and efficient, and the pile of completed parcels at her side was growing more quickly than either Milly's or Nora's. Not that it was a competition, she told herself sternly. But, after her earlier fears that she had nothing to offer the Home Depot, at least she was more than just 'adequate' at this. Thank goodness for all those days and hours wrapping parcels in the shop under Ma's watchful and critical eye.

Ma.

Ma, who was so disappointed in and furious with her.

No.

Nothing good would come from dwelling on that.

Instead, Beth looked around the table at her newfound friends. Milly was quick and dextrous and had the potential be very good at repacking – better even than Beth – but she tended to rush and Beth noticed that she often had to stop to redo her work. Nora, on the other hand, worked steadily and willingly but was all fingers and thumbs. She often couldn't see how best to package something so that its weight was evenly distributed and the packaging was secure. Beth couldn't help wondering how she had passed the selection process – her parcels wouldn't survive Miss Parker's unceremonious three-foot drop onto the table – but Beth was inclined to give her the benefit of the doubt. Maybe her talents lay elsewhere.

Anyway, while their hands were occupied, the three girls talked.

And talked.

And talked.

Unlike school, there seemed to be no rule against chatting while they worked and, even though Miss Parker came around from time to time to check how they were getting on and to offer advice, she didn't tell them to be quiet. Indeed, the first time she came over, they had all instinctively stopped talking but she had just given them a small smile and said 'as you were'. And if that wasn't a tacit invitation to gossip, Beth didn't know what was!

Beth learned that Nora lived in a house on the other side of the Regent's Park. It sounded similar to the 'icing-cake houses' Beth had passed that morning on her way from the Tube and she couldn't help envying Nora both her grand home and the fact that she could walk to work. No trekking halfway across the South of England every day for her! Nora's father was a Harley Street doctor who was too old to serve abroad, and her mother his much younger second wife. Nora was the oldest of four children and her only brother was just eleven, so was of course much too young to have signed up. There had been servants – butlers and housekeepers and governesses and a cook – but it was hard to hold on to them in this day and age and Mother was having to make do with a much smaller staff. This, apparently, was playing havoc with her nerves, as was of course the fact that her eldest daughter was doing something quite unsuitable to help with the war effort. If it all sounded a million miles away from

Woodhampstead, at least Beth and Nora had something in common: their mothers both hated what they were doing.

Milly was quite different. Her father wasn't around; Milly didn't elaborate but Beth got the impression that he had been gone for a long time and for reasons that had nothing to do with the war. Milly's mother worked in a munitions factory with a younger sister; an older sister worked in a toy factory; and there seemed to be several other younger siblings as well. It sounded like Milly had got the job at the Home Depot through her uncle who worked for the post office and because a family friend had supplied a glowing reference. Her decision to accept the job seemed to be as much to do with money as to doing her bit for the war and her mother had been very much behind her decision to apply.

A very different situation to the other two girls indeed.

'I can't believe this,' said Nora, suddenly. 'This person,' she studied the parcel, 'this Mrs Williams from Solihull, has sent raw eggs through the post without even *trying* to wrap them individually.' Her face was screwed up in distaste and yolk dripped slickly from her fingertips onto the table.

Milly glanced over, tutting. 'What a waste,' she said. 'Six eggs – just ruined. And they've ruined the newspaper she's sent as well. It hardly seems worth sending it on.'

'Never mind that,' grumbled Nora pulling out a handkerchief. 'What about my hands. What about my fingernails? What about my *skirt*?'

Beth and Milly laughed at Nora's distaste.

'We're *all* filthy,' said Beth. 'And I *itch*.'

'Me too,' said Nora. 'Look at this.' She ran a finger under her collar and brought it out covered in a light brown film. 'This dust gets *everywhere*.'

'Yes, we're covered in it,' said Milly. 'It's even in my mouth – I can taste it.'

She stuck her tongue out with such an expression of disgust that the others laughed all the louder.

'It's dust from the sacks and from all the building work, isn't it?' said Beth. They had the odd sack at the shop, so she recognised sack dust when she saw it, but she'd never experienced anything like . . . *this*.

'Yes. It's the same dust that caught fire earlier on,' said Nora. 'It's really making my eyes sting but there's no getting away from it so we might as well just get used to it.'

'But it's so *hot*,' said Milly. 'And so stuffy.'

'And those skylights might let in light, but they're making it even hotter,' added Nora.

There was a silence while the girls carried on with their labours.

'Oh, but it's *all* so messy and dirty,' said Milly suddenly. 'Look at these bleedin' chocolate caramels. They're all over my shirt.' She put her hand up like a child at school and called over to Miss Parker. 'Miss, Miss, my shirt is ruined. Can I claim back the money so I can buy another one?'

Miss Parker walked over calmly. 'I'm sorry but you can't, Milly,' she said. 'Keeping your own clothes clean and tidy is your responsibility, I'm afraid.'

Milly made a face at Miss Parker's retreating back. 'Well, that's bloody marvellous, innit?' she said. 'My best white shirt ruined on me first day and most of me wages going on making a new one.'

Beth couldn't help thinking that if Milly took things a bit more slowly and made use of the sponges and cloths and bowls of water on the floor by each table then this wouldn't have happened. But she already knew enough about her new friend to know that she might be taking her life into her own hands by suggesting such a thing.

'How very annoying,' said Nora. She paused. 'Now don't take this the wrong way, but I know Mummy has put aside a lot of our old shirts to give away. Maybe I could "intercept" them and bring them in. They're in all shapes and sizes and I think we'll all be in need of some spares.'

For a moment, Beth thought Milly was going to take offence and, anxious to keep the peace, she said, 'That's a lovely idea, Nora. I don't have many spare shirts myself, so I would be very grateful if you would. Especially if they are light and cool ones!'

Milly narrowed her eyes but then grinned. 'Thanks,' she said. 'That would be grand. But I'm still not sure how getting chocolate all over my shirt is important war work.'

'Yes,' agreed Nora. 'It's hardly going to help us beat the Germans, is it?'

'Oh, but it is!' burst out Beth.

Or was it Liza?

Where had *that* come from if not from Liza?

The others turned to look at her and Beth felt herself blushing. It wasn't like her to be quite so passionate and outspoken. But it was too late to stop now. Hopefully Liza could find the words that Beth might not.

'It really is going to help us beat the enemy and it's important war work,' she started. Why did she 'get' it and they didn't? And then she realised why: it was – it must be – because she had loved ones at the front, and they did not.

That must be the difference.

But how on earth to explain what that meant to her?

'My brother Ned has just left for the war,' she started. 'Of course he wants to do his duty, but he doesn't want to be there. *We* don't want him to be there. It's a separation that none of us asked for, that has been forced upon us, and sometimes it feels almost unbearable knowing what he's going through and that he's risking everything.'

She stopped and blinked a couple of times.

It really wouldn't do to blub. Not here. Not now. Not when

the others had stopped work and were giving her their full attention. And not when, as far as she knew, Ned hadn't even gone out to France yet.

Beth took a deep breath and carried on. 'The things that we send Ned each week are partly, of course, to supplement his rations and to keep him warm. But it's far more than that. We send him things we're eating so that it feels that we are still eating as a family. If Ma makes sausage rolls or apple tarts or . . . anything, really, we will pop a couple in the post to Ned so that he can enjoy them with us, too. If I see some pretty flowers, I might pick one and send it to him or I'll send him a magazine article that has caught my attention. In the same way, my sister's husband sometimes sends back French cheeses and postcards of where he's based. He even sent a poppy he found growing by the roadside. We need to keep in touch. We're a family. It's what we have to do to still feel like one.'

'Oh,' said Nora, looking a little shame-faced. 'I hadn't thought of it quite like that.'

'Me neither,' added Milly.

'It's more than that, though,' said Beth, only now working it out for herself. 'It's important to send stuff so they know home is here waiting for them and that there is somewhere to fight for and to come back to. We're also showing them that, as far as possible, things are carrying on as normal and that the shortages aren't making too much of a difference. They worry about that, you know. They worry a lot about what's going on in Blighty and what they might be coming home to.'

She stopped, feeling unexpectedly emotional. The other girls were staring at her silently.

'Right,' said Nora, giving herself a brisk little shake. 'I'll clear up this newspaper as best I can and get it on its way.'

'And I'll get what's left of this parcel off to Bert Swinbourne,'

said Milly soberly. 'I can save the biscuits, even if the chocolates are ruined.'

And the two girls silently turned back to their work.

If Beth was tired by the time her shift finished at five o'clock,
she was almost beside herself with exhaustion by the time
the train finally limped back into Woodhampstead.

The journey home had been just as bad as the one into
London that morning. She had walked to King's Cross rather
than taking the Underground, in the hope that it might wake
her up a little. It hadn't and she had arrived at the terminus
hot, sticky, footsore – and late. The through train to
Woodhampstead had already departed and she had to wait
half an hour for the stopping service that also necessitated
another half-hour stopover at Hatfield. Even two sticky buns
and some hot, sweet tea at the station cafe had failed to perk
her up.

It was past eight o'clock by the time the train finally pulled
into Woodhampstead and a gorgeous early summer evening.
Beth was the only person to disembark. She made her way
past the signal box and the sidings and up onto the road,
feeling totally discombobulated. Woodhampstead was so
different to London. The only sounds were the birds and
chickens getting ready for the evening with a great deal of
muted kerfuffle, and the chatter of a group of girls playing
five stones on the pavement.

Sally answered her front door as soon as Beth rang the
bell.

'How was it?' she asked, ushering Beth in and fussing
around her like an old mother hen. Beth's coat and hat were
taken from her and hung up by the front door and she was
shepherded into the armchair by the fire. *This* had never
happened when she worked at the shop.

'It was . . .' Beth trailed off. How to describe everything

that had happened in one short day? 'It was . . . over-whelming.'

She started explaining everything: the horrible journey and being late, the wooden building, Sergeant Major Cunningham's briefing.

'You'd have been so proud of me because I actually answered a question,' said Beth taking a sip from the cup of tea Sally pressed into her hand.

'I am proud of you,' said Sally. 'I know just how shy you can be with strangers.'

Beth smiled at her sister over the rim of her cup. How she wished her parents could be proud of her too. Lovely and supportive though Sally was, she wished she could be regaling Ma and Pa with her adventures as well. Ma would sigh with pleasure at her daughter 'doing her bit', Pa would reach over and ruffle her hair and even good Queen Vic on the wall would look like she was smiling.

Beth gave herself a little shake. She had made her decision and she would have to live with the consequences. And none of this was Sally's fault. She turned to her sister with a determined smile. 'And then, when he asked my name, for some reason I told him I was called Liza.' Beth laughed, a little embarrassed. She still wasn't sure why she had done that.

'Liza?' Sally cocked her head to one side. 'You mean *E*liza?'

'No,' said Beth. 'And not Lisa either. *Liza*. I don't know where it came from. I don't know if it's even a name. It just came out of my mouth!'

'It does sound very exotic,' said Sally with a giggle. 'Miss Liza Healey. It sounds like you're a rich debutante with a different French frock to wear every night of the week. Much grander than plain old Beth Healey from Woodhampstead.'

Beth laughed, relieved that Sally understood 'What name would you choose?'

'Oh, I don't know,' said Sally with a little shrug. 'Maybe Sara without an H to make it more unusual.'

'But Sarah's your real name anyway,' scoffed Beth. 'Come on, you can do better than that.'

'Hmmm.' Sally pondered, head back on one side. 'Selma,' she said after a few moments. 'Yes I like that.'

'Selma it is, then,' said Beth, holding out a hand. 'How do you do, Miss Selma Hazelden?'

'Very well, thank you,' said Sally, shaking it with a laugh. 'Now, if Miss *Liza* Healey would like to follow me, dinner is served. I hope chops are to your liking?'

10

The next morning, several more tables had been added to the Broken Parcel Department and a dozen new girls were reporting for 'duty'. The sounds of banging and sawing were even louder than the day before and, at breaktime, Beth, Milly. and Nora took a peek behind the Home Depot and saw the skeleton of a huge, single-storey extension, as large as several barns, being tacked on to the building.

It looked like the world's largest wooden structure was about to be made even larger.

The day after, the number of tables had doubled and soon, there were nearly fifty women hard at work keeping the nation's parcels intact and on the move.

Beth, Milly and Nora were friendly and sociable with everyone, but after that momentous first day, the three were fast friends, sitting together in 'their' original seats at 'their' table and sticking together at breaks and lunchtimes. They became used to the work, repackaging the never-ending stream of parcels as quickly and efficiently as they could.

Beth loved it.

She loved feeling that she was doing something that was important to the whole war at one extreme and to the man the parcel was intended for at the other. She loved discovering that she was good at it and the fact that her parcels never failed the Parker Drop Test. But most of all, she loved the camaraderie and her growing friendships with Milly and Nora. Her job in the shop had been sociable enough with a steady stream of customers coming and going all the time, but this was different. In the shop, the encounters were brief and often superficial and many of the customers were much older and positively Victorian in attitude. But here, with Nora and Milly and the others, it was vibrant, it was fresh – it was exciting.

If only Ma and Pa weren't so disappointed in her.

So *furious*.

'Let's play a game,' said Milly a couple of days later. Beth had never met anyone quite like Milly and her energy, enthusiasm and sense of fun were infectious. 'The new canteen on the corner has opened, so whoever loses has to buy the treats at breaktime. You have to parcel something beginning with A, and when you've done that, move on to B and so on. The one who's the least far through the alphabet when we're dismissed is the loser.'

Beth had noticed the canteen being built across the grass near the entrance to the site, but she hadn't realised it was actually opening. That was exciting. The Home Depot had laid on a rudimentary lunch thus far each day, and she had brought some apples and hardboiled eggs from home as snacks, but something different – particularly something hot or sweet – would be a welcome change.

'One of the new girls in this department is the niece of the lady superintendent running the canteen,' said Nora, 'and I overhead her saying there are jammy buns! So, let's get going. One, two, three . . . or should I say A, B, C?'

The three girls set to work. All three had repackaged something beginning with A within the first twenty minutes; Beth was wrestling with a couple of ale bottles that had broken free from their flimsy packaging, one of Milly's packages contained some apples and Nora had unearthed some apricots in hers. B was easy too (books, Bovril and bread) as was C (condensed milk, chutney and currants). The three girls were neck and neck.

D, however, proved much more problematic; the clock was ticking and all three girls had repackaged a good ten parcels without so much as a whiff of one.

'Dates,' cried Milly, triumphantly, waving some of the dried fruit around in rather too exuberant a manner and earning herself a 'look' from Miss Parker.

Blast, thought Beth. The whistle for the morning break would be going any time soon and while she didn't, of course, mind buying her friends a morning treat, her competitive streak had been activated and she wouldn't go down without a fight.

She picked up the next parcel and the contents obligingly fell out for her. Sardines – socks – why couldn't the letter have been S! And here was some chocolate; it was Bournville, so she might just get away with 'dark' chocolate. It was worth a try. She really didn't want to come last—

'Damson jelly' squealed Nora suddenly, waving a jar triumphantly under Beth's nose.

Beth thought about protesting. Surely that counted as a 'J' for jam and the flavour was irrelevant? But then, she didn't want to appear a bad sport, so she just smiled and said, 'Well done,' and two seconds later Miss Parker blew the whistle for break.

The three girls walked arm in arm out of the Home Depot. It was a short walk across the grass to the new canteen on the corner of the site and they followed little clusters of people who were headed in the same direction. Some came from the Home Depot and others from the handful of other buildings that had also sprung up in the Regent's Park to house government and army offices and warehouses.

Inside, all was steamy and smoky but not as hot as inside the Home Depot, thank goodness. Beth left Milly and Nora to grab a table while she joined the little queue to be served.

She could see a huge tray of the oozy, sticky, jammy buns that Nora had mentioned on the counter.

Maybe they would even be filled with damson jam . . .

'Hello, Miss Healey.'

Beth swung round at the sound of her name. It was Mr Blackford and it was only when Beth looked up into his deep, clever grey eyes that she realised she'd been waiting – hoping – to bump into him again, ever since she'd seen him on the grass outside the Home Depot at the beginning of the week. Was it wrong to be so pleased to see him when she was writing to Sam?

'Hello, Mr Blackford,' said Beth. And then stopped because she couldn't think of anything else to say. Liza, damn her, didn't step in to help this time.

'So, you got the job?' said Mr Blackford, raising one eyebrow.

'I did,' said Beth. 'I'm not quite sure how, but yes, I did. And you? What are you doing here?'

Liza wanted to add, 'Were you sent to the Home Depot for excessive fraternisation?' but Beth stopped her just in time.

'I asked to be posted here,' said Mr Blackford. 'I'm a supervisor in the Honour Envelope Department and they're setting up a section over here. I'll be backwards and forwards over the next couple of weeks.' He paused and gave her a little smile. 'I wasn't sent here as a punishment for excessive fraternisation, in case you were wondering.'

'Indeed,' said Beth, wondering if her flush was giving her away while also marvelling at the fact that they had thought of the exact same joke at the same time, right down to the wording.

She had questions. Lots of questions. Like – for one – what on earth were honour envelopes?

'Talking of fraternisation,' Mr Blackford continued, 'things seem to be much more relaxed over here – at least, they are when Sergeant Major Cunningham isn't paying us a visit. So, I hope I'm not being too forward if I tell you my name is James.'

Oh!

That *was* rather forward, but Beth found that she didn't mind at all.

Not one bit.

James.

Over his shoulder, Beth could see Milly and Nora staring at her and grinning in a most unladylike manner. She gave them a severe glance and turned back to James.

'And I'm Liza,' said Beth, firmly. 'Not Eliza or Lisa,' she added, when James opened his mouth. '*Liza*.'

Something in her badly wanted to tell him that her name was Beth. But how could she? It would just make everything far too complicated . . .

'Very good to meet you, Liza,' said James, offering his hand with a jokey little bow. 'And how are you finding working at the Home Depot?'

'I'm enjoying it,' said Beth, honestly. 'The work's interesting and the people are nice and, of course, it feels good to be doing my bit.'

She expected James to nod and smile and agree – the sorts of things that everyone did when talking about helping the war effort. But he didn't. He just nodded gravely at her. There was no time to ponder his strange behaviour because, all of a sudden, it was her turn to be served. She turned from James to the plump, cheerful woman behind the counter.

'What can I get you, my dear?' the woman asked.

Beth hesitated, suddenly realising she had no idea what her new friends might like to drink. There was tea and Velma coffee and hot chocolate and Bovril and lemonade . . . and she was all too aware of James's eyes on the back of her head.

Neither Beth nor Liza had any wish to holler across the busy canteen packed to the gills with chattering customers, so in the end, she plumped for tea and jammy buns all round. You couldn't go too far wrong with that, she reasoned. She stood there surreptitiously scratching her itchy neck, still very aware of James standing just behind her but not sure what else to say to him, while the lady superintendent loaded up a tray with cups and saucers, teapot, strainer, milk jug and sugar.

'I'm sorry,' she said, when the tray was full to capacity, 'but all the larger trays have gone. I'm afraid you'll have to take this over to your table and come back for the buns.'

'Of course,' said Beth, fishing in her purse for the right change and handing it over. She was about to set out on her first journey when James, who had just brought a packet of cigarettes off the second server and had already paid, said casually, 'Allow me to carry the tray over for you, Miss Healey.'

Beth smiled at him. 'Thank you,' she said, picking up the buns. Together they walked through the canteen to where Milly and Nora were still goggling none too subtly at her.

James put the buns down on the table and nodded to the two girls. Then he straightened and glanced round the room. Beth followed his gaze. Every table was occupied, every chair was taken. Except . . .

'Do join us, Mr Blackford,' she said. 'Otherwise I fear you may be sitting on the floor.'

Nora stifled a giggle but Milly was already busy removing her shawl and bag from the back of the empty chair.

'Yes, do please join us,' she said. 'There doesn't seem to be any rule against men and women sitting together here.'

James smiled. 'We can but hope that Sergeant Major Cunningham doesn't make an appearance,' he said, sitting down and lighting a cigarette.

Everyone laughed and Beth made the introductions. How

strange this was! When she had first met Mr Blackford –
James – in the corridor at the King Edward Building and
later under the loggia, she could never have dreamt that less
than two weeks later she would be introducing him to her
new friends. The four chatted animatedly but politely about
this and that: the lovely weather, the size and scale of the
Home Depot, the jammyness of the buns. Social chit-chat;
nothing risky, nothing untoward. Beth watched James as he
joined in the conversation. His mannerisms were calm –
languid, even – but Beth sensed a tension in him. There was
a tiny muscle flickering in his cheek and his empty hand was
folded into a tight fist on his knee. He was like a coiled
spring, Beth thought – at any moment, the pressure might
all get too much and he'd unravel at speed.

Oh, stop it, Beth. Stop over-thinking everything.

He was just a handsome man, spending his morning break
with them because there was nowhere else to sit, and trying
not to notice that Milly was making the hugest and most
unsubtle cow eyes at him!

'James is a supervisor in the Honour Envelope Department,'
said Beth when there was a little pause in the conversation.

'Ooh, a supervisor,' said Milly, practically fluttering her
eyelids at James. 'I'm not sure we should be consorting with
our superiors. Better mind our tongues, girls!'

James gave her a polite smile, but Beth was pleased to see
that he didn't otherwise engage with her flirting.

'I'm not sure I know what an honour envelope *is*,' admitted
Beth. She might as well come clean.

James took a drag from his cigarette. 'Most home-
ward-bound letters are censored at the front by the junior
officers,' he said. 'But that can be awfully rum all round when
everyone knows each other so well and is living in such close
confinement. If the men want to write something they don't
want their officer to see, they can apply for an honour enve-

lope. They promise their letter doesn't break any rules, pop it in a green envelope and the officer waves it on its way. And then it comes here and we have the pleasure of reading it instead and checking that the soldier has kept his word.'

'I see,' said Beth.

'I'm surprised you haven't come across them before,' said James.

'I'm not,' said Beth with a laugh. 'My twin's only just signed up and letters were never his strong point. It's only a matter of time before he resorts to those pre-printed cards and simply ticks the "I am well and healthy" box.'

Everyone laughed, but Nora's laughter quickly turned into a fit of coughing.

'It's the ruddy sack dust,' said James sympathetically. 'It gets everywhere. I see you've got tide marks already. We *all* have.' Their faces must have been blank because James laughed and added, 'That's what we all call the rings of dust on our collars and cuffs. Hellish to get out.'

Beth couldn't help feeling vaguely scandalised. A young man talking so openly about a lady's clothes!

Mr Blackford – James – really was most unusual.

'Well, it's worth it if it frees up a man to go to the front,' said Nora staunchly.

There was a little awkward silence.

Beth's gaze slid to James. So did everyone else's. Beth knew Nora wouldn't have meant it, but somehow the inference hung in the air.

Why wasn't James at the front?

James looked round at them all and laughed. Then he rocked back in his chair and laced his fingers behind his head.

'I'm very grateful for your service, Nora,' he said. 'But you can rest absolutely sure in the knowledge that I will not be signing up any time soon. In fact, you can rest absolutely sure in the knowledge that I will not be signing up at *all* – even if the war goes on for years.'

Oh.

Oh!

How utterly embarrassing.

There was obviously some medical reason James was unfit for service. There were so many reasons that men could be turned down – anything from flat feet to colour-blindness or short-sightedness to more serious ailments like heart defects or lung disease. Just because they couldn't see anything wrong with him . . .

James was still laughing.

'I can see what you're thinking,' he said, 'but I'm not unfit for military service. At least, I don't think I am.'

'Of course,' said Beth hastily. 'You're doing important war work here. We didn't mean—'

'No,' said James firmly, bringing his chair down flat and holding up one hand. 'I don't want there to be any misconceptions – and I haven't anything to be ashamed of – but I haven't signed up because I don't believe in the war.'

Now Beth really was confused.

The war wasn't something you believed in or not, like fairies or Father Christmas. The war just *was*. It was happening, whether you liked it or not. You couldn't just 'not' believe in it.

But, to her surprise – her *shock* – Milly was nodding. 'To be perfectly honest, I don't really believe in the war either,' she said.

Beth's hand was shaking as she rattled her teacup back into its saucer. You would never hear something like that in Woodhampstead – never! – and she still didn't really understand what Milly and James were saying.

'How can you not believe in the war?' Nora asked, looking from Milly to James and back again.

Milly sighed. 'It's not the war itself,' she said. 'It's more that it's deflecting and distracting from things that are more important.'

To Beth, she sounded almost like she was parroting something. Or someone.

'Like what?' asked Beth, intrigued. After all, what could be more important than fighting for King and Country?

'Oh, like fighting for a living wage, housing you can actually *live* in, equal pay, food price controls, pensions . . .' said Milly. Her violet eyes were flashing in a way Beth hadn't seen before and her hands were gesticulating widely. She was excited, animated, *passionate*. 'I could go on – there are loads of other things – to say nothing of the women's vote.'

Goodness. Beth had never thought of it quite like that.

Nora gave a bark of laughter. 'You sound like a suffragette, Milly,' she said, and in her tone of voice, Beth could hear her own father muttering 'those bloody women' and her mother adding that Milly had unsexed herself—

'I *am* a suffragette,' said Milly. Far from being defensive, there was pride in her voice. 'I'm a fully paid-up member of the East London Federation of the Suffragettes. But, despite what people seem to think, votes for women is only one of many things we are campaigning for.'

Another silence.

Beth – Liza – turned to James. 'And are you a suffragette, too?' she asked somewhat tartly. She hadn't really planned to say that but the whole conversation had become very strange indeed.

James grinned at her. 'I'm not,' he said. 'At least, not officially, although it's hard to argue with anything Miss Woods has just said. No, my conscience doesn't let me fight. I can't bring myself to kill a load of German boys who are as much victims in all of this as we are. There you are. That's what I believe. I don't care who knows it and I don't care if I get enough white feathers to stuff an eiderdown.'

Coward!

The word came unbidden to Beth.

Coward!

'My brother and my brother-in-law are fighting out there, risking their lives for all of us—' she said.

'My brother too,' said James softly. 'As I said, they are as much victims in all this as everyone else—'

'They're *heroes*,' burst out Beth, fighting a strong temptation to slap James very hard across his thin, clever, handsome face. She felt so strongly, she didn't even need Liza to step in for her.

The two stared at each other and Beth wasn't sure what would have happened next if the whistle hadn't been blown to signal the end of break.

'I'm sorry,' said James, still looking straight at her.

Beth nodded. And found that she had absolutely no idea exactly what he was sorry for.

Or if she had forgiven him.

Or why she cared.

It was a rather subdued threesome who returned to work after the break.

There was no attempt to carry on the game they had started earlier on and the girls worked in near silence. Beth's head was reeling. Her initial anger towards James hadn't dissipated – how dare he refer to Ned and the others as victims? – but she found herself fascinated by all the different views she was hearing. Whether or not she agreed with them, it was very different to Woodhampstead where everyone just blindly and staunchly believed in the war effort.

Anyway, why did it matter what James thought?

He was just a chance acquaintance, and beyond being

polite, she had no need to talk to him ever again. She wasn't going to call him a coward or give him a feather. It wasn't in her nature and, anyway, no one *had* to sign up. Besides, James was doing important war work so he was helping the cause in his own way. Apart from expressing his views so – too? – strongly, he wasn't actually doing anything wrong.

Neither was Milly.

After all, all she had said was that she believed the war was getting in the way of other necessary reforms. While Beth might not agree with her – or, more to the point, had never even considered such things – the two had to carry on working together and there was no need to fall out over it.

So, she turned to the others and said, 'Hard-boiled eggs.'

The others looked up with blank expressions.

'Hard-boiled eggs,' Beth repeated with a smile. 'Unless you two are going to try and suggest that they start with an "H", I'd say that's my "E" and that you two have some catching up to do!'

When Milly disappeared off to the bathroom a little later, Nora turned to Beth. 'That was a bit of an eye-opener, wasn't it?' she said.

'It certainly was,' agreed Beth. She hesitated. 'And now's the time to tell me you're against the war as well.'

'Of course I'm not,' said Nora, giving her a friendly punch on the arm. 'I want us to win as much as the next patriot. Daddy says it's akin to treason to even talk of peace, and even though I don't agree with much of what he says – like getting married and having babies as soon as possible! – I do agree with him on that.'

Beth sighed, thinking hard. 'It's really interesting to hear these different points of view but I can't bear to think of my brother and friends and all the rest of them fighting and risking their lives for something that people don't believe in.'

'Most people believe in it,' said Nora. 'And maybe we can change Milly and James's minds.'

Beth paused. She wasn't entirely sure if she wanted to change Milly and James's minds. Oh, she didn't exactly agree with them but, if she was honest with herself, she wasn't entirely sure what it was she did believe in and what she had just picked up from Ma and Pa. She sighed quietly. It seemed she was Beth-in-the-middle here too – caught between two opposing points of views.

Who was she?

Where did she fit in?

'I've got something for you,' said Nora, cutting across her thoughts. 'I was going to give it to you at break, but we all got somewhat distracted.'

She reached into her bag and handed Beth a picture post-card. Beth took it and looked at it curiously. Entitled 'the secret language of stamps', it had a number of small illustrations of stamps in different positions on a letter together with a short explanation of what the position of the stamp was supposed to communicate. Hence, a stamp in the traditional top right-hand corner but tilted to the right said 'will you be mine?' while one in the same place but tilted to the left meant 'I am longing to see you'. An upright stamp to the left of the surname denoted 'no', while one that had been placed upside down in the same position told the recipient an emphatic 'yes'. A stamp on its side in the top left-hand corner said 'I cannot be yours' while an upside down one in the bottom right-hand corner meant simply 'do write soon'.

It was so simple but so brilliant. How had she not heard of this before?

She tried to remember what message Ralph had been sending to Florence when she had naively assumed he had just been ignorant or in a hurry?

'You can keep it,' said Nora with a laugh. 'You don't have to memorise it all now.'

'Are you sure?' said Beth looking up.

'Of course,' said Nora. 'Uncle Alf has given us loads. There's also another one you can have if you like. It's more recent, with more of a military theme.' She handed Beth a second card. This one had a picture of a soldier holding a letter in the centre of the card together with a short poem – '*Mark well the stamp and you will see – a message there to you from me!*' As with the other card, there were stamp positions around the edge together with their intended meanings.

'I love this,' said Beth. 'So simple and yet so clever. Thank you.'

Did she dare try any of the messages out on Sam?

A few short days ago, Beth wouldn't have dreamt of it and she probably still wouldn't.

But Liza might.

Yes.

If Sam ever wrote back to her, Liza might very well.

11

Not that writing letters was top of either Beth or Liza's agenda.

By Friday morning she was exhausted in mind, body and soul, and she prayed that the day would pass quickly and smoothly.

The Great Northern Railway had other plans. The through train was cancelled and all the others were running late. Beth finally limped into work almost an hour late and close to tears.

Was it really worth falling out with her parents for . . . this?

Miss Parker was unsympathetic. Beth was late and, regardless of the reason, she needed to make up the lost time. She would lose her lunch hour and complete her missed quota of parcels then.

Beth took her place in the Broken Parcel Department feeling dejected and demoralised. She enjoyed the work, but the journey really was a pig. Everyone else seemed to live somewhere sensible like Islington, Hackney or Shepherd's Bush. Had she made a terrible mistake and bitten off more than she could chew? Should she have got a job with the Women's Land Army or something closer to home? Probably. Despite the fun and her new friends, all the sacrifices probably hadn't been worth it. Not really. Not when she couldn't even sleep in her own bed anymore . . .

Sighing, she picked up the first parcel and started transcribing the address label, which had been saturated by something sticky.

After half an hour, she had relaxed into the gentle rhythms and routines and was winning that day's alphabet race. It was all fine, she decided. She was making a difference here and she had too much to lose if she gave it up after only a week.

She would stick it out.

She had to.

Apart from breaks, the only time the ladies of the Broken Parcel Department left their stations was to go to the unloading bay. Here, they helped to manhandle the incoming sacks off the lorries, place them in huge baskets on casters and then wheel them back into the Home Depot to stack in strict order of arrival.

The other girls moaned and groaned about this aspect of the job. Nora, unused to any form of manual labour, found it especially hard. Beth, on the other hand, didn't mind it. Yes, it was hot, sweaty, back-breaking work, but it was nice to stretch her legs and to have a change of scene and to get out into the fresh air, if only for a few minutes. Anyway, she was used to unloading the delivery van and carrying the sacks into the storeroom at home. This really wasn't so very different.

Their turn came again that morning. Beth, Milly and Nora duly headed to the unloading bay where the incoming lorry was already in place. Two men had just finished pulling the sacks of parcels from the back of the van into position.

'Mornin' ladies,' said the first, touching his cap.

The other man seemed not to be in the best of tempers. Mumbling something under his breath, he didn't make eye contact and physically turned his back on Nora when she wished him a pleasant morning.

Charming!

The unloading began.

Misery-Man stood on the tailboard of the lorry and handed down the first bag to Milly and Beth. Together, they grabbed hold of it and lowered it on the ground.

'Bugger! There aren't any baskets,' said Milly. 'Bloody Censoring Department never return them! I'll go and track some down and I'll give whoever's hoarding them hell.'

'I'll give you a hand,' said the friendly man, jumping down from the back of the lorry and disappearing into the building with her.

Nora and Beth exchanged a glance and lined up for the next sack. Misery-Man dragged it into position and started to lower it down to them, but suddenly he seemed to let go. Nora took most of its weight but lost her balance, sprawling backwards onto the ground, the bag across her lap. It was all Beth could do to avoid falling on top of her. She straightened up and glared at Misery-Man, who was standing with his hands on his hips and smirking down at them.

'Oi!' Beth wanted to shout. 'You did that on purpose.' But she was too timid to accuse out loud – and she couldn't be *entirely* sure it hadn't been an accident. Besides, she was more concerned with checking that Nora wasn't badly hurt.

Nora was hunched over, rubbing her ankle. 'Ouch,' she said. 'Ouch, ouch, ouch. I've gone right over on it and it hurts like buggery.'

Beth blinked at the very unladylike word from her usually very ladylike friend and bent over to take a look. The ankle above the dainty kid boot had already puffed up to twice its usual size. It would be black and blue by lunchtime.

'It does look nasty,' said Beth, crouching down beside Nora. 'Let's get you inside and tell Miss Parker, then see about getting you home.'

'Yer la-di-da friend take a little tumble, did she?' said

Misery-Man with another smirk. 'That's right, better take her home to Mummy.'

Beth ignored him. 'Come on, Nora,' she repeated. 'Let's get you inside and get some help.'

'No!' hissed Nora with surprising vehemence.

'No?' Beth looked at her in surprise. 'Whyever not?'

'Don't you see?' said Nora in an urgent whisper. 'That's just what Daddy and Uncle Alf want!' said Nora. 'They'll use it as an excuse to say I can't cope with the work and then they'll make me leave. Please don't tell them. Please don't tell anyone.'

'But it's not your fault!' said Beth.

'That won't make any difference,' said Nora, mournfully.

'Daddy will be cross, will he?' mocked Misery-Man, who had obviously picked up at least part of their conversation.

Beth had had enough.

Forgetting her reticence, she stood up and strode over to the lorry. 'Stop it,' she said furiously. 'You did that on purpose!'

'No, I didn't,' said Misery-Man said a sneer. 'Your posh friend just can't take the pressure, that's what happened. I'm surprised she hasn't brought her maid along to do the heavy lifting.'

''She can take the pressure! You *dropped* that bag on us and you know you did.'

'Nah! You can't prove nuffink,' said Misery-Man. 'Bloody women, coming here, taking our jobs!' he added, apropos of nothing.

'Excuse me – we haven't taken anyone's job,' said Nora with considerable dignity, given she was sprawled on her bottom on the ground. 'These are new jobs created because of the increase in post going to the fronts. Our jobs wouldn't even exist if it wasn't for the war.'

'If yer say so, love,' said Misery-Man. 'But whatever the

reason, a bit of fluff like you just ain't up to the job, are yer?'

Beth took a sharp intake of breath at his rudeness. She was about to respond but at that moment both Misery-Man's colleague and Milly reappeared, pushing several unwieldy wheeled trolleys between them.

'What's happened?' said Milly, taking in the little spectacle.

Beth and Nora looked at each other.

'Nothing,' said Beth firmly. 'Nora's tripped and sprained her ankle, so we're going to help her into a more comfortable position and then we're going to finish unloading this lorry so that these . . . gentlemen can be on their way.'

Milly gave Beth a sharp look and for a moment Beth thought she was going to demand more details. But then she just said, 'Poor you, Nora. Let's prop you up somewhere more comfortable while we finish off here and then we'll help you inside.'

Nora smiled at Milly gratefully. Then, Beth and Milly helped her onto her feet and steadied her as she hopped over to the depot wall and settled behind a pile of sacks out of sight of Sergeant Major Cunningham, Miss Parker or anyone else who might be passing. Then, with the assistance of Friendly-Man, they quickly manhandled the rest of the sacks out of the lorry and into the huge baskets.

'So, what really happened?' demanded Milly as soon as the lorry had disappeared.

Beth filled her in. 'Part of me really wants to report it,' said Beth. 'He was very rude to Nora and he *definitely* dropped that sack on purpose.'

'Please don't,' begged Nora. 'If my sprained ankle gets written into the Injury Book, it's bound to get back to Uncle Alf and he'll tell Daddy and then they'll definitely stop me working here.'

Milly sighed. 'It's not your fault at all,' she said. 'But if your sprained ankle gets back to anyone in authority, they'll think that none of us "gals" are up to working here and we really don't want that. We want them to know that we can do the job as well as any man.'

'Which is why they're not going to find out,' said Beth briskly, thinking hard. 'I don't think your foot's broken, so if we can get you back to your chair, do you think you can work there for the rest of the day?'

Nora nodded. 'I think so,' she said. 'It's only agony when I try to put weight on it. But what about lunchtime? Surely people will see there's something up as soon as I try to get up?'

'Then, don't,' said Beth. 'Look, I've got to work during lunchtime because I was late this morning. What about if you say you're being a good sport and keeping me company? Miss Parker can hardly complain about you doing extra work. Then, at the end of the day, we'll help you home and you can tell your family you sprained your ankle walking across the park. That could happen to anyone at any time. Your parents couldn't possibly hold *that* against the Home Depot.'

'Good plan, Liza,' said Milly, approvingly.

'You'd really do all that for me?' Nora looked from one to the other with shining eyes.

'Of course,' said Beth.

'You saved my bacon over the fag end and you saved Liza from humiliation over the stamps, so I think you've earned it,' said Milly. 'There's just one small problem. How are we going to get you back to the department without arousing suspicion?'

There was a silence.

Then Beth nudged the nearest basket on wheels with her foot.

'Your carriage awaits, Miss,' she said with a little giggle.

* * *

The plan worked like a dream.

Leaving Nora hidden, Beth and Milly wheeled the incoming sacks to the Broken Parcel Department and stacked them carefully in the storage area. If anyone noticed that Nora wasn't giving them a hand, they didn't comment. Then the two girls went back for Nora, still secreted near the – luckily still quiet – unloading bay. They bound her ankle as best they could with their handkerchiefs and then, with muffled giggles – and the odd squeak of pain from Nora – they manhandled her into an empty basket. They placed the last couple of sacks around her and a couple of empty sacks went over her head, and they were on their way. No one batted an eyelid as Beth and Milly wheeled the basket back across the Home Depot floor, past the newly formed Censoring and Registered Parcels and POW departments and over to their own section.

Damn!

Miss Parker was there, giving someone's parcel the Parker Drop Test. Beth and Milly exchanged glances. Without breaking their stride, they wheeled the trolley behind a huge sack of parcels and, with their hands under Nora's shoulders, they hauled her out of the basket.

'How am I going to get back to my place without everyone seeing that I'm limping?' whispered Nora.

Oh goodness. That was a point.

Had they come so far only to fall at the final hurdle?

Milly gave them a grin. 'I'm going out,' she said. 'When you hear a . . . consternation, come out as quickly as you can and sit down.'

'But . . . how? . . . what? . . .' spluttered Nora.

Milly put her finger to her lips. 'Shh,' she said. 'Just do it. You'll know.'

She slipped out from behind the tower of sacks. Beth held her breath and moments later there were loud exclamations of shock and annoyance.

'Now!' hissed Beth.

She put her arm around Nora's shoulder and supported as much of the taller girl's weight as she could and together they emerged, making for their table as quickly as they could. Milly had obviously upset some water or glue on the table at the far end of the department and all heads were turned her way to see what was going on. Beth could see Milly gesticulating apologetically and hear her saying 'sorry, sorry' as Nora slipped into her chair with a little 'oof' of pain.

As far as Beth could tell, no one had seen that Nora was incapacitated.

They'd done it!

Nora stayed in her seat the whole day. Miss Parker had barely commented when Nora 'volunteered' to keep Beth company at lunchtime – and it was just as well Nora had stayed, because her ankle seemed to be getting even more swollen and painful by the minute.

'How on earth am I going to get home?' she whimpered, mid-afternoon. 'I really don't think I can put any weight on it. I suppose I could try to get a message home and Collins could come and pick me up in the motor, but that would rather give the game away, wouldn't it?'

'It's all sorted,' said Milly with a little glint in her eye. 'You're going home the same way you arrived back here in the department. In a basket.'

'Milly!' said Nora with a little laugh. 'We'd never get away with that!'

'We already have,' said Milly, grinning. 'The ordnance stores further up Gloucester Green have asked to borrow two baskets from the Home Depot this weekend and I've already told Miss Parker that we're happy to wheel them across. We'll even get dismissed a little early this afternoon to do it. What they don't know is that one of the baskets is going to go for a little detour with some unexpected cargo!'

This time it was Beth's turn to gawp at her. How did the girl do it? Oh, they all knew that the various army buildings springing up in the Regent's Park helped each other out with supplies and equipment from time to time, but this seemed almost too convenient to be true.

'Did they really request the baskets?' she asked, with a grin. 'Or could it be that the idea was planted?'

Milly giggled and patted her pocket. 'I sometimes have a ciggie with a nice girl who works in the procurement department over there and, let's say, she's been very helpful. When I told her what had happened, she sprang into action. She's even given me a letter requesting two baskets. With an official stamp and everything! Miss Parker couldn't say a word.'

The three girls dissolved into giggles and then found they couldn't stop. Even Miss Parker fixing them with a beady stare couldn't dampen their spirits. The rest of the afternoon whizzed by and before long it was time to set off on their errand.

'Liza?' It was Miss Parker, standing at their table and looking down at Beth, her face expressionless. Beth had been in the middle of a conspiratorial conversation with Milly and Nora and hadn't heard her arrive. 'Would you mind stepping into my office for a moment?'

Beth gave Milly and Nora a stricken look as she got to her feet and followed Miss Parker. Without all three of them involved, their plan couldn't work. Oh, why hadn't Milly said that the ordnance stores only wanted to borrow one basket? Then Milly could wheel Nora home and it wouldn't matter if Beth was detained.

And why exactly did Miss Parker want to see her?

Had she discovered that Beth had smuggled Nora back

to her work station in a basket? Was planning to wheel her across the park? Had lied about her name?

Goodness, whatever had happened to Goody-Two-Shoes Beth in just one week? She hardly recognised herself.

Miss Parker smiled at Beth and gestured for her to sit. 'I won't keep you, Liza,' she said. 'I know you have an errand to run with the other girls. But I just wanted to compliment you on your first week. You are one of the quickest and most efficient members of my team. You take instruction well and you didn't complain when you had to work through lunch today. You are a credit to the team and I just wanted to say well done and to keep up the good work.'

Beth left Miss Parker's office on cloud nine. How wonderful! Far from being a failure, she had caught the eye of Miss Parker in the best possible way. Humming under her breath, she went with Milly to get the two baskets and then, thoroughly emboldened, turned to Nora and said, in full ear shot of everyone, 'Would Miss perhaps like a ride?'

Nora, laughing, allowed herself to be helped into the basket and – with much whooping and cheering from the rest of the department – the little party departed.

'Nothing like carrying out an operation in broad daylight,' said Milly with a grin as they wheeled Nora out of the front entrance and over to the sentry at the gate. They showed him the paperwork and he waved them through. 'Can we all have a ride?' was all he said – and they were out!

Mission accomplished.

From then on it was easy. They set off up the path to the ordnance stores and, when they were out of sight of the Home Depot, turned left and set off at a run across the park, Nora kneeling up in the basket and giving them directions towards one of the icing-cake houses on the other side of the park.

'Emergency transportation for an injured army post office

worker,' said Beth to an old man who gave them a questioning look, and he gave them a little salute as they passed.

On they ran, until the wind blew back their hair. In front of them, Nora let out a little whoop of pure exhilaration.

This was wonderful, thought Beth.

She was doing her bit.

She had made friends.

She belonged.

Life, despite all its hardships, was sweet.

12

Back in Woodhampstead, the summer air was soft and sweet and even the tang of manure seemed gentler than in London. Weary and footsore but still happy as a sandboy, Beth set off down the high street towards Sally's cottage.

But wait!

What was that equally weary clip-clop behind her?

She would recognise it anywhere. It was . . . it was . . .

She spun round and – yes – it was Mayfair pulling the shop's delivery cart and gaining ground on her, fast.

Heart pounding, she stepped to the side of the road and waited. It was her chance. Her chance to see Pa, to talk to him, to explain. And to tell him about her first week. The things she had learnt. The people she had met. Pa would pull Mayfair to a halt and she would climb up beside him and all would be well.

The cart drew level to her . . . and moved on. Not by flicker of eye or muscle did Pa acknowledge he had seen her – but Beth knew that he had. He *must* have. But the cart carried on rumbling over the rutted road and Beth was left staring after it, her heart dropping faster than the sun in the sky.

Tears prickled Beth's eyelids but she felt angry as much as sad.

How *could* he?

It wasn't as if she had taken a lover or run away to join the circus, or even taken a job at one of the munitions

factories. She was working for the army post office, for
goodness' sake, and packaging damaged parcels so that they
could continue on their journey to the front. She could
hardly have found a more respectable, a more genteel . . .
a *safer* job if she'd tried. Of course, lying in order to get to
the interviews hadn't been ideal – and the telegram incident
had been very unfortunate. She was very sorry for that and
for upsetting Ma, but . . . really! All Pa was doing was
making himself look stubborn and out of touch and provincial and—

Beth stopped herself. She wasn't used to thinking about
her parents in this light and she wasn't sure it reflected very
well on herself. But she wouldn't go after Pa and beg him
to reconsider and to let her move home. She wouldn't turn
up at the house and start pleading to Ma. She would go back
to Sally's cottage and help her make supper and tell her all
about her marvellous, funny, exhausting day.

But Sally was out.

She'd left a note on the kitchen table to say that she'd had
her supper already and had gone to do a shift at the pub.
There was supper left for Beth in the pot on the stove and
she hoped that Beth had got home safely and was not too
tired after her long day.

Beth sighed.

She had been looking forward to telling Sally all about the
day's adventures. Then she lifted the pot lid and sighed again.
Sally had made a broth. It contained pieces of liver and some
other unidentifiable meat and suet dumplings. Beth stirred
it disconsolately dreaming wistfully of sausage and mash in
the canteen or one of Ma's richer and more savoury stews.
How she missed Ma's cooking! She expected that Sally did
too; after all, Beth moving in with her meant that neither
sister was now taking their meals over at the family home.
Goodness, how messed up everything was.

Beth doled out her lonely supper.

It was only when she took it over to the table and lit the gas lamp against the gathering gloom that she saw the letters propped up against the teapot. One was from Ned, and her spirits lifted. She hadn't heard from him for several days. She didn't recognise the handwriting on the second and, curious, she checked the back . . .

It was from Sam!

Suddenly, the evening took on a whole new texture. Studiously ignoring the fact that Sally had obviously brought the letters back from 'home' – thus underlining the fact she really wasn't welcome there – she propped them back against the teapot. It wouldn't do to read them while she was eating, even if she was by herself. She still had some standards.

Only when she had eaten her food and gone back for seconds (she was, she realised, absolutely ravenous after missing her lunch), rinsed her bowl in the scullery and put the kettle on, did she allow herself to open the letters. She chose Ned's first and slid the single page out.

Was he still in Blighty?

Was he safe?

She started to read.

Dear Sis,
I hope this letter finds you well. Nothing from you for a week? Blasted post. You'll know my news from my letter to the family.

Beth's breath hitched. She didn't know, of course, she hadn't been there when Pa – presumably – read it out at the dinner table. She carried on reading.

We're on Salisbury Plain now and training is in full swing. We've started specialist training and the word on the street is that we won't be waiting long before we get in front of the enemy. Not more than a month or two, I'd say. France, Beth, we're off to France. I hope you were impressed by how brave and patriotic I was in my letter to the parents but the truth is that I'm terrified. Everyone knows it's not exactly a picnic out at the front and to be honest I'm hoping I can hack whatever lies ahead!

Anyway, I'm taking comfort from picturing you all at home. You standing in the shop and writing everything neatly in the ledger and everything as it should be in the world. Keep the home fires burning for me and pray that I'll be home soon with you all.

And, in the meantime, please get busy with the home comforts. Tobacco, sherbet lemons, more socks, whatever you're having for dinner tonight!!

Your loving brother,
Ned

Beth finished reading with a pang in her heart.

France was a shock, of course, especially so soon, but even worse was the fact that Ned had no idea about her new job and the rift it had caused in the family. That felt wrong. Totally wrong. And even worse, it meant that she hadn't written to her twin as often as she otherwise would have done, and he had noticed. That was terrible. Unforgiveable. Oh, she knew Ma had asked her not to tell Ned what had happened, but equally, she had promised Ned to tell him everything that was going on at home. So, either way, she would be letting someone down.

What to do? Then she realised that, without consciously meaning to, she had taken out Sally's writing things and already loaded the pen with ink.

She knew exactly what she needed to do.

My Dearest Ned,

I was so pleased to get your letter and so shocked to hear you are probably going to France so soon. I know it's all beastly but I do know that you are brave and strong and I know you will be able to cope with whatever the war throws at you and that we will soon all be together again in Woodhampstead.

Now, I don't want to worry you but we did agree we would tell each other everything so I want to let you know that I have got a job in London working for the Royal Engineers Postal Service! It's based in the new Home Depot that has just been built in the Regent's Park and they're saying it's the biggest wooden building in the world. At the moment I am repackaging badly wrapped parcels destined for the various fronts – you wouldn't believe the things people send. One family sent a portion of a roast dinner to their son in France – even the gravy! It made a horrible sticky mess. Anyway, the whole thing has caused an awful fuss at home, I'm afraid. They don't want me working in London, and I must confess to a certain amount of deceitfulness in going up to London for the interview. You mustn't worry about anything but I am living with Sally at the moment and Ma and Pa don't seem to want anything to do with me. I suppose I can hardly blame them, but oh Ned, I am so happy to be doing something – if only in the smallest way – to help out and you must promise that you won't be angry or concerned because I know that my problems are tiny compared to yours. I had told Ma that I wouldn't trouble you with all of this but we did promise that we would tell each other everything and I felt terrible keeping it from you.

Well, dearest brother, I don't have much more to say now, so will close with fondest love and from your loving twin, Beth.

PS: Parcel to follow.

Beth sat back with a sigh as she sealed the envelope. Telling Ned the truth might cause more trouble at home but it was definitely the right thing to do. Then her eye fell on Sam's letter. She had almost forgotten it was there and she snatched it up in excitement.

Two sheets of paper. Densely written.

What a treat! She started to read.

Dear Beth,

I knew you would get the job! The way that you can read even the most beastly of handwritings with no trouble at all means there wasn't a cat's chance in hell that they wouldn't snap you up! But well done anyway on getting the job and an extra well done on accepting it – even though it is in London and a fair trek from good old Woodhampstead! (And yes, of course I knew it was in London. Didn't I tell you that?!)

So, do tell – what have they got you working on? Sorting? Censoring? Spying?

As for me, life with the 2/8th London is quiet. While the 1/8th has been fighting at Festubert, I am still in Blighty. In fact, until recently, can you believe I was actually in Hertfordshire – billeted at a lunatic asylum near Kings Langley. It wasn't too bad, except we had to sleep on the very hard floor of the hall using our boots as a pillow and we were surrounded by hundreds of lunatics (although sometimes I wonder who the lunatics actually are!). I've now been sent to the coast (can't say exactly where) with some of the other boys to patrol the towns and look out for the Hun Invasion fleet. No pillows here either! Looks like I won't get out to France for a while, although, of course, things can change at a moment's notice.

If you get a chance to look in on Ma and the girls, I would really appreciate it. I do worry about them all of

course, especially with winter on the way, and I worry
particularly that Ma won't tell me if there is anything really
amiss for fear of worrying me! And please do write again
– you can have no idea how all the letters and parcels bolster
us poor chaps so far away from home!
    Keep those letters moving and enjoy REPS!
    Yours,
    Sam

At least *Sam* was safe and likely to remain so for the fore-
seeable future. She shut her eyes and could almost see him
standing in front of her, dark eyes dancing, ready smile on
his lips. She would send him a pillow! The postage would
cost a fortune but she was earning good money now and
could afford it. And she knew that Sam would love the
gesture. She could hear his laughter as he unwrapped the
parcel. He was always so positive, so cheerful – even as he
put aside his own wishes to go and do his duty. Unlike
James . . .

She snapped open her eyes, bewildered.

Where on earth had *that* thought come from?

What on earth had *James* got to do with anything?

Never mind all that! She would write back to Sam straightaway. After all, who knew when she would next have the
time again. She made herself a pot of tea and wrote a bright
and breezy letter, thanking him for his, promising to check
in on his family and telling him all about life at the Home
Depot. She even told him about the fire on the first day and
Nora's twisted ankle that morning and how they'd got her
home, hoping it would all amuse him and that such indis-
cretions wouldn't come back to haunt her.

She popped the letter into one of Sally's envelopes and
addressed it. Then she paused. And paused a little longer.
And then she smiled as she stuck on the stamp at a slight

angle. The sort of angle that – if it was a little more pronounced – could possibly be stamp code for 'I'm missing you'. The sort of angle that might also easily be explained away as carelessness, a lack of attention to detail or being in too much of a hurry to do things properly. Who knew if Sam would pick up on it? Oh, he'd know the code all right, being a postman, but would he know that Beth did? And would he ever think that she might dare to send him such a message?

Oh, stop it, Beth. Stop overthinking everything!

And, just to prove that it didn't have to mean anything, she stuck the stamp on the letter to Ned at the angle that meant 'write soon'.

She was still giggling to herself when she heard Sally's key in the lock. Beth was about to pop the letter she'd just written to Sam behind the clock on the shelf, but Liza stopped her. She had absolutely nothing to feel guilty about.

Sally came into the kitchen. 'Hello, Beth,' she said, tucking a loose strand of chestnut hair behind her ear and throwing her hat onto a chair.

'Don't you mean, "Hello, Liza"?' said Beth with a giggle. 'I've had a *such* a day being Liza and, to be honest, I'm struggling to shake her off!'

'I think it must be Liza who stuck the stamps on like that,' said Sally with a laugh, pointing at the envelopes on the table. 'Unless Beth has been having a drink.'

'Of course I haven't,' said Beth with a laugh. 'It's a code. A stamp code.'

'Really?' Sally sounded intrigued. 'So, what does this mean?' She pointed at the stamp on the letter to Ned.

'"Write soon",' said Beth with a grin.

'And this one? To . . .' Sally turned over the letter. 'Sam Harrison.' She turned to Beth, eyebrows raised, an amused smile playing at her lips.

'"Missing you",' said Beth with a shrug of her shoulders and a little self-deprecating grin.

'Beth! For shame!' said Sally, laughing out loud. 'So are you and Sam stepping out together? I saw that he'd written to you.'

'Yes. No. I don't know,' said Beth, feeling a little confused. 'He asked me to write to him and . . .'

'Well, enjoy your "yes, no, I don't know",' said Sally. 'I've always liked Sam Harrison. He's a nice boy. And that stamp angle could just about be explained away as a mistake so you've nothing to lose. Now, let's get a fresh pot of tea and you can show me how this stamp code works. I want to use it on Bertie. Right away.'

Thank goodness for Sally, thought Beth as she swung the kettle onto the range. Her parents might want nothing more to do with her, but she could always rely on her siblings.

13

A month later – the middle of July – London greeted Beth with a hot, sooty, smelly hug and she got off the train with almost a spring in her step. This was her town or, if it wasn't now, it very soon would be. The Tube no longer held any fear for her and she managed to knit a few more rows of her latest sock before it pulled into Portland Road Station. She set off up the road with the icing-cake houses at a steady but not panicked pace. She was not in a hurry. She had plenty of time. She had this journey down to a T. Ned and Sam were still in both England, despite Ned's earlier fears. Ned had been most encouraging about her new job. Sam had been delighted to receive the pillow she'd sent him, and his last stamp had definitely been at a slight angle.

Life was good.

If only her parents were talking to her.

'Good morning, Miss Healey.'

Beth swung around. She'd been so lost in her own thoughts she hadn't heard the footsteps from behind. She wasn't sure how she felt when she saw that it was James Blackford. She hadn't seen him since that rather awkward conversation in the canteen in her first week at the Home Depot, although she had thought about him several times since then. Each time, though, she had ended up feeling rather cross.

'Good morning,' she replied with a cautious smile. 'I haven't seen you for a while.'

'No indeed,' said James, falling into step with her. 'I've been back at Mount Pleasant, but the Honour Envelope Department is formally moving to the Home Depot today, so I shall be around a lot more from now on.'

'I see.'

'Any news of your brother?' asked James pleasantly. 'I do hope he is safe.'

It was on the tip of Beth's tongue to say, 'Yes, thank you.' It was just what one did.

But, somehow, she couldn't.

'I didn't think you'd care,' she said, knowing she was being ungracious but unable to stop herself. 'After all, isn't he just another potential victim?'

James stopped. Then took hold of Beth's arm and gently swung her round to face him. 'Now, that's not fair,' he said softly. 'I might want nothing to do with the war, but I care very much about the people caught up in it.'

Beth felt tears pricking at his rebuke. 'I'm sorry,' she muttered. 'That was very rude of me.'

'It was,' said James matter-of-factly. 'But I forgive you. Don't forget I have a brother caught up in all this as well, so I understand exactly how you're feeling. And I'm happy to talk to you any time you want about what you're going through and I hope, as a friend, I can count on the same from you.'

Beth wasn't sure how to answer.

Is that what they were?

Friends?

Beth found she rather liked the idea and suddenly had the urge again to tell James that she was really called Beth. But just as she was about to, the loud tooting of a horn made them both jump and a very smart black motor pulled up alongside them. Milly was smiling and waving from the back seat and, for one strange moment, Beth felt disorientated.

She had had it all wrong. Milly was rich – very rich. The East End of London story was a ruse, a stab at normality, a wish to infiltrate the workers—

And then she saw Nora beside her, leaning over and beckoning to them, and everything fell back into place. It was Nora's car. Or at least her family's.

'Hop in,' said Nora. 'Both of you,' she added with a laugh when James hung back. 'We'll give you a lift the rest of the way. Daddy was out early this morning and Mother's still in bed and I was running late so I persuaded Collins to give me a lift. We picked up Milly further down the Outer Circle.'

They set off and Beth hugged her excitement to herself. Life was a series of moments and, in the present one, she was a lady driving in a smart motor with her friends.

If the folks at home could see her now.

Collins parked as close to the Home Depot as he could because there were far more lorries backing up outside the building than usual and the place in general seemed much busier. The girls and James went through to the gate, across the grass and through the front entrance together. Then they stopped in amazement.

Wow!

The space had been totally transformed. Where before it had been a cross between a wood and an empty, cavernous cathedral, today it was a market. A very bustling market – perhaps St Albans market just before Christmas. It looked for all the world like dozens of costermongers standing behind stalls and selling their wares while crowds of shoppers milled around and porters darted about with a sense of business-like urgency.

Or maybe it was Father Christmas's workshop the day before Christmas Eve and all these men and women were his elvish helpers.

Oh, stop it, Beth. Don't be so childish.

It wasn't a market, of course. Or Father Christmas's workshop. It was the army post office sorting office, or at least a part of it, which seemed to have arrived lock, stock and barrel from elsewhere over the weekend and was already fully populated.

'Oh Lordy,' breathed Milly. 'All those *men*.'

'You mean "all those men who will be fighting us over the jammy buns"?' said Nora. 'And making the place even hotter.'

Beth didn't say anything.

Sensible Beth, Logical Beth just stood there, trying to make sense of it all and not to feel nervous and resentful that 'their' Home Depot had been taken over by a multitude of strangers. They'd always known they were only the advance guard – had been told so right from the very beginning – so it shouldn't have been a surprise. Yet still it felt strange. Strange and chaotic. There were just so many people and so many parcels. She looked a little closer. There were hundreds of sacks slung between wooden frames, many with cardboard signs on metal sticks above them. Some had a single mysterious letter on them, others words – Royal Engineers, Indian Infantry, Egypt, Mesopotamia. Many more Union Jacks had been hung from the wooden beams, which gave everything a most jolly and patriotic air despite the gunmetal grey heavens visible through the skylights. And everywhere there were sacks. More sacks than Beth could ever have imagined. Propped up against the walls, sometimes almost to the ceiling; piled up against the wooden frames, in baskets, on trolleys, being carried . . .

'All those letters,' breathed Beth. 'All those parcels.'

Beth already knew enough about the Royal Engineers Postal Section to know that it might look chaotic but, under the surface, it would be anything but. Any organisation that managed to get 12 million letters out to the various fronts every week had to be doing *something* right!

'If you think that's a lot of parcels, wait until you see the broken ones,' said Miss Parker who had come up behind them unseen and unannounced. 'Now, come along girls. To your stations. These parcels won't mend themselves.'

Beth nodded goodbye to James and she and the others made their way over to the Broken Parcel Department. It was still shielded from the main space by the same wooden screens but everything felt completely different because of all the noise and activity beyond them. There were several more tables and many more new girls and, as Miss Parker had warned them, countless new parcels.

It was all rather overwhelming.

Beth couldn't help noticing, however, that many of the old familiar faces were missing.

'Where's Mabel?' she said to no one in particular. She liked Mabel – a game sort, if not the speediest. Surely, she hadn't been sacked? Would they all have to be on their guard from now on? Would they have to up their game?

'Flu,' said Hettie on the next table. 'She were sneezing something rotten on Friday and she told Ruby who lives near her that she was too poorly to come in today. There's at least four girls off with it today.'

'Poor things,' said Beth. 'We'll all have to work twice as hard today to make up for them.'

They set to work.

'Another alphabet race, ladies?' suggested Nora. 'Loser buys the buns at breaktime.'

'Good idea,' said Milly. 'But can we start with a different letter, for a bit of variety?'

'Of course,' said Nora. 'Liza, you choose.'

Beth choose the letter M. She'd assumed it would be easy,

but it proved surprisingly elusive and the girls worked without any joy for at least fifteen minutes.

'Mince pies,' cried Nora suddenly.

Beth glanced across. Nora did have some small pies in front of her – rather bashed around the edges but not so badly that the contents had spilled out.

'Mince pies?' she said suspiciously. 'It's July! I know they say pack early for Christmas, but that's ridiculous.'

'Yes. You can't prove they're mince pies,' said Milly. 'It doesn't count.'

'Ah, but you can't prove that they aren't,' said Nora with a little glint in her eye.

'Want to bet?' Milly looked around her and then, without warning, pinched a tiny piece off one of the pies and popped it in her mouth. 'Apple,' she said. 'Minus marks for attempting to cheat, Nora. You go back to L.'

Beth laughed along with the others, but inside she was rather shocked. Milly had no business spoiling the little pie. It wasn't her property and she had no right to mess with it like that, especially not just to win a point in a silly game. Miss Parker would have had a fit if she had seen, and quite rightly so. And the way she spoke to Nora. If the war hadn't come along, Nora would have been her superior in every way and while Nora didn't seem to mind . . .

Hang on, what was the clear liquid in this glass jar? Water?

It must be water. Yes, the handwritten note said 'tonic water'. And *that* was very much the same as . . .

'Mineral water,' Beth called out in a sing-song voice. She would *not* lose every round of the game. Even if it was mainly luck, her pride was at stake. As were the contents of her purse.

'Water?' said Nora dubiously. 'That's a W not an M for a start. And why would anyone send water to the front?'

'Lots of reasons,' said Beth. 'The water out at the front might be disgustingly dirty. Besides, mineral water is a tonic and will help keep them healthy.'

She knew both these things to be true. Lots of people bought water from the store to send on to their boys, especially those in the Dardanelles.

'Let me see that,' said Milly. Before Beth could stop her, she had reached across the table and grabbed the bottle. Flicking back the stopper, she dipped her finger into the liquid and then licked her finger.

'Not water,' she said matter-of-factly. 'Gin.'

Beth recoiled. *Gin!*

Her first case of attempted smuggling!

It wasn't that alcohol was banned at the front; far from it, everyone knew the rank and file received a ration of rum before they went into battle and officers could drink more or less what they wanted. But you weren't allowed to send spirits through the post.

Beth stood up. 'I'll take it to Miss Parker,' she said, half wondering if Milly would try to persuade her not to. She knew many people felt soldiers should be allowed to receive alcohol to help drown out the horrors of the war. After all, she'd been allowed to wave through all those small packages of cocaine from Harrods complete with syringe and spare needles and tagged 'A Useful Present for Friends at the Front'. Was a little alcohol really that much worse?

But Milly was nodding. 'Yes, get it handed in,' she said quite seriously. 'Dreadful stuff.'

So off Beth went and, by the time she got back, Nora had claimed malted milk tablets and Milly mixed fruit.

It really wasn't fair.

By that evening, Beth found she was almost too tired to move. Her arms ached. Her back ached. Her throat was sore.

Her eyes itched. And now she had the journey back to Woodhampstead to face. After a shift in the shop, she simply walked back through the storeroom and into the house and got herself a cup of tea. Now it was going to take her the best part of two hours to get home, and that thought was almost unbearable.

She put her head on her knees with a deep sigh.

'You all right, Liza?' It was Milly, standing over her and shaking her shoulder.

Beth woke with a start, blinking up at her friend. 'Oh goodness, I must have drifted off,' she said, standing up. She wiped her mouth on her hanky, leaving behind a light brown smear. 'I was just getting the strength together for the journey home.'

'How long does it take you?' asked Milly curiously.

Beth sighed. 'It will be two hours before I'm home,' she said, 'and that's if everything goes to plan. If the train is delayed or decides to stop everywhere en route, then it could be even longer.'

'Gawd,' said Milly. 'I had no idea. Why don't you come back and stay with me? It's only half an hour away – I'm usually home by six.'

'Oh, doesn't that sound wonderful?' said Beth. 'But wouldn't your mother mind?'

'Mind?' said Milly. 'No, of course she wouldn't. She works shifts anyway, so she probably won't even be there.'

'That's lovely,' said Beth. 'But I can't today of course. My family would be worried sick.' Well, Sally would be worried sick, that is. But her parents wouldn't even know. The thought made her feel sad, all of a sudden.

'Not tonight,' said Milly, putting on her hat. 'But why don't you come tomorrow? Stay the night? We'll get a pie down the Roman to save us cooking.'

How odd all this was! A few weeks ago she barely left

Woodhampstead from one month to the next and yet here she was arranging to stay overnight in the East End of London with a girl she now counted as one of her closest friends.

'If you're sure your mother won't mind, then yes, please, that would be wonderful,' said Beth. 'Thank you so much.'

14

'I forgot to tell you I have a meeting tonight,' said Milly casually as she and Beth were getting on the Tube at Portland Road Station the next evening.

'Oh.' Beth's heart sank. She had been looking forward to staying with Milly that evening. She'd bought an overnight bag into work and the two of them had mentioned it several times during the day and had walked down to the station together. Why this sudden revelation? 'Well, never mind. I can just jump off the train at King's Cross and no harm done.'

Milly laughed. 'I don't mean that, you dolt,' she said. 'I've said you can billet with me and you still can. I want you to come.'

Beth smiled, relieved and pleased the plans hadn't changed and amused at Milly using the word billet. She liked all the terminology that was bandied round the Depot. She liked reporting for duty and discussing who might be going on leave. They weren't in the army, but it made her feel useful. Important. Part of something bigger than herself.

Milly was still talking. 'I was just letting you know,' she said, voice rising as the train swooshed into the station. 'You can come to the meeting with me, if you like, or you can stay at my house, or you can just hang around the Roman.'

'Hang around the Roman'? Is that really what Milly had said? It sounded very strange. Like loitering near a gladiator or something. Whatever could Milly mean? But she just smiled and said 'thank you' as they boarded the train. She would find out soon enough and there was no point in showing her ignorance.

'What's the meeting about?' Beth asked instead as the train pulled out of the station.

'It's an ELFS meeting,' said Milly absentmindedly scratching inside her collar and making Beth do the same. It was catching. Like yawning.

'Elfs?' echoed Beth

Elves?

Little men with pointed ears?

Milly really seemed to talk double-Dutch sometimes.

'East London Federation of the Suffragettes,' elaborated Milly, moving on to scratching behind her ears. 'I've got to go because I'm helping out with the teas, but you don't.'

Beth hesitated.

Ma had always been very clear on how she felt about the votes for women brigade. Queen Victoria had been outraged by the very notion of suffrage, and so was she. And, to be honest, Beth had never really questioned it. Things had been the same throughout history and worked well enough. She'd seen first-hand that women could – and did – exert influence within the home (no one, not even Pa, dared cross Ma when she got a bee in her bonnet) but everyone knew their place and there was no need to rock the boat.

But did she feel like that anymore?

The war was opening up all sorts of hitherto unheard-of opportunities for women and her gender seemed to be rising to the challenge quite admirably. So maybe it wasn't that outrageous for women to demand a say in voting for the things that affected them . . .

So, she'd go to the meeting.

Of course, she would.

But . . . the suffragettes!

She often got a bit confused but, if she remembered correctly, the suffra*gists* went about things peacefully while the suffra*gettes* caused a lot of mischief. Weren't the suffragettes the ones who went around throwing things through windows and slashing paintings, to say nothing of throwing stones and the like? She was pretty sure they were and, really, was that the right way to go about anything? Didn't it just give the whole movement – and women in general – a bad name?

So, she wouldn't go to the meeting.

Of course, she wouldn't.

Ma would be horrified!

It was on the tip of Beth's tongue to tell Milly all this, but then she hesitated. Why not go? Why not make up her own mind? Surely no one was going to force her to chain herself to railings or run out in front of a horse or set fire to a shop if she didn't want to. What was the worst that could happen?

'I'd like to come,' said Beth firmly.

'Right you are,' said Milly lightly. 'Mrs P will be there tonight. I'll introduce you.'

'Mrs P?' echoed Beth. 'Does she work at the Depot?'

Milly burst out laughing. 'No!' she said. 'Mrs Pankhurst. Sylvia Pankhurst. She set up ELFS and she's bleeding marvellous.'

'Of course,' said Beth, feeling a little foolish. She'd heard of the Pankhursts – of course she had. Everyone had.

Milly smiled at her. 'Let me tell you who's who,' she said. 'I don't want you showing me up! Emily Pankhurst and her daughter Christabel were involved with the Women's Social and Political Union and the other daughter, Sylvia, has broken away – or been chucked out, depending on who you believe – and formed the ELFS.'

'I see,' said Beth. She really wasn't sure how she felt about meeting Sylvia Pankhurst. Ma would give her a good slap around the legs if she knew . . .

But there was no time to dwell on that because, minutes later, the train whistled into Bow Road Station and Milly said, 'We're here.'

The two girls alighted and Beth realised she had butterflies in her tummy. Just very slightly but definitely there because she knew 'here' meant the heart of the East End of London. Beth had very little to go on but she knew that Ma, who had probably never been east of the Tower, viewed the whole area as one homogenous mass of Ripper-esque deprivation and depravity. The street Milly led her down looked ordinary enough, though. Wide and tarmacked with redbrick buildings on either side, there was no obvious violence or debauchery and if there were more horse-drawn vehicles than motors, Beth reminded herself that Woodhampstead was much the same.

'We have to practically pass home but there's no time to pop in,' said Milly, walking at such a pace that Beth almost had to break into a run to keep up with her. Beth's first impression was that, far from being a homogenous mass, the area varied hugely, often street by street. There were large homes with their own stables a stone's throw away from souls living cheek by jowl in oppressive tenements, the unmade alleys slick with 'mud' and dozens of small, round eyes peeking out of doorways at them as they passed.

'Home,' said Milly, waving as they passed Arnold Street. Somewhere between the two extremes: it looked poor but respectable – a road of identical redbrick terraced houses with tiny front gardens. But there was no time to linger because Milly was speeding up.

'Where are we going?' asked Beth.

'The Mothers Arms,' said Milly without breaking stride.

That meant nothing to Beth. She was about to question Milly further when they rounded a corner and were suddenly in the middle of a market in full swing and further conversation was impossible. Barrows and stalls spilled along the edge of the pavement and onto the road. Hawkers and stall-holders shouted their wares, an organ-grinder cranked a merry tune and a horse and cart clattered across the cobbles. And the *people*. Thronging the street, gossiping in little groups, queueing three abreast outside some shops and stalls – it was next to impossible to walk in a straight line. Beth followed Milly down the street, weaving around a couple of tired old donkeys and a skinny dog scavenging in the gutter, and was relieved when Milly turned right down a side street and the assault on her senses subsided.

'That was the Roman,' said Milly.

'The Roman?' said Beth.

Why did she seem to be repeating everything Milly said like an idiot?

'The Roman Road market,' said Milly. 'We'll stop there for pie and mash on the way home. Nearly there now.'

Just as well. Beth was exhausted. Up the street, past a wood merchant, and then, on the corner, Milly stopped outside a large public house. Coloured bricks proclaimed that it was called The Gunmakers Arms.

'Here we are,' said Milly.

'The Gunmakers Arms,' said Milly.

Was the meeting taking place in a public house?

Ma would be apoplectic!

'It *used* to be a pub,' said Milly. 'But earlier this year, ELFS took it over and now it's called The Mothers Arms. Look, we've painted ELFS in gold on the outside. It's got a nursery and a mother and baby clinic and a free milk distribution centre and plenty more besides.'

'How lovely,' said Beth, warming to ELFS. It didn't *sound* like the kind of organisation that was hell-bent on creating mischief. Indeed, Beth reflected, if there were more buildings called The Mothers Arms and fewer called The Gunmakers

Arms, maybe the world might not be in the sorry state of affairs it now found itself in.

'It is a *wonderful* place,' said Milly, eyes shining in a way Beth hadn't seen before. 'My sister Margaret's son comes to the nursery here and Margaret works at the toy factory the ELFS set up around the corner. I can't help out much anymore but I always come up here on a Saturday morning. A nurse comes in to weigh the children and to give the mothers advice and sometimes there's free eggs and barley and Virol. I fetch and carry and help out where I can. There's always something to be done.'

Beth looked at Milly with newfound respect. Never mind that she had broken a bit off one of those little apple pies yesterday; look at all she was *doing* – and without making a big song and dance about it, either. And compare it with what Beth had done over the weekend. A bit of letter writing. A visit to Mrs Harrison. And a great deal of feeling sorry for herself because Ma and Pa had chucked her out for lying to them.

'I'm really impressed,' said Beth, standing back as a group of women went up the steps into The Mothers Arms.

'Don't be,' said Milly briskly. 'We're all just trying to lend a hand, aren't we? Now, come on.' She took Beth's arm. 'People are arriving and we'd better go and help set up.'

The meeting took place in a room on the first floor. It was clean and freshly whitewashed but Beth still fancied she could smell – taste, almost – the beer ingrained into the very fabric of the place. It must still be there: in the tread of the worn floorboards and the heavy flock wallpaper and the sturdy wooden chairs. There must be an echo of all the gunmakers who had frequented the pub over the years – many of whom would now be at the various fronts using the very weapons they had helped to fashion.

How strange life could be.

Tonight, though, there was just tea and Rowntree's hot chocolate on the menu and Beth was kept busy standing behind the trestle table helping Milly to pour and serve. Milly insisted on introducing Beth to everyone – Elsie Lagsding, Jessie Steven, Melvina Walker. There was no mistaking the pride in her voice, but the names meant nothing to Beth. She just kept nodding and smiling and hoped fervently she wouldn't be put on the spot later on.

'And this is Miss Pankhurst,' said Milly suddenly. 'She takes two sugars, Liza. Miss Pankhurst, might I present my friend Liza Healey?'

Beth looked up from her sugar tongs with interest, impressed that Miss Pankhurst had queued up with everyone else rather than expecting her refreshments to be brought to her. At first glance she looked formidable, even grave, with her severely parted dark hair, beetling brows and heavy-lidded eyes but then she started laughing, her mouth turning up in merriment and altering her whole countenance. Whatever could she be finding so funny?

'Good evening, Miss Healey,' said Miss Pankhurst in a surprisingly deep voice. 'And might I surmise that you have employment in the same place as your friend Miss Woods?'

'Good evening, Miss Pankhurst,' replied Beth, hoping her voice wasn't shaking. A little queue had formed and everyone had fallen silent, listening with interest to the exchange. 'And, yes, I do. Milly – er, Miss Woods – and I both work at the new Home Depot in the Regent's Park. We're attached to the Royal Engineers Postal Service.'

Despite her nerves, Beth couldn't help a note of pride in her voice. The Home Depot was a place *anyone* would be proud to work and she knew jobs there were in much demand. But how could Miss Pankhurst know? Had Milly told her before? Or was there something in her face, her bearing . . . ?

'I thought so,' said Miss Pankhurst with a huge guffaw. 'You've both got exactly the same film of light brown dust all over your white collars!'

Oh!

What did Ma always say?

Pride comes before a fall . . .

The little queue erupted into laughter. Beth wondered if she should feel affronted, but Miss Pankhurst's eyes were kind rather than taunting.

'That's true, Miss Pankhurst,' she replied with a little giggle. 'The dust is from all the sacks and believe me, it gets *everywhere*.'

'Everywhere,' echoed Milly with a grin.

'I can quite imagine,' interrupted Miss Pankhurst drily and everyone laughed again.

'Still, it's a small price to pay to help the war effort,' said Beth, lest anyone thought she was complaining.

'Indeed,' said Miss Pankhurst. 'One has only to think of the poor girls at the munitions factories. They come here from time to time and they are absolutely bright yellow. But still, they seem to think of it as a badge of honour and that's how you must think of your dust. From now on, I shall refer to you as the Dusty Elves. Yes, that's exactly what you are. The Dusty Elves.'

She smiled at the girls, picked up her cup of tea – goodness knew how many sugars Beth had ended up putting in there – and headed off. Beth looked at Milly with amazement. Sylvia Pankhurst had not only spoken to them but had given them a nickname to boot.

The Dusty Elves . . .

Fancy that!

Wait until she told . . . only, who *could* she tell? Who would be interested, let alone impressed? Ma and Sally would be horrified – the East End of London, the suffragettes. Ned might be curious and Sam might be vaguely amused.

Nora would love it, of course. And James. *James*. For some reason, she knew he would both 'get' it and be tickled pink.

The Home Depot was beginning to feel like her family.

Now she just had to get through a meeting, which was probably going to be deathly boring. Either that or horribly militant. She knew she would be counting the minutes before they got back to the Roman and a slice of pie.

The meeting was fascinating.

Fascinating.

The early conversation was all about a Distress Bureau the ELFS had set up to help local women obtain the separation allowance they were entitled to when a son or husband joined the army. Horror stories abounded about forms and legal documents going missing or the money granted being wrong and the distress and poverty that could result. Had Ma and Pa applied when Ned went? Perhaps even more importantly, had Mrs Harrison applied when Sam signed up? Beth found that she had no idea, but she was deeply impressed to hear ELFS had taken up numerous cases on behalf of soldiers and their families, writing to the relevant government departments to make applications and to challenge decisions. They sounded more like family solicitors than the 'bloody women' her parents railed against.

Even more impressive was the League of Rights for Soldiers' and Sailors' Wives and Relatives, which Miss Pankhurst had created earlier that year. It encouraged women to take up their own grievances supported by expertise from ELFS members. How much better was that than treating these women as passive victims? Beth had to sit on her hands when Miss Pankhurst asked for more volunteers because she was itching – literally – to get involved. But how could she? She didn't live here. She lived twenty miles away in a village where suffragettes were either figures of scorn or suspicion.

The meeting moved on to ELFS' 'cost price' restaurants, so called, as Miss Pankhurst explained, 'because the name should be a slogan against profiteering, and should carry no stigma of charity'. There were more initiatives, too: an unemployment bureau, the toy and boot factories, the children's feeding centres, and the mother-and-baby clinics that Milly had already told her about.

Beth drank it all in, her awe for Sylvia and all the other women growing in waves. This was what making a difference was all about! Oh, she was making a difference in her own way, of course, but at the end of day, her work at the Home Depot was just a job – and a well-paid and reasonably comfortable one at that. In fact, some might argue that she wasn't really 'doing her bit', but merely profiting from a job that had been created by the war – and that thought didn't make her feel very comfortable at all.

'Just one more thing before we finish,' said Miss Pankhurst. 'I expect you all know the beautiful rocking horse that Mr and Mrs Dickin kindly donated to the children's nursery? A most splendid thing and a very generous gift. Well, I'm sorry to report that it has been quite vandalised. Nearly every hair from its mane and tail has been deliberately pulled out. The poor creature is almost denuded!'

Oh dear, thought Beth.

This was where she would see the other side of Miss Pankhurst. The one where she totally lost her temper. It was quite justified, of course – deliberate vandalism was never to be condoned – but what form would it take? Would she punish the children concerned or even expel them from the nursery? Fine the parents?

What would she, Beth, do in Miss Pankhurst's place?

Miss Pankhurst paused and looked round the room. 'We mustn't forget, of course,' she said, 'that the youngest members of our society are as much affected by this wretched

war as the rest of us. More so, if anything – as they are
unable to understand and rationalise what's going on. Their
destructive behaviour no doubt stems from this and, of
course, many children using this nursery also come from
deprived backgrounds. I've been racking my brains as to
what we might be able to do to help and I've set up a meeting
with a lady called Maria Montessori. Mrs Montessori has
developed a new way of learning, which allows children to
explore ideas in their own way and at their own pace. We
might look to introducing some of those ideas here so that
any future Dobbin has at least a fighting chance of keeping
his tail!'

Well!

That was that!

Miss Pankhurst was officially a saint. Henceforth, she could
do no wrong in Beth's eyes.

As the two girls walked back down St Stephens Road in the
gloaming, Beth found she couldn't stop talking about the
meeting.

'I can't believe all the things ELFS are doing to help,' she
gushed. 'It's wonderful! And I can't believe you said they
don't believe in the war when they're doing so much good!'

Milly laughed. 'But it's not the same thing at all,' she said,
tucking her hand under Beth's arm. 'It's perfectly possible
to think the war's a bad thing and still try to help people
who're suffering. Believe me, Miss Pankhurst does not like
the war.'

'Oh, but she's quite marvellous,' said Beth, ready to forgive
Miss Pankhurst anything and everything. Anyway, there had
been no hint of any anti-war sentiment in the meeting, let
alone any intention of creating public mischief. Milly must
have been exaggerating. After all, it wouldn't be the first time.

'Miss Pankhurst *is* quite marvellous,' said Milly, quickening her pace. 'And I'll tell you what else is quite marvellous. Clarkson's pie and mash! I can almost smell it from here. Hurry up, I'm ravenous.'

Now here, Milly certainly *wasn't* exaggerating. The slice of pie that Beth ate sitting on a garden wall was quite heavenly. Light, flaky pastry encasing big pieces of beef in the richest, most savoury gravy. Now that she could most certainly get used to – even though she knew Ma and good Queen Vic would be terribly disapproving of her eating in public. And on a *wall* to boot . . .

Beth hadn't been sure what to expect of Milly's home, but it really wasn't very different from Sally's cottage. Outside, everything was neat and tidy. The black-and-red tiled path from the gate to the front door was newly swept and washed, the step was scrubbed and the front door knocker gleamed dully in the twilight. Inside there was a long narrow passage, just like Sally's, with two doors leading off it.

'That's Mr Wildermuth's room,' said Milly, gesturing to the closed parlour door. Or, at least, what would normally be the parlour. 'He's at work at the moment.'

'Mr Wildermuth?' echoed Beth, hanging her hat and coat on the stand.

'Yes,' said Milly. 'He's staying here because his previous lodgings were bombed. He works at a bakery in Brick Lane and he often does an evening shift so all the women who are now working can still buy fresh bread.'

Beth didn't care what Mr Wildermuth did for a living. 'Isn't that a German name?' she said, scandalised. In Hertfordshire, everyone with a German name had been put straight in camps. Beth was sketchy on the details but she knew they certainly weren't working in bakeries and lodging wherever they chose.

Milly laughed. 'Mr Wildermuth's lived in London since

before you and I were born,' she said. 'He uses the name Wildsmith sometimes when he's out and about – especially after the Zeppelin strike – but you don't need to worry about him.'

She carried on down the passage and into the kitchen. 'Tea?' she asked over her shoulder, while she lit the lamps.

'Yes please,' said Beth following Milly into the scullery. And then, as Milly splashed water into the kettle, she gasped. 'Oh, my goodness! You have running water.'

A tap was the height of luxury to Beth. Running water hadn't made it out to Woodhampstead – even the very largest houses had to make do with pumps and wells. How strange to find plumbing in an ordinary terraced house!

Milly was laughing. 'The whole East End's got running water,' she said. 'Even the tenements have had it for ages. We've got a water closet out the back too. Haven't you?'

Beth shook her head, thinking of the ancient privy in the backyard. 'No!' she said. 'No one does. I'm beginning to feel like a complete country bumpkin.'

'That's cos you are!' said Milly, wrinkling up her nose in merriment as she swung the kettle onto the range. 'I'm sorry there's no one here to meet you this evening. Ma's doing the night shift at the munitions factory with my sister Alice and my other sister, Caroline, is looking after a neighbour's children this evening while they're at work, and she'll probably stop over there for the night. And my youngest brother Charlie should already be tucked up in bed ready for his newspaper round before school tomorrow morning. So, it's just you and me. Kick your boots off and make yourself at home.'

Beth and Milly spent a lovely hour chatting in the kitchen until their yawns became more and more frequent and Milly pronounced it time for bed. Beth, always used to her own bed – and indeed her own room – found sharing a bed with Milly a little strange. She had tried to relax and join in with Milly's cheerful chatter as the two girls did their ablutions, but she found it hard to sleep and lay ramrod straight much of the night, staring up at unfamiliar shadows dancing on the unfamiliar ceiling.

What a day! She had woken that morning sure that the suffragettes were little more than public nuisances bent on mischief. Now, she had seen that this simply wasn't true – far from it! And, even more surprisingly, she could feel her beliefs about the war beginning to be challenged. *Was* it fair that the poor seemed to be suffering more than the rich? *Was* the war really worth winning at all costs? Beth wasn't at all sure what the answers were, but she did know that she couldn't – wouldn't! – continue to blindly trot out the same views as her parents and the rest of Woodhampstead. She was her own person with own opinions and beliefs.

She just had to work out what they were.

What a day, indeed!

15

When they arrived at the Home Depot the next morning
– Beth feeling refreshed after an extra hour in bed –
there were lots of new faces and another couple of tables
had been added to the group. Despite that, Beth could see
that many people were missing. No Ruby and no Hazel again
– and that was just for starters.

'Morning, Liza,' said Nora cheerfully as Beth sat down.
At least *she* looked hale and hearty. 'How was last night?'

'Oh, it was wonderful,' said Beth, grabbing the first parcel
out of the communal basket. 'Milly took me to along to a
suffragette meeting.'

'Really?' Nora gaped at her.

'Really!' said Beth. 'And I met Sylvia Pankhurst,' she added.
'I was all prepared not to like her but what's she's doing is
actually quite marvellous. *And* she nicknamed us the Dusty
Elves! Can you believe it? A nickname! From Miss Pankhurst.
Fancy!'

Beth paused, fully expecting Nora to sit forward or clap
her hands together. Or *something*. After all, to be given a
nickname by someone who was practically a household name
was surely worthy of some comment. But Nora just gave a
little frown as she wiped some oozing jars of marmalade.
'I'm not sure about Sylvia Pankhurst,' she said. 'I'm sure
she's very passionate and amusing, but she has some strange
ways of going about things.'

Beth put the string down. She'd felt the same as Nora just

a couple of days before and now it was up to her to convince Nora that they had both been wrong.

'Honestly, she's doing so much good,' said Beth earnestly. 'Setting up the nursery *and* the Distress Bureau *and* the cost-price restaurants. That's not strange. That's . . . *heroic*!'

'She also burned down the refreshment pavilion in the Regent's Park a few years ago,' said Nora quietly. She was concentrating very hard on sticking on a new address label and didn't quite meet Beth's eye.

What?

What?!

Beth thought of the little abandoned building they'd passed when they'd pushed Nora home. 'I'm sure Miss Pankhurst wouldn't do that,' said Beth firmly.

She wouldn't.

She *couldn't*.

'She did,' said Nora, equally firmly. 'We saw the flames from our living room and watched the firemen try and put it out. But they couldn't. It was too big.'

'But that could have been anyone,' said Beth, indignantly.

'The "anyone" scrawled *Votes for Women* on the ground outside,' said Nora. 'They also left a muff behind.'

A *muff*?

'But that could have been any women's group,' said Beth. 'And even if it was ELFS, it certainly doesn't mean that it was Miss Pankhurst.'

Personally, Beth thought that even if Miss Pankhurst had been there, she certainly wouldn't have been foolish enough to leave a muff at the scene. That was such an elementary mistake.

Miss Pankhurst would have been slick.

She would have been *clever*.

Nora sighed. 'Liza, I think she admitted to it. It was all over the papers. And I'm sure she's wonderful and inspirational but just be aware maybe you're not seeing the full picture.'

Beth grabbed the next parcel out of the basket. 'Come to the next meeting, Nora,' she said. 'Come and see and make up your own mind.'

Nora just gave a little sniff in reply.

That lunchtime, Beth was about to head over to the canteen with the others when James appeared by her side.

'It's a lovely day,' he said casually. 'I was planning to take a stroll about the park and I wondered if you would like to join me?'

Beth blinked up at him in surprise. That had come out of the blue! For a moment, she was tempted to turn down his offer; to tell him that she always went to the canteen with her friends.

But . . . why not?

What harm was there in taking a stroll around the park with him?

In fact, Beth found that she wanted to. Despite his views, he was clever and intense and just a little mysterious and Beth realised that she wanted to find out more about him.

It didn't have to mean anything.

So, she smiled up at him and said simply, 'I would like that very much.'

Despite its proximity, Beth had never ventured out into the park at lunchtime, preferring to spend the time with her friends in the canteen or under the plane trees in the compound. Now she wondered why they never went further afield. It was a little slice of normality in the midst of a world that revolved around the war. There were sweeping lawns, fine trees and borders in all their summer glory and, despite the labour shortages, everything was still somehow beautifully maintained.

Nature at its best combined with human artistry. A true tonic for the soul.

James picked a path seemingly at random. Beth had wondered if he might offer her his arm, but he didn't, so they set off together, side by side, at a comfortable stroll.

'Lovely day,' said James after a while.

Beth stifled a smile. It really wasn't a lovely day – it was cool for a summer's day and the high scudding clouds suggested it might even rain later. But James's clumsy comment suggested that he felt somewhat nervous, and that served to give Beth both confidence and a little thrill. She wasn't used to making handsome young men feel nervous and she found that she rather liked it.

But there was nothing to be gained by calling James out on the weather and making him feel even more uncomfortable so she just said demurely, 'Yes, isn't it?'

'Any news of your brother?' His eyes, she noticed, had deep green flecks among the grey.

'There isn't,' she replied. And then she checked herself. 'At least, I don't think so. Or, rather, I don't know.' Goodness, what must she sound like? 'I stayed in Bow with Milly last night so I haven't been home.'

'Ah. So, what did you think of the East End?' asked James.

'I liked it,' said Beth. 'I loved the pie down the Roman and Milly took me to see the suffragettes in action at The Mothers Arms.'

'Oh, you went to an ELFS meeting, did you?' said James. They had reached the boating lake by now, a huge, open expanse of water, and James led her over to one of the benches which dotted its banks. 'Was Miss Pankhurst there?'

'She was,' said Beth, sitting down. 'You seem to know rather a lot about these things,' she added, hoping that didn't sound rude.

'I've got a lot of time for Sylvia Pankhurst,' said James.

'I've even been known to go along to her meetings on occasion.'

'Really?'

'Yes. I think she's a remarkable woman.'

Beth clapped her hands together in pleasure. 'Oh, I couldn't agree *more*,' she said. *This* was the reaction she had been hoping for from Nora earlier on. 'I think she's marvellous. Just marvellous.'

James laughed. 'Do you?' he said. 'When we were all in the canteen together that time, you didn't seem to be too keen on the suffragettes.'

Beth frowned. 'Yes, that's true,' she said, slowly. 'But it's fair to say that I didn't really know that much about them then. I thought they were just mischief-makers and now – well, I'm not really sure what I think . . .' She trailed off, embarrassed.

How little she knew about everything.

James reached out and squeezed her hand. 'It *is* all right to change your mind about things, you know,' he said gently. 'It's how we learn and grow.'

Beth smiled at him gratefully. That had been generous of him – he could so easily have teased her about blowing with the breeze. 'I'm not sure I approve of Miss Pankhurst burning down the refreshment pavilion in this very park, though,' she said with a grin.

James squeezed her hand again. 'Maybe, just sometimes, if people really aren't listening, you need to do something to make them notice,' he said. And let her hand go.

'Yes,' said Beth slowly. 'It depends on what that something is, of course, but maybe you do.'

The conversation moved on to families. James was a grammar-school boy from Suffolk who had been doing well working for the post office in Ipswich; his mother had died two years earlier, leaving his much older father grief-stricken and bereft. James's brother Johnny had enlisted as soon as war was declared and everyone had assumed that James would do the same, 'if only to get away from the awful atmosphere at home'. Instead, James had stunned everyone by applying for a transfer to the army post office in London. 'I wanted to do my bit without actually signing up,' he said, 'but my father took it badly. Felt it reflected badly on him and the family and he's hardly spoken to me since.'

'Oh, James.' It was Beth's turn to reach out and touch his hand. 'I'm so sorry. And I know exactly what you're going through because my parents haven't spoken to me since I took the job here. They more or less made me leave home too and I'm living with my sister now. It's all just beastly.'

'You and me, both, eh?' said James softly. 'And is it worth it, Liza? Tell me, is it worth it?'

The moment stretched between them – was even, who knew, poised to become something more – when the noise of loud laughter and splashing shattered the calm. A moment later, three rowing boats full of young men and women emerged from behind an island in the middle of the lake. Beth could feel her cheeks flushing even though absolutely nothing untoward had happened between the two.

'Watch out, you're going to crash,' said James jumping to his feet and running to the bank. Beth stood up too and smoothed down her skirt. The boats were being manned by blind soldiers who were being 'supervised' by young women, who seemed to be having really rather too much fun. But their joviality was infectious and James was laughing as he put a foot out to stop one of the boats from crashing into the bank at speed. 'That was a near miss,' he called. 'We could easily have had a man or woman overboard there!'

The boat retreated with laughter and splashing and shouted thanks. Beth and James, as one, turned and headed back to the Home Depot.

'Who were they?' asked Beth.

'St Dunstan's Hostel,' said James. 'Some Lord or another has given his London house to be used by blind soldiers and sailors while they recuperate and retrain. You often see them around here, boating or walking or having tea on the lawns of the hostel and they always seem to be having a lot of fun. One of the chaps said it was almost like a marriage agency over there given the number of romances that have started up between soldiers and volunteers.'

'Goodness,' said Beth lightly. 'Sergeant Major Cunningham would be horrified to hear about all that fraternisation! But it did look like fun. Maybe I should have volunteered to work there instead!'

She knew she was being pert and provocative but somehow she just didn't care. Sometimes, Liza just wouldn't be stopped!

James was smiling at her. 'Surely you've signed up to do your bit rather than find yourself a husband?' he asked.

'Of course,' said Beth playfully. 'But there are perks to every job and it would be a shame to overlook them.'

She glanced at James with a little smile to show she was joking but he had stopped walking and was looking at her quite seriously with his head on one side. 'So you aren't stepping out with anyone?' he asked in a faux-casual voice.

There was a pause.

Liza wanted to tell him pertly that that was for her to know and for him to find out. But Beth found herself wanting to tell him the truth. Whatever the truth actually was. She'd told Milly and Nora that she was writing to a boy in the village and left it at that. But what – exactly – should she tell James?

'No. Yes. I don't know,' she said as they flashed their admission cards at the bored-looking sentry.

James turned to her. 'What does that mean—?' he started.

'Chop, chop! Men to trenches, women to benches!'

It was Milly with Nora, heading back from the canteen and smiling at them. They took Beth's arms and, laughing, started walking her back into the Home Depot. Beth, relieved that Nora wasn't upset with her after their conversation that morning, allowed herself to be marched away.

'Come and stay again next week,' said Milly.

'Come and stay with me too,' said Nora.

Beth-in-the-middle said yes to both invitations. Then she allowed herself a brief look over her shoulder to say goodbye to James, but he had gone.

Nora's house was sumptuous.

It was not a word Beth had had cause to use very often in her life but there really was no other word to describe 11 Gloucester Gate.

Sumptuous.

As Nora led her from one grand room to another, non-chalantly reeling off their names – 'morning room', 'library', 'dining room' – Beth could only marvel at the elegant propor-tions, the elaborate plasterwork, the richly textured upholstery. Most of all, it was *light*; the house was decorated throughout in a subtle palette of cream, coffee and gold, with accents of turquoise and bronze. And it could afford to be light, Beth reflected: there were electric lights throughout and so no need to mask the stains from the gas lamps with dark patterned wallpaper, like everyone else did.

Oh, it was all just glorious.

Nora, though, was dismissive. Their place in the country, in Hampshire, was much better; *it* had space to breathe and grounds to get lost in. But here, she said, it was don't touch this, don't knock that and she was always in trouble for running down the corridors, sending things flying. Daddy was worried they wouldn't be able to afford the country place after the war and that really was quite devastating. Liza would know what she meant. After all, she lived in the country.

Beth smiled to herself and didn't answer. She couldn't help thinking that her family home in Woodhampstead bore less resemblance to Nora's place in Hampshire than the Home Depot did to Buckingham Palace.

'I'm ravenous,' said Nora when the little tour was over. 'Shall we go and see what's for supper?'

Beth's tummy was rumbling too but she feared it was as much from nerves as from hunger. What was 'supper' going to require of her and was she up to the challenge? To her relief, though, there were only two places laid at one end of the huge dining table.

'Mummy and Daddy are at the Albert Hall and ate before they went out,' explained Nora. 'Clara Butt is doing a concert for some soldiers' charity – they tried to take me along but thank goodness I could say I'd already invited you over.'

Fancy!

Ma loved Clara Butt – probably because Queen Victoria had also loved her. Beth could remember all the fuss and excitement when Ma and Pa had gone to see her sing in Hertford once. They had talked about nothing else for days before or afterwards, and here was Nora brushing off the opportunity as if it was a drag!

'Where are your brothers and sisters?' asked Beth.

'Oh, they'll have eaten in the nursery already,' said Nora. She rang a little bell on the table, and moments later a young girl in a black and white uniform arrived.

'Evening, Miss Nora,' she said. 'Mrs Benham asked us to serve you just soup and the main this evening. I hope that's satisfactory.'

'Yes, of course, Sylvie,' said Nora with a smile.

Sylvie bobbed a curtsey and disappeared. She came back moments later with the richest, creamiest fish soup Beth had ever sampled, complete with little croutons and sauces to go on the top. Beth discreetly watched Nora to see what to do with them so that she didn't show herself up.

Nora kept up a steady stream of chatter about some drinks party her mother wanted to take her to that weekend in search of a husband. It all sounded absolutely ghastly and Nora looked so horrified by the whole thing that Beth couldn't help but laugh, doing her best not to drip soup down her front.

Conversation trailed off as Sylvie cleared their bowls and brought in the main course. Beth's mouth started watering as soon as she saw the platter of lamb in its caper and anchovy sauce – the very dish that Ma had served on her and Ned's eighteenth birthday. It was absolute melt-in-the-mouth heaven, of course, but how strange to have something so luxurious on what was just a run-of-the-mill Monday. Whatever must Nora eat on high-days and holidays? And the portions! Beth was full fit to burst and there was still food left on her plate. It didn't seem right somehow. Not when so many were going hungry and when food was so expensive. If only the Benhams and those like them would buy a little less, there would be more to go around. She just hoped that the leftovers got re-used or given to the servants and didn't go to waste.

'I just want to make one thing clear,' said Nora, after Beth had run out of superlatives on the food front. 'After our conversation the other morning, I want you to know that I do think votes for women is a worthy cause. It's just ELFS I'm worried about. They just seem a bit . . . militant.'

Beth sighed. 'I don't want to argue about it, Nora,' she said. 'I went to a meeting and I was really impressed, and that's all I can say about it.'

'But there are lots of other groups you could think about joining instead. My friends Daisy and Binky sometimes go along to the Women's Social and Political Union, which I know for a fact is much more patriotic even though it's run by Miss Pankhurst's mother and sister. Daisy said they changed the title of their newspaper from *The Suffragette* to *Britannia* when the war broke out, and you can't get more patriotic than that! Shouldn't we give that a try?'

Beth wiped the last bit of sauce off her plate with a piece of bread, not caring if her manners were appalling. Surely no one in their right mind would waste even a drop of sauce this sublime. Then she looked up at Nora.

'Maybe,' she said. This new group sounded very grand – Nora made it sound almost like a social club for women who lived the high life. Beth wasn't sure that she would fit in there any more than she fitted in at the East London Federation of the Suffragettes. 'I'll tell you what,' she added. 'You come along to ELFS with me and I'll come along to this other one with you.'

Nora laughed. 'You drive a hard bargain,' she said.

Later, though, in her sumptuous bedroom, Beth couldn't help sighing to herself. Was she doomed to always be in the middle, sitting on the fence, neither one thing nor the other? Not the tallest, not the shortest. Not the richest, not the poorest . . .

When and how would she know who she was meant to be?

The next morning, at breakfast, Beth met Mrs Benham for the first time. Tall and willowy like her daughter, she was helping herself to something from under a cloche on the sideboard, her back to Beth. She was wearing a silk robe with a dragon on the back, which struck Beth as the epitome of style and grace.

'Good morning,' she said turning, as Beth approached, silver tongs dangling from her fingers.

'Good morning,' replied Beth, feeling surprisingly nervous. Mrs Benham had blond hair like her daughter, but where Nora's face was open and friendly, her mother's pursed mouth and narrowed eyes looked determined to find fault with the world. Beth hazarded a guess that she wouldn't want to get on the wrong side of Nora's mother.

'Help yourself, Liza,' said Nora, already seated at the table and waving her fork around.

'Manners, darling,' said Mrs Benham, taking her plate over to the table.

Beth started opening and closing the cloches, trying not to let anything clang or clatter. My, what a choice there was! Kippers, kedgeree, sausages, bacon . . . She took a little of everything, wondering again what happened to the leftovers, and went over to sit next to Nora.

'I don't believe we've been introduced,' said Mrs Benham, her disapproval at this omission barely concealed.

'Oh, Mummy, sorry,' said Nora, hastily. 'Mummy, this is Liza Healey, who works at the Home Depot with me. Liza works in the Broken Parcel Department with me. Liza, this is my mother, Mrs Eula Benham.'

'How do you do?' said Mrs Benham and Beth parroted the same back to her.

'Liza,' said Mrs Benham, reflectively. 'Not Eliza or Lisa? Where are you from, Liza?'

'Hertfordshire, Mrs Benham,' replied Beth. She wasn't going to elaborate. She was happy to let Mrs Benham think she was from a grand country house for as long as she could get away with it.

'Indeed,' said Mrs Benham. 'And are you out?'

Drat.

She'd fallen at the very first hurdle.

Of *course* she wasn't out. No one of her acquaintance had been presented at court. Not unless you counted Lady

Alexandra at Maitland Hall . . . and she was hardly an acquaintance.

'No, Mrs Benham,' she admitted.

'Liza's family have a general provisions store in Woodhampstead,' elaborated Nora cheerfully, 'so she's absolutely fabulous at parcelling anything and everything up. She doesn't even need glue most of the time. She just has to stop herself making little handles out of the string out of habit.'

'Indeed,' said Mrs Benham again, but this time her tone was dismissive. She took a bite of her toast and then looked from one to other of the girls. 'Well, you'll both have to find husbands straight after the war,' she said. 'This working lark is all well and good but neither of you is getting any younger. Put it off much longer and you'll both end up on the shelf.'

'Oh, Mummy,' said Nora laughing. 'We're *eighteen*. Anyway, Beth is going to be all right. She already has the eye of a very dashing supervisor in the censoring department. He's frightfully important and very clever.'

Beth glanced at Nora in surprise. Is that how Nora saw it? That she 'had the eye' of James? Beth rolled this piece of information around her mind and found that she didn't mind if that was what people were thinking. She didn't mind it at all.

But, what about Sam . . . ?

'What's his surname?' Mrs Benham was saying.

'Blackford,' said Beth, shooting Nora a 'look'. 'But I really don't think—'

'The Blackfords of Carlton Hall?'

'I'm afraid I really don't know.'

Beth and Nora were still giggling as they set off across the park to work.

'I'm sorry about Mummy,' said Nora. 'At least you see what I have to put up with!'

Beth grinned. 'I think I'll have to check that James *is* a Blackford from Carlton Hall before I deign to talk to him again,' she said.

'Absolutely,' agreed Nora. 'After all, one has standards to keep up.'

'One does. But really there's nothing going on between me and James. And, of course, there's Sam . . .'

'The boy you're writing to?' Nora gave her a grin. 'Well, I think sometime soon you are going to have to make a choice between the two. Aren't you the lucky one?' She stopped and fished in her bag for her admission card. 'Right, here we are. Battle stations!'

Beth flashed her own card deep in thought.

Would she really have to make a choice between the two?

And, if so, who would she choose?

16

July slipped into August and then into September. The nights started drawing in and there was a definite nip to the air. Summer was nearly over.

'At least this place is getting a little cooler,' said Nora one Monday morning towards the end of the month, fanning herself with the letter from the parcel she was repackaging.

'It will be ruddy freezing in winter,' laughed Milly. 'Then we'll wonder what we were moaning about.'

'And I'll be travelling back to Woodhampstead in the dark pretty soon,' sighed Beth. 'That's not exactly going to be a barrel of laughs. Gosh, I hate that journey!'

'Come and stay!' cried Milly and Nora almost in unison.

Beth looked at her friends with affection. How fond she was of them both and how she had come to rely on them. In three short months they had become the closest friends she had ever had. Oh, the fun they had had and the laughs they had shared; there always seemed to be a hint of mischief – especially with Milly about.

But it wasn't all flippancy and frolics. Both girls had been kindness personified when Ned and Sam had written within a week of each other to say they were finally off to France. Ned had then written that his battalion had crossed the channel overnight from Southampton to Le Havre on board the *Empress Queen* before moving forward to the front line – but thereafter his trail went cold and she knew that he wouldn't be allowed to tell her any more. And, despite his continued letters, she had no idea where Sam was or what he was doing. There had been almost no action on the Western Front all summer – but who knew when that was going to change. The newspapers certainly seemed to think that something was imminent and there was suddenly a permanent lead weight in her chest. When it all got too much, she could confide her worries with her friends. Sometimes she didn't even have to do that; both seemed to instinctively know when she was feeling at odds with the world and whether to offer a listening ear, a kind gesture or a silly joke.

She found herself getting closer and closer to James as well, both bound together by the fact they had brothers at the front as well as parents who disapproved of what they were doing. They took a turn around the Regent's Park a couple of times a week and put the world to rights, bemoaning how intransigent the older generation could be . . .

Because if Beth had hoped that her parents' attitude towards her would mellow once Ned left for France, she would have been sorely mistaken. It was now well over three months since she had started work at the Home Depot and she had barely spoken to either Ma or Pa since. And that hurt. It hurt a lot. Sally was lovely but she missed the family home, she missed her parents' love and support, missed helping in the shop and her own bedroom in the eaves. She even missed her mother's many references to Queen Victoria. In her darkest moments, she wondered if she would ever speak to her parents again. But then she told herself not to be so melodramatic and reminded herself of all she was doing to help the war effort.

It was worth it. It had to be . . .

Meanwhile, Milly and Nora were both staring at her and waiting for an answer.

'Well, I'd love to come and stay with both of you,' said Beth. 'I think Milly said it marginally more quickly, so I shall come and stay with you first . . .'

'Come tomorrow,' said Milly.

'Come to mine next week,' added Nora.

'Nora. Milly. I need to speak to you straightaway.' It was Miss Parker, poring over her clipboard.

Milly and Nora exchanged a glance. 'Of course, Miss Parker,' they said, getting to their feet and brushing their skirts down.

Milly made a little rueful face to Beth as she was led away and Beth couldn't help but wonder what her friend had done wrong this time. As far as Beth could tell, both girls were blameless – they weren't late, they both had their admission cards and neither of them had been smoking on the premises. Nora didn't smoke at all!

'And Liza, if you could go and help with the next unloading,' said Miss Parker over her shoulder. 'Take a couple of the new recruits with you. Mrs Harper and Mrs Peters, would you go with Miss Healey, here, please? She will show you what to do.'

Unloading duties so early in the day! And without either of her best friends to help her. Still, it couldn't be helped. Beth smiled at the two women Miss Parker had pointed out.

'If you'd like to come with me, ladies,' she said, getting to her feet.

Mrs Harper stood up at once and returned Beth's smile. 'Right you are,' she said. 'Lead on, MacDuff!'

Mrs Peters seemed far more reluctant. She had a face like thunder as she hauled herself to her feet. Tall and broad in the beam, she glowered at Beth through heavy brows. 'You're awfully young to be working here,' she said, apropos of nothing. 'You're younger than my daughter. Why, you can't be a day over twenty.'

'I'm eighteen,' said Beth, weaving through the tables. There was no point in hiding it, although she knew it might antagonise Mrs Peters even more. 'Now, when we get to the unloading bay, the men will lower the sacks down from the lorry to us. We put them into baskets and—'

'That sounds like awfully heavy work,' came Mrs Peters's voice from behind her. 'I thought I was here to patch up parcels. Can't the men do the heavy lifting?'

Beth sighed to herself. 'We're here precisely because the men *can't* do it,' she said, trying to keep the tinge of impatience from her voice. 'It's hard work but we're certainly up to it. If we take turns, help each other out and all do our bit, I assure you we'll be just fine.'

'That's the spirit!' said Mrs Harper stoutly.

Mrs Peters just grunted, but at least she didn't argue. But when they arrived at the unloading bay, Beth's heart sank again. Standing at the back of the lorry, waiting to pass down the bags, was Misery-Man.

Beth gave him a wary smile and clapped her hands. 'Mrs Harper, Mrs Peters, this gentleman will lower the sacks down to us. Grab them with both hands and put them into this basket; it's on casters so make sure they are secure or the basket will run away from you.'

'Good morning, young man,' said Mrs Harper cheerfully. 'I didn't catch your name.'

'George Bateman,' said Misery-Man.

Well, that was useful to know. Maybe Beth should have asked before now.

'How do you do, Mr Bateman?' said Mrs Harper. 'Go easy on us new girls, won't you?'

To Beth's surprise, Misery-Man – George – smiled at Mrs Harper and sketched a little salute. 'How do, Mrs Harper?' he said. 'Just make sure you keep your back straight and you'll be dandy.'

Mrs Harper nodded and smiled, Mrs Peters just grunted and Beth stepped forward for the first sack.

'See you've got yourself some new recruits,' murmured George.

'Yes,' said Beth. 'Thanks for being nice to them.'

'Oh, I don't mind the old sticks,' said George handing down the first sack. 'They won't want to hang around when the war's over. It's you young'uns we've got a problem with. Coming here, taking our jobs . . .'

Beth concentrated on taking the weight of the sack and didn't answer.

But, as she manoeuvred the sack into the basket, she acknowledged that George had a point. She had never asked herself what she wanted to do when the war was over. At the moment, it felt as though it would never end, but end it must at some point – and then what? Did she want to keep on working at the Home Depot, even if it meant that Ma and Pa would never speak to her again, or would she be happy to go back to Woodhampstead with her tail between her legs and carry on working in the shop? Beth found that she did not have an immediate answer . . .

Nora and Milly didn't come back to the Broken Parcel Department all morning.

Beth carried on repairing parcels and showing the new women the ropes, but she was growing increasingly concerned. Where were they? What on earth could Miss Parker possibly want with them all this time? Or had they both suddenly been struck down by the flu that was doing the rounds? When Beth went off to the bathroom, she had a good look around to see if she could spot either of them, but there was no sign.

At morning break, Beth fairly ran over to the canteen. Her eyes scanned the chattering crowds through the smoky haze and . . . there they both were, over at a little table by the window and waving enthusiastically at her. Thank goodness for that. With a smile on her face, Beth wound her way through the tables and over to join them. To her pleasure, she saw that there was a cup and saucer and a jammy bun already waiting for her.

'And what happened to you two this morning?' she asked, before taking a huge mouthful of the jammy creation. 'Loitering by the bike sheds? Crafty cigarette out the back? Dressing down from Sergeant Major Cunningham?'

'None of the above,' said Nora with a smile.

'We've been promoted,' added Milly with an altogether more exuberant grin.

Oh!

Oh!

Beth looked from one to the other in confusion. Promoted to what, exactly?

And . . . why hadn't she been promoted too?

No, Beth! Be happy for your friends.

'That's wonderful,' she said warmly. 'And what exactly are you going to be doing?'

'Oh, Liza,' said Nora reaching out and taking her hand. 'It's not really a promotion. Because so many people have been taken ill with the flu, the Returned Letters Department is really short of workers so Milly and I have been drafted in to help out. I'm not even sure if it's permanent.'

Beth clearly hadn't been as successful with her I'm-so-happy-for-you-face as she'd hoped.

Because it *was* a promotion. Or, at least, it sounded like one.

Everyone knew that when a soldier died, any letters that had been written to him were returned to the sender – but only after the official telegram from the War Office had been released. The Home Depot was meant to hold on to all returned letters until they had confirmation the telegram had been delivered, but things occasionally went wrong and, when they did, newspapers and public opinion had been far from sympathetic. Who wanted to find out a love one had been killed by your letter to them being returned 'killed in action'? Plans were in hand to send all the returned letters on to the War Office itself precisely to make sure that things like this didn't happen but, in the meantime, it was down to the men – and women – of the Home Depot to keep things on track.

It was down to girls like Nora and Milly.

'Well, permanent or not, I'm thrilled for you,' she said firmly.

And she was, she really was. It was an important role – there was no doubt about *that* – and it was wonderful that her friends had been picked to fill it.

But why hadn't she been chosen as well? Had she done something wrong? Was she not seen as having a sensible head on her, of being a safe pair of hands?

Or was it because she didn't have an important uncle or one in the post office to petition for her? Was it because, despite her attempts to reinvent herself as Liza, she was still just plain old Beth Healey, a nobody from Woodhampstead – and always would be?

Oh, Beth.

Stop being such a sourpuss. Stop feeling so sorry for yourself. It's not your friends' fault they've been chosen and you haven't.

It's yours.

So, she smiled very determinedly and said 'good luck.'

And headed back to the Broken Parcel Department alone.

Beth found that she missed Milly and Nora.

She missed them a lot.

It wasn't that anyone in the Broken Parcel Department was particularly nasty or unfriendly – although Mrs Peters was more than a bit trying. It was just that she, Milly and

Nora had been thick as thieves – maybe to the exclusion of everyone else. Maybe they should have made a bit more of an effort with the other girls. Maybe then she wouldn't feel like she was on the outside looking in, the unpopular girl hovering on the edge of the playground.

Still, she had a job to do and she was going to continue to do it to the best of her ability. It was time to get her head down and get on with it.

Miss Parker called for her mid-afternoon.

'I expect you're wondering what on earth is going on?' she said without preamble.

Beth smiled. She had always liked Miss Parker. 'Yes, miss. I mean, no miss. A little, miss,' she said.

Now Miss Parker was smiling too. 'Well, I won't keep you in suspense any longer,' she said. 'As the Broken Parcel Department is growing so rapidly, we need to change the management structure to cope with it. And I would like to make you one of my three supervisors.'

Beth was so surprised she didn't know how to respond. She gulped a couple of times, felt herself blushing scarlet and looked around the small office in confusion.

'You look surprised,' said Miss Parker gently.

'Well, *yes*,' said Beth, finding her voice at last.

She, Beth Healey, an eighteen-year-old shop girl from Woodhampstead, far from being overlooked, was being put into a supervisory role after only three months at the Home Depot. And when she felt she had only just scraped into the position to boot. Of course, she was surprised.

She was blooming amazed!

Wait until Ma and Pa heard about this.

If only . . .

Miss Parker was still speaking. 'You must know that we've been very impressed with you,' she said. 'Not only have you proved yourself a fast and efficient worker, you have a natural authority about you and you have commanded the respect of everyone you work with. The way you dealt with Mrs Peters this morning, for example – not the easiest of characters, I know – shows that you are ready for more responsibility. I think you will rise to the challenge with aplomb.'

'Thank you!'

Miss Parker stood up and started pacing around the small office. 'I hope I can trust you to be discreet about this, but my one worry about promoting you was the close friendships you've formed with Miss Benham and Miss Woods,' she said. Beth was about to interrupt in defence of her friends but Miss Parker held up her hand. 'I'm saying nothing against either of them,' she said. 'Both are most admirable in their own ways. But they are not right or ready for promotion in this department and I did worry how they might react to you being elevated into a position of authority above them. Hence the move to the Returned Letters Department. No, don't interrupt; I can see that you are about to be indignant on their behalf. Let me reassure you that we genuinely are in need of extra workers in the Returned Letters Department both due to the recent influenza outbreak and the – ah – increased volume of letters we are expecting to be returned. The latter, I fear, is something that will only get worse in the next couple of weeks. It's a very important role and a good move for both of them.'

'Yes, miss,' said Beth, her thoughts racing.

'So then, what is your answer?' asked Miss Parker.

Beth was about to trot out, 'Yes, miss – of course, miss,' when something made her hesitate. Something that told her she could be totally honest with Miss Parker. 'I'm ever so honoured to have been chosen,' she said. 'But I'm worried I won't be able to do it! I mean, how many women will I be responsible for, miss? And what exactly will I have to do?'

'You will be responsible for four tables, Liza,' said Miss Parker. 'That's thirty-two women, most – as you know – considerably older than yourself. You will be responsible for supervising the loading and unloading of the lorries, managing the workload and keeping to target, managing any staff issues, checking the quality of the work, dealing with any obvious contraband or censorship issues—'

'But I'm just a shop girl,' burst out Beth with something that was almost a laugh. 'I'm used to weighing out the butter and bagging up the tea—'

Miss Parker smiled. 'And do you think that *I* was born to this sort of work?' she asked. 'Do you think I grew up managing a team of several hundred women in the army post office?'

Beth hesitated and thought about it. She had, she realised, never given any thought to what Miss Parker might have done or not done before the war. Like Beth's teachers at school, Miss Parker was just *there* and always had been there. She probably failed to exist once she stepped outside the Home Depot building!

Miss Parker didn't wait for an answer. 'I was a student at the Royal Academy of Arts,' she said. Beth's face must have been a picture because Miss Parker started laughing again. 'I can see that's surprised you,' she said. 'I don't mind admitting that I was quite well regarded for my watercolours and my oils weren't bad either. But, of course, the war put paid to all that and, anyway, I was anxious to do my bit. But that's not what matters now. What matters is that I saw something in you as soon as you came for that interview at the King Edward Building and Sergeant Major Cunningham was so, er . . . *challenging*, shall we say? I saw a quiet determination to help – yes, of course – but also to succeed. Not to take no for an answer. You commute a long way in each day and I obviously have no idea how much support you have at home, but I'm sure it hasn't always been easy for you. Don't underestimate yourself, Liza. And don't underestimate women in general. Just because you've been a shop girl – just because we haven't had these opportunities before – don't think we can't do things just as well as a man and that we aren't deserving of the same opportunities.'

Beth didn't reply for a moment.

Why, Miss Parker almost sounded like Miss Pankhurst. Almost like a suffragette.

Beth realised that she didn't mean that as an insult or a slight – but as a compliment. After all, why shouldn't women have the vote and the same chances as men?

Why *shouldn't* they?

'I would be very happy to take on the role,' said Beth stoutly. 'I promise to perform my duties to the very best of my abilities.'

'I know you will, Liza,' said Miss Parker with a smile. 'You will start your new position on Wednesday.'

Beth couldn't wait to tell Sally the news that evening. She fairly ran from the station to the little cottage, too fired up even to worry about bumping into Ma and Pa.

'I have news,' she announced, bursting through the front door and throwing her hat onto the stand. 'You'll never guess what's happened!'

Sally was in the kitchen as usual. She gave a little grunt and poured Beth a cup of tea.

'I've had the most extraordinary day,' said Beth, throwing herself back against the cushions. 'Nora – I've mentioned her, the upper-class one, whose uncle is in charge of the whole Home Depot, if you please – and Milly – the one from the East End who doesn't believe in the war – well, they've been moved to the Returned Letters Department and—'

Sally sat down heavily into a chair and held up her hand. 'Beth—'

'Liza—'

'*Beth*,' repeated Sally, firmly. 'Can you just stop talking please – just stop! – for one *minute*?'

Her tone was sharp and it took Beth by surprise. It was unlike Sally to talk to her like that. And it was unfair too – Beth had important news and it wasn't her fault that Sally was stuck in Woodhampstead with not very much to do. Maybe her sister was jealous.

'I've not finished,' she replied, a trifle tartly. 'And I don't see—'

'Beth,' said Sally, more loudly this time. 'Reggie's missing in action. He went over the top with the rest of them and then . . . nothing.'

Beth's mind started churning. 'Over the top?' she repeated stupidly. 'Over the top where? There aren't any battles going at the moment where they are.'

'There are now,' said Sally, dully. 'A place called Loos. Huge battle. Tremendous casualties . . .'

Icy water ran down Beth's spine.

Reggie.

Bertie's brother.

Sally's brother-in-law.

An image of Reggie popped into her head. A good four years older than Beth, they had of course paid each other absolutely no attention at school. He still didn't pay her any attention, even though his younger brother had married her older sister, but he'd at least nod at her if they passed in the street. He'd never been much for talking, had Reggie. He was tall and gangly with mousy, curly hair, a high forehead and a smile that showed as much gum as teeth. He'd always been utterly unremarkable except that he had a passion for golf and as soon as he was able, he'd started hanging around the golf courses on the outskirts of town, picking up lost balls and selling them back to the clubhouse. Then he'd started doing caddying around his shifts in the pub and he had become, by all accounts, a pretty useful player.

No, Beth.

Not 'had'.

He was missing in action, not dead.

Sally was still talking. 'So, if you don't mind, Beth, we'll have no more talk about people who might or might not believe in the war. Not tonight. Because, while it's lovely for them to have a choice, a lot of young men are putting their lives on the line for their country and those are the people I want to think about tonight. And if Reginald is missing in action, what about Bertie? They're in the same regiment. Oh Beth, what about Bertie?'

For a moment, Beth was stunned into silence. Then she got up and knelt at Sally's feet, putting her head into her sister's lap.

'I'm sorry,' she said. 'I'm so sorry. But it doesn't necessarily mean . . .'

It didn't mean Reginald had died.

People sometimes really were just missing. And then they were found. Anything could happen in the confusion of war.

But more often . . .

More often . . .

It took a while, but finally Sally wrapped her arms around Beth and the two girls rocked together in silence.

Beth found that she was thinking, not of Reggie, but of Ned and Sam who may well also be going over the top to an equally uncertain future.

And then she cried.

For all of them.

For the whole ruddy topsy-turvy world and for the war, of which there seemed to be no end in sight.

17

Beth had wondered if she should postpone her stay at Milly's the next evening and go back to Woodhampstead instead to support Sally, but she decided against it. There was no more news of Reginald. Beth knew that they might not hear anything for weeks. They might not hear anything at all. Everyone knew that was the grim reality of the situation.

She had read the newspaper from cover to cover and looked at Sally's atlas, trying to work out where Loos was. It was a tiny village suddenly thrust centre-stage. She had no way of knowing if Ned or Sam were stationed nearby.

So, she packed an overnight bag and headed into London for her last day before she became a supervisor.

Miss Parker announced her promotion to the team and Beth was relieved to see that the news was well received. There were smiles and words of congratulations and even a little ripple of applause. Only Mrs Peters looked less than pleased, her mouth so pursed that her lips looked in danger of disappearing. Beth realised there may trouble brewing from that quarter but hopefully she would at least be allowed to find her feet.

Beth, of course, gave a very edited version of her new position to Milly and Nora. Over buns in the canteen, she told them that she had been promoted and what her new role entailed, but of course she made no mention of the fact Miss Parker had effectively moved the two of them to clear her path. Instead, she went out of her way to imply that all three of them had been equally promoted and that perhaps Milly and Nora's change in circumstances was much more impressive than hers. But she needn't have worried as Nora and Milly seemed so excited about their new jobs that it didn't seem to occur to them to think otherwise.

Milly and Beth went straight to Milly's house that evening as there was no ELFS meeting. Milly's mother and her sister Alice had again already left for their shift at the munitions factory and Mr Wildermuth was presumably still out at the bakery, but Milly's youngest sister Caroline and her brother Charlie were both at home and her older sister Margaret was paying a visit with her plump toddler, Arthur.

As soon as Milly arrived home, she took her younger siblings off to the shops to pick up a few bits and bobs for tea. She insisted Beth stay behind, so Beth sat and chatted to Margaret in the kitchen. Margaret looked like a faded, washed-out version of Milly – all the looks, none of the sparkle – and Arthur, cute as a button with the Woods' trademark curly dark hair, was sitting on the hearth rug, grizzling.

'Teethin',' said Margaret, as Arthur attempted to jab one fat fist into his mouth. 'You can always tell by them bright red cheeks. Seems to have been going on forever this time, though. One breaks through, we get a week's rest and then he starts up again. Poor little bugger.'

'Yes, the poor thing,' said Beth, touching Arthur's other little hand and marvelling at the tiny fingers and even smaller nails. Teething troubles or not, it would be lovely to have a baby in the family – but the war had, of course, put all that on hold along with everything else. Not for herself, of course – she had no intention of marrying for a while even if anyone would have her. Even if . . . and here she paused because alongside the usual picture of Sam, James popped into her mind.

'You're the girl what lives miles away, ain't yer?' said

Margaret suddenly, reaching down and pulling Arthur onto her lap.

'I am,' said Beth, firmly banishing such thoughts of James. 'I live in Hertfordshire so I'm very grateful to Milly for putting me up like this. It can be a two-hour journey each way.'

'That's a lot of travelling,' agreed Margaret, running a finger through one of her son's curls. 'Ain't there any suitable employment up where you're from?'

Beth hesitated. 'I don't know,' she admitted. 'Someone recommended the Home Depot to me and I felt like it would be a good way of lending a hand and doing my bit. I'm actually really enjoying it.'

Margaret nodded. 'Yeah, Milly's been full of it all. Talks non-stop about you, she does. You and the other one – the hoity-toity one – what's her name?'

'Nora,' said Beth.

'Yes, that's right. Nora. To be honest, we've all been that pleased she took the job. Seems to have settled her down something proper after all the trouble last year.'

Beth sat forward, puzzled. 'Trouble?' she said. 'What sort of trouble?'

Margaret gave a little snort. 'I'd have thought she'd have told you all. The trouble with ELFS. Got herself into a right little pickle, did our Milly.'

Beth shook her head. 'I had no idea,' said Beth. 'I mean, she took me to a meeting at The Mothers Arms, but it was all very respectable. Very impressive, actually.'

'Oh, yes.' Margaret pulled out a hanky and wiped Arthur's nose and mouth vigorously. 'They do a lot of good work nowadays. Of course, you'll know that I work at their toy factory up Norman Grove and Arthur here is in their nursery, so I won't have a bad word said about them. But before the war, things was a bit different. They was much more militant then, of course – and there's some that says that weren't a bad thing when no one's listening to you – but some who should have known better took it too far and dragged our Milly along with them.'

'Really?' Beth found she was not very surprised. And then, 'I hope you don't mind me saying so, but I can't imagine Milly being dragged into something she didn't want to do.'

Margaret laughed. 'You're right there,' she said. 'You've got the measure of our Milly, no doubt about that! But she were only sixteen or so. And arson, public mischief, hunger-striking, force-feeding . . . those aren't the sort of things that anyone should be encouraging a child to get involved with, no matter how fiery and sure of herself she might seem. No, there's some at ELFS should be thoroughly ashamed of themselves. I'm real glad Miss Pankhurst saw fit to put in a good word for Milly up at the Home Depot when it looked like her record might stop her getting a decent job anywhere at all.'

'Wait!' Beth was thoroughly confused. 'I thought she – you – had an uncle who worked for the post office.'

'We do,' said Margaret. 'Uncle Eddie. Helps out in a little post office over East Ham way. But what's he got to do with anything?'

Beth wrinkled her nose. 'I . . . thought Milly had got the job at the Home Depot because she worked for him and he'd recommended her,' she said.

Margaret laughed. 'I don't think those people would listen to anything that Eddie Woods might say. Anyway, he hasn't had a good word to say about Milly since he caught her nicking sweets from his shop when she was twelve. I don't think he'd recommend her for anything!'

'But Milly *said* . . .' Beth trailed off. What exactly *was* it that Milly had said? She tried to recall. Milly had definitely said she had an uncle who worked in the post office. Maybe

Beth had just *presumed* that he had been the one who had got Milly the job at the Home Depot. Maybe she'd got totally the wrong end of the stick.

Anyway, it didn't matter a jot.

Except, Beth realised with a little glow of pride that – if you didn't count Sam – she had been the only one of the three to have got the job entirely on her own merits.

And that made her feel really rather good.

Beth was exhausted by bedtime and nothing, not even the hubbub of a full household, was going to stop her from sleeping that night.

Beth was bunked in with Milly again. She snuggled down. There was a streetlight right outside the window, shining a shaft of light across her face, but it didn't look as if the curtains would meet in the middle even if she padded across the room to give them a tug. She would just have to make the best of it. Tomorrow she started her new role. It was more important than ever to get a good night's sleep . . .

BOOM!

Beth woke with a start, thoroughly disoriented. What on earth had that been?

A loud, resonant bang, not near but not too far away either. Had she dreamt it? She'd certainly been at the front, ducking and diving across no-man's-land, dodging the shells, looking for Ned, looking for Sam . . .

But Milly had woken too and was sitting bolt upright in bed beside her.

A storm? A clap of thunder?

'A Zeppelin,' hissed Milly, jumping out of bed. And then more loudly, calling to the others, 'Quickly everyone. Zeppelin raid! To your places. Now!'

Beth was out of bed without registering how she had got there, her shawl pulled tight around her shoulders. The clock on the mantel said just after two o'clock. She followed Milly out of the bedroom and into the narrow hallway, pausing while Milly shook her brother and sister awake. Then the little gang trooped downstairs together. It was all surprisingly calm – grumbles of irritation rather than whimpers of fear – but Beth found her mouth was dry and that her heart was in her throat. This sort of thing had happened before in London but it was unheard of in Woodhampstead and, if she was being totally honest with herself, it was scary.

Really scary.

At the bottom of the stairs, the parlour door was open and a good-looking blond man was standing in the entrance in a silk dressing gown. 'Come on, Charlie,' he said in barely accented English. 'We know the drill, don't we? By the time we've counted backwards from ten thousand in sevens, it will be all over.'

The two younger children disappeared happily enough and Beth couldn't help but wonder at the irony of their being protected by a German while his countrymen attempted to bomb them all to pieces.

Too strange to contemplate.

'Off you go, Caroline,' said Milly, pushing her other sister towards the kitchen. 'Under the table. Liza and I will be there in a mo.'

Why not now? thought Beth wildly. Why the *dickens* not now? She didn't want to be standing there totally exposed in the middle of the passage in her nightie when the next bombs started falling!

And what was Milly doing now?

Opening the front door, that was what. Honestly, was the girl stark staring mad?

Mad or not, Milly had slipped outside. She was standing outside on the front path, hugging her shawl around her and beckoning for Beth to join her. 'Come and take a look,' she whispered, one finger to her lips.

Against her better – or indeed, *any* – judgement, Beth tiptoed outside to join her friend. The flagstones were icy under her bare feet; she hadn't thought to put on her slippers as Milly had done. She glanced around. All around, people were peering out of windows, standing in front gardens or out in the road. All were staring upwards in the same direction.

Milly followed their gaze and there it was. A menacing, sinuous airship a mile or so away towards the centre of London. It was slipping slowly and silently across the sky towards them and Beth was struck by how low it was – only a few hundred yards above the ground. In its wake, the glow of several fires stained the night sky. Further away, to the west, two more airships were faintly illuminated by search-lights and were hovering with ghastly intent, shells bursting below them.

'It's at the Tower, or thereabouts,' said the woman next door, clutching a sleeping baby to her chest and pointing to the nearest ship. 'And it's heading towards the docks. It'll miss us, I'm sure . . .'

'The munitions factories, though,' said Milly, one hand shielding her eyes. 'Ma! Alice!'

The woman shook her head. 'More like Woolwich,' she said. 'But it'll bolt for home now it's had a good go at us, you mark my words.'

'I hope so, Mary,' said Milly. 'But maybe I should—'

'Maybe you should nothing, Milly,' said Mary, her voice sharp. 'You'll not go haring off to the factory and you'll not go down to the Tower to help. Your ma will have your guts for garters – mine too, if I let you hare off on a fool's errand. Your place is at home looking after your brother and sisters. Your friend'll tell you the same, won't you, love?'

Beth realised Mary was talking to her and tore her eyes

from the sky. She found she was struggling with a mix of emotions. There was horror and fear, certainly, to see the Angels of Death so close by. But now she realised they weren't in imminent danger, there was also a (totally inappropriate, she knew) thrill of excitement.

You didn't get this in Woodhampstead!

This was living!

This was *really* living.

Maybe they should go and help. Maybe they should leave right away.

Then she caught herself. The neighbour was right. She turned to Milly. 'Yes,' she said. 'We've got to stay here and look after the others.'

'I suppose you're right,' Milly said reluctantly. 'But at least we've got time to brew up and play some cards before any of them buggers come within striking distance of us.'

Nodding a goodnight to Mary, the two girls went inside, made some tea and took it under the table. It seemed ages later that Mr Wildermuth knocked on the kitchen door and told them it was all clear. They got to their feet, stiff and cold and crampy and eventually, having settled the younger ones back to sleep, Beth and Milly were finally able to do the same.

Although now, of course, Beth couldn't sleep. She lay there stiffly next to a gently snoring Milly until the cold grey light of dawn crept through the gap in the curtains – and only then, naturally, did she sleep the sleep of the dead.

Beth woke woolly-brained and foggy-minded.

Two seconds later she was out of bed. She was a leader of women. The Broken Parcel Department and the army post office – make that the *country* – needed her. Sleep or no sleep, she couldn't let any of them down.

The stand at Bow Road Underground Station had already

sold out of newspapers, but from snippets of conversations overheard on the Tube, Beth managed to piece together what had happened.

'. . . Dozens dead, they're saying. Gawd only knows how many injured . . .'

'. . . Those poor souls . . .'

'. . . It smashed the ancient stained-glass of the chapel . . .'

'. . . Awful damage to the City . . .'

Milly nudged Beth. 'That's the one we must have heard,' she said. 'About two miles away – straight along the Bow Road.'

Goodness.

Two miles at home was *nothing*.

Two miles would take you to Maitland Hall or to the watercress beds where Bertie worked or the pub on the Luton Road that his parents ran. Beth personally knew many, many people who lived two miles away from home and a Zeppelin raid at that distance would be huge news – a life-defining moment. But in London, of course, it was different. Thousands and thousands of people lived between Milly's house in Bow and the poor souls two miles away. You couldn't compare it at all.

'Oh bugger. I can't find my admission card,' said Milly, changing the subject abruptly. She started rummaging ever more frantically in her handbag. 'I'm sure it was in here,' she muttered pulling out various items. Her purse, her ticket, a hanky, her lipstick and compact, her keys . . .

No card.

'Don't worry,' said Beth reassuringly. Annoying though it was, it hardly compared to being bombed! 'I'm sure it's at home somewhere.'

'Maybe,' said Milly. 'Or maybe I left it in the office at work. Either way, Miss Parker and Sergeant Major Cunningham are going to haul me over the coals.'

'No, they won't,' said Beth. 'You might get a ticking off, but what's new?'

Milly grimaced back. 'That's why I'm afraid they might dismiss me,' she said.

'I expect they'll just be glad you're reporting for duty the morning after a raid. We're bound to be short-staffed.'

Milly grunted and returned to her rummaging, but she still hadn't found the errant card by the time the Tube squealed to a halt at Portland Road Station. The two girls set off around the side of the park together, Milly grumbling that her days at the Depot were numbered.

'It's all going to be perfectly fine,' said Beth reassuringly. 'They know you on the gate and, anyway, I'll be with you to vouch for you.'

And Beth was right. Milly didn't even need to sweet talk the soldier on duty to let her in. He just made a note on a form, got her signature and waved her in.

Beth hurried over to the Broken Parcel Department.

This was it.

She was a supervisor. Time to rise to the challenge and make her mark.

As Beth had predicted, numbers were well down that morning.

Even when all the stragglers had been accounted for, Beth counted fully ten women in her 'section' who had not yet reported for duty. It wasn't surprising: while her journey from the East End had run smoothly enough, not all the Underground lines were running as regular a service and, of course, many omnibus routes would have been badly affected.

Beth set to work with a confidence she suddenly didn't feel. Oh, she was sure she could handle the work – it wasn't particularly taxing – but she was much younger than just about everyone else in her team. How were these women –

most of them mothers, two already *grand*mothers – going to react to being given orders by an eighteen-year-old slip of a girl from Hertfordshire?

She needn't have worried.

The women settled down to work happily enough, a couple even congratulating Beth on her promotion. And if one or two made a point of suggesting that Beth had only been given the role because she had been working at the Home Depot longer than the others, then so be it. Maybe they were right. Either way, they went to load and unload the delivery trucks when Beth asked them to and didn't – noticeably, at least – grumble when she asked one or two to redo some shoddy repackaging.

It was going to be all right.

And then Mrs Peters arrived.

A Mrs Peters who was loud, complaining and even more out of sorts than normal.

'I didn't get a wink of sleep last night,' were the first words she said to Beth. 'Those bombs! Those airships! The wicked, wicked Germans. I was frightened for my life. It's a wonder I'm here at all but I thought, "I've got to do my duty. I can't let King and Country down".'

Beth swallowed a sigh. Honestly! Mrs Peters was nearly two hours late and, from the way she was talking, you would think she was the only person who had seen a Zeppelin last night. And Beth knew for a fact Mrs Peters lived in Kensal Rise, further even from any of the airships than Beth had been.

What to do?

What on earth to do?

For a moment, Beth was tempted just to usher Mrs Peters to her seat – even to thank her for coming in to work, as the older woman clearly expected. Anything for an easy life! But then she pushed her shoulders firmly back and lifted her chin. No! That wouldn't do at all. If she let Mrs Peters get away with this sort of behaviour now, goodness knew what she would be like in the days and weeks ahead. No. Beth would have to stamp her authority on the situation right here and right now.

'Were you out helping last night, Mrs Peters?' Beth asked pleasantly.

It was only fair to check the facts. After all, if Mrs Peters *had* been up all night tending injuries or pulling people from the rubble, or even making cups of tea for terrified neighbours, then surely the Home Depot could afford to be lenient about today's tardiness.

'Well, no,' blustered Mrs Peters. 'I was down in the basement as we are all meant to be. But the worry. Oh, my dear, the worry. My daughter in Cambridge is in the family way and . . .'

Beth barely suppressed her sigh this time. Over Mrs Peters's shoulder, she could see members of her team looking over with interest. The moment hung, as pregnant as Mrs Peters's daughter. What Beth did now *mattered*.

It mattered a lot.

'Mrs Peters, if you'd like to come with me,' said Beth, gesturing towards the supervisor's office which she now had access to.

'No, dear,' said Mrs Peters. 'I'm sure you can have nothing to say to me that you can't say in front of all of us.'

Oh!

Those words were a direct challenge to her authority if ever Beth had heard one. It was emphasised the more by Mrs Peters's disrespecting tone and the totally inappropriate endearment. Beth knew she had to act fast.

'Very well, then,' she said, drawing herself up to her full height – still a good four inches below Mrs Peters's. 'As you were late today for no good reason, I would like you to make up the lost time during breaks this week. You reported for duty two hours late today so I would like you work an extra half an hour each break from today until the end of the week.'

There was a deathly silence. You could have heard a mouse in the stack of parcels squeak. Then Mrs Peters's mouth opened and Beth braced herself.

'How dare you?' she bellowed. 'I'm not taking orders from a slip of a thing like you!'

'I think you'll find you have to,' said Beth calmly. She grasped her hands in front of her so that Mrs Peters couldn't see they were shaking and hoped that the slight quaver in her voice wouldn't give her away.

'Stuff and nonsense,' cried Mrs Peters. 'Let's see what Miss Parker has to say about this, shall we? Because I rather think she'll agree with me, my girl, and then where will that leave you?'

Beth opened her mouth to reply, but Mrs Peters had gone, pushing past her rudely. Beth turned her back to her gawping team so that they couldn't see her flaming cheeks and took a couple of deep breaths to calm herself down. Then she fixed her face into what she hoped was a composed – nay, *serene* – expression, and turned back around.

'Right, back to work, everyone,' she said, clapping her hands lightly and hoping against hope that no one would think to contradict her.

Everyone turned back to work.

A couple were smiling.

18

By lunchtime, Beth was exhausted but quietly jubilant. Mrs Peters had returned from raising a stink with Miss Parker and looked really quite cowed and crestfallen. Not another word was spoken on the subject throughout the morning shift but, when the other women cheerfully packed up shop for their midday meal, Mrs Peters stayed in her seat and carried on with her work, though slamming down the glue and cutting the canvas with much more force than was entirely necessary.

So, despite her lack of sleep, there was a spring in Beth's step as she set out across the park with James for their arranged walk that lunchtime. She'd had her first real test as supervisor – somewhat earlier than she might have hoped – and she had come up trumps.

James, though, seemed out of sorts. He barely said a word as the two set off on their usual route across the lawns, and his face was set and stern.

'I spent last night with Milly in Bow,' said Beth, brightly.

James turned to her with a wry smile. 'Ah. Then you must have been kept awake as well?'

'Oh, yes – rather!' said Beth. 'We spent most of it under the table in the kitchen. How about you? Were you affected?'

'Yes. Cupboard under the stairs. Well, that was after I'd gone to see if I could help the poor sods whose lodgings got a direct hit.'

'Oh no, James,' said Beth, laying a hand on his arm and

then removing it quickly, lest he thought her forward. 'You got caught up in the last Zeppelin raid as well, didn't you? The one the night before I had my interview.'

'Yes,' said James. He reached out and took her hand, tucking it into the crook of his arm. 'Jerry must be after me.'

'Don't be silly,' said Beth, trying to ignore the thrill of his touch. 'It does seem awfully bad luck though.'

'Doesn't it?' said James. 'I'm going to have to move again, I think. My building is all right, but the whole area's taken a terrible pounding. They're opening lodgings near here for supervisors at the Depot and I'm hoping I might get a place. I don't mind admitting I feel a trifle shaky and I was glad we'd arranged to walk together today. Just the thing to calm my nerves.'

'Thank you,' said Beth. She took a deep breath. 'The whole thing is just so awful, isn't it? And now the new battles in France. My sister's brother-in-law is missing in action and of course everyone is frantic with worry.'

'I'm so sorry,' said James. 'It's a rum business – I dread to think what's happening over there. I don't know what I'd do if anything like that happened to my brother. It'll be a fine day when this bloody war is finally over one way or another.'

Beth paused. Then she said, 'Amen to that,' adding, 'When the war is *won*,' under her breath. She couldn't wish the war to end in defeat, not even if it saved lives. She just couldn't. Not quite yet.

The two had reached their usual bench near the boating lake. The blind servicemen were boating again, having a hoot with the female volunteers as usual, but today they failed to raise a smile in James. He remained quiet and apparently deep in thought. Beth was about to tell him about her promotion and her small victory over Mrs Peters when he suddenly reached into his pocket and pulled out a green envelope.

'What's that?' asked Beth.

'An honour envelope,' said James.

'Yes, I know that,' said Beth. 'But why have you got that particular one out here?'

And, Goody-Two-Shoes Beth wanted to add, everyone knew that it was strictly forbidden to remove any post from the depot, so what on earth was he thinking?

'Oh, there's nothing particularly special about this one,' said James, slipping the envelope open. 'It's just one of the thousands we've processed this morning. But I wanted to show you the sort of thing we're dealing with all day and every day.'

He held the letter out to Beth. She hesitated before she took it, hand trembling slightly. It felt all wrong but she took out the folded sheets of paper anyway and opened them slowly.

The writing was spidery and loopy and it took Beth a moment to get her eye in.

Dearest Mother,
I would be brave but I've had my fill of this war. Nothing is as I thought it would be. The trench I am living in smells of rotting bodies and blood; it hangs heavy in the air our every waking moment. My feet are rotting – some poor sods have had to have theirs amputated – and the rats and the lice don't bear thinking about. Today I killed sixteen men and I still have horrendous visions in the back of my mind . . .

Beth couldn't read any more. She put the letter down and turned to James in horror

'Is that really what's going on out there?' she demanded, fear prickling her insides. There was nothing noble, nothing patriotic about such squalor, such butchery. 'It's . . . horrific.'

'It is,' said James. 'And I'm reading the same thing hundreds of times every day, so it must be true.'

'Oh, my word. Poor Ned. Poor Sam. Poor Reggie. Poor all of them.' Beth fell silent, tears prickling her eyelids. It just didn't bear thinking about. 'But this can't be allowed to happen,' she burst out suddenly. 'Can't someone do something to stop it?'

James smiled sadly. 'Liza, my job is to stop these letters getting to their intended recipients,' he said. 'Anyone requesting an honour envelope is promising that their letter contains nothing but personal matters and they are breaking their word by writing something like this. I'm not allowed to send it on its way, tempted though I am to wave it through – and the countless others like it – to the folks back home. If people knew . . . if they only knew.'

Beth fell silent, looking down at her hands. For the first time she realised that there were no easy answers. The rules were there for a reason, she understood that, but supposing this letter was from Ned, desperately wanting to tell her what life was like at the front. What then?

She turned back to James. 'What are you going to do?' she asked.

James blinked at her. 'I'm going to follow the rules, of course,' he said. 'If I start allowing letters through that break the rules, where do I stop? I may not like it, Liza, but I'm going to do my job to the best of my ability. I just wanted to show you that it isn't always easy, and why I feel the way I do about the war.'

It was Beth's turn to be quiet as they walked back across the park. How hard James's job was – and how trivial hers by comparison. And what would she do if she was in his position?

But there was another reason Beth was quiet. She suddenly felt very close to James and the thought made her feel uncomfortable. What about Sam, blithely and bravely writing to her – and from the front, no less. He might be going over the top any day now. How could she let him down when he already had so much to lose?

'Chop, chop,' said Nora, coming up to them as soon as they were back in the Home Office compound. 'You don't want to be late back on duty. Not now you're a supervisor!'

James turned to Beth in surprise. 'Well, aren't you the dark horse!' he said. 'That's wonderful news. But you never breathed a word.'

Beth could feel herself blushing. 'It just never came up,' she said. 'And we've all been promoted. Milly and Nora have been moved to the Returned Letters Department.'

'Then it's congratulations all round,' said James. 'I'd say that's worth a sherry in the Queen's Head after work. My treat. I'm sure the King will understand.'

And so it was that Beth, Milly, Nora and James headed to the pub after work.

James brought along a couple of colleagues, Denny and Cuth, from the Honour-Envelope Department and it was a very jolly group that toasted all the promotions. Beth looked around at the flushed, smiling faces and realised that she hadn't been as happy for a long, long time. How her life had changed in the past few months!

Afterwards, James and Milly accompanied her on the Tube as far as King's Cross, and, feeling distinctly light-headed and giggly from three glasses of sherry, Beth got onto the connecting train to Woodhampstead with a spring in her step.

Despite the war, despite everything, in that moment, life was sweet.

She leaned her head against the glass and closed her eyes.

Beth was still feeling floaty, if exhausted, when the train pulled into Woodhampstead Station an hour and a half later.

A cup of tea, a bite to eat and she would be ready for her bed. She made her way to the door, slid down the window, reached outside to turn the handle.

There – on the platform – was *Ma*.

19

Beth disembarked from the train as if in a dream. Light-headed, thoughts a-whirl, she stumbled towards her mother. What was it?

More importantly, *who* was it?

What dreadful news had compelled Ma to come to the station to meet her train?

She stopped in front of Ma, too afraid to say, to hear the words. 'Ned?' she croaked. 'Oh, Ma, not *Ned?*'

Time seemed to stand still.

And then Ma's hand fluttered to her chest. 'No,' she said. 'You, Beth. *You.*'

Beth looked at her mother, totally perplexed.

'*Me*, Ma?' she said. 'But why? I'm perfectly all right, as you can see.'

Ma's face crumpled and she suddenly looked every one of her forty-three years. She put both hands on Beth's shoulders and gave a little shake, tears starting to stream down her face. 'Yes, but I didn't know that, did I?' she said. 'Zeppelins in London last night. Dozens dead. No word from you and I've been to hell and back!'

'Oh Ma. Oh Ma.' Emotion built up in Beth's chest and burst free. Suddenly she was crying too and she didn't quite know who had made the first move, but somehow she was in her mother's arms and being rocked to and fro, right in the middle of the station platform.

'Oh Beth,' sobbed Ma. 'I was so scared. So scared that something had happened to you and that you wouldn't be coming home.'

'I'm safe, Ma. I'm safe. I'm here.'

'And after I'd thrown you from the house too. I'm sorry, Beth. So sorry.'

'*I'm* sorry for lying to you about the job,' sobbed Beth. 'I'm sorry for taking it when I knew you and Pa didn't want me to . . .'

'Oh, Beth,' said Ma, stroking her hair. 'If you only knew how proud I am of you for taking the job, putting yourself in danger every day, working late.'

Beth buried her face deeper into her mother's neck.

Now probably wasn't the time to explain that she hadn't been working late. She'd been in the pub with her friends and without a care in the world. Did that make her a terrible person? Beth was rather afraid that it did – as did the fact she hadn't stopped to consider her family might have been fretting about her. There wasn't much she could have done beyond sending a telegram to say that she was safe – but maybe she *should* have done just that. She *certainly* shouldn't have lingered in town any longer than she needed to.

The two pulled apart and smiled shakily at each other. Then Ma, her arm tight around Beth, started steering her off the platform.

'You'll come home now, won't you?' she said, wiping her eyes. 'Pa and Sally are both there, waiting for news . . .'

'Of course, Ma,' she said. 'Of course, I will.' But something wasn't quite adding up in her mind. 'But how did you know what train I was on? How did you know which to meet?'

Ma turned to her. 'I didn't,' she said. 'How could I know? I've been meeting them all.'

★   ★   ★

'She's home then?' someone cried, as Beth and Ma walked up Station Approach together.

Ma smiled and hugged Beth closer. 'Yes, praise the Lord she's safe!' she said.

Guilt.

Much more guilt.

Of course, something like this would be big news in their little town. Of *course*, the news that Beth-From-The-Shop hadn't returned from London the day after a Zeppelin raid would have spread like wildfire.

That just made her lingering in the pub after work all the more heinous. As was the fact that she was very slightly drunk . . .

Luckily, Ma was talking enough for two and didn't seem to have noticed Beth's silence.

'Did you see the Zeppelins?' she asked, and then without waiting for an answer, 'We've already got your things from Sally's and I've put them back in your room. We were all just waiting . . . waiting.'

Beth hadn't been home for over three months.

Another life.

Certainly another her.

She watched Ma open the front door as if she was returning from the grand tour. Everything seemed smaller. Diminished. The narrow hallway. The—

Oh, stop it, Beth.

Stop being so dramatic!

And here was Pa. The news had clearly already reached him that she was safe because he looked happy and relieved rather than shocked. He folded her into a bear hug. 'My little warrior,' he whispered into her hair, as if Beth had been singlehandedly fighting off the Zeppelins rather than carelessly swigging sherry in the Queen's Head. Beth buried her head into his shoulders to hide sudden, scalding tears.

Now it was Sally's turn. She hugged Beth to her and the hug seemed warm and genuine. But then she whispered, with a funny edge to her voice, 'The prodigal daughter returneth . . .'

Beth pulled away and looked at her sister in surprise. Whatever had Sally meant by that? But Sally just gave her a bland smile in return; a smile, Beth noticed, that didn't quite meet her eyes.

'Come on, help me set the table for supper,' she said. 'Ma's cooking chops. It's a celebration, don't you know?'

The news about Reginald arrived the very next day.

The news they had all been dreading.

The telegram that told Reggie's distraught parents their son was no longer 'missing in action' but was now confirmed 'killed in action'.

Beth was already in London by the time the telegram arrived so didn't discover the news until she arrived home from work that evening. The shop was shuttered and Ma and Sally were sitting in the kitchen drinking tea.

'The very worst thing was that I never wrote to him,' said Sally. 'I feel dreadful, I really do. I meant to, but what with one thing and another . . . And his parents said he was upset he hadn't had many letters . . . and now, it's too late.'

Beth couldn't help thinking that not receiving a letter from a not particularly close sister-in-law was unlikely to have been high on Reginald's list of regrets, but now wasn't the time to say so. She poured herself a cup of strong, stewed tea and put her arm around her sister.

'But it's not too late for you to write lots of letters to Bertie,' she said. 'And I shall write to him too – this very evening, as soon as I have written a letter of condolence to his parents. We must all keep writing,' she said more generally. 'It's letters that will win us this war.'

Ma nodded gravely. 'Whoever thought my Beth would come up with something so profound,' she said. 'Queen Victoria herself—'

'It was Sergeant Major Cunningham, not me,' said Beth hastily. 'I'm still just Beth, not profound at all.'

There was no funeral.

Of course there wasn't, Beth reminded herself.

There was no funeral because there was no body. The earthly remains of Private Reginald Hazelden, such as they were, were to be left in the corner of some foreign field, less than a mile from where he had fallen.

Instead, there was a sad little service in the Woodhampstead Parish Church and a congregation that looked grief-stricken, shell-shocked and – most sadly – almost resigned.

All those hopes, all those dreams, all those wishes – just gone.

Beth clutched her hanky to her nose, breathed in the ancient dust of the church and tried not to wonder who would be next and how many 'nexts' there would have to be before the war was over. And for once – just once – she found herself not much caring *how* the war would be over.

Just over would be enough.

20

It was lovely to be back at home.

Lovely to be back in her own familiar room with her books, her pictures, her sewing patterns, her *things*. Lovely to sleep in her familiar bed, which somehow managed to be comfier and cosier than any other she had slept in – even the sumptuous one at Nora's. Lovely to gaze out of the window at the familiar view overlooking Mayfair's stable and the chickens roosting in the apple trees beyond. Now she could really tell how much time had passed; when she had left for Sally's, the leaves on those trees had been fresh and verdant in all their early summer glory and now they were heavy with fruit and tinged with autumn . . .

Yes, it was good to be home. Good to spend time with her parents who were clearly thrilled to have her back. In a way, nothing had changed. But, in another way, everything had. *She* had changed. Where once she had accepted her parents' wholehearted support for the war at absolutely any cost, now she winced a little at some of the things they casually said. Where once she had wholeheartedly agreed that the suffrage movement in general, and the suffragettes in particular, were the work of the Devil, now she had to bite her tongue when her mother talked about women unsexing themselves. Beth wasn't sure exactly what she did believe in, but what she knew now was that there was another side to her parents' views and beliefs. Another point of view which, at the very least, was worthy of consideration and debate. But she held her tongue. She didn't want to rock the boat.

Beth enjoyed being back in the shop – being able to help at weekends and being able to buy things herself. One of the first things she did was to pack a huge parcel for Sam crammed full of every delicacy she could think of and paid for out of her wages at the Home Depot. And then she felt guilty and packed an even bigger one for Ned.

There was just one downside to all this.

She missed Sally.

Missed her a lot. Even though Sally slipped back into her old routine of eating most evenings with Beth and their parents, it wasn't the same as being curled up in the kitchen, just the two of them. And Sally was distracted nowadays. Short with her, even. Of course, she was – her brother-in-law had been killed in action and her husband was serving with the same regiment and fighting on the same front.

Who wouldn't be tense and preoccupied?

Back at the Home Depot, Beth's friends were full of support and sympathy over Reginald's death.

'Come and stay,' pleaded Milly. 'We could go along to an ELFS meeting.'

And then: 'Come to a show with me tomorrow night? One of the chaps in my team has got tickets he can't use now and I've bought them off him. It's light and funny to cheer you up.'

That last one was from James. And, almost despite herself, Beth found herself saying yes.

So, she arranged to see the show with James the next day

and to go an ELFS meeting with Milly and Nora the day after.

Thank goodness for lovely friends.

'We're going to the music hall at the Palladium,' announced James casually as he and Beth walked down the Outer Circle together the following evening.

Beth turned to him in surprise. That wasn't at all what she had been expecting – what she had put her best navy skirt and blouse on for. The music halls had a reputation for being bold and scandalous and really rather working class. Oh, Beth knew they had been cleaned up no end since Victorian times and had even acquired a veneer of respectability but still, she couldn't imagine that they were the sort of places that James frequented. She would have thought that a Shakespeare play or a classical concert would have been more his style. Then she remembered that he had bought the tickets off one of his staff members. Maybe he hadn't checked exactly what they were for before he'd parted with his cash. No matter. She was sure that Liza would be able to cope with the worst that the music hall had to throw at them even if Beth could not.

She smiled up at him. 'I have a confession to make.'

'What's that?' said James, returning her smile. 'You've vowed never to set foot inside a music hall?'

'No,' said Beth. But whatever would Ma say? Going to any performance during the war was deemed dubious enough, let alone one such as this. 'No, it's that I've never been to a show. Well, any London show, that is. I've been to lots of performances of varying quality at the Woodhampstead Village Hall!'

James laughed and tucked her hand into the crook of his arm. 'Well, what a way to start,' he said, with a delighted chuckle.

★ ★ ★

The show was *wonderful*.

There were a variety of acts – comedy sketches, magicians, ballet, acrobats – and Beth loved them all. But it was the music that took centre-stage and, far from being scandalous, it was deeply patriotic and moving. Beth knew most of the songs and, cheeks flushed and heart aglow, belted out 'It's a Long Way to Tipperary', 'Keep the Home Fires Burning' and 'We Don't Want to Lose You (But We Think You Ought to Go)' with everyone else.

This was wonderful!

Even Ma would love it.

It was only towards the end of the show that another, more disquieting, thought began to dawn on Beth. Lovely and optimistic though this all was, it was really nothing short of propaganda. In fact, the singer – 'Tommy the Trench' – was openly pushing potential recruits to sign up and, at one point, there was even a basket of white feathers on the stage. James would be horrified . . . furious. Beth risked a little glance at him, but he seemed unmoved, smiling back at her before lustily joining in with the next song.

Beth turned back to the stage, confused.

Afterwards, James insisted on accompanying Beth in a taxi back to King's Cross Station.

'I'll pay for you to get another taxi from Hatfield,' he said, when they were on their way. 'Can't have you hanging round waiting for the connecting train at all hours of the night.'

'No, that's quite all right,' replied Beth. She had already decided that she was going to get a taxi but she would pay for it herself. It was lovely having her own money.

'I would like to,' said James firmly and Beth knew when she was beaten.

'Thank you,' she said. And then she added, 'Did you know it would be like that this evening?'

'Like what?' asked James.

'Well, almost a recruitment rally for the army.'

James shrugged. 'I had an idea, yes,' he said.

'Then why on earth did you buy the tickets?' said Beth. 'Why did you agree to go if you knew it would make you feel uncomfortable? At one point I thought they were going to hand out those white feathers to every man of fighting age who wasn't in uniform!'

James hesitated. 'Because I also knew that it would be cheerful and patriotic and I hoped it might be some comfort to you after the loss that your family – your sister – has just endured. I hoped it might help you make sense of things and remind you that his death is not in vain.'

Beth blinked at him. 'But you don't believe that,' she whispered.

'No. But you do.'

Beth felt tears pricking at her eyelids. 'I don't know what I believe in anymore,' she said, 'but thank you. Thank you very much.'

The taxi pulled up at King's Cross and Beth, desperate not to cry in front of James, was out of the door before he had a chance to come round and open it for her. 'I'd better run,' she said. 'The trains . . . Thank you for a lovely evening.' And she was off, practically running through the doors and across the concourse.

That had been kind of James. So very kind and thoughtful.

And she liked him.

She liked him a lot.

But what about Sam?

How could she let him down when he was away at the front, risking his life?

And when she got home, there was a letter waiting for her from him. The contents were cheerful and upbeat – nothing romantic about it – but the stamp was definitely at an angle. Not enough to be too obvious but definitely well off the perpendicular.

'*Be mine.*'

21

The next morning, Beth was still confused.

But there was no time to dwell on her problems. Mrs Peters had hurt her back and was at her most cantankerous. Worse, some of her repackaged parcels, which Beth had waved through the day before, had been rejected at the quartermaster's inspection and needed to be redone. And – the final straw – the whole team was down on its quota. She needed to be very careful to keep on top of things today or she would end up being hauled over the coals.

'Incoming delivery, Liza,' said Miss Parker, walking past with a clipboard. Usually, full of smiles and warm support, Miss Parker seemed positively disapproving today.

Mrs Peters was next on Liza's list for unloading duties but she was clearly out of action with her bad back – *and* she had yesterday's shoddy work to re-do. Beth feared that if she took anyone else away from packing, her team would fall even further behind on its quota. She decided to go and help out herself.

Please let it not be George that morning.

It was George.

'Good morning,' she said, trying to ooze cool politeness.

George just grunted in return and started lowering the sacks down. Beth, Mabel and Helena worked quickly and efficiently together and the lorry was emptied in no time. Beth breathed a sigh of relief. That had gone surprisingly well. Now to get the baskets back to the Broken Parcel Department and try to get back on track . . .

'Oi!' George had jumped off the back of the lorry and was waving a clipboard and pencil in the air. 'Someone needs to sign for this.'

Helena was standing closest to him and Beth assumed she would step forward and sign for the delivery – anyone was authorised to do so. But Helena was new and obviously not sure of the correct procedure.

'Oh, I think you need Miss Healey to do that,' she said, gesturing towards Beth. 'She's the supervisor.'

Beth was about to intervene, but Helena and Mabel had already started to wheel the basket away from the unloading bay. Never mind.

One quick signature . . .

'Supervisor, eh?' said George with a smirk. 'Been promoted, have yer?'

'I have,' said Beth, with what she hoped was brisk professionalism. 'And now if I could just sign for the delivery, I'll let you get on your way.'

She took a step forward but, instead of handing her the clipboard, George placed it on the floor of the open lorry. Beth started in surprise as he came right up to her, so close she could smell the tobacco on his breath.

'Give us a kiss, blondie,' he said with a leer.

Beth's heart started thumping painfully in her chest.

She took a quick look around. The unloading bay was empty and George's colleague, whoever he might be, was nowhere to be seen. Very probably he had nipped inside the Home Depot to use the bathroom. Maybe George had even asked him to make himself scarce. Either way, they were all alone.

'Don't be silly, George,' she said, taking a step backwards and trying to inject a playful laugh into her voice. Hopefully she could defuse the situation by staying calm and business-like. Hopefully George would realise how inappropriate he was being and back down.

'Come on, give us a kiss,' persisted George. 'You ain't as grand as yer tall friend or as pert as the little dark one, but I reckon you's the prettiest of the lot. An' a supervisor to boot.'

'No,' said Beth, firmly. '*No.*'

George took no notice. He put one meaty hand on Beth's waist and pulled her towards him. Beth – furious, *scared* – pushed both her hands against his chest as hard as he could, but he was far too strong. Pulling her towards him even more tightly, George dug the fingers of his other hand into her hair and lowered his head, his lips searching for hers. Beth twisted her head away, but George yanked it back.

Her first kiss . . .

It *mustn't* be like this.

It was going to be like this.

No.

No.

'Stop right there!'

The voice behind her was calm but steely and authoritative. George released his grip and Beth stumbled backwards, trying to keep her balance while simultaneously wiping her mouth on the back of her hand.

Then she felt herself being pushed gently out of the way and – *wham*!

Someone had stepped forward and punched George full in the mouth. George recoiled and put one hand gingerly to his face. It came away covered in blood. Beth swung round to see who had saved her.

It was James. 'What was that for?' George mumbled through swollen lips, continuing to dab his mouth with the back of his hand. 'Little lass were asking for it. She were bloody asking for it, I'm telling yer.'

'Piss off,' said James, cradling his fist. 'And if you try anything like that again, I promise you I'll find out about it. Now fuck off, there's a good chap.'

For a moment, George squared up to James and Beth held her breath. James may have had the obvious advantage in height but George was broader, stockier. But his fists dropped and he turned away. Beth exhaled quietly.

And here was George's companion, the lorry driver, coming out of the Home Depot. He stopped short when he saw George's bloody mouth.

'What's going on here?' he asked warily, taking in the little tableau.

'Nothing,' muttered George sulkily. 'Accident.'

'Too right,' said James. 'And let's hope it doesn't happen again.'

He gave George a long, last stare, then shepherded Beth away, back inside the Home Depot. There was a little pile of sacks just inside the entrance and he helped Beth to sit down on them. She was glad to do so; she suddenly felt light-headed and her legs were shaky beneath her.

'Are you all right?' James asked gently, hand on her shoulder.

Beth was so full of conflicting emotions that she didn't know how to reply.

'I am . . . I suppose. Thank you.' And then she added, without really meaning to, 'I thought you didn't believe in violence!'

James gave her a small lopsided smile. 'I never said that,' he replied. 'If I recall correctly, I said I don't believe in the *war*. And, of course, I don't believe in unnecessary violence. What civilised person does? But sometimes it's necessary. Now, shall I go and get one of the others? Miss Parker? Milly? Nora?'

'No, thank you. I shall be quite all right.' She mustn't make a fuss. After all, she wasn't hurt. 'But can I buy you lunch to thank you for last night? And for just now?'

The handsome grey eyes slid to hers, focusing with a little

squint. 'Thank you,' he said. 'But I'm debating whether or not I should be here today. My father's ill – pneumonia – and I had a letter waiting last night from my aunt who says he's really most unwell. I'm wondering if I should be on a train back to Ipswich.'

'I'm sorry,' said Beth. 'That's a difficult decision. But maybe if your father is ill and there's no one else nearby, you should go . . .'

James was shaking his head. 'I don't know. There's so much to do here.'

'I'm sure you'll make the right decision,' said Beth. 'But if it was my father . . .'

'Yes.' James straightened up and brushed down the front of his trousers. 'Now, are you sure you are all right?'

'Yes.'

But the kiss.

Her first kiss.

Like . . . that!

It didn't bear thinking about.

James leaned in towards her. 'This probably isn't the right time to say this,' he said, 'but I can't help wishing it was me who had tried to kiss you.' He paused and then continued. 'And I can't help hoping that your response would have been quite different.'

And he was gone.

James wanted to kiss her.

James wanted to kiss her!

The day had totally turned around and the rest of the morning passed in a happy blur.

Regardless of what George had tried to do and Mrs Peters's carping and Miss Parker frowning over her clipboard, Beth felt on top of the world. She worked through her morning break in an effort to make up for lost time, and at lunchtime she fairly skipped across the grass to join Milly and Nora in the canteen.

James wanted to kiss her and she rather wanted to kiss him back!

Beth swung open the door to the canteen and scanned the rooms for her friends. She spotted Milly immediately by the perfect smoke ring above her head. It looked almost like a little lopsided halo.

Nora and Milly were sitting alone, deep in conversation, and Beth twinkled across the room to join them.

'Hello,' she said cheerfully. 'I hope you haven't eaten all the buns.'

She knew they hadn't. There was one waiting for her on the plate in front of them. She would queue up for her lunch and then enjoy it afterwards.

Nora looked up. She didn't smile.

'We've got something sad to tell you,' she said.

'What's happened?' asked Beth, looking from one to other. 'Not bad news, I hope?'

'It's to do with you, Liza,' said Nora.

'Well, not exactly . . .' added Milly.

'Yes, it is,' said Nora.

The familiar icy water dripped down Beth's spine.

'What?' she burst out. 'What is it?'

Milly sighed. 'It's really not a big deal,' she said. 'And now we've gone and got you all hot and bothered for nothing.'

Beth resisted the temptation to pick up one of the buns and throw it at her friends. Why wouldn't they just *tell her*?

'I'll tell her,' said Nora. 'Look, Liza, it's nothing big. It's just a bit of a coincidence. Earlier this morning, Milly came across a letter that your sister Sally had written to Reggie and it's been redirected to her.'

Oh!

Thank goodness for that.

Not Ned . . .

Not Sam . . .

Not . . . anything really.

It was just, as Nora said, a bit of a coincidence and sad for Sally to have her letter to her brother-in-law returned to her with 'killed in action' scrawled across it. It was almost a pity she was staying away from home that night or she could have warned Sally it was on its way and softened the blow.

'I thought about giving it to you so you could give to your sister in person,' Milly was saying. 'But then I remembered how much you like to play by the rules and I knew you'd give me a good ticking off for even considering it. After all, you are a *supervisor* now. So, I sent it on its way.'

Nora punched Milly on the arm and even Beth giggled. Milly had a point – she was a little goody-two-shoes sometimes! Smiling, she turned to go and queue up for her lunch.

But, wait a minute. Something didn't sound – *feel* – quite right.

What was it Sally had said after Reggie had been confirmed killed in action?

'I wish I'd written to him . . .'

Beth spun on her heel, the world grinding to a halt around her. *Sally hadn't written to Reggie.*

And that meant . . .

'Milly, we need to go back into the Home Depot right now and check your list,' she said.

Nora and Milly stared back at her.

'*Right now*,' repeated Beth, punching both fists down onto the table for emphasis. The tea in the cups shuddered and Beth could see curious faces turning to stare at them.

'We're not allowed back into the office at lunchtime—' started Nora.

'I don't care,' barked Beth. 'Sally didn't write to Reggie.'

'She did,' said Milly, putting a hand on Beth's arm. 'It was definitely a letter from Sally Hazelden to Private R Hazelden. I double-checked it against the list. It's all above board.'

Beth shook her arm free, panic building in her chest. 'Sally. Didn't. Write. To. Reggie,' she repeated slowly and clearly.

'She must have done,' said Milly. 'Maybe she just didn't tell you?'

'No!' Beth was almost shouting now.

Why weren't the others standing up? Why weren't they coming with her? Then she realised she hadn't actually told them what she was afraid of – what was only just crystallising in her own mind.

'I'm worried it might be Bertie,' she said. 'Oh God, it might be Bertie too!'

There was a short, stunned silence.

Then Milly shook her head. 'It's not,' she said. 'The envelope was addressed to Private R Hazelden. It was definitely an R. Not B for Bertie. Not even A for Albert. R.'

The canteen started to swirl around Beth. She put both hands on the table and took a deep breath. It wouldn't do to faint. Not at a time like this. 'Bertie is short for *R*obert,' she said dully. 'Not Albert. *R*obert. Did you double-check the number?'

Milly had gone ashen white. 'No,' she said in a tiny voice.

Nora's hand fluttered to her mouth. 'Milly—' she started.

Beth brushed her aside. 'And where was the stamp, Milly?' she demanded. 'Can you remember where the stamp was?'

Milly paused and shut her eyes. 'On its side in the bottom right-hand corner,' she said in a little voice.

Her eyes, when they opened and met Beth's, were wide with dawning horror.

I love you.

A stamp placed in the bottom right-hand corner meant *I love you.*

Beth knew that.

Milly knew it.

Sally knew it too, and Beth knew that for a fact because it was she who had told Sally all about the stamp code.

Oh God.

'Please will you come with me?' she said to the others, her sudden calmness merely a bandage over her desire to scream. 'Please will you show me the list?'

The others were *finally* standing up and pushing unfinished lunches aside. Hats were crammed onto heads and, somehow, they were all outside and running across the uneven grass. They flashed their admission cards to the bored soldier standing outside the entrance and he waved them in absent-mindedly. He would have no reason not to, to be fair; everyone's lunchbreak started and finished at different times. Then they walked as fast as they could down the corridor that skirted the main hall, down towards the office where Milly and Nora worked. No one stopped them. No one confronted them. In fact, no one took a blind bit of notice of them at all.

But wait.

Here was James coming down the corridor towards them. He was looking straight at Beth and there was a smile playing at the corner of his lips.

'Liza—' he started as they drew level.

'*No*,' Beth replied, pushing past him.

James stepped back but not before Beth had seen the look of hurt and confusion on his face.

He thinks I'm upset, she thought.

He thinks I'm upset . . . shocked . . . horrified that he said he wanted to kiss me.

But there was no time to stop and explain. No time to even turn around. Beth set her jaw and rushed into the Returned Letters Department after her friends.

To Beth's relief, the office was empty.

'Show me, show me,' she said as soon as they had slammed the door behind them.

She might be wrong.

She *had* to be wrong.

It might not be Bertie. The officer in charge might have sent back the wrong letter. The two brothers were in the same regiment and he might have got confused and returned the wrong brother's letter. Yes, that was probably it. It was just a silly mistake.

Nora produced a sheaf of type-written sheets and handed them to Milly.

'Many more names than normal,' she commented. 'The latest battles . . .'

So many pieces of paper.

So many names.

So many young men cut off in their prime.

'Show me,' said Beth again.

White-faced, Milly took the sheaf and flicked over a couple of sheets. 'There,' she said stabbing her finger about two-thirds of the way down the page.

And there it was. Reginald Hazelden followed by his army number. Even though Beth knew he was dead, it was still a shock to see it there in black and white . . .

'Right,' said Beth. 'The question is, is Bertie in there too?'

Without waiting for an answer, she snatched the sheaf of papers from Milly and started rifling through them, running a shaking finger down the lists of names as quickly as she could.

Nothing.

Nothing . . .

It was all going to be all right.

But then, jumping out at her from halfway down the very last page . . .

Robert Hazelden.

Beth shut her eyes.

She was imagining it.

She *must* be imagining it.

She was stressed and worried and the words and letters were jumping around and she had got confused. She would open her eyes and it wouldn't be him. It would be some other sister's husband, some other mother's son.

She opened her eyes slowly.

Robert Hazelden.

Bertie.

'There,' she said, pointing. 'There.'

And she slumped back into a chair.

Bertie, with his faint but unmistakable whiff of manure, was dead.

Bertie pulling her plait at school, kicking a football round the road with the other kids, smiling proudly but self-consciously on his wedding day to Sally.

Dead.

Nora picked up the sheet of pages. 'I'm so sorry, Liza,' she said. 'Your poor sister. He's on the list of very recent casualties that have just been sent through. And – oh no! – his official telegram is not due out until tomorrow morning.'

Beth and Nora both swung round to look at Milly.

'I didn't think to look further,' she said in a small voice. 'You'd told us about Reggie and I just assumed. I just assumed it were him. I'm so sorry, Liza.'

Oh, Milly! thought Beth. Carefree, careless, slapdash Milly.

Suddenly Beth was calm and in control again.

Sally was *not* going to discover her beloved husband had been killed by her letter to him being casually returned and marked 'killed in action'. That was absolutely unthinkable. It must *not* be allowed to happen. 'We've got to stop the letter,' she said decisively, standing up and wiping her eyes.

Milly and Nora were started at her blankly.

'When did this happen?' asked Beth briskly. Maybe it was still in the Depot.

'First thing this morning,' said Nora. 'Quarter past nine or so. Usually our work is double-checked but the supervisor is off with flu today and we were told to supervise each other. I'm as much to blame as Milly. I let it through. I'm so sorry . . .'

Beth nodded. Now wasn't the time for recriminations or apportioning blame. Now was the time for action. Because – damn! – the letter wouldn't still be in the Depot. The returned letters went back into the civilian post and would probably have left the Depot by ten at the latest. It was now nearly two o'clock and the letter had probably already left London. While there was of course the possibility that it wouldn't be delivered until the next morning, it was more likely to be delivered that afternoon or early evening with the last delivery.

Think, Beth, think.

Think quickly!

At any moment someone could walk into the room and the cat would be out of the bag. Of course, that someone might be able to help. They might be able to telephone ahead, get hold of the depot, intercept the letter before it was too late. But, of course, Milly would be in no end of trouble if this got out. Beth's loyalties lay with her sister. She did not want Sally finding out that Bertie had died by her letter to him being sent back to her. Then again, she didn't want Milly getting the sack . . .

Oh, it was all so *hard*.

'We could telephone,' suggested Nora. She was standing by the door, wringing her hands together but otherwise outwardly calm.

Beth looked around the room. No telephone. 'Where from?' she said. 'Who to?'

Nora gave an infinitesimal shrug of her shoulders. 'I don't know,' she said. 'I suppose I could get word to Uncle over at the King Edward Building . . .'

Milly shot Beth a look of alarm.

'No, thank you,' said Beth firmly. There had to be a better way than getting the head of REPS involved. Anyway, that would take time. Time they didn't have.

'We have a telephone at home,' said Nora. 'We could sneak back there—'

'But who would we call?' said Beth.

There wasn't, as far as she was aware, a single telephone in the whole of Woodhampstead. Oh, the big houses scattered around the village had them, of course, but what use was that to her? She could hardly call Maitland Hall and ask the butler to put her through to Florence in the kitchens. What on earth could Florence do about it, anyway? Equally, she could hardly give Lady Cavan at Woodhampstead Hall a ring, tear her away from one of her committee meetings and ask her to lurk around the high street to intercept the post girl.

It was so preposterous it was almost funny.

Only it wasn't.

There was only one thing for it . . .

'I'm going,' said Beth, standing up and clapping her hands together.

'Going where?' asked Milly in alarm. It was the first time she had said anything since her mumbled apology.

'Back to Woodhampstead,' said Beth. 'All I can do is hope that I get there before Ivy does her rounds and try to intercept her.'

Nora swung herself to her feet. 'Let's go,' she said, cramming her hat on her head.

Beth looked at her in surprise. 'Thank you,' she said, 'but there's no need. I'll be fine on my own.'

Much as Beth might appreciate the company, there was no point in both of them getting in trouble or worse for being absent without permission.

'I'm not going *with* you,' said Nora. 'You go back to Woodhampstead and I'll head straight to the depot to see if I can stop it there.'

Oh.

Beth found easy tears brimming again, for quite a different reason. But this was no time for silly sentimentality . . .

'Thank you,' she said briskly. 'That would be a great help. But you'd need to go to Euston Station and then up to St Albans. That's where the depot is. Even though it's only six miles to Woodhampstead, it's on a different train line.'

Nora nodded. 'Right you are,' she said. 'Let's be off then. We can share a taxi most of the way.'

'What I can do to help?' said Milly in a small voice.

Beth and Nora turned around in the doorway.

'Nothing,' said Beth, resisting the obvious temptation to add 'you've done enough already'. That wouldn't help anything or anyone and she didn't blame Milly. Not really. There were so many coincidences and mitigating circumstances, it had been a mistake waiting to happen.

'Just tell anyone who asks – especially Miss Parker – that Beth and I have been taken ill and have had to leave in a hurry,' said Nora

And they were off, practically running down the corridor, through the large wooden doors and back across the grass. Beth found her shoulders were hunched, waiting for someone to shout after them, to ask them why they were going off duty at such an irregular time, but all remained quiet.

'Urgent postal business,' panted Nora to the unfamiliar guard on the periphery gate. She flashed her admission card for some quite unknown reason and the soldier opened the gate, his eyes flickering over the pair of them.

Very much in her milieu, Nora managed to flag down the very first taxi coming down the Outer Circle and in no time at all they were on the Euston Road.

'Quick as you can, please,' said Nora as the motor puttered to near halt behind an ancient-looking horse and cart. 'This is an emergency.'

The taxi driver touched his cap, said 'yes, miss,' and swung out into the path of the oncoming traffic. Before Beth knew it, they were pulling up in front of Euston Station. As the driver came around to open the door, Nora pressed some notes into Beth's hand.

'Here you are,' she said. 'Don't be silly – I won't accept no for an answer. This is all partly my fault anyway.'

And she was gone.

The driver pulled out into the traffic again, and in no time at all, pulled up in front of King's Cross Station. Beth paid him – *how* much?! – and ran into the station as quickly as she could. Of course, it made not a jot of difference. The next connecting train to Woodhampstead was due to leave in fifteen minutes. It could have been a lot worse, but fifteen minutes was still fifteen minutes of doing nothing! Fifteen minutes in which the letter would be inching towards Woodhampstead . . .

The train was already at the platform so Beth installed herself into a corner seat and pulled out her knitting. It quickly descended into one good stitch, one dropped and she set aside her work with a sigh. A hole-y sock would be no good to anyone.

As the train finally lurched off, her thoughts turned to Nora. That had been such a surprising – such a *kind* – thing for her to do. She was a queer old stick, so la-di-da in her upbringing, but ready to get stuck in with the rest of them when it mattered. Beth wondered if she was already on her way. Maybe the letter was on the same train as she was on.

Maybe she would ask if she could look at the mail and start rifling through the sacks while she was still on the train. Maybe if she showed them her admission card . . .

No.

Don't be so ridiculous, Beth. It was a preposterous thought. Nora wasn't even in uniform and who would let an eighteen-year-old girl loose on the mail bags, even if she was posh and in possession of a Home Depot admission card? Anyway, if the letter was on her train, it would head to the sorting office at St Albans and Nora would be able to intercept it. The problem was – as was most likely – that the letter had made its way up to Hertfordshire on a much earlier train.

Thoughts like these got Beth as far as Hatfield. There was another half-hour wait for the connecting train to Woodhampstead and Beth was halfway to the station cafe to grab something to eat – she had missed her lunch, after all – when she realised that there was still quite a lot of Nora's money left and that maybe she could catch a taxi all the way from Hatfield as she had the night before. No sooner was the thought in her head than she was bolting up the stairs from the platform, over the bridge and out onto the road. To her relief, there was a taxi waiting and, in a matter of minutes, she was on her way. The closer to Woodhampstead they got, the more nervous Beth felt and the more she sat forward in her seat, half willing the driver on and half dreading the moment they arrived. The fields sped by more and more quickly and suddenly here they were, at the cottages and houses strung out along the road—

'Drop me off here, please,' said Beth suddenly. It really wouldn't do to be seen getting out of a taxi in the centre of the village. It would give rise to all sorts of questions and potentially let the cat out of the bag.

She paid off the taxi, which turned around and headed back in the direction of Hatfield.

Right.

Now what?

Beth started walking towards the centre of the village with a confidence she didn't feel. What would she say if anyone stopped her? Why was she home in the middle of the afternoon? And why was she *here*, on the outskirts of the village, where she really had no reason to be?

Maybe the taxi should have dropped her off closer to home.

Maybe she should have got the train after all.

Maybe she was just making a complete hash of the whole operation.

But no one stopped her. Nobody took any notice of her at all. And suddenly here was the shop. Beth didn't dare to go too close, but she could just make out Sally behind the counter with Ma. They were both serving customers and everything seemed calm enough; Beth even fancied she heard Sally laugh. It certainly didn't look or sound like she had recently received the very worst of news. It certainly didn't seem as if she knew her husband was dead . . .

That was good, but Beth mustn't be caught loitering outside the family shop. She quickly nipped around the corner and let herself in the front door. Pa would be out on his deliveries so she should safe enough. A quick check confirmed there was no recently delivered post on the doormat, none stacked up on the hall table. It was unlikely as Ivy usually took the post straight into the shop, but at least she could rule it out.

That was good, too.

What next?

She crept out, shutting the front door quietly behind her. Then she walked around the long way to Sally's house so she wouldn't have to walk past the shop window and risk being seen. She still had a key to the cottage and she let herself silently in to check for recent post. This was unlikely too, but best to be sure.

Nothing.

Now what?

Beth slipped out of the cottage and locked the door behind her. It was four o'clock and Ivy would be arriving in the village any time now. The post was sorted in St Albans and Beth was pretty sure Sam had told her that whoever was delivering the afternoon post didn't get involved in sorting it. So Ivy should have no idea of what was in her bag. She would be dropped off by the postal van on the other side of her village and then set off on foot.

Should Beth go and intercept her?

Lurk near – but not in eyesight of – the shop?

What would be best?

'Yoo-hoo. Elizabeth.'

Beth jumped guiltily. It was Mrs McBride standing right in front of Sally's gate and barring Beth's way onto the street. Beth felt a surge of frustration. Was there anywhere Mrs McBride didn't get to? What on earth was the old lady doing up here, right on the edge of the village?

'Good afternoon, Mrs McBride,' said Beth politely.

Get out of my way.

Please get out of my way.

'I've just brought round a milk pudding for Mrs Abrahams next door', said Mrs McBride. 'She has a dreadful cold. But . . . I believed you to be working in London.'

There was a question mark in her voice and Beth nodded.

'Yes, I am,' she said. 'At the Home Depot in the Regent's Park.'

And it's all going horribly, *horribly* wrong.

'Is it a part-time position?' asked Mrs McBride.

'No,' said Beth. 'No . . . not at all. I've just come home early today because I'm . . . a little unwell myself.'

It was true.

Sort of.

She *did* feel rather weak and light-headed. And she had the mother of all headaches brewing.

Oh, goodness. And here was Ivy coming around the corner onto the high street. It wouldn't be long now until she reached the shop . . .

'Yes, I can see you're poorly,' said Mrs McBride. 'Your complexion is most flushed this afternoon.'

'Is it?' Over Mrs McBride's shoulder, Beth was watching Ivy working her way steadily up the high street. Oh good, she had stopped to chat to old Mr Johnson. And now she was going into the haberdashery. But Beth didn't have long and she certainly hadn't come all the way home to be thwarted at the last moment . . .

'If you could just let me past,' she said, taking a couple of steps down the path.

Mrs McBride didn't budge; her considerable bulk remained in Beth's way.

'Why are you at Sally's house?' she asked, her keen eyes boring to Beth's. 'I understood there had been some sort of altercation with your parents and that you'd moved in with your sister temporarily, but I thought all had been resolved?'

Oh, the nosy old so and so . . .

What on earth did it have to do with her?

'Yes, it has,' said Beth, 'but I thought I might have left something here . . .'

Ivy was out of the haberdashery and very close to the shop now. Supposing Ma or Sally came outside to take the post from her? It wasn't unheard of, if the shop was quiet and the day was clement. If they did, and the returned letter was there, the game was up . . .

'Do excuse me, Mrs McBride,' she murmured, pushing bodily past the older woman.

'*Well!*' exploded Mrs McBride. 'Of all the rudeness—'

Beth didn't stop to listen. She didn't *care*. Breaking into a run, she bolted down the road, holding her skirts up to avoid the worst of the mud. Ivy heard her coming and swung round, pretty face radiating surprise. 'Beth!' she cried. 'Whatever is the matter?'

'Nothing,' panted Beth, unconvincingly. 'I just thought I'd—'

'But why are you running? And why aren't you at work? Are you sure you're quite all right?'

Beth realised how she must look. Flushed . . . frantic . . . dishevelled.

'I *am* a little hot, Perhaps a fever brewing.' What on earth was she talking about? 'But I've come to see if I can take the post in for you? Ours from the shop and anything for Sally. You know, to save you a trip up to the cottage . . .'

Ivy gave her a curious glance and Beth couldn't blame her. Beth's unladylike sprint down half the length of the high street could hardly be explained away by an offer of taking the post in! Through the shop window, Beth could see that Ma and Sally had noticed her and her heart rate ratcheted up a gear. She gave them what she hoped would come across as a gay, unconcerned little wave and turned back to Ivy. Ivy gave her another piercing glance followed by a little shake of her head, but she did at least start rifling through her pile of letters. This was ridiculous. The letter obviously wouldn't be there and she had made a complete fool of herself for absolutely nothing.

Only it was!

Beth saw it as soon as Ivy started flicking through the pile.

A totally unremarkable white envelope with Sally's writing on it. Nothing that would stand out to anyone else, but it was definitely *the* letter. Beth even thought she glimpsed the words 'killed in action' as Ivy flicked by and, for a moment, she thought she might be sick.

A dozen possibilities flickered through her mind.

Maybe Ivy already knew the letter was there and, further-more, knew exactly *why* it was there. She had sorted the letters herself at the depot or else whoever had done so had told her about it. She would, of course, presume the telegram giving the sad news had already been delivered and she would be full of sympathy and bland, embarrassed platitudes. Worse, because she was giving the letter to Beth rather than to Sally, she would be emboldened and would express those sympa-thies more fully than perhaps she would have done. And then Sally would come out of the shop to see what was going on and . . .

Or she didn't know. She had no idea but her suspicions would be roused by the fact that Beth was standing over her and so she would scan the letters and packages far more diligently than she otherwise might have done. And then she would see it, register it and . . .

Either way, the news would be all over the village and Beth – by her foolish actions – would have made things twenty times worse.

It was all an unmitigated disaster.

But . . . wait.

Ivy was separating out the post for the shop and the post for Sally and now she was stacking them carefully together – with the incriminating letter for Sally safely at the bottom.

'There you are,' she said, casually.

Beth took the pile of the letters and clutched them to her chest. 'Thank you,' she replied, trying to keep any shred of emotion from her voice. Her vocal cords seemed to have developed a mind of their own, though, and despite her best efforts, her voice cracked.

'You take care of yourself,' said Ivy. 'Sounds to me like you're losing your voice on top of everything else.'

'Yes, I think I might be.' Goodness, it looked like Sally was on her way out of the shop. If she didn't hide the letter quickly, it would be a case of out of the frying pan and into the fire . . .

'I think what you need is a nice hot toddy,' said Ivy.

She smiled at Beth, swung her bag onto her shoulder and carried on up the high street. Beth took a deep breath. She really hadn't considered what was going to happen next. It was a relief that Sally wouldn't receive her returned letter out of the blue, but what now?

Bertie was still dead.

And Beth still knew this and Sally still didn't.

Whatever was she going to do?

22

If it had been Ma who'd come out of the shop, Beth might well have made a different decision.

If it had been Ma, Beth might have shown her the letter.

In fact, if it had been Ma, Beth might well have thrown herself into her mother's arms and blurted out the whole sorry tale.

But it wasn't. It was Sally, coming out of the shop, wiping her hands on her pinny and giving Beth a quizzical smile.

Time seemed to slow down. What was Beth going to do?

Give Sally the letter and leave her to work out the implications?

Hold the letter back but explain that she knew Bertie had died?

Don't tell Sally, hide the letter and let events unfurl in their own time?

What was the best thing to do?

What was the *right* thing to do?

Think, Beth.

Think!

Beth had no idea which alternative she was going to plump for. She watched, almost entranced, as Sally came across to where she was still rooted to the spot in the middle of the road.

'Hello, Beth,' said Sally matter-of-factly. 'You're back from London very early.'

Without consciously planning to, Beth found her fingers separating the bottom letter from the pile she was holding. The bottom one, she knew, was *the* letter; the one her subconscious was just at that moment deciding that Sally must not see. She held out the rest of the little stack while secreting the incriminating letter in the folds of her skirt with the other.

'Post for you,' she said with as bright a smile as she could muster. 'And I've come from work early because I'm not feeling very well. There's a rotten cold and flu doing the rounds and I'm very much afraid that I might be coming down with it.'

Sally wrinkled her brow. 'I thought I saw you running from the direction of my cottage,' she said with a little frown.

Oh God. What on earth to say now?

In the end, the words chose themselves. 'I was hiding and then running from Mrs McBride,' she said, making a little face. 'I'm afraid I just couldn't face her this afternoon.'

Sally gave an easy laugh, 'I'm not surprised,' she said. 'She's bad enough at the best of times.'

She reached out and took the post and then flicked through it, dark hair falling forward and blocking her face. Beth took the opportunity to open her bag and slip the letter inside, at the same time pulling out her handkerchief and blowing her nose loudly. It came away covered in light brown dust. How long ago, how far away the Home Depot seemed . . .

'Oh, there's one for you,' said Sally, handing Beth a letter back. 'I'm surprised you didn't notice. Now I know you really *are* feeling ill.'

The letter was another from Sam, but Beth couldn't think about that now. All she could do was exhale very gently as Sally turned on her heel and headed back into the shop. Beth followed her slowly.

Had she done the right thing?

Surely she had done the right thing?

Surely it was better to let things take their natural course and to allow the news to arrive in the usual way rather than through a garbled story about mess-ups at the Depot. Surely Sally, surely *Bertie*, should be afforded that dignity. She could only hope that Milly had not let through *several* letters and that, elsewhere in Woodhampstead, Bertie's parents weren't at this moment receiving their own letters being sent back to them. Should she follow Ivy and try to check the post that was about to be delivered to Bertie's parents? *No!* Beth gave herself a little shake as the shop door jangled shut behind her. If that was the case, it was not her business and she could do nothing about it. She had done her bit . . .

'Beth's feeling ill, Ma,' Sally was saying. 'That's why she has come home early.'

'Poor poppet,' said Ma, swinging open the hatch and coming into the shop. She put a cool hand on Beth's forehead. 'Yes, you do feel hot. Go on upstairs and I'll bring you up tea and water shortly.'

Yes. Upstairs. That was the best thing to do.

So, why then, was she crying? Huge tearing sobs that started from somewhere in her chest and wrenched themselves free. What on earth was *wrong* with her?

'Oh, Beth, Beth.' Ma's arms were around her, one hand stroking her hair. 'Whatever is the matter?'

'I don't know,' sobbed Beth. 'Nothing. *Everything.*'

'I know,' said Ma soothingly. 'Sometimes it all gets too much, doesn't it? Now, up you go.'

Beth nodded and walked behind the counter, through the storeroom and into the hallway. Then, still hiccupping with sobs, she trudged slowly upstairs to her bedroom. Despite her bleary eyes, everything was thrown into sharp relief. The faded patterned carpet, the chipped banister spindles, Queen Victoria fixing her with a beady eye at the top of the stairs . . .

Oh, the guilt.

It was only when Ma had disappeared safely downstairs again that Beth dared to take the letter out of her bag.

Heart thumping, she turned it over and over in her hands, studying it for she didn't know what. It was, as she had registered before, a perfectly normal envelope addressed, as Milly had already told her, to Private R Hazelden. The stamp was at a heartbreakingly jaunty angle in the bottom right-hand corner; even though Beth already knew this to be the case, it still tugged at her heartstrings. The letter had been opened by the censor on the outward journey and had been duly stamped as such . . . and there were the neat letters in a black pen just above Bertie's name . . . *killed in action.*

Beth's easy tears started up again. She mustn't let them get onto the letter and smudge the ink and make everything worse. She had already deceived and lied to her sister . . . that was bad enough. With a heavy heart, she slipped both it and the letter from Sam under the mattress and lay down.

If today had been awful, tomorrow would be even worse.

Beth woke to a light rap on her door.

She had no idea whether it was seconds, minutes or hours later. It was dark outside, but that didn't give her much of a clue. She wriggled to a seated position and pulled the counterpane under her chin. It was unlike her family to knock – unless it was Pa, of course. She called for whoever it was to come in.

It was Nora.

In Woodhampstead.

In her *house.*

Beth blinked a few times, trying to take it in, trying to work out what it might mean. 'Nora! What on earth are you doing here?' she hissed.

Then she noticed Ma hovering nervously in the hallway.

'This young lady just arrived outside,' said Ma. Her voice was flipping between outrage, excitement and deference. 'Asking for "Liza". She said you knew her. She *insisted* on seeing you.'

Oh goodness.

What to do?

What to say?

Beth's eyes slid to Nora's. 'I came home because I don't feel well,' she said carefully. 'I'm sorry I didn't come round to your house as arranged and I'm sorry that I couldn't get a message to you in time.'

'I see.' Nora's voice was just as careful. 'I looked all over but I couldn't . . . find you, so I thought I'd better come over to see if I could help at all.'

'You've come all the way from London – and in a taxi to boot – because our Beth came home with a cold?' said Ma incredulously. And then she almost bobbed a curtsey.

Despite the circumstances, Beth smothered a smile. 'Might I have a word with Nora alone?' she said. 'I *was* meant to be staying with her tonight and I've been very remiss. I should like to apologise . . .'

'Of course,' said Ma. 'It sounds to me that an apology is in order. But wouldn't you like to receive your friend in the parlour?'

'Oh no. There's no need for that, Mrs Healey,' said Nora. 'Not if Liza is feeling poorly. I'll just have a word and then I'll be on my way again.'

'Liza?' asked Ma, wrinkling her brow.

'It's what they call me at the Depot,' said Beth, feeling her cheeks flush.

She didn't dare look at either of them.

'Nora, how are you getting back to London?' asked Ma. 'Can we help in any way? Another taxi or—?'

'Oh, don't worry, Mrs Healey,' said Nora cheerfully. 'The taxi from earlier is waiting for me. I've asked the driver to keep the meter running.'

Ma backed out, her eyebrows almost getting lost in her hair, and the girls could hear her muttering, 'A taxi to and from London. Oh, Lordy me,' as she headed towards the stairs.

Nora grinned and dropped heavily onto the bed, grabbing Beth's hands.

'What's happened?' she asked. 'Are you really ill?' She ploughed on without waiting for an answer. 'I went to the depot as we agreed. They were really suspicious and not very helpful at first but when I explained what had happened, they sprang into action. The manager – Mr Webster, was it? – said that if the letter had left London this morning, it would most probably already have been sorted and be on its way to Woodhampstead. He said it was a pity they didn't have more local checks and balances to stop this sort of thing happening but that it wasn't up to him and—'

'Shhh,' said Beth, wriggling one hand free and putting her finger to her lips. '*Shhh!* It's here!'

She pointed to under the mattress and then put her finger to her lips again.

'Oh.' Both Nora's hands flew to her mouth. 'You've got it? Oh, thank goodness for that. But . . . you haven't told your sister?'

'No,' Beth screwed up her face. 'No, how could I? Oh Nora, do you think I've done the wrong thing?'

Both girls were talking in urgent whispers as if Ma might still be listening outside. Nora got up, went to the door, shutting it firmly. Sitting back down on the bed again, she took one of Beth's hands in hers.

'I think you've done what you think is the right thing and that's all anyone can ask of you,' she said.

Beth allowed herself the ghost of a smile. 'But is it the right thing for Sally?' she said. 'That's what I'm asking myself. I won't go into work tomorrow, of course. I'll stay here, wait for the telegram to arrive and do my very best to comfort her. It's the least I can do.'

'But what about the letter?' asked Nora.

Beth shrugged. 'I'll slip it into the post,' she said. 'There's no point in letting on what's happened. It would just add to her distress knowing I knew before she did.'

Nora nodded. 'You're a good sister,' she said. 'But . . . Beth?' She wrinkled her nose.

Beth could feel herself blushing. There was no point in bluffing – even if she could think of something appropriate quickly enough. Not to Nora. Not after everything Nora had done for her that afternoon.

'I made up Liza,' she admitted in a small voice. 'I thought it was more interesting than Beth.'

To her surprise, Nora burst out laughing. 'Well, thank goodness for that,' she said. 'I'm actually called Leonora – *never* anything shorter – but I decided everyone would think that was far too stuffy.'

'Not really?'

'Really.'

The two girls smiled at each other. 'Our secret?' said Beth. 'Our secret.'

Beth didn't sleep well.

She tossed and turned, the letter burning a hole through the mattress.

At eleven o'clock she almost ran up the street to Sally's cottage to confess all. At one in the morning, she had to fight a shameful urge to open the letter and see what Sally had written. And, at three o'clock, she remembered that she'd received another letter that afternoon – one that she could very much open. She pulled out the letter from Sam and noted that the stamp was at an angle. More of an angle, even, than the stamp on the envelope she had sent to him. She ripped the envelope open and scanned Sam's news of patrols and inspections and dreary mess food.

Oh, what was she going to do?

How could she let him down when he could be in mortal danger?

How could she even consider doing so?

She settled back down to sleep with a heavy heart.

She hoped Nora was right.

She hoped all would be well.

The next morning, the terrible little scene played itself out as Beth knew it must.

A boy messenger – smooth-cheeked and aged no more than fourteen – arrived on cue with the telegram for Sally. Beth, up early and dressed but still ostentatiously poorly, could see him through her bedroom window, which looked out on the high street.

He was on his way to Sally's house and she could do nothing to change the awful course of events. She knew that, finding the cottage empty, he would be directed to the shop by villagers with curious, sympathetic and, yes, relieved eyes that today the very worst of news was not for them. With a heavy heart, Beth made her way downstairs.

When he finally arrived at the shop doorway, Beth for the first time really understood why the young boy messengers were nicknamed the 'angels of death' – just like the Zeppelins. Although she also couldn't help noticing how the young lad's hand shook and his lip trembled as he handed over the telegram.

A sister losing a husband at the height of the war was, Beth knew, a story as universal as it was deeply, tragically personal. For her, of course, the element of shock was missing and she experienced the little tableau as though through a pane of glass. But as she saw the colour drain from her sister's face, heard the raw howl of pain and hugged the shaking shoulders, she knew that she would never forget it for as long as she lived.

She played her part as she knew she must. She slipped Sally's returned letter into the afternoon's post and never breathed a word as to how it had got there. And, as her head pounded and her vision blurred and the professed nausea became real, she kept that as quiet as she could too and knew that she deserved it all.

23

Beth was back at work again the next day.

Much as she wanted to stay and comfort the inconsolable Sally, she had a job to do and, as Ma reminded her, Sally had plenty of support at home. So, Beth got back on the train to London with a certain relief at escaping the deep gloom that had descended on her little corner of Woodhampstead and her guilt over what had happened.

However, she had no sooner hung up her hat and jacket and squared her shoulders in readiness for another day at the coalface, than she found herself hauled in front of Miss Parker.

'I must say I'm most disappointed in you, Liza,' said Miss Parker before Beth had even had a chance to shut the door behind her.

Beth hesitated before sitting down, her heart pounding. She was ready to apologise – she *wanted* to apologise – but she needed to know exactly what it was she was apologising for. How much did Miss Parker know? Did she know that Sally's letter had been returned to her before the official telegram had been released? Did she know Beth had set off cross-country in a bid to intercept it? Did she know Beth had practically wrestled a letter that wasn't addressed to her off the Woodhampstead post girl?

Why exactly *was* Miss Parker disappointed in her?

With nothing in Miss Parker's expression to illuminate her, Beth just looked at her feet and mumbled 'yes, miss,' in reply.

Most unsatisfactory all round.

Miss Parker sighed. 'I stuck my neck out getting that promotion for you, Liza,' she said. 'In fact, I stuck my neck out getting you the job at all. And the very day I pull you up on falling behind on your quota, what happens? Instead of pulling your socks up as I'd expected, you disappear at lunchtime without so much as a by-your-leave. No note. No message. No attempt at all to clear it with anyone. You just upped and offed and left your team without a manager for the afternoon. What do you have to say for yourself?'

Beth paused.

How she wanted to just tell Miss Parker the whole sorry tale.

Even if it resulted in her being dismissed, at least she would be being true to herself, to Play-by-the-rules Beth. But she couldn't. How could she? If she told the truth, she would be exposing Milly and Nora as well.

'I'm so sorry, miss,' she said instead. 'I was feeling poorly so I . . . went home.'

How inadequate that sounded.

'Feeling poorly?' spluttered Miss Parker. 'Do you really expect me to believe that you, Nora Benham and James Blackford all felt sufficiently poorly at *exactly* the same time that you had to run out of the building together? What was it? Too many of the lady superintendent's jammy buns? The lure of the public house?'

'No, miss! None of those, miss . . .'

But *James*? What on earth did *he* have to do with anything? Of course, she couldn't ask, but she was burning with curiosity.

'I can't speak for Mr Blackford,' she said carefully, 'but Nora and I did ask Milly to let you know that we were both . . . inconvenienced.'

'That may well be the case, but that message didn't get

back to me until later in the afternoon,' said Miss Parker. 'By which time, of course, the information was quite useless to me. In Milly's defence, I gather she was sent over to the War Office and so she couldn't pass the message on. But, either way, she's not in your department anymore. You should have ensured you got a message to me or to someone in our department as protocol dictates.'

'Yes, Miss Parker. Sorry, Miss Parker.'

Miss Parker was drumming her fingertips on the desk. 'Now,' she said. 'You did manage to get a message to Miss Benham that you wouldn't be coming in yesterday – and I gather you have lost a family member, my condolences – so I won't discipline you for that. But Wednesday afternoon is a different matter and I would like you to make up the hours.'

'Yes, Miss Parker.'

Beth felt a swoop of relief. At least she wasn't being dismissed.

'Oh, and from the week after next, we are starting a new shift pattern from noon until eight in the evening as we continue our recruitment drive. Most of your team have already agreed to switch, as have Milly and Nora. I know you are not twenty-one, but needs must – and this would be a very good way to start getting back in my good books.'

'Yes, Miss Parker. Thank you, Miss Parker.'

This was actually a Good Thing. No more early starts.

But, oh, how she hated Miss Parker being disappointed in her.

Beth scarpered from the office with her tail firmly between her legs.

She hadn't even got back to the Broken Parcel Department when she bumped into James. The swooping in her stomach told her how thrilled she was to see him – closely followed by the old familiar guilt over Sam.

'Hello, Liza!' he said, with a smile that didn't meet his eyes. He looked even more pale and serious than usual. 'How are you? Can we talk?'

'I'm well, thank you,' said Beth. 'But I really mustn't be caught gossiping. I'm in enough trouble with Miss Parker as it is.'

James gave her a sympathetic grimace. 'What about a walk at lunchtime?' he said.

Beth's heart soared. She could think of nothing nicer than a stroll in the park with James. She'd even tell him the whole sorry story about Sally's letter . . .

But then she remembered. 'I can't, I'm afraid,' she said. 'I've got to work this lunchtime. In fact, I've got to work every lunchtime . . .'

James didn't answer for a moment. He just stood there, pulling on his ear and staring at her. Then he said, 'Have I done something to anger or upset you?'

'No, of course not,' said Beth, glancing over her shoulder to make sure Miss Parker hadn't noticed her chin-wagging in the middle of the Depot.

'It's just that you don't want to talk now, you can't talk at lunchtime and when I bumped into you a couple of days ago, you practically pushed me out of the way. What's going on?'

'Oh, James,' said Beth. It did sound really bad when he put it like that. 'You haven't done anything wrong. I really am in trouble and I really do have to work. Look, what about breaktime? I'd love to chat then.'

'Thank you,' said James.

'Don't *thank* me. The canteen?'

'Not the canteen, no,' said James. 'I'll come and find you. Show you somewhere else.'

And he was off, leaving Beth staring after him in confusion. Less than an hour later, he was back. He beckoned for

Beth to follow him and set off though the Home Depot, skirting the Letter-Sorting Section and the Registered Letters Section and then past the office where Milly and Nora were presumably hard at work in the Returned Letters Department.

At the end of the corridor was a doorway – more of an opening, really – that Beth hadn't noticed before. James beckoned again for her to follow him and they slipped through the gap together. It led into the new extension that had been going up over the past few months – and the source of the sawing and hammering that had plagued their working hours. Nothing exciting, the extension was a largely empty space with a small pile of sacks piled haphazardly towards one end. Beth knew that in just a few short weeks it would be packed to the rafters.

'Are we allowed in here?' she asked tentatively.

'Nothing to say we aren't,' said James, leading her behind the sacks. 'Besides, you and I are supervisors now, so don't we get to make the rules?'

'Not really . . .' said Beth with a nervous laugh. She trailed off, suddenly nervous. Why had James brought her in here? Then a thought struck her. Maybe he wanted to kiss her. After all, he had mentioned it only the other day and now, here they were, quite alone . . .

Sam . . .

'We've been coming here for a smoke when it's been too wet outside,' said James, sitting down on a little pile of sacks. 'Me and Milly and some of the others. In fact, we've been coming here ever since it was just a roof without walls. Made the perfect shelter, you see.'

Beth nodded and sat down beside him, smoothing down her skirts. It was a sunny autumn day. None of the smokers would be coming inside.

'Dreadful fire risk,' said Goody-Two-Shoes Beth, lightly. 'Anyway what's wrong? What's happened? And why didn't you want to meet in the canteen?'

Are you going to kiss me?

James's face suddenly crumpled and he started crying – huge, tearing sobs that fought to wrench themselves free. 'My father died,' he said simply.

Oh!

'I'm sorry,' said Beth. She had shuffled closer to him and put her arm around him before she realised what she was doing. 'I'm so, so sorry.'

James took hold of her hand. 'Thank you,' he said. 'Pneumonia, the doctor said, but really we all knew it was the war that ground him down after Ma died.' He gave an even deeper sigh. 'I should have stayed at home – I know I should – but I wanted to come to London to do my bit and I left him alone up there. I was a bad, *bad* son.'

Beth touched his shoulder. 'No, you weren't,' she said. 'None of it is your fault.'

James glanced at her. 'It *is* my fault,' he said fiercely, dashing tears from his eyes. 'And even when he was dying, I didn't get there in time. I just came into work, even though I knew how bad things were. It was only when you said I should go to him that I came to my senses. But by then it was too late. Too bloody late. The old bugger had slipped away by the time I got home.'

'I'm sure he was very proud of you. His clever son, a supervisor at the Home Depot—'

'Oh, what does that matter?' said James roughly. 'I'm just stopping the poor chaps at the front from telling their folks what it's really like out there. Probably better all round if I just waved their letters through. This bloody place. This bloody war.'

Beth hugged him tighter. There was nothing really that she could say. Imagine if it was Pa dying, slipping away all on his own. It didn't bear thinking about. So, instead, she told him the whole story of Sally's returned letter and, by the time she'd finished she, too, was in tears.

'Oh Liza, I'm so sorry,' said James. He twisted round and took her into his arms, rocking her gently to and fro. 'You did the right thing,' he said. 'Absolutely the right thing.'

Beth, her head against his chest, allowed herself to be soothed. 'I've just had enough of the war,' she finally admitted.

'Me too,' said James. 'Me too.'

Milly was full of remorse and contrition for having sent Sally's letter on its way.

'And I can't believe that you're now in trouble for it,' she said at lunchtime. She had come to visit Beth during her lonely vigil in the Broken Parcel Department and had smuggled a jammy bun for her. Beth couldn't help thinking that being caught eating on duty would not be the wisest thing at present, but Milly looked so down and dejected that she couldn't help but laugh.

'Thank you,' she said. 'But you eat it. Or give it to Fluffy.'

One of the Home Depot mousers – all nicknamed Fluffy – was hanging around, although that was probably because of the kippers in the parcel that Beth was repackaging, rather than the bun.

'I'm going to own up to Miss Parker,' said Milly, taking a bite of the bun. 'It's really not fair that you're taking the blame.'

'Don't,' said Beth. 'It's done now. You'll get in worse trouble than I'm in if you own up now. Best to let it lie.'

'But what can I do to make up to you?' said Milly.

'Nothing,' said Beth. 'But another meeting of the ELFS would be good – as would be more pie up the Roman.'

'Consider it done,' said Milly. 'Come and stay next Monday. And the pie is on me.'

'It's a deal. And we'll get Nora along too.'

24

After a sad and subdued weekend at home, Beth was relieved to get back to work at the Home Depot on Monday. The prospect of a night at Milly's was the icing on the cake – although the thought made her feel even more guilty.

To Beth's delight, Nora had agreed to come with them to the ELFS meeting that evening so, after work, the three girls boarded the Underground train at Portland Road Station. As they took their seats, Nora admitted with a little giggle that she had never ventured east of Liverpool Street Station.

'Never been to Petticoat Lane Market?' cried Milly, aghast.

'No.'

'Or down the Roman?'

'What's that?'

'Oh, I despair,' said Milly, putting her head in her hands comically. 'But I'm genuinely surprised you haven't been to the Whitechapel Gallery. I'd have thought that was right up your street!'

'Not even there!' said Nora, with a grin.

Beth was about to join in the good-natured ribbing when she caught herself. Until a few weeks ago, she had never even been as far east as Liverpool Street Station – let alone beyond it. She would be a fine one to talk!

'Well, here we are at Bow Road Station,' said Milly twenty minutes later as the Tube lurched to a stop. 'Brace yourself for the East End, Nora!'

★ ★ ★

Beth was excited about attending the ELFS meeting. She went into The Mothers Arms with a smile on her face and a spring in her step. Her enthusiasm and excitement only grew when Sylvia Pankhurst stopped to greet her. If Sylvia knew her name, it must mean she was really one of them.

But, to her dismay and consternation, everything was different this time. In fact, it started to go wrong as soon as the meeting started.

'I want to talk about our belief that working people have nothing to gain from a war that is being waged solely for the material gain of society's elite,' said Miss Pankhurst almost as soon as they had all sat down.

Wow. No beating around the bush this time!

Nora made a – presumably involuntary – sound that was akin to an indignant squawk.

'Did someone want to say something?' asked Miss Pankhurst, swinging in their direction. 'One of the Dusty Elves perhaps?'

Beth, who was right in Miss Pankhurst's line of sight, shook her head and carried on looking ahead, but she was aware of Milly turning to look straight at poor Nora.

Nora cleared her throat and said, perhaps more loudly than she meant to, 'Surely we all have *everything* to gain from winning the war? Everything's at stake. Our cultural identity, our very freedom – everything!'

She finished, looking Miss Pankhurst straight in the eye, and Beth held her breath. But, if the general assembly hadn't yet noticed her exquisite embroidery or the poised tilt to her head, they would certainly pick up on the perfectly modulated vowels. It shouldn't matter, of course. It really shouldn't matter . . .

Sure enough, the mumbling and murmurings had started to take on quite a different tone.

'Surely you accept that working people have different

interests to their supposed betters, even at a time like this?'
said the woman Beth knew to be called Betty.

'Careful, Nora, careful,' Beth mumbled under her breath.
She had noticed previously that Betty could be very sharp
of tongue. It really wouldn't do for Nora to get on the wrong
side of her.

Nora didn't hear Beth's caution – or, if she did, she chose
to ignore it.

'Not really,' she said. 'At a time like this, I think we should
be *all* be thinking of the men and boys at the front, regardless of our own personal circumstances—'

'Daddy tell you that, did he?' someone muttered in a
sneering tone.

Beth felt her heartbeat ratchet up a gear and, next to her,
she felt Milly stiffen.

'So, you wouldn't agree that the war isn't in the best
interests of some sectors of society?' persisted Betty, with a
dangerous tone to her voice.

Nora shot Beth a slightly desperate look. 'I just think we
should all be playing our part to make sure that we win the
war and not thinking about ourselves and our different
circumstances at the moment,' she said. 'We should be
focusing on what unites us, rather than what divides us.'

There was a silence, which persisted until it threatened
to become awkward. Beth wanted to help Nora out, but
somehow, she just couldn't. She found herself rooted to
her chair, mouth glued firmly shut, despising her own
cowardice but also wondering if she agreed with Nora.
Winning the war was important – of course it was – but
surely the poor shouldn't have to suffer more than the rich
in order to do so. Surely the poor should be protected from
further hardship and, if necessary, the rich should do much,
much more.

Oh, it was all so *complicated*.

On the other side of her, Milly sat apparently equally dumbstruck, her mouth a thin red line and pink blotches staining her cheeks.

This was *awful*.

Then Miss Pankhurst smiled pleasantly. 'Why don't you tell us why you're here, Miss . . . ?' she said pleasantly.

Nora glanced at Beth again. 'Miss Benham,' she said. 'And I'm here because Milly invited me and because I believe in votes for women. I thought that was the whole point of the suffragettes, to be honest.'

Silence.

Beth hoped against hope that no one recognised Nora's surname. Not that they should – Major Benham was far from a household name. Oh, why couldn't they just be talking about nurseries and rocking horses like last time?

Miss Pankhurst was still smiling. 'Votes for women is, of course, one very important strand of what we stand for,' she said. 'But, as you no doubt know, active campaigning for women's suffrage has been placed on hold for the duration of the war. In the meantime, we believe that workers across international boundaries actually have more in common with each other than they do with their ruling class.'

'That's preposterous!' exploded Nora.

Beth hardly recognised the usually mild-mannered Nora.

'Not preposterous at all,' said Betty. 'What's preposterous is that British transport workers are being called upon to shoot at German transport workers when, not so long ago, those same German transport workers sent five thousand pounds to help their British counterparts fight for better conditions.'

'Indeed,' said Miss Pankhurst. 'All sorts of reasons that sound glorious and patriotic are invariably put forward in support of war but practically every single one in history has been fought to protect the interests of powerful and wealthy financiers. One has only to look at the cost of food spiralling because of all the stockpiling and profiteering—'

'No!' Now *Beth* found herself on her feet, staring down Miss Pankhurst. 'No! That's simply not true. My family has a shop in Woodhampstead and Ma and Pa would *never* stockpile in order to put prices up like that. Never! That sort of behaviour is dishonest and just . . . beastly!'

Betty raised her eyebrows in a gloriously dismissive gesture. 'Well, I can't speak for what happens in *Woodhampstead,* of course,' she said, 'but my family are dockers and it's useless to talk about a scarcity of flour and sugar when there's tons and tons of it stacked up in the docks. Our men go in and see it, dearie. They *know.*'

'No!' said Beth, but with less conviction. She sat down, shaking. '*No!*'

'No one is accusing your parents of anything,' said Miss Pankhurst kindly. 'We're not talking about the middle class. It's the ruling class – factory owners, shipping company owners and so on – who are the problem. If we could only stop employers making such vast profits, I swear we would bring the war to an end.'

The conversation moved on. Beth sat there shaking slightly and looking down at her hands. Nora gave her a little nudge and a sympathetic smile but, on her other side, Milly was still staring straight forward and didn't acknowledge either of them at all.

'It's a pity we're not still using some of our pre-war tactics,' said Betty. '*They* were very good at getting the establishment's attention.'

'Remember, we're still organising demonstrations and sending deputations to government,' said Miss Pankhurst.

'Yes, but think what more we could achieve with more radical action,' said someone else with relish. 'Those bricks through the window always caused a stir.'

'Handcuffing ourselves to the railings was a guaranteed front page—'

'As was setting fire to postboxes. And if we could disrupt the post to the front lines, then so much the better—'

'No!'

Beth found herself on her feet again without any real idea of how she had got there. She had obviously stood up very abruptly this time, because her chair had clattered to the ground behind her – one upturned leg digging painfully into her calf.

'No,' she said again, more quietly but just as vehemently. 'The post is important. *Really* important.'

'I *know* it's important,' said the same woman. 'That's why I suggested it. In fact, there's some that say that the whole war could be won or lost on the back of it . . .'

Beth glanced round the room. Two dozen pairs of eyes stared back at her – except for Milly, who stayed looking straight ahead. Beth took a deep breath. 'I'm a supervisor in the Broken Parcel Department at the Home Depot,' she said. 'I see everything from small parcels of cigarettes and chocolates to large food hampers of home-made cakes and bread to packets of bandages and cocaine. Regardless of how big or small they are, it's all about the tie with home. You can't seriously be suggesting we set fire to them?'

Betty pursed her lips. 'If we damage them, we damage morale and the war will be over more quickly,' she said.

Nora stood up. 'I'm not listening to any more of this,' she said. 'I bid you all good evening.'

She picked up Beth's chair for her, touched her shoulder . . . and she was gone.

Beth wondered whether to follow her. But the white-hot bolt of anger that had flashed through her instructed her to stay and to finish her piece. 'Our boys at the front are living with the fear of death all the time,' she said. 'I can't believe you'd even think of destroying their only connections to their homes and loved ones.'

Beth was relieved that a couple of people replied with a 'hear, hear'. But Milly and Miss Pankhurst were not among their number.

'I think we should move on,' said Miss Pankhurst. 'Now, let's talk about funding . . .'

When the meeting finally broke up, Beth was the first to rush outside. There was no sign of Nora anywhere – not even in the street.

When she went back inside The Mothers Arms, Milly was holding out her hat and coat.

'Let's go,' she said shortly.

The two girls walked in stony silence most of the way down St Stephens Road. Just before they reached the Roman Road, Beth couldn't bear it any longer.

'Why didn't you stick up for me in the meeting?' she demanded.

Milly started as though she'd been slapped. 'What do you mean?' she said, stopping in the middle of the pavement.

'You know exactly what I mean,' replied Beth furiously. 'You didn't say *anything*. I can sort of understand why you didn't want to stick up for Nora, but you just sat there when they laid into me for saying trying to disrupt the post wasn't right.'

Milly still didn't say anything for a moment. Then she swung round to face Beth. 'So that's how you see it, is it?' she snapped.

'That's how I see it?' echoed Beth. 'That's how it *was*!'

'Well, shall I tell you how *I* see it?' said Milly. Her face, very close to Beth's, was screwed up with rage. 'I invite my *friends* – or at least people I thought were my friends – along to something that's important to me and instead of being polite and actually listening, they both start arguing and kicking up a fuss – and then one storms out. That's how I see it! *That's* how it was and I was mortified. I ain't ever taking either of you back there again.'

Beth hesitated. She hadn't thought of it quite like that before. 'But stopping the *post*, Milly!' she said. 'Surely you can't think that's a good idea?'

'That's not the point!' cried Milly. She pulled a handkerchief out of her coat pocket and blew her nose very vigorously. 'Bloody dust,' she added apropos of nothing.

'It's entirely the point,' said Beth. 'You promise me *right now* that you will never get involved in anything like that.'

Milly's violet eyes bored unblinkingly into Beth's blue ones.

'I don't have to promise you nothing,' she said, matter-of-factly, her cockney accent more pronounced than usual. Or maybe Beth was just noticing it more than usual, allowing it to underline the differences between the two girls and to show that what separated them might be more than what bound them together. 'I like you, Liza, and you're my friend an' that, but I don't have to promise you nothing.' All this time, Milly had been feeling in her pockets, her face growing more and more stricken. 'And what's worrying me more at the moment is that I don't seem to be able to find my admission card,' she added. 'I'm sure it was in my pocket, but it's not here anymore. Oh, for goodness' sake! That's the second one I've lost. I'll be fined for sure!'

'Stop changing the subject,' said Beth. 'Surely you don't – you *can't* – think it's a good idea to set fire to postboxes? I dread to think how Ned, how Sam – how all of them! – would be without their post.'

'Sometimes you got to look at the bigger picture,' said Milly, looking all around her on the pavement. 'Drat – where is it? It can't just have disappeared!'

'Shut up about your card!' Beth was nearly shouting by

now. 'And you can't believe disrupting the post is ever a good idea. Not after everything you've learned at the Home Depot. After everything they've done for you.'

'They ain't done nothing for me,' said Milly stoutly. 'They've just paid me for the work I've been doing. No more. No less. And it's a darned sight less than they'd pay a man for doing the same job.'

'So, you'd be willing to do something against the army post office would you?' said Beth. 'Oh, Milly, I can't believe I'm hearing this.'

'I never said that,' said Milly.

'Then promise me you're not going to do anything,' said Beth. 'Promise me you'll do nothing against the Home Depot or the army post office.'

'Listen to yourself,' said Milly. 'Like I said, I don't have to promise you nothing. But shame on you for asking. Now I'm going to go back to The Mothers Arms and see if my card's there. Do you want to come with me, or shall I see you at the pie shop?'

Beth hesitated, furious. 'Do you know, I don't think I'll do either,' she said, thoroughly riled. 'I think I'd much rather go home.'

'Suit yourself,' said Milly. 'I think I'd rather that too! And the sooner you work out who you are and what you stand for, the better it will be all round.'

Beth was back on the Underground and almost at King's Cross before she decided that she wouldn't go straight home. She was cross and upset and she had no wish to inflict her problems and her mood on her already suffering family. She would go around to Nora's first – it was only a few more stops on the same Tube line after all – and hopefully the two could try to make sense of what had happened that evening. Besides, surely it was only good manners to check that Nora had got home safely and maybe, if she was very lucky, Nora would invite her to stay the night and then there would be no need to arrive home unexpectedly with all the awkward explanations – or lies – that that would entail.

It was only when she was standing outside Nora's icing-cake house that Beth doubted the wisdom of her plan. Surely nicely brought-up young ladies didn't present themselves unchaperoned and uninvited at the front door of such dwellings at past nine o'clock at night on an autumn evening? It was most unseemly. Maybe she would be better off going down the basement steps and announcing herself at the servants' entrance.

Maybe she would be better off going home.

No, Beth. Stop overthinking everything. Just knock on the blasted door.

She rapped the door firmly with the gleaming brass knocker and stood back. Seconds later it swung open. A maid in a black and white uniform and – thank goodness – Nora just behind her.

Nora rushed forward. 'Oh, Liza,' she cried, all smiles. 'Come in, come in. Thank you, Sylvie,' she added to the maid. 'I'll see to Miss Healey.'

'Who's there, Leonora?' said a voice and, seconds later, Nora's mother appeared in the hallway, her mouth pursed with disapproval, glass tumbler in her hand.

'It's only my friend Liza, Mother,' said Nora. 'She was at the work thing with me tonight and had to stay later than expected. I said she could stay the night if it dragged on and on. It's far too late for her to go back to Woodhampstead tonight.'

'I see.' Mrs Benham sounded supremely disinterested. 'Well, the Rose Bedroom is made up.' And, without another word, she drifted back into the drawing room, leaving the air heavy with her musky scent.

'I hoped you'd come,' said Nora, grabbing Beth's hand. 'Let's go upstairs and you can tell me what happened after I left. Or,' she paused, 'are you hungry? Shall we grab something from the kitchen?'

'Starving,' admitted Beth.

Ten minutes later, the girls were sitting on the sumptuously appointed bed in the Rose Bedroom tucking into a lavish selection of cold cuts. Beth had laid out her napkin but Nora seemed unconcerned about getting pickle on the exquisitely embroidered counterpane. Beth supposed it wouldn't be her job to try and wash out any mishaps . . .

'So, tell me. What happened?' said Nora, pulling her knees under her chin.

Beth filled her in about the argument on the pavement.

'I am never, *ever* going back to an ELFS meeting,' said Nora, wiping her mouth on her napkin. 'I've never met such a bunch of rude, unpatriotic, dare I say *traitorous* women in my whole life. It was all I could do not to march out of there.'

Beth laughed. 'Err, you did march out,' she said.

Nora gave a rueful smile. 'I prefer to think I left with elegant haste,' she said. 'And I think I did very well to stay in there as long as I did. It was . . . hideous.'

'It was,' said Beth with a sigh. 'That meeting wasn't at all like the other one I went to. If it had been, I'd never have dragged you along.'

'Oh, I'm not blaming you,' said Nora. 'You weren't to know. But they're so against the war. It's *horrible*. And what on earth is Milly doing going there week after week?'

Beth hesitated, remembering what Milly's sister had said about Milly getting out of her depth and into trouble the year before. It was on the tip of her tongue to tell Nora but that wouldn't be fair. She didn't know the details. She didn't know exactly what Milly had or hadn't done.

'I suppose we have to take them at their word that they're not doing anything militant anymore,' she said instead.

But Nora was shaking her head. 'I know they *claimed* that,' she said, pushing her plate away from her. 'But I'm afraid I don't trust them. I won't be going there again.'

'Me neither,' said Beth sadly, remembering how excited, how inspired, she had been after her first meeting. But to continue going would feel like a slap in the face to Bertie and Reggie who, after all, had made the ultimate sacrifice for their country.

Late that night, Beth lay awake and thought about Milly.

She understood that Milly was upset that her friends had disrupted the meeting, and maybe she had a right to be so. And maybe it *was* unfair that the poor seemed to be taking the brunt of the war. Beth was certainly coming around to that way of thinking. But why had Milly just sat there when people started talking about sabotaging the postboxes and disrupting the mail? That, surely, was beyond the pale?

Oh, she knew Milly liked to sail close to the wind. She knew Milly could be pert and outspoken. Indeed, she knew Milly had a wild and impetuous streak – a bit like a horse that had yet to be broken in. She knew all that but, despite it all, she had always trusted that Milly's intentions were sound.

Now she couldn't help but wonder if that trust had been misplaced.

Maybe Milly intentions *weren't* honourable. Maybe she really *was* hell-bent on making mischief.

And maybe – just maybe – she had taken on her role at the Home Depot with mischief in mind. Maybe ELFS had encouraged her, helped her get the job, *masterminded* it even – so that they had someone on the 'inside' of the army post office. Beth sat bolt upright in bed. Gosh, maybe she was on to something here.

And the missing admission cards?

Maybe that wasn't simply the action of a careless, slapdash girl. Maybe there was something more sinister going on. Could Milly possibly have given her card to someone else? Beth felt a shiver of unease and pulled the bedcovers up around her shoulders. Why Milly might be doing that, she wasn't sure, but it was certainly a plausible theory. It would allow an unknown somebody to slip into the Home Depot and . . . what? Slip censored materials into the post? Spy on correspondence to and from the various fronts? *Meddle* with such correspondence? And when you factored the mysterious Mr Wildermuth lodging in her house into the mix . . .

Oh goodness, it really didn't bear thinking about.

Should she speak to Miss Parker? Voice her fears?

Even though ratting on one of her best friends went against just about everything that Beth believed in, maybe that was the right thing to do.

Beth sighed deeply and lay down again.

Here she was in the most lavish room she would probably ever have the opportunity of sleeping in, and she was thinking about Milly! Damn the girl! She would luxuriate in her surroundings, flick the light switch on and off a few times just because she *could*, and not think about Milly again until the morning.

25

Beth was no clearer as to what to do the next day.
Her suspicions about Milly seemed a little ludicrous in the cold light of day. This was Milly – her friend!

Of course she wouldn't rat on her to Miss Parker.

Then again, it was indisputable that Milly was heavily involved with ELFS and the more Beth had got to know the organisation, the clearer it was that they were only a hair's breadth away from creating public mischief again. And there was the case of the second missing admission card. The second that Beth knew about, to be precise – who knew how many more there might be? To be fair, Beth had no proof that Milly hadn't genuinely lost the cards – and for that reason she had decided not to mention it to Nora – but it did all seem more than a little suspicious.

She really should say something to Miss Parker.

But then again, Milly was still her friend . . .

Round and round Beth went, driving herself crazy with indecision. By the time she got into work, she had decided she should say something to Miss Parker. She could trust Miss Parker to be discreet and to do the right thing.

But Miss Parker wasn't in. Flu, Mrs Peters told her. She'd overheard Sergeant Major Cunningham talking about it.

Beth sighed. For very many reasons, she couldn't face talking to Sergeant Major Cunningham about Milly. The best thing to do would be to avoid Milly, bide her time and wait until Miss Parker was back in.

Milly clearly had the same idea about avoiding Beth. When Milly passed the Broken Parcel Department on the way back from the bathrooms, she totally blanked Beth. Oh, Beth knew Milly had seen her – the quick glance and the pursing of Milly's mouth were testament to *that* – but there was no smile, no greeting.

Nothing at all.

Despite it all, Beth felt a pang of sadness. Milly had been such a good friend. Along with Nora, the best friend she had ever had. It was awful that it had come to this, and it must be ten times worse for Nora if she was getting the same cold shoulder treatment in the same small office.

To make it all worse, James wasn't around for her to confide in. He was in Ipswich for his father's funeral. And, by the time he was back, she would be off work herself for Bertie's service. She wouldn't see James again until next week.

Beth sighed and picked up her clipboard. There was a lot to do, she was understaffed and she just needed to get on with it.

Milly didn't turn up in the canteen at breaktime. It was a drizzly early autumn day, so presumably she was having an illicit fag in the extension. Maybe Milly should report her for that, too . . .

Goodness, she thought, taking a sip of her tea. She was turning into a right little sourpuss.

'That was awful!' said Nora, plonking herself down beside Beth and throwing a newspaper on the table. 'Milly didn't say a word to me all morning.'

Beth gave her a sympathetic smile. 'I was afraid that might be the case,' she said.

'Were you meant to be staying with her tonight as well?' asked Nora.

'I was,' said Beth. 'I'll just go home though. I should spend some time with my—'

'No, you won't,' said Nora. 'Come and stay with me again. Because look what I've just seen.'

She pushed the newspaper towards Beth. Beth took a look, but the paper had been opened to an article about politics and Beth couldn't see what the fuss was about. 'What?' she said, slightly impatiently. 'Why would I come and stay with you because of the boring old Liberal party?'

'Not that, silly,' said Nora. '*This*.' She pointed at an advertisement below the article. 'The Women's Social and Political Union are holding a rally at Hyde Park. It's *tonight* at five thirty. If we leave work promptly, I reckon we could get down there in time.'

'Oh, Nora,' said Beth wearily. 'I've had enough of the suffragettes for one week.'

'But it's not ELFS,' said Nora. 'The WSPU are pro-war, I'm sure of it. So, we'll be able to support the votes for women cause without being unpatriotic. Come on, it's the perfect opportunity. It's just so lucky that Sergeant Collinson left his paper open on his desk or I'd never have seen it.'

'Another time—' started Beth.

'Liza! You promised,' interrupted Nora. 'You said if I came along to an ELFS meeting, you'd come along to a WSPU one. Don't go all provincial and "Beth" on me,' she added, with a sideways look.

Oh. That stung.

'Fine,' said Beth. 'I'll come.'

At five o'clock sharp, Beth and Nora met by the gate to the Home Depot compound. Milly had made no mention to Beth of coming to stay that night and Beth had had no wish to seek Milly out either. The earlier drizzle had given way to late afternoon sunshine and the two girls set off at a brisk pace.

'It's probably quickest to walk across the park,' said Nora.

'Oh, I'm so glad you agreed to come. Apart from anything else, it gives me the perfect excuse to miss cocktails with dreary Mr Cooper and his dreadful son. I can just say I was working late.'

Beth gave her a sharp look. 'I thought you wanted to support the women's movement,' she said.

'Oh, I do,' said Nora. 'And my friend Binky might be there too, which will be lovely. But my godfather is coming for drinks before they go to the theatre and I'm sure my mother wants me to marry his awful son. I can't say I'm sorry to be missing that.'

Nora gave a horrified shudder and Beth couldn't help but laugh. She linked her arm through her friend's.

It was only a meeting. What could possibly go wrong?

The WSPU event was already underway by the time Beth and Nora found the right part of Hyde Park. The rally was quite small – much smaller than the pictures of thousands upon thousands of massed people that Beth had seen in papers when Emmeline Pankhurst used to hold forth before the war. There must have been only a couple of hundred people there, many of them very well-to-do, but what they lacked in numbers they were making up for in noise and enthusiasm. A woman on a makeshift stage was bellowing into a megaphone about interning all people of enemy nationality and her supporters were duly cheering and waving a variety of placards echoing 'intern them all'.

Nora grabbed Beth's hand and they pushed their way to the front. 'Look, there's Binky,' Nora said. 'Let's go and say hello.'

Beth allowed herself to be led over to a ginger-haired freckled girl standing near the stage. She and Nora practically fell on each other with enthusiastic hugs and kisses and, from the ensuing conversation, Beth deduced that Binky had been trying to persuade Nora to come along to a WSPU meeting for months, was frankly amazed and delighted to see her there today, and however had she managed to give her mother and father the slip?

Nora pulled Beth forwards. 'It's all thanks to Liza,' she said. 'I would never have dared to come before I joined the army post office but this wonderful girl has given me so much courage.'

Beth blinked. That certainly wouldn't have been her version of events, but who was she to argue?

'Ah yes, the army post office,' said Binky. 'I was amazed when I heard you'd persuaded your parents to let you work there, Leonora. Good show! And you too, Liza. If only we could get more women into national service, more men could be conscripted and this bloody war would be over before we knew it.'

Beth smiled. At ELFS she had felt like she was rather seedily profiteering from the war by taking a job that had been opened up because of it, but here she was being positively praised for it.

'Now, do you fancy helping out tonight?' Binky was saying. 'There are loads of jobs you could do – or you could just stand and listen.'

'Happy to help,' said Nora and Beth nodded.

'Marvellous,' said Binky. 'Let me just ask Alice what she'd like you to do.' She turned and started conferring with a stout woman sitting behind a table next to the stage and swung back to Beth and Nora holding two little baskets.

'If you wouldn't mind starting to distribute these, that would be a great help,' she said.

Beth wondered what was in the baskets. Leaflets of some description, she supposed. It would be a little embarrassing handing them out to perfect strangers – Beth was still naturally shy, despite all her new experiences – but those strangers were presumably here because they had some sympathy with the WSPU and, of course, Liza would revel in it all.

'Be very polite,' Binky was saying and Beth felt a tinge of impatience. Of *course,* she would be polite. Who did Binky think she was? 'One to every man of military age in civilian dress.'

Beth felt a twinge of alarm and glanced into the proffered basket. White feathers.

The symbol of cowardice.

Beth stood still and the world seemed to stop with her. She couldn't do it.

Wouldn't do it.

A vision of James – lovely, proud, idealistic James – came into her mind. As brave as any man she had known but who had his own reasons for not signing up. Who were WSPU to decide that those who hadn't yet signed up were cowards?

How dare they?

She glanced over at Nora. She was holding the basket and laughing at something that Binky had said like she didn't have a care in the world.

The whole world was going mad.

Quite, quite mad.

Beth let the basket drop to the ground. Feathers fluttering out, twisting and turning in the breeze. Faces turning to her.

Beth ran.

Once on the train to Woodhampstead, Beth found that she couldn't stop shaking. It was all a disaster.

She was a disaster.

She was thrashing around, turning with the tide, with no idea who she was or what she believed in. She had upset Milly the day before and she had no doubt upset Nora today.

She was in love with a man – yes, finally she could admit

that to herself – who didn't believe in the war and yet she was giving hope to a man who was still at the front.

It was all just a terrible mess. She was out of control, out of her depth . . .

And her head was pounding away.

Home.

She would stay at home.

She would take an extra day off, stay at home for the rest of week, support her sister as best she could at Bertie's funeral on Thursday and not go back to the Home Depot until Monday.

Maybe she wouldn't go back at all.

26

It was lovely to be home.

Even though Bertie's service was unbearably sad, it was wonderful to be back with people who knew and understood her. To be back with people who didn't expect anything of her.

To be in a place where being Beth was enough.

On the Saturday morning, she volunteered to help in the shop. Ma was uncharacteristically poorly with the flu and it was the least she could do. And then Sally appeared, pinched and red-eyed.

'I can't just sit and do nothing,' she said.

'Oh, Sally,' said Beth. 'Have a lie in. I'll come and check on you in a while.'

'No, no. I'm better off keeping busy.'

And the two sisters set to work. Just like old times.

I'm back in the shop and nothing has changed.

I'm back in the shop and nothing has changed.

The words started beating like the clatter of hooves on cobbles through Beth's head, tightening across her skull and making her temples throb.

And I haven't changed.

I haven't changed at all.

These words were higher, shriller, like the clang of trolleys or the whistles at King's Cross. They made Beth's breath catch and her hands shake – as though they belonged to someone else . . .

'That's under, Elizabeth.' Mrs McBride's voice was sharp. 'Don't be tricky with the butter. There's a war on, don't you know!'

Sweat prickled the roots of Beth's plait under her neat, white cap. She was *never* tricky with the butter. She was never tricky with *anything*. It wasn't in her nature and . . .

Actually, that wasn't quite true, was it?

She had proved she could really be quite tricky when tricky was called for.

Not that she was especially proud of the fact, but she couldn't deny that it was true. And what was also true was that she'd had enough of Mrs McBride's constant carping and criticising.

'Now, Mrs McBride,' she said lightly. 'You know by now that J.A. Healey, General Provisions of Woodhampstead, is built on honesty and that we are *never* tricky with the butter. And you know too that, while the first piece I take off the main block might well be under half a pound, by the time I've patted on more with the wooden pats – like so – the scales will balance perfectly.' Beth stopped talking and gave Mrs McBride a friendly smile as she smacked the misshapen lump into a smooth, neat rectangle. 'Now, will there be anything else?'

For a moment, Mrs McBride looked as though she might have plenty to say but then she swallowed her response. 'Two pounds of tea, please,' she said meekly.

Beth gave her another smile. 'I'm sure you have a very good reason for asking for all that tea – a fete, perhaps, or maybe packages for the prisoners of war – but we're running low on tea at the moment. Unless customers have a special letter of dispensation, we are asking that they restrict their purchases to half a pound for the time being so that there is enough to go around. Will that be all right for you?'

Again, there was a little pause while Mrs McBride considered her alternatives.

'Half a pound will be acceptable,' she said finally.

'Excellent.' Beth put both purchases carefully into Mrs McBride's basket and entered the sale into the ledger. 'Have a lovely day, Mrs McBride,' she said.

'You too, Elizabeth.'

And Mrs McBride was gone.

Sally turned to Beth, her mouth a round O of surprise.

'What on earth got into you there?' she said.

'I don't know,' said Beth, feeling almost as surprised. 'I think I've just had enough of being put down by old ladies like Mrs McBride.'

'But the "letter of dispensation"!' said Sally. 'What on earth *is* a letter of dispensation when it's at home?'

'I have no idea!' said Beth. 'I just made it up on the spot.'

And Sally very nearly smiled.

Later, Beth brought some tea up to her mother. Ma, lying in bed, was flushed and coughing weakly.

'Is the shop busy?' she asked, shuffling to a sitting position as Beth put the cup and saucer down on the nightstand.

'Not at the moment,' said Beth. 'Mrs McBride has been and gone and there's a bit of a lull.'

Ma patted the bed. 'Sit, then, and talk to me,' she said. 'Tell me about your grand job in the city.'

Beth sat down. She really didn't want to talk about the Home Depot. She didn't know if she wanted to go back there.

'I'm sorry I took the job without telling you,' she said. The words were out of her mouth before she could stop them. She hadn't planned to say that.

'Oh, Beth, I'm not blaming you,' said Ma, patting Beth's

hand. 'We were wrong trying to keep you in Woodhampstead. And look at you now, all grown up. A supervisor in the army post office, no less. We're so proud of you. The whole *village* is so proud of you.'

Beth forced a smile, feeling even worse. What was the 'whole village' going to think if she gave up her glamorous job and slunk back to Woodhampstead?

'Tell me about your friends,' persisted Ma. 'I must say that the young lady who came to visit you when you were poorly was most charming.'

'Yes, Nora is super,' said Beth. Although she couldn't help but think that Nora was hardly likely to return the compliment after Beth had flung the feathers to the ground like that.

'Who else are you friendly with?' asked Ma.

Beth hesitated. She was still devastated that she had fallen out with Milly – that it had all gone wrong – but she didn't want to talk to Ma about that. Then there was James, of course . . .

She took a deep breath. 'There's another friend I'm fond of,' she said slowly, feeling her way. 'We've both got brothers at the front and we were getting . . . close. But this friend has had an awful run of bad luck. Their father has just died and their mother is already dead and they've moved into lodgings near the Home Depot and . . . I'm worried about them. That they're all right, I mean. And I don't know what to do.'

Ma was quiet for a moment. 'Such a terrible time for you young people left behind, this war,' she said. 'We tend to forget that. I'm sure you will be a great comfort to your friend, Beth – you're sensible and you're kind. And if she ever needs somewhere to come and stay away from London, she's welcome here for as long as she wants. I'd like to think someone would do the same for you if the need arose.'

Beth was touched beyond words. 'Thanks, Ma,' she said. 'I'm sure it won't come to that, but . . . thank you.'

She bent over and kissed her mother's soft cheek, then stood up. To think she had almost become estranged from Ma and Pa. How important your family were. How important to keep them close.

'How is she?' asked Sally, when Beth arrived back in the still empty shop.

'Still coughing,' said Beth. 'Still quite hot. It's a nasty bug. I wonder where she got it from.'

Sally looked at her curiously. 'What do you mean?' she said. 'She got it from you of course. That day you came home early from work and were feverish. The day before . . .'

She trailed off as a customer came into the shop and Beth exhaled a ragged breath.

Oh goodness. That was close.

She must be more careful in future. *Much* more careful.

There was a sudden flurry of customers and Beth and Sally were kept busy for the next few minutes. But, when the shop was empty again, Sally turned to Beth with a look that made Beth's toes curl.

'You weren't poorly, were you?' she said and her voice was . . . different.

Beth hesitated.

What to say? 'I felt awful,' she said honestly. 'But I'm better now. Back to normal.'

'No, what I mean is that I don't think you were *ever* poorly.' Sally was staring at her, her red-rimmed eyes suddenly icy. 'Something hasn't been adding up in my mind ever since that day, but that comment about Ma just confirmed it. It's just too much of a coincidence that you arrived home unexpectedly the day before we heard about Bertie. Something happened, Beth, didn't it? Something you haven't told me.'

Beth's mind went totally blank and she stared at her sister in horror. What on earth could she say?

Sally's eyes narrowed. 'You knew,' she whispered. 'Oh my, Beth. You *knew* Bertie was dead, didn't you? You knew the day before I found out.'

Trapped and cornered, Beth could only give the tiniest of nods and bury her head in her hands.

'How!' said Sally. She sounded icy cool and that somehow was worse than her breaking down. 'How on *earth* did you know before I did?'

And Beth could only blurt out the whole story. Sally's letter being redirected to her by mistake before the official telegram had been dispatched. Beth racing up to Woodhampstead to intercept it and slipping it in the following day's post.

'I'm sorry,' Beth finished. 'I thought I was doing the right thing.'

Sally had listened to the whole sorry tale without saying a word. Now she was shaking her head. 'How could that possibly be the right thing?' she demanded.

'I didn't want you to find out that Bertie had died by getting your letter returned to you!' cried Beth.

'Yes, that much I understand,' said Sally.

'Can you?' whispered Beth. Maybe it was going to be all right.

'Yes,' said Sally. 'I can understand you coming home and intercepting the letter. That was kind. But what I'm failing to grasp is why you didn't then tell me the truth. Why make me wait to receive that unbearable telegram from that poor boy the next day?'

'Because . . . because . . .' Beth trailed off.

Why, exactly, *had* she done that?

'Cat got your tongue?' said Sally, her anger showing at last. 'I'll tell you exactly why you did it. You did it because you wanted to stop your precious friend at the Home Depot getting into trouble.'

'No . . .' stammered Beth. 'No.'

'Oh, admit it,' said Sally in disgust. 'You had a choice and you put them before me. Even though there's no way I'd have ever kicked up a fuss.'

Beth was stung into silence. What could she possibly say to defend herself? 'I didn't want you finding out the wrong way,' she said at last. That, at least, was the truth.

'Ha! As if there's a right and wrong way to find out your husband's died. You've changed, Beth,' Sally spat. 'You've changed so much I hardly recognise you anymore. Perhaps I should start calling you Liza. Liza! What a ridiculous name.'

'You thought it was funny before,' said Beth, hurt.

'Well, I certainly don't think it's funny now. How do you think Ma felt when your hoity-toity friend called you Liza? As if the name we call you isn't good enough for you anymore. As if you're ashamed of us all.'

'I'm still Beth,' said Beth in a small voice.

'No, you're not,' said Sally hotly. 'Beth would never have done this. Beth wouldn't have lied and hidden that letter from me. Beth would have been brave and she would have told me Bertie was dead. I knew Beth but I really don't know who *you* are anymore.'

'I'm so sorry,' whispered Beth.

'And while you're being sorry, what about writing to your twin? Ned says he hasn't heard from you for weeks.'

Beth felt a stab of shame pierce her. 'Sally, I'm sorry!'

'Don't apologise to me! Meanwhile you seem to have plenty of time to send letters with crooked stamps to Sam Harrison when the whole village knows that he started stepping out with Ivy Hastings just before he left!'

What?

The room started swirling and Beth gripped onto the counter for support.

Sam was stepping out with Ivy.

'Are you sure?' she said. 'You're sure Sam is stepping out with Ivy?'

'Quite sure,' said Sally scornfully. 'I heard Mrs Harrison talking about it a couple of days ago. I'd stop sending him letters with crooked stamps before you make a complete fool of yourself, if I were you.'

After her shift, Beth went up to her room, her mind buzzing with all sorts of thoughts and feelings.

She deserved that reaction from Sally. She knew she did.

But now everyone was angry with her at home as well as at work. Sally for not telling her about the returned letter. Ned for not writing to him. She'd really let herself down there.

But *Sam*.

Sam and Ivy were sweethearts.

And that meant that the path was clear for her to be with James . . .

27

Beth went back to the Home Depot.

Of course, she did. She and Sally had reached an uneasy truce – Sally obviously mortified that she had told Beth about Sam's romance with Ivy so bluntly – but the atmosphere at home was still so oppressive, it was a relief to get away. Nothing Nora or Milly could throw at her could be worse than that.

It was the first day of the new shift pattern and she sat on the almost empty mid-morning train wondering ruefully how she could have got the situation so wrong with Sam. How on earth had she conjured up a budding romance out of a few off-kilter stamps? Decided that she and Sam were practically sweethearts? Sent him a *pillow*, for goodness' sake? She cringed at the thought of it. She clearly had a lot to learn in matters of the heart and really, she should be feeling thoroughly ashamed of herself, but what she really felt was relief. Sweet, exquisite relief that this cleared a path to James. And he'd wanted to kiss her . . .

James wasn't in the Home Depot. Discreet enquiries led to conflicting reports. He had been seen first thing that morning but had now gone to the War Office for the rest of the day. He had been in but had been sent home poorly. He was still up in Ipswich.

Beth sighed. Whichever was true, she clearly wasn't going to see him that day.

Nora was very much in. She pounced on Beth in the

first break. 'Liza! Doesn't this all feel topsy-turvy? Morning break at two in the afternoon! And how was Bertie's service? And—'

'I'm sorry about the feathers,' said Beth quickly. 'I just thought it was such a dreadful thing for them to ask us to do.'

Nora looked her silently for a moment and then, to Beth's surprise, she burst out laughing. 'Me too,' she said. 'It was *terrible*.'

'So . . . you didn't give them out?' ventured Beth.

'Of course I didn't. I only wish I'd been brave enough to throw them on the ground like you. Really, it was marvellous. A big white cloud of feathers; it looked like there'd been a pillow fight.'

'Oh!' Beth smiled ruefully. 'I didn't mean that to happen! I was just so shocked. I'd been thinking that I agreed with the WSPU and then . . . that!'

'I know,' said Nora. 'The only bad thing is that it got back to Milly that we'd been to a WSPU rally and now she seems even more upset with us than before. She's in trouble anyway, so she's none too happy. Something about her admission card.'

Beth felt a swoop of relief. If Miss Parker was already aware of what was going on with Milly's cards, then surely there was no need for Beth to get involved. She would just give Milly a wide berth in future. It was sad, but it was the best thing to do.

Beth worked hard all day. When the new day shift left at 5pm, the Home Depot felt like a different place. The usual background chorus of thousands of people going about their daily business had gone, leaving a strange eerie calm. The electric lights cast harsh shadows over sacks and baskets and deepened the deep, disapproving lines radiating from Mrs Peters's mouth. (Beth wished fervently that the woman had remained on the day shift, but was determined to make the best of it.) At first, Beth had kept reminding herself not to stare directly at the lights, and then laughed at her silliness. Everyone nowadays knew that electric lights couldn't blind you – not even the big industrial ones lighting the Depot.

She reached for another parcel. With only ten of them working that evening, she found she was less a supervisor and more a team member with a mountain of packets to deal with before 8pm. The piles of sacks seemed never-ending – and everyone said this was the calm before the Christmas rush . . .

Beth pulled apart the brown paper wrapping of the latest parcel. It was big and very heavy and the whole thing was disintegrating in her hands. She would have to start from scratch with this one, possibly repacking the contents into a sturdy cardboard box if she could find a suitably sized one. She pulled out the only item inside. It was a fruitcake, and an absolutely massive one at that. She knew soldiers tended to share their packages from home and it looked like Private George Williams and his compatriots were in for quite a treat.

Beth was leaning down to rummage under the table for a suitable box when something in the cake caught her eye. Something amber, just breaking through the surface. At first glance, it looked like dried fruit – some angelica, maybe? – but it was larger and shinier than she might expect. Curious, she touched it, and drew her finger back sharply when she felt the cool, hard surface of what was unmistakably glass.

What the dickens?

With a sneaking suspicion of what she might find, she scraped a little of the cake away. Yes, more amber. And more. Finally she nudged Ruby next to her.

'Look what I've found,' she said in a sing-song voice. She reached into the cake and, with a triumphant scatter of crumbs, pulled out the bottle of whisky that had been secreted there.

And so, she and the whole group were laughing when James's friend Denny poked his head around the partition into the Broken Parcel Department and looked around at them curiously.

'Can I help you, Denny?' asked Beth, composing her features and wondering if they were about to be ticked off for being too raucous on duty.

'I just wondered if you've seen James?' the soldier asked.

Beth looked at him in surprise. 'I haven't, I'm afraid,' she said, her spirits lifting at the thought of James. 'I didn't think he was on duty tonight.'

The groove between Denny's eyebrows deepened. 'He's not. But he turned up an hour or so ago, went off for a smoke and hasn't come back.'

Beth was aware of the other women looking at her curiously and got up to join Denny so that they could speak together more quietly. 'Surely he could be anywhere,' she said. 'In the canteen? Maybe he's popped out to buy tobacco?'

Denny shook his head. 'He's not in the canteen,' he said, 'and the chap on the gate says he hasn't left. Still,' he added, rubbing his hands together, 'I'm sure he'll turn up sooner rather than later.'

And off he went.

Beth sat down again, feeling the first prickling of unease. Still, as Denny had said, James was a grown man and he could be anywhere. And, in the meantime, she had the little matter of the smuggled bottle of whisky to sort out . . .

It was when she was halfway through the paperwork that Beth realised exactly where James would be. He would be having a cigarette in the – as yet empty – new extension; the place he had taken Beth just after his father had died. Of course, that was where he'd be. He probably just needed a little time to himself.

But it was a bit strange that he'd come in at all, if he wasn't due in.

The question was, should Beth go and join him? Would James welcome her company, or would he rather be left on his own? There was no real way of knowing. She would finish off processing the errant parcel and repack two more parcels and then she would go in search of him.

Yes, that's exactly what she would do.

Two parcels later, Beth duly headed through the Home Depot in search of her friend. The vast open area was emptier now than usual, but there were still at least a hundred men and women sitting in rows in front of their wooden sorting frames. Beth walked past the familiar signs – Gallipoli, Serbia, Salonica, Mesopotamia – and on to the Honour Envelope Department.

There was no sign of James.

Denny came over to her. 'He's still not back. I've no idea where he's gone.'

Beth nodded. 'I'll take a look around.' There was no point in giving away James's hiding place, if indeed he was there.

'Thank you,' said Denny. 'I must admit I'm a bit worried. Since he found out his brother died, he's been acting very erratic . . .'

Wait.

What?

'His *brother* died . . . ?' said Beth.

Surely there was some mistake.

'Yes,' said Denny. 'I assumed—'

'Do you mean his brother,' interrupted Beth. 'I mean, I know his father—'

'Yes. I mean his brother. And his father. Both. He came

into work this morning, but we sent him home. And then he just pitched up an hour or so ago—'

Beth didn't wait for him to finish. She set off back across the Home Depot at a run, skirting the Broken Parcel Department and the Returned Letters Department and on to the entrance to the new extension.

A door had been added since the last time she was here and there was light coming from underneath it.

Beth hesitated for a moment. There was nothing specifically to say 'do not enter' or to otherwise imply that the room was out of bounds – but still. There was nothing on Sergeant Major Cunningham's office door to say the same and everyone knew that you didn't just barge in.

Still, needs must.

Beth took a brief look around her, pressed her ear to the door and then gingerly turned the handle. It wasn't locked. She pushed the door open and poked her head inside, taking a good look around. Where once had been empty echoing space, were now thousands upon thousands of sacks, slumped on top of each other in tottering piles, some reaching almost to the rafters. It was obviously being used as an overflow storage area because there didn't seem to be anyone around. Beth's first thought was to wonder, with a sinking heart, how many of the sacks contained broken parcels and how on earth she and her team were supposed to get on top of them this side of Christmas. Then she remembered her mission.

She slipped inside and shut the door silently behind her. Then she crept cautiously forward, almost on tiptoe, to a pile of sacks that was obscuring her view of the centre of the room.

'James?' she whispered.

Suddenly, there was an almighty, ungodly yowl and something shot in front of her. Beth stepped backwards with a little screech, hand to heart, before realising with relief that she had disturbed one of the Home Depot mousers.

'Bloody cat,' she muttered.

It was only as her heart rate returned to normal that she registered the low chuckle coming from behind the pile of sacks.

'Fluffy frighten you, did he?'

'James!' Half-embarrassed but mainly relieved, Beth skirted the pile of sacks and there he was, lounging against a table, cigarette in hand. 'You've got half the Home Depot looking for you . . .'

'Have I indeed?' said James, with a crooked half-smile.

'Well, no, not exactly,' admitted Beth. 'But Denny was worried. He told me about your brother so I've come to check you're all right. Well, not all right, but you know what I mean. Oh, James. I'm so, so sorry. I almost can't believe it.'

James didn't answer for a moment. He just took a deep drag from his cigarette, exhaled deeply and looked at Beth through half-closed eyes.

'I hoped you'd come,' he said simply.

Oh, the joy! 'Did you?' she said.

'Yes. I wanted to say goodbye.'

Joy turned to confusion and unease. 'Goodbye?' she echoed stupidly. 'Why? Where are you going?'

Then she looked around and, for the first time, took in her surroundings. On the floor in front of James, one of the sacks had been upended and some of the letters had been pulled out into a little trail. The trail led directly to a sack, which had been lined up to touch another, which in turn touched another, and another, all the way over to the big tottering pile.

The prickle of uneasy fear turned to icy fear.

Beth's eyes slid to James in horror.

'What in God's name do you think you are doing?' she whispered, although the plan was abundantly clear.

'It's the best way,' said James, holding his lit cigarette up. 'In fact, it's the *only* way!'

'No, it's not,' said Beth. 'What on earth are you talking about? This whole room would go up in smoke.'

'That's the general idea,' said James with a disturbing little smile. 'In fact, I'm hoping the whole Home Depot will burn down.'

Oh God! James had gone mad.

Stark. Staring. Mad.

He did, in fact, look deranged: lounging against the table, smiling up at her, cigarette dangling from his fingers, but she saw it immediately for what it was. The loss of his father and his brother in quick succession had tipped the poor man over the edge.

This wasn't James. It wasn't the real James, anyway.

But it was the James she had to deal with in the present moment.

The question was, what was she going to do about it? Should she make a run for it? There was nothing between her and the door, and she could dash out and get help.

No. That would take time.

Time she didn't have.

By the time help arrived, the whole place could be ablaze. She had seen how quickly the sack dust caught fire when Milly dropped her cigarette all those weeks ago . . .

Maybe she could tackle James, or at least try to take him by surprise and snatch the cigarette off him? No, that was a ridiculous idea: he was far bigger and stronger than her and, anyway, he had only to toss the cigarette butt and the game would be up.

No, she would just have to try and calm him down. Talk him out of it.

It was the only thing she could do.

She took a deep breath. 'Come on, James,' she said cajolingly. 'You've had a huge shock and you're not being yourself. Why don't we go to the canteen and have a good chat? If nothing else, I can tell you about the bottle of whisky I've just found hidden inside the most enormous fruitcake.'

She held her breath.

Would that work?

Or had it been a mistake to try to lighten the tone? Sure enough, James was shaking his head.

'No,' he said. 'I don't want to hear about the elaborate lengths people are going to, to smuggle goods to the front and prolong the war. I'm serious, Liza. I'm serious about all this.'

He gestured to the envelopes and the sacks with the cigarette and Beth's heart sank.

What now?

What could she possibly say now?

She said the first thing that came into her mind. 'I'm not really called Liza,' she said.

James narrowed his eyes as he took another drag. 'What do you mean?' he said. 'What is your name then? And why have you changed it? Are you undercover? A spy?'

'No!' Beth couldn't help laughing despite the gravity of the situation. 'No, I'm not a spy! I *am* really called Elizabeth but my family and everyone else call me Beth.'

'So why does everyone call you Liza here?' asked James, his eyes never leaving her face.

'Because I told them to,' said Beth. 'Because . . .' Her eyes cast around the room while she sought an explanation. Why *had* she thought it would be a good idea to reinvent herself as Liza? 'Because I was afraid that being Beth wasn't enough,' she finished in a tiny voice. Might her honesty help bridge the gap between herself and James?

But James just shook his head in frustration. He pushed himself away from the table and started pacing around the table.

'Bloody hell,' he said. 'No one and nothing is what it seems.

Even *you*,' he added accusingly, spinning on his heel and glaring at Beth. 'Everyone is hiding behind a façade, pretending to be something they're not. Even this great Home Depot, the largest bloody wooden building in the world, is built on a lie. It pretends to be all about getting home comforts to dear old Tommy at the front – "a little slice of home" – whereas it's really just part of the conspiracy. Keep the lies going, blind the little people, keep morale high. Sell the lie, sell the lie. Don't you think I would be doing everyone a favour by letting this cigarette drop right here? Maybe – just maybe – if we destroyed all these parcels, all this Christmas post, all the propaganda we know is going to the various fronts – well, maybe then the little people might actually revolt and the war might be over.'

'Oh James, stop it. *Stop* it!' said Beth. 'Your brother wouldn't want you to be doing this. Think of him if no one else.'

'How do you know?' James was practically shouting now. 'How do you know all the poor saps at the front aren't longing for someone to do something like this? Something – *anything* – to try and make the killing stop more quickly?'

'But this isn't the way,' Beth cried. 'It's really not the way. And, if we don't go up with the building, *you* would certainly be hanged for treason.'

'Oh, what does it matter?' yelled James. 'Men are dying by the million. The world wouldn't notice another one. And who would miss me anyway? My whole family is gone. At least this way I might go out doing some good.'

'*I* would miss you,' shouted Beth. 'I would miss you very much.'

She hadn't meant to say that. It wasn't another attempt to calm James down and to alter his course of action.

She had just said it . . . because it was true.

She would, she realised, miss James very much.

She had to convince him of that too. And hope against hope that it mattered to him.

'I would miss you very much,' she repeated. 'Our talks and the way we can discuss our differences. Our walks in the park and to the Tube. You rescuing me from that horrid man in the unloading bay that day.'

To her relief, James's shoulders dropped and he smiled at her. Not a mad, staring smile, either, but his familiar crooked grin. 'Do you remember what I said to you that day?' he said.

'Of course, I do,' said Beth. 'You said you wanted to kiss me. And can I let you into a little secret?'

'What?'

'I wanted you to.'

James gave her a proper smile this time. 'Did you?' he said. 'Did you really, Liza – I mean Beth?' He stopped and laughed. 'Actually, I much prefer Beth to Liza,' he said. 'It's much softer. It's much more you.'

Suddenly, Beth was laughing too. 'Is it?' she said. 'Who knew there was so much in a name? I really don't know why I ever said my name was Liza. Showing off, I suppose. Trying to pretend I'm something I'm not. I'm so stupid. I'm just Beth from the general store in Woodhampstead.'

'You're not stupid,' said James gently. 'And you're not "just" anything. Well if you're "just" anything, you're "just" finding your way. Just like the rest of us are. You don't have to have all the answers. You only have to be true to yourself.'

He was walking towards her and Beth suddenly realised, with a great big exhalation of relief, that it was all going to be fine. It had been close – grief had driven James to the edge – but disaster had been averted and everything was going to be fine. And now he was going to kiss her. Or she was going to kiss him.

James stopped and frowned. 'The man you're writing to . . . ?' he said tentatively.

Beth hesitated. It was on the tip of her tongue to tell James that she had ended it, but she stopped herself. There were to be no lies or half-truths between them.

'It's over,' she said. 'Well, to be honest, I don't think it ever really started. I thought it might be something, Then I met you and we got to know each other, and I cursed myself for ever writing to him and I didn't feel I could let him down when he was away at the front. But in the end I think his stamps were crooked by accident since he's stepping out with someone else.'

James started laughing. 'Well, thank goodness for that, you idiot,' he said affectionately. 'You don't know how relieved I am to hear that. But isn't the stamp code actually meant to *help* communication? Now, where were we?'

'Here,' said Beth. She took a step towards James and tilted up her face towards him. James lowered his and—

'Ouch!'

James had staggered backwards. 'Damn,' he shouted, waving his hand around. 'Damn! Ouch!'

Beth looked at him, confused. They had been about to kiss – she had been sure of it – and now, this. Then she saw the smouldering cigarette stub on the ground and she understood. Unnoticed by either of them, the cigarette had burned down to James's fingers and he'd dropped it. She rushed to stub it out but, before she could, the floor around the cigarette stub whooshed into flame. Beth and James caught each other's eyes with surprise rather than alarm. It was only a small blaze. Just a little drama on top of everything the evening had already thrown at them. They'd get it under control and—

They both started stamping on the little flames to extinguish them. But the fire was spreading. It was eating the sack dust and dancing along the floor, red and orange fingers fanning out in all directions. She and James both started stamping ever more quickly and ever more desperately. There was a moment when it looked like everything would be all right. It hung pregnant, hopeful, and then evaporated. The fire was just spreading too quickly and when the first envelope burst into flames, Beth realised their stamping would be in vain. Her fear crackled white-hot, her senses on red alert.

This could be bad. Really bad!

Think, Beth. Should they run . . . ? Get help . . . ?

No time. Have to think of something else . . .

But what?

She stopped stamping and tried to survey the situation calmly and dispassionately. 'Break the chain!' she suddenly shouted at James.

The scattered envelopes and the open sack next to them were a lost cause. The priority must be to create a gap in the line of sacks on the floor so that the fire couldn't reach the tottering stack.

But James was still intent stamping on the envelopes, flames licking his ankles, and didn't seem to have heard her.

'Forget those, James,' shouted Beth, giving him a little push for emphasis. 'We need to break the chain!' James glanced up at her, his face blank. 'James! Pull the sacks away from each other and from the piles,' she reiterated. 'Now!'

For a moment, Beth wondered if he would continue to ignore her; even, indeed, if he was doing it on purpose. But then, thank goodness, he gave her a nod and ran up the chain of sacks. Beth wondered if she should help him but maybe she would be of more use getting the fire bucket down so that when James had moved the sacks, she could tip the sand into the gap to make absolutely sure the fire couldn't bridge the divide. *Yes.*

Definitely the right thing to do.

Beth ran to the wooden post on the other side of the table

and started to wrestle the heavy bucket down. James crouched over and started to pull the sacks out of line. He'd chosen to start with the ones closest to the huge stack and, while that did mean the first half dozen sacks might be lost, it was probably the most sensible thing to do.

It was going to be all right, she thought as she pulled the bucket down with both hands. It really was going to be all right. She would get the sand over to James and together they would tip it into—

Suddenly, there was a loud yowl, audible even over the ever-louder crackling of the fire. A cat – probably the same cat that had frightened Beth earlier – shot out from the pile of sacks and streaked across the warehouse floor. James, startled, staggered backwards into the huge pile of sacks. The stack shifted and stirred and a couple of dislodged sacks thumped to the floor. Beth let out a little scream as a third hit James full on the head.

He was falling, falling, heavy as a stone.

Crumpling onto the ground, head hitting the wood with a sickening thud.

Still. So still.

So horribly, desperately still.

It had all happened so quickly.

Beth was over to him in a flash, the sand bucket forgotten. 'James, James,' she shouted, crouching down beside him and giving his shoulder a little shake. 'James, wake up!' Under his inert head, a pool of sticky blood was beginning to form and for a heart-stopping moment, Beth wondered if he was dead. But then he gave a little moan and his eyes flickered, and Beth cried out in relief. Alive. Alive but hurt. 'James, you've got to get up!'

Nothing.

Beth stayed very still and the world stopped with her, grinding to a halt while she considered her alternatives.

She had a choice. And what she did next mattered. Really mattered. Mattered more than anything else that had ever happened to her. Indeed, it mattered more than anything that would happen in many people's lives – even if they lived to be one hundred years old.

If she made one choice and ran for help an innocent person might die. And James *was* innocent; in spite of everything, deep down she was absolutely sure of that. He might be flawed, deeply flawed, but who wasn't? He might have teetered on the edge of making a disastrous decision but, at the end of the day, he hadn't gone through with it. No, he'd been trying to stop the fire, she was sure of it. And wasn't he really as much a victim of the war as if he'd been fighting at the front?

But if she went the other way and dragged him to safety, who knew then what might happen? The fire could really take hold, while her back was turned. The sacks would burn, the whole extension might be lost. There could be devastation beyond measure, that much was certain. And, if the whole Home Depot went up in the smoke, might not morale take a dip? Might not the very outcome of the war be affected?

So, what to do?

One – special – person versus the greater good. An explosion – another whisky bottle? – a moan from James, and the world started to speed up at the very instant Beth leapt into action.

At the end of the day, she knew – had always known – exactly what she would do.

She would save her friend.

She would save James.

Of course, she would.

Before she started, she pulled one of the sacks out of line, to try to break the chain. Even as she manhandled it to one side, though, she could see that it was hopeless: the fire was skipping along the sack dust covering the ground and was going to reach the tottering pile with or without James's line of sacks. She could only hope that she would manage to pull James out the way before the whole rapidly igniting edifice fell on top of the pair of them!

'Come on, James,' she pleaded, trying to sound calm and in control. It was getting very hot in there and the background noise was changing from a crackle to a steady roar. 'Come on, James, up you get.'

James didn't respond so Beth put her hands under his shoulders and started to pull. He was heavy, a dead weight and, to begin with, nothing happened. But then he began to slide along the floor, his head lolling from side to side, and she got some momentum going. Beth tried to ignore the blood matted in his hair and smearing on the ground – there was nothing she could do about the wound right now. The most important thing was to drag him well out of harm's way and then she would consider what to do next. She glanced over her shoulder. There was a door, presumably leading outside, over on the far wall. She would aim for there and even if it was locked, it should be far enough from danger to leave James while she ran for help. But it was a long way away – a very long way – and progress was slow. She needed to speed up; the fire had now reached the base of the pile of sacks and fingers of flame were beginning to inch their way upwards. If the sacks contained letters, they would go up like a shot; if they contained parcels, the contents might explode or give off fumes or . . .

No!

Don't think like that, Beth. Just get James over to safety and then call for help.

The room was getting hotter. How much of that was the fire and how much the effects of her exertion, Beth had no way of knowing. Her palms were slippery and sweat was running down her face and into her eyes but, inch by inch, she was making progress.

Finally, *finally*, here was the door and, best of all, she could open it from the inside. With fumbling fingers, she pulled the metal bolts across and flung it open. Oh, the blessed feeling of the cool air against her flaming cheeks. The exquisite relief of reaching safety. She pulled the still unresponsive James outside and lowered his head and arms down onto the damp grass.

She had done it. James was safe.

She bent down and kissed his cheek. Now what?

Beth stood up and looked around her. Then, for the first time, she thought to shout for help. She had been so focused on getting James out of the burning warehouse that it simply hadn't crossed her mind to start shouting as she was manhandling him out.

'Help,' she called. 'Fire! Help!'

There was no response.

There was no one around to hear.

28

The door from the warehouse led onto the grass on the far side of the Home Depot, facing the now empty ordnance stores in the plot next door. Even as she shouted, she doubted anyone in the Home Depot on the other side of the extension would be able to hear her and she was well away from the canteen, the security guards at the entrance to the compound and anyone else who might be able to assist her. Heart sinking, Beth realised she would have to go and summon help when all she really wanted to do was to flop down on the cool grass beside James and never get up again.

But she didn't have time for thoughts like that. James might be out of danger but the Home Depot was burning down! She would have to move – and move quickly.

What was best? she wondered. Run back through the warehouse or round the side of the Home Depot? Through the warehouse was definitely quicker, if it wasn't too dangerous. She could be through the warehouse and reach help in a matter of seconds. Otherwise, she had to go all the way round. Her mind made up, she crouched down beside to James. 'I'll be back,' she said, touching his shoulder, and she fancied that he gave a low groan in reply.

Then she set off at a run, flying back through the warehouse. To her shock, flames were running amok through the pile of sacks, spitting and hissing. Letters, scorched and ghostly, had escaped, dancing and swooping in the eerie breeze and Beth flinched as one brushed against her hand, fizzing and stinging. Several more sacks had tumbled from the stack and she saw that two had landed right where James had been lying. She had made the right choice in getting him out first. He may well have died if she'd left him and summoned help first. But all those letters.

All those parcels.

All literally going up in smoke.

She was almost there! She flung open the door to the Home Depot, shut it behind her and ran down the corridor.

'Fire,' she yelled, through the open door to the Returned Letters Department. 'Fire!'

Beth wasn't sure if she was yelling for people to come and help her or warning everyone to evacuate the building. She just kept shouting 'fire' and pointing towards the warehouse until the shocked faces that had turned to her started to spring into action.

First to come running were Milly and Nora. For one heart-stopping moment, Beth wondered if the increasingly anti-war Milly would refuse to help – even if she had somehow been in on the plan with James to set fire to the Depot – but Milly followed Beth down the corridor readily enough and her eyes were as wide with horror as Nora's as she took in the blaze romping over the pile of sacks.

Thank goodness for that!

More and more people arrived on the scene and amid the chaos and confusion, people were taking command and barking orders. The huge stack of sacks already on fire was deemed too risky to touch, but maybe some of the sacks nearer the door could be saved. Beth, however, had thoughts only for James.

'There's a man – Mr Blackford – badly hurt outside,' she kept shouting and it felt an age until she saw one of the

Home Depot medical orderlies and could show him where James was lying. James was still inert on the ground but stirred when the orderly bent over him, eyes flickering. Then he staggered to a half-sitting position and, without warning, was violently sick on the grass.

'Oh, James, James,' cried Beth in relief, trying to get closer.

'Away with you,' said the medic, gently shooing her away. 'Let us attend to him, miss.'

Disoriented and discombobulated, Beth wandered off.

What should she do now? Should she quietly slip away? That way she wouldn't have to answer any awkward questions about how and why the fire started.

But no, she couldn't do that. It wouldn't be right.

She headed back towards the warehouse and was immediately leapt upon and assigned to one of the human chains attempting to remove as many sacks as they could from the building. As instructed, she took up position by a smaller stack of sacks on the other side of the warehouse away from the fire and started lugging the sacks towards the door. It was hard and hot and sweaty work but Beth found she was grateful for it. Apart from anything, it took her mind off everything else . . .

Behind the front façade, some of the sacks had been pulled into a low U-shape and, in the middle, was a jam jar with some cigarette stubs in it.

'It's a den for those bloody smokers,' said one of the soldiers, pulling one of the sacks out and passing it down the line. 'No wonder the whole place has gone up in flames.'

Beth ignored him. She couldn't think of anything to say and she was too exhausted to reply anyway. Besides, her attention had been taken by a small blue card, which had fluttered to the floor when the soldier moved the sack. Beth picked it up. It was an admission card. She turned

it over curiously, but somehow knew what she would find.
Milly Woods.

The words, in Milly's familiar looping scrawl jumped out
at her.

Milly's missing admission card.

Beth felt her heart beat faster. She stepped out of her place
in the line and picked up the jam jar containing the cigarette
stubs.

'What you doing, love?' one of the soldiers next to her
said. 'Looking for evidence?'

'The fire didn't start here. You're barking up the wrong
tree,' said another. 'Come on, let's get these sacks shifted.'

Beth ignored them both, looked closely at the cigarette
stubs in the jam jar. Several bore a lipstick mark that looked
suspiciously like Milly's.

Oh my goodness!

Milly wasn't a *spy*. She hadn't hatched some evil plan to
let outsiders hell-bent on mischief into the Home Depot. Far
from it! She had had a surreptitious cigarette in the den in
the warehouse with some friends – admittedly not ideal, but
hardly treason – and had somehow dropped her admission
card. Beth's relief at discovering this fought with her guilt at
misjudging her friend, and the confusion made her laugh
out loud. The trouble was, once she'd started laughing, she
found she couldn't stop.

'Poor lass is hysterical,' said the soldier on one side of her
sympathetically.

'Aye, that she is,' said the soldier on the other side. 'We'd
better get her out of here before she swoons.'

And so, still giggling, Beth found herself being escorted
out of the warehouse by two extremely solicitous soldiers.
She tried to explain that there was no need, that she was
quite all right and that they should return to their duties but
by now, the fire brigade had arrived and, with a good deal

of shouting and whistles being blown, everyone was ordered out of the warehouse.

James wasn't where she had left him. The orderlies had presumably moved him further out of harm's way but she couldn't see where he'd been taken. Maybe she should go and find out. Yes, she definitely should . . .

Legs suddenly weak, she slumped down onto the grass.

She'd go in a minute, when she felt stronger.

'Liza!' It was Nora, plonking herself down next to Beth. 'Liza, are you all right? Were you in there with James when the fire started? What on earth happened?'

Nora was gabbling – excited, nervous, shocked – and for a moment, Beth didn't answer. She didn't know what to say, hadn't yet got it clear in her own mind how she was going to explain what had just happened. What would she say? She could trust Nora with most things but could she really tell even her that James had planned a deliberate act of arson, even if he hadn't actually gone ahead with it? Or would she be better keeping that to herself, now and always?

Nora was looking at her, waiting for an answer and without really planning to, Beth found herself reaching into her pocket and brandishing Milly's admission card in front of Nora's nose.

'Look what I've just found,' she said, as much to change the subject as anything else.

Nora took the card from her and read the name on it. 'Milly's!' she said. 'Where on earth was it?'

'In the warehouse,' said Beth. 'Some of the sacks had been rearranged to form a smoking hideaway and when we moved them, it just floated to the ground. I expect she'd been sitting there and it got stuck between two sacks. Of course, I have no way of knowing whether it's the first or second card she lost, but at least that's one mystery solved.'

'It's the first card,' said Nora with certainty.

'How can you be so sure?' said Beth, frowning down at the card. There was nothing to make that clear.

Nora hesitated. 'Because I took the second one,' she whispered, making a little face.

Beth rounded on her. 'You did what?' she said. 'You *took* the second one?'

'I did,' said Nora. 'I know I shouldn't have done but—'

'But when?' said Beth. 'And *why*? You could have got Milly in real trouble.'

'I know,' said Nora, not meeting Beth's eyes. 'I'm not very proud of myself – especially after what you've just told me. But, I was worried that Milly might . . . not be all she seemed. It was the night of that ELFS meeting when she was acting so strangely. Almost as if she thought it might be acceptable to attack the Home Depot. And certainly not sticking up for her friends. And then I remembered that she had already lost one admission card and I was suddenly worried that maybe it had fallen into the wrong hands. And then I thought that if I took her card, then at least she couldn't slip it to anyone there who was planning some sort of mischief.' She glanced at her hands, looking a bit crestfallen. 'I feel a bit rotten now I know there was an innocent explanation for the first card. I've been a bit beastly, haven't I?'

'We've both been beastly,' said Beth. 'I thought exactly the same – in fact, I could hardly sleep that night at yours, I was so worried about it all.'

'And all the time she was innocent,' said Nora.

'Yes,' said Beth. 'A bit careless and fiery but essentially one of us. I wonder where she is now?'

At that moment, right on cue, Milly staggered out of the door to the warehouse carrying Fluffy. She rushed over to them, panting.

'The poor thing was hiding in the corner,' she said. 'I couldn't leave until I'd got him out, even though one of the firemen was threatening to have me arrested if I didn't leave immediately.'

'That "poor thing" was responsible for a sack falling on James's head and knocking him unconscious,' said Beth as Milly let the cat go and it streaked off into the shadows. 'But you were very brave to rescue him. And – oh, Milly, I'm so sorry about the night at ELFS. I should never—'

'Don't be daft,' said Milly. 'We're all entitled to our own opinions, after all. Now, where's James? Is he all right?'

'They moved him around the corner of the building,' said Nora. 'And I'm pretty sure someone said an ambulance had arrived. But, Liza, what happened?'

Beth sprung to her feet. She suddenly couldn't believe she was sitting there with her friends while James was lying injured just around the corner. Even though she'd been dismissed when the medical orderlies took over, she should have stayed close by. Why had she just wandered off? That, she supposed, was what shock did to you.

Without answering the others, she was off, round the side of the Home Depot. There, indeed, was the ambulance, with several people clustered around it. Heart in mouth, she ran over. James was propped up on a stretcher on the ground with medics gathered around him. He seemed barely conscious but at least he was alive.

'James!' she exclaimed, pushing through the little throng of people. '*James.*'

There was a little muttering of disapproval and Beth feared that she might be sent packing again. But then she heard the medical orderly say, 'That is the girl who showed me where he was. I think she's the one who pulled him out of the building,' and suddenly all eyes were on her.

'I wonder if we might have a word, miss.'

For the first time, Beth noticed the policemen. There were two of them, steering her away from the little group. 'Of

course,' said Beth, heart thumping. What on earth was she
going to say?

'You were the one who rescued Mr . . . er . . . Blackford
from the fire?'

'I was.' Those clever eyes were open now and seemed to
be trying to focus on her.

'If you could take us through what happened? How Mr
Blackford came to be injured.'

Knowing it was not really what they wanted to hear, Beth
started telling the policemen about trying to move the sacks
to stop the fire from spreading, and how the startled cat had
startled James in turn and he'd staggered back against the
pile of sacks. And then came the question she dreaded.

'And how did the fire start, miss? Was the warehouse
already on fire when you got there? And why were you and
Mr Blackford in the warehouse to begin with? I understand
it is usually out of bounds . . .'

Careful, Beth, what you say next is very important . . .

The truth was important, of course it was, and there was
nothing that Play-by-the-rules Beth wanted to do less than
tell lies to an Officer of the Law. But how could she tell
them the whole truth? That James had planned – albeit in
a moment of madness – to set fire to the Home Depot and
hang the consequences. How could she do that to him,
when she knew very well that he had changed his mind at
the last minute? She could, of course, tell another version
of the truth: that James had accidentally dropped a cigarette
stub and that that had started the fire. But even that would
get James into trouble and probably lose him his job – or
worse.

What to do, Beth.

What on earth to do?

Everybody was staring at her by now and Beth was glad
that the darkness would hide her glowing cheeks and her

shaking legs. She glanced at the semi-conscious James and took a deep breath.

'I can't tell you exactly what happened,' she said, marvelling at just how steady her voice sounded. 'But I know that Mr Blackford has had two recent bereavements and that he went into the warehouse to have a moment alone. And I can't tell you exactly what happened to start the fire. I know that sometimes smokers go into the warehouse – we found evidence of that when we were trying to get some of the sacks out just now. Maybe someone accidentally left a smouldering stub lying around? Or it could be one of the really badly wrapped parcels containing tobacco and matches. I work in the Broken Parcel Department and I constantly come across them. It's really not safe and I've been saying for a long time that this was an accident waiting to happen.' She stopped and took another deep breath. 'One thing I can promise you, though, is that Mr Blackford was trying his utmost to stop the fire when the sacks fell on him and knocked him out. That much I know for sure.'

Beth stopped talking and looked at the policemen. She hadn't lied. Or, at least, everything she had just said had been technically true – albeit with a huge omission. But would it be enough? Would it be enough to get James off the hook?

The policemen looked at her sharply for a moment and then one of them gave a nod.

'Thank you, miss,' he said. 'These places do tend to be bloody tinderboxes. We had another fire – on a smaller scale, mind you – over in Edgware just last month. Shame about the letters but I think we can count ourselves lucky that no one was killed and that the main building wasn't affected.' He snapped his notebook shut. 'That will be all for now, but we may have more questions later when we've had a chance to question the young man.'

Beth's eyes met James's again and she fancied she saw him smile.

And here was Mrs Peters, pushing through the little throng with a tray of tea. She bustled around pouring it out and then handed the first cup to Beth.

'That's nice,' one of the policemen said. 'Bringing the wee shocked lass a cup of tea.'

Beth braced herself for Mrs Peters to say something sarcastic. Mrs Peters duly straightened up and turned to face the policeman. 'I don't know what "wee lass" you are refer-ring to,' she said. '*I* am bringing my supervisor a cup of tea. A very fine supervisor she happens to be too, and one who has just saved a man's life.'

'Spotted her potential the first moment I saw her,' added Sergeant Major Cunningham, who had turned up out of nowhere.

Beth turned from one to the other in speechless amaze-ment.

The ambulance man straightened up from James. 'We'll need to observe this young man overnight,' he said, 'but after that he'll need somewhere to convalesce. I gather he lodges nearby and I'm not happy about sending him back there alone—'

Beth's mouth opened by itself. 'That won't be a problem,' she said, 'because he won't be going back to his lodgings. He's very welcome to come and convalesce in Hertfordshire with my family. I believe the country air will do him good.'

'Right you are, miss,' said the ambulance man. 'We'll have to sort out transport, of course—'

'That won't be a problem either,' said Nora, joining the little group. 'My driver would be very happy to give him a lift.'

'All the way to Hertfordshire?'

'All the way to Hertfordshire.'

'Problem sorted,' said the ambulance man cheerfully.

'There's just one more problem,' said Milly slowly. Everyone turned to look at her. 'I seem to have lost my admission card.'

Beth and Nora grinned at each other.

'We can help with that,' they said together.

Epilogue

It was the strangest and, in its own way, the most wonderful Fundraising Dance she had ever been to, and one that Beth could never, ever have predicted, even a few short months ago.

James *had* come back to Woodhampstead to recuperate. Ma, somewhat surprised to discover that Beth's friend was, in fact, a man, had rallied around superbly and welcomed him with open arms. Beth spent as much time as she could with James and, over the next few days, he seemed to be getting much stronger, both physically and mentally. And, if it wasn't quite yet a romance, well, Beth had every hope that it would be very soon.

And then Beth discovered that James's twenty-third birthday fell on the night of the dance in aid of the Soldiers' Fund. Everyone was going, and it was just too good an opportunity to miss. Invitations were duly issued to Milly, Nora and Denny and, best of all, Ned wrote that he would be back on leave for that weekend.

Beth's cup overflowed.

And now here they all were, dancing the night away in the Woodhampstead Village Hall, which was decorated to the gills with patriotic bunting. Milly was dancing with James and Nora with Denny and even Ma and Pa were taking a whirl around the dance floor. Over there, Bertie and Reggie's parents were wrapped in each other's arms and – goodness, was that really Mrs McBride smiling up at the vicar as they took a sedate turn or two?

Beth stood and watched it all, knowing soon that it would be her turn to join in again. And then Sally came and joined her. Beth gave her a wary smile. Cordial relations had been restored but things still weren't the same between the two sisters.

Sally followed Beth's eyes to where James and Milly were attempting an elaborate series of spins. 'I wondered why you weren't more upset when I told you about Sam and Ivy,' she said with a little smile.

Beth spun round to her. Were her feelings really that obvious?

'He's a nice man,' said Sally softly. 'And your friends have been telling me just how brave you were in rescuing him. So, I want to say sorry. Sorry for saying that you've changed and that you don't put others first anymore.'

'There's no need, Sally,' said Beth, tears pricking her eyes. 'I should have told you about the letter, I know I should.'

'You thought you were doing the right thing,' said Sally. 'And, do you know what, you probably did. Otherwise the news of Bertie's death would have got all muddled up with the mistake over the letter.'

Beth turned to her sister and gave her a hug. 'Thank you,' she said simply.

The dance finished and everyone changed partners. And here was James striding across the dance floor to her, as she had known he would. She slipped into his arms – the arms that felt like home – and leaned her head against his shoulder. Behind him, she could see Ned and Nora dancing together and there was just something in the way they were looking at each other that made her breath catch. She caught Milly's eye with a little delighted grin.

But this wasn't about Nora and Ned or anyone else.

This was about her and James.

The beginning of their story.

She smiled up at him and he kissed her cheek gently in return.

Britain might be at war with Germany, but – just for now – all was well in Beth's little slice of the world.

Acknowledgements

I am so lucky to have many wonderful people in my life who have helped *The Post Office Girls* see the light of day.

Firstly, enormous thanks to my wonderful agent Felicity Trew – advocate, therapist and co-conspirator – for her unstinting support and belief in me and my writing. Thank you for making my dreams come true. To Thorne Ryan, Madeleine Woodfield and the team at Hodder & Stoughton, thank you for giving me the opportunity to tell this story – and for all your help in making it better. You've been brilliant – professional, enthusiastic and enormous fun to work with. But just a reminder that you owe me a lavish lunch or two after lockdown disrupted our plans!

The Post Office Girls was largely researched and written during the 2020 Covid-19 pandemic – at a time when lockdown forced absolutely all museums and libraries to close. As such, I'm really in debt to all those individuals who kindly took the time to share their extensive knowledge with me. It really is deeply appreciated; needless to add, any mistakes or inaccuracies in the book are down to me.

In no particular order:

1. Woodhampstead is very loosely based on the town of Wheathampstead in Hertfordshire and I'd like to say a huge thank you to Ruth Jeavons, Honorary Secretary of the Wheathampstead History Society, for her enthusiasm and generous help in my research – pointing me in the

right direction for everything from train timetables to descriptions of chickens roosting in the trees. Thank you so much, Ruth.

2. I'd also like to acknowledge David Ivison, Vice Chairman of The Royal Parks' Guild and thank him for all his help and advice. David's book, *The Royal Parks In The Great War*, was a great source of information of inspiration about the Home Depot and he was terrifically patient in answering my many and varied questions. Thank you, David.

3. *Men of Letters* by Duncan Barrett is a fabulous history of the post office workers who fought in the Great War and is highly recommended. One of its anecdotes was the inspiration behind how Beth first met James.

4. Another big thank you to the staff at the research room at the Postal Museum for all your help. I spent a happy day there virtually the day before lockdown and think I covered the main bases but I look forward to returning as soon as I can.

5. And last, but not least, many thanks to my lovely friend Tim Bowler for a crash course in all things WW1. You're a star.

Writing can be a lonely old business, so thank goodness for lovely chums who are always there to support, encourage and pour the drinks – albeit mainly virtual at the moment. Huge thanks to: the LLs – Catherine Boardman, Vanessa Rigg, Jane Ayres, Chris Manby, Maddie Please, Sue Bavin, Christina Banach and Kazzy Coles and the Coppa Crew – Claire Dyer, Marilyn Groves and Becci Fearnley. Mine's a Limoncello!

A huge thank you to you, the reader, for choosing *The Post Office Girls* and for supporting a debut. I hope you enjoyed it and, if so, that you'll consider reviewing it far and wide.

Finally, thank you to my husband, John and to my fabulous children, Tom and Charlotte. Thank you for your love, your support and all the fun – even during lockdown! You're the best. xx

I love these pictures showing the 'organised chaos' of the Home Depot. You might recognise the baskets in the top left photo from the story . . .

Three young women hard at work mending parcels in the Home Depot, just like Beth, Nora and Milly.

This is how I picture Beth, Nora and Milly at their tables
in the Broken Parcel Department.

Bookends

When one book ends, another begins...

Bookends is a vibrant new reading community to help you ensure you're never without a good book.

You'll find exclusive previews of the brilliant new books from your favourite authors as well as exciting debuts and past classics. Read our blog, check out our recommendations for your reading group, enter great competitions and much more!

Visit our website to see which great books we're recommending this month.

Join the Bookends community:

www.welcometobookends.co.uk

 @Team Bookends   @WelcomeToBookends